OF
POSEIDON

ANNA BANKS

SQUARE
FISH

FEIWEL AND FRIENDS
NEW YORK

For Mom, who believed I could do anything, and for Dad,
who also believed I could do anything—except wrong.

SQUARE
FISH

An Imprint of Macmillan
175 Fifth Avenue
New York, NY 10010
MACTEENBOOKS.COM

Square Fish and the Square Fish logo are trademarks of Macmillan and
are used by Feiwel and Friends under license from Macmillan.

Square Fish books may be purchased for business or promotional use.
For information on bulk purchases, please contact the
Macmillan Corporate and Premium Sales Department at
(800) 221-7945 x 5442 or by e-mail at SPECIALMARKETS@MACMILLAN.COM.

Library of Congress Cataloging-in-Publication Data Available

ISBN 978-1-250-02736-8

Originally published in the United States by Feiwel and Friends
First Square Fish Edition: May 2013
Square Fish logo designed by Filomena Tuosto

10 9 8 7 6 5 4 3 2 1

AR: 4.2 / LEXILE: HL650L

1

I SMACK into him as if shoved from behind. He doesn't budge, not an inch. Just holds my shoulders and waits. Maybe he's waiting for me to find my balance. Maybe he's waiting for me to gather my pride. I hope he's got all day.

I hear people passing on the boardwalk and imagine them staring. Best-case scenario, they think I know this guy, that we're hugging. Worst-case scenario, they saw me totter like an intoxicated walrus into this complete stranger because I was looking down for a place to park our beach stuff. Either way, *he* knows what happened. *He* knows why my cheek is plastered to his bare chest. And there is definite humiliation waiting when I get around to looking up at him.

Options skim through my head like a flip book.

Option One: Run away as fast as my dollar-store flip-flops can take me. Thing is, tripping over them is partly responsible for my current dilemma. In fact, one of them is missing, probably caught in a crack of the boardwalk. I'm betting Cinderella didn't feel this foolish, but then again, Cinderella wasn't as clumsy as an intoxicated walrus.

Option Two: Pretend I've fainted. Go limp and everything. Drool, even. But I know this won't work because my eyes flutter too much to fake it, and besides, people don't blush while unconscious.

Option Three: Pray for a lightning bolt. A deadly one that you feel in advance because the air gets all atingle and your skin crawls—or so the science books say. It might kill us both, but really, *he* should have been paying more attention to *me* when he saw that I wasn't paying attention at *all*.

For a shaved second, I think my prayers are answered because I do get tingly all over; goose bumps sprout everywhere, and my pulse feels like electricity. Then I realize, it's coming from my shoulders. From his *hands*.

Option Last: For the love of God, peel my cheek off his chest and apologize for the casual assault. Then hobble away on my one flip-flop before I faint. With my luck, the lightning would only maim me, and he would feel obligated to carry me somewhere anyway. Also, do it *now*.

I ease away from him and peer up. The fire on my cheeks has nothing to do with the fact that it's sweaty-eight degrees in the Florida sun and everything to do with the fact that I just tripped into the most attractive guy on the planet. Fan-flipping-tastic.

"Are—are you alright?" he says, incredulous. I think I can see the shape of my cheek indented on his chest.

I nod. "I'm fine. I'm used to it. Sorry." I shrug off his hands when he doesn't let go. The tingling stays behind, as if he left some of himself on me.

"Jeez, Emma, are you okay?" Chloe calls from behind. The calm fwopping of my best friend's sandals suggests she's not as concerned as she sounds. Track star that she is, she would already be at my side if she thought I was hurt. I groan and face her, not surprised that she's grinning wide as the equator. She holds out my flip-flop, which I try not to snatch from her hand.

"I'm fine. Everybody's fine," I say. I turn back to the guy, who seems to get more gorgeous by the second. "You're fine, right? No broken bones or anything?"

He blinks, gives a slight nod.

Chloe sets her surfboard against the rail of the boardwalk and extends her hand to him. He accepts it without taking his eyes off me. "I'm Chloe and this is Emma," she says. "We usually bring her helmet with us, but we left it back in the hotel room this time."

I gasp. I also try to decide what kind of flowers I'll bring to her funeral after I strangle the life from her body. I should have stayed in Jersey, like Mom said. Shouldn't have come here with Chloe and her parents. What business do I have in Florida? We live on the Jersey Shore. If you've seen one beach, you've seen them all, right?

But noooooooo. I had to come and spend the last of my summer with Chloe, because this would be our last summer together before college, blah-blah-blah. And now she's taking revenge on me for not letting her use my ID to get a tattoo last night. But what did she expect? I'm white and she's black. I'm not even tan-white. I'm Canadian-tourist white. If the guy could mistake her for me, then he shouldn't be giving anyone a tattoo, right? I was just *protecting* her. Only, she doesn't realize that. I can tell by that look in her eyes—the same look she wore when she replaced my hand sanitizer with personal lubricant—that she's about to take what's left of my pride and kick it like a donkey.

"Uh, we didn't get your name. Did you get his name, Emma?" she asks, as if on cue.

"I tried, Chloe. But he wouldn't tell me, so I tackled him," I say, rolling my eyes.

The guy smirks. This almost-smile hints at how breathtaking a real one would be. The tingling flares up again, and I rub my arms.

"Hey, Galen, are you ready to—" We all turn to a petite black-haired girl as she touches his shoulder. She stops midsentence when she sees me. Even if these two didn't share the same short dark hair, the same violet eyes, and the same flawless olive skin, I'd know they were related because of their most dominant feature—their habit of staring.

"I'm Chloe. This is my friend Emma, who apparently just head-butted your boyfriend Galen. We were in the middle of apologizing."

I pinch the bridge of my nose and count to ten-Mississippi, but fifty-Mississippi seems more appropriate. Fifty allows more time to fantasize about ripping one of Chloe's new weaves out.

"Emma, what's wrong? Your nose isn't bleeding, is it?" she chirps, enjoying herself.

Tingles gather at my chin as Galen lifts it with the crook of his finger. "Is your nose bleeding? Let me see," he says. He tilts my head side to side, leans closer to get a good look.

And I meet my threshold for embarrassment. Tripping is bad enough. Tripping into *someone* is much worse. But if that someone has a body that could make sculpted statues jealous—and thinks you've broken your nose on one of his pecs—well, that's when tripping runs a distant second to humane euthanasia.

He is clearly surprised when I swat his hand and step away. His girlfriend/relative seems taken aback that I mimic his stance—crossed arms and deep frown. I doubt she has ever met her threshold for embarrassment.

"I said I was fine. No blood, no foul."

"This is my sister Rayna," he says, as if the conversation steered naturally in that direction. She smiles at me as if forced at knifepoint, the kind of smile that comes purely from manners, like the smile you give your grandmother when she gives you the rotten-cabbage-colored sweater she's been knitting. I think of that sweater now as I return her smile.

Galen eyes the surfboard abandoned against the wood railing. "The waves here aren't really good for surfing."

Galen's gift is not small talk. Just like his sister, there's a forced feel to his manners. But unlike his sister, there's no underlying hostility, just an awkwardness, like he's out of practice. Since he appears to be making this effort on my behalf, I cooperate. I make a show of looking at the emerald crests of the Gulf of Mexico, at the waves sloshing lazily against the shore. A man waist-deep in the water holds a toddler on his hip and jumps with the swells as they peak. Compared to the waves back home, the tide here reminds me of kiddie rides at the fair.

"We know. We're just taking it out to float," Chloe says, unconcerned that Galen was talking to me. "We're from Jersey, so we know what a real wave looks like." When she steps closer, Rayna steps back. "Hey, that's weird," Chloe says. "You both have the same color eyes as Emma. I've never seen that before. I always thought it was because she's freakishly pasty. Ow! That's gonna leave a mark, Emma," she says, rubbing her freshly pinched biceps.

"Good, I hope it does," I snap. I want to ask them about their eyes—the color seems prettier set against the olive tone of Galen's skin—but Chloe has bludgeoned my chances of recovering from embarrassment. I'll have to be satisfied that my dad—and Google—were wrong all this time; my eye color just can't be that rare. Sure, my dad practiced medicine until the day he died two years ago. And sure, Google never let me down before. But who am I to argue with living, breathing proof that this eye color actually does exist? Nobody, that's who. Which is convenient, since I don't want to talk anymore. Don't want to force Galen into any more awkward conversations. Don't want to give Chloe any more opportunities to deepen the heat of my burning cheeks. I just want this moment of my life to be over.

I push past Chloe and snatch up the surfboard. To her good credit, she presses herself against the rail as I pass her again. I stop in front of Galen and his sister. "It was nice to meet you both. Sorry I ran into you. Let's go, Chloe."

Galen looks like he wants to say something, but I turn away.

He's been a good sport, but I'm not interested in discussing swimmer safety—or being introduced to any more of his hostile relatives. Nothing he can say will change the fact that DNA from my cheek is smeared on his chest.

Trying not to actually march, I thrust past them and make my way down the stairs leading to the pristine white sand. I hear Chloe closing the distance behind me, giggling. And I decide on sunflowers for her funeral.

2

THE SIBLINGS lean on their elbows against the rail, watching the girls they just met peel the T-shirts off their bikinis and wade into the water with the surfboard floating between them.

"She's probably just wearing contacts," Rayna says. "They make contacts in that color, you know."

He shakes his head. "She's not wearing contacts. You saw her just as plain as you're seeing me. She's one of us."

"You're losing it. She can't be one of us. Look at her hair. You can't even call that blonde. It's almost *white.*"

Galen frowns. The hair color had thrown him off too—before he had touched her. The simple contact of grasping her arm when she fell dispensed any doubts. The Syrena are always attracted to their own kind—which helps them find each other across miles and miles of ocean. Usually that attraction is limited to water transmission, where they can sense the presence of one of their own. He's never heard of it occurring on land before—and never felt it so strongly, period—but he knows what he felt. He wouldn't—*couldn't* react that way to a human. Especially given how much he despises them.

"I know it's unusual—"

"Unusual? It's impossible, Galen! Our genes don't come with the 'blonde' option."

"Stop being dramatic. She *is* one of us. You can see how bad she is at being human. I thought she was going to brain herself on the rail."

"Okay, let's say by some off chance she figured out how to bleach thousands of years of genetics out of her hair. Now explain why she's hanging out—no, *vacationing*—with humans. She's breaking the law right in front of our faces, splashing around in the water with her obnoxious human friend. Why is that, Galen?"

He shrugs. "Maybe she doesn't know who we are."

"What do you mean? Everyone knows who we are!"

"Obviously not. We've never met her before, remember?"

She snorts. "Are you dehydrated? She can see our mark. It's not like we were hiding it."

"Maybe she thinks it's a tattoo," he offers.

"A what?"

"Look around, Rayna. See the markings on that human girl's ankle?" He points toward a man walking up the stairs. "See that male? He's got markings—humans call them tattoos—all over him. Maybe she thought—"

Rayna holds up her hand. "Stop. She'd recognize the trident. *If* she was one of us."

Galen nods. She's right. A Syrena knows a Royal by the small blue trident on their stomach—and dressed for the human beach, it's visible on both of them right now. So, she has blonde—white—hair, and didn't recognize them as Royals. But he knows what he felt. And she does have the eyes. . . .

Rayna groans. "Oh, no."

"What?"

"You're making that face."

"What face?"

"The face you make when you think you're right."

"Am I?" He watches Emma straddling the surfboard, splashing waves of saltwater in her friend's face without mercy. He grins.

"We're not going home, are we?" Rayna says, propping herself against the rail.

"Dr. Milligan doesn't call for just anything. If he thinks it's of interest, then it probably is. You can leave if you want, but I'm looking into it." Dr. Milligan is one of the only humans Galen trusts. If the doctor were going to tell anyone about the Syrena's existence, he would have done it the day Galen had saved his life all those years ago. Instead, Dr. Milligan returned the favor by denying he'd ever seen Galen—even when his scuba companions called the press. Since then, they had built a friendship by sharing sushi, afternoon swims, and most importantly, information. Dr. Milligan is a well-connected and highly respected oceanographer and the director of the Gulfarium here on the coast, in a prime position to monitor the activities of his professional colleagues.

When Galen received Dr. Milligan's urgent voice mail yesterday about a blonde Syrena visiting the Gulfarium in human form, he swam the gulf in a day. If Dr. Milligan is right about Emma's abilities, he's found more than just a rule-breaking Syrena. The good doctor might have found the key to uniting two kingdoms.

But since Rayna's specialty is not discretion—she would even tell on *herself* when she was younger—Galen knows he must keep this secret from her. Besides, he's not sure he believes it himself. Even if he *did* believe it, if he *could* confirm it, would Emma do what she must? And where has she been? And why? Everything about Emma is a mystery. Her name doesn't originate with the Syrena—or her hair or skin. And the way her lips turned red when she blushed almost knocked the breath out of him.

"What?" his sister asks.

"Nothing." He wrenches his gaze from Emma. *Now she's got me muttering my thoughts out loud.*

"I told you, you're losing it." Rayna makes a phlegmy gagging sound and wrings her hands around her neck. "This is what Father will do to me if I come home without you again. What should I say when he asks where you are? When he asks why you're so obsessed with humans? 'But Father, this one is a pretty blonde with nice contacts'?"

Galen scowls. "He's going to regret not taking an interest in them. At least Grom's reasonable about it. It's only a matter of time before they discover us and—"

"I know, I know," she drawls. "I know how you hate humans.

Sheesh, I was just kidding. That's why I follow you around, you know. In case you need help."

Galen runs a hand through his hair and leans back over the railing. His twin sister does follow him around like a sucker fish, but being helpful has nothing to do with it. "Oh, are you sure it doesn't have anything to do with settling down with—"

"Don't even say it."

"Well, what am I supposed to think? Ever since Toraf asked Father for you—"

"Toraf is foolish!"

Toraf has been their best friend since birth—that is, until he recently made his intentions toward Rayna clear. At least he had the good sense to hide out and wait for her death threats to subside. But now she gives him something worse than threats—complete indifference. No amount of pleading or coaxing from Toraf has thawed her. But since she turned twenty this spring—two years past the normal age of mating—Father couldn't find a good reason not to agree to the match. Toraf is a good candidate, and the decision is made, whether Rayna chooses to ignore it or not.

"I'm starting to think you're right. Who would want to attach himself to a wild animal?" Galen says, grinning.

"I'm not a wild animal! You're the one who isolates yourself from everyone, choosing the company of humans over your own kind."

"It's my responsibility."

"Because you asked for it!"

This is true. Galen, stealing an old human saying about

keeping your friends close and your enemies closer, asked his older brother, Grom, for permission to serve as an ambassador of sorts to the humans. Grom, being the next in line for kingship, agreed with the need to be cautious about the land dwellers. He granted Galen exclusive immunity to the law prohibiting interaction with humans, recognizing that some communication would be necessary and for the greater good. "Because no one else would. Someone has to watch them. Are we really having this conversation again?" Galen says.

"You started it."

"I don't have time for this. Are you staying or going?"

She crosses her arms, juts out her bottom lip. "Well, what are you planning to do? I say we arrest her."

"We?"

"You know what I mean."

He shrugs. "I guess we'll follow her for a while. Watch her."

Rayna starts to say something but gasps instead. "Maybe we won't have to," she whispers, eyes big as sand dollars.

He follows her line of sight to the water, to a dark shadow pacing beneath the waves where the girls share the surfboard. He curses under his breath.

Shark.

3

I SPLASH enough water in Chloe's face to put out a small house fire. I don't want to drown her, just exfoliate her eyeballs with sea salt. When she thinks I'm done, she opens her eyes— and her mouth. Big mistake. The next wave rinses off the hangy ball in the back of her throat and makes it to her lungs before she can swallow. She chokes and coughs and rubs her eyes as if she's been maced.

"Great, Emma! You got my new hair wet!" she sputters. "Happy now?"

"Nope."

"I said I was sorry." She blows her nose in her hand, then sets the snot to sea.

"Gross. And sorry's not good enough."

"Fine. I'll make it up to you. What do you want?"

"Let me hold your head underwater until I feel better," I say.

I cross my arms, which is tricky when straddling a surfboard being pitched around in the wake of a passing speedboat. Chloe knows I'm nervous being this far out, but holding on would be a sign of weakness.

"I'll let you do that because I love you. But it won't make you feel better."

"I won't know for sure until I try it." I keep eye contact, sit a little straighter.

"Fine. But you'll still look albino when you let me back up." She rocks the board and makes me grab it for balance.

"Get your snotty hands off the surfboard. And I'm not albino. Just white." I want to cross my arms again, but we almost tipped over that time. Swallowing my pride is a lot easier than swallowing the Gulf of Mexico.

"Whiter than most," she grins. "People would think you're naked if you wore my swimsuit." I glance down at the white string bikini, offset beautifully against her chocolate-milk skin. She catches me and laughs.

"Well, maybe I could get a tan while we're here," I say, blushing. I feel myself cracking and I hate it. Just this once, I want to stay mad at Chloe.

"Maybe you could get a burn while we're here, you mean. Matterfact, did you put sunblock on?"

I shake my head.

She shakes her head too, and makes a tsking sound identical to her mother's. "Didn't think so. If you did, you would've slipped right off that guy's chest instead of sticking to it like that."

"I know," I groan.

"Got to be the hottest guy I've ever seen," she says, fanning herself for emphasis.

"Yeah, I know. Smacked into him, remember? Without my helmet, remember?"

She laughs. "Hate to break it to you, but he's still staring at you. Him and his mean-ass sister."

"Shut. Up."

She snickers. "But seriously, which one of them do you think would win a staring contest? I was gonna tell him to meet us at Baytowne tonight, but he might be one of those clingy stalker types. That's too bad, too. There's a million dark little corners in Baytowne for you two to snuggle—"

"Ohmysweetgoodness, Chloe, stop!" I giggle and shiver at the same time and accidentally imagine walking around The Village in Baytowne Wharf with Galen. The Village is exactly that— a sleepy little village of tourist shops in the middle of a golf-course resort. During the daytime anyway. At night though . . . *that's* when the dance club wakes up and opens its doors to all the sunburned partiers roaming the cobblestoned walkways with their daiquiris. Galen would look great under the twinkling lights, even with a shirt on. . . .

Chloe smirks. "Uh-huh. Already thought of that, huh?"

"No!"

"Uh-huh. Then why are your cheeks red as hot sauce?"

"Nuh-uh!" I laugh. She does, too.

"You want me to go ask him to meet us, then?"

I nod. "How old do you think he is?"

She shrugs. "Not creepy-old. Old enough for *me* to be jail-bait, though. Lucky for him, *you* just turned eighteen.... What the ... did you just kick me?" She peers into the water, swipes her hand over the surface as if clearing away something to see better. "Something just bumped me."

She cups her hands over her eyes and squints, leaning down so close that one good wave could slap her chin. The concentration on her face almost convinces me. Almost. But I grew up with Chloe—we've been next-door neighbors since the third grade. I've grown used to fake rubber snakes on my front porch, salt in the sugar dish, and Saran wrap spread across the toilet seat—well, actually, Mom fell prey to that one. The point is Chloe loves pranks almost as much as she loves running. And this is definitely a prank.

"Yep, I kicked you," I tell her, rolling my eyes.

"But ... but you can't reach me, Emma. My legs are longer than yours, and I can't reach you.... There it is again! You didn't feel that?"

I didn't feel it, but I did see her leg twitch. I wonder how long she's been planning this. Since we got here? Since we boarded the plane in Jersey? Since we turned twelve? "Yeah right, Chloe. You'll have to do better than that if—"

Her scream is blood-congealing. Her eyes balloon almost out of their sockets, and the creases on her forehead look like stairs. She grabs her left thigh, holding it so tight one of her fake nails pops off.

"Stop it, Chloe! It isn't funny!" I bite my lip, trying to keep up my show of indifference.

Another nail pops off. She reaches for me but misses. Her leg jerks back and forth in the water, and she screams again, only much, much worse. She clutches the board with both hands, but her arms are shaking too much to stay anchored. Real tears mix with seawater and sweat on her face. Her sobs come in huge gulps, like she can't decide if she wants to cry or scream again.

And I am convinced.

I lunge, grasp her forearm, scoot to her on the board. Blood clouds the water around us. When she sees it, her screams become frantic, un-human. I lace my fingers through hers, but she barely grips back.

"Hold on to me, Chloe! Pull your legs up on the board!"

"No, no, no, no, no, no, no," she sobs, choking between breaths. Her whole body shakes, and her teeth chatter as if we've somehow drifted into the Arctic Ocean.

And the fin is all I see. Our hands separate. I scream as the surfboard tilts and Chloe is wrenched from it. The water snatches away her shriek as she's pulled under. Blood trails behind as she becomes a shadow, moving deeper and deeper, farther and farther away from light, from oxygen. From me.

"Shark! Shark! Help! Somebody please help us! *Shaaaaaaaaaark!*"

I flail my arms and scream. Kick my legs and scream. Bounce up and down on the surfboard—and scream and scream and scream. I slide off, stick the board in the air, wave it with all my strength. The weight of it forces me under. Terror and water cocoon me. For a second, I'm four years old again, drowning in my grandmother's pond. Panic settles on me like stirred-up muck. But unlike then, I keep tethered to reality. I don't detach; I don't let my imagination take over. I don't dream of catfish and striped bass pushing me to the surface, rescuing me.

Maybe it's because I'm older. Maybe it's because someone else's life depends on my staying calm. Whatever the reason, I keep my grasp on the surfboard and pull myself up, swallowing part of a wave as I surface. The saltwater stings my raw throat even as the fresh air chases it.

The people on shore are specks, moving around like fleas on a dog. No one sees me. Not the sunbathers, not the shallow-water swimmers, not the moms hunting shells with their toddlers. There are no boats, no Jet Skis nearby. Just water, sky, and a setting sun.

My sobbing turns into lung-bursting hiccups. No one can hear me. No one can see me. No one is coming to save Chloe.

I push the surfboard away, toward shore. If the waves carry it in, maybe someone will see that its owner didn't return with it. Maybe they will even remember the two girls who took it out. And maybe they will look for us.

Deep inside, I feel I'm watching my life float away on that glistening board. When I peer down into the water, I feel I'm watching Chloe's life float away with that faint trail of blood, blurred and weakened by each passing wave. The choice is clear.

I breathe in as much air as my lungs can take without popping. And then I dive.

4

TOO LATE.

As fast as he is, Galen is too late. He powers through the current as the floor of the gulf slants steeper and steeper. Every time he hears Emma's desperate screams, he pushes harder, harder than he's ever pushed himself before. But he doesn't want to see it. Whatever is happening to her to make her scream like that, he doesn't want to see it. Already, he knows he'll be haunted by those screams forever. He doesn't want to add to his torment with the sight of it. Chloe has already stopped screaming—he doesn't want to think about what that means. And he refuses to acknowledge how much time has passed since he heard Emma. He clenches his teeth and slices through the water faster than he can see ahead of him.

Finally, finally, he finds them. And he is too late.

He groans when he sees Emma. She clutches Chloe's limp

arm, pulling and tugging and twisting, struggling to pry her friend from the bull shark's jaws. She doesn't see that each jerk, each yank, each inch she gains only tears more flesh from Chloe's leg. And she doesn't see that her friend stopped fighting long ago.

She and the beast are at war. It shakes and writhes, mirroring her actions, pulling them both into deeper water, but Emma won't let go. Galen glances around, wary for other contenders the blood might attract. But the haze of red is dissipating—Chloe is almost drained.

Why didn't Emma change? Why didn't she save her friend? Doubts mingle with remorse. He swallows the eruption of bile shooting up his throat. *Rayna is right.* She isn't one of them. If she was, she would have saved her friend. She would have changed, would have carried Chloe away to safety—all healthy Syrena can swim faster than sharks.

I was wrong. Emma is human. Which means she needs oxygen. Now. He starts toward her but stops.

The several minutes she has been fighting that shark should have sapped her strength. But her tugs are becoming *stronger.* A few times, she even makes headway toward shallower water. *She is making headway with a bull shark.* Galen remembers Dr. Milligan saying humans make something called adrenaline, which makes them stronger, gives them more energy when they need it to survive. Maybe Emma's body is making extra adrenaline. . . .

Why are you thinking about it? Even if it is adrenaline, she's still human. She needs help. And where is Rayna? She should have been here by now, with those useless humans who call themselves lifeguards. Lifeguards who sit in their tall wooden stands, keeping careful vigilance of the beach to make sure no one with a bikini drowns in the white sand.

Galen doesn't have time to wait for any adolescent savior. Even if Emma's making enough adrenaline to *stay* down here, it's a miracle the shark hasn't given up on Chloe and attacked *her.* He starts toward her a second time. And for a second time, he stops.

It's just that . . . she doesn't *look* as though she needs help. Her pale face is contorted with anger. Not fear. Not distress. Just fury. Her white hair floats around her like an aura, jerking in delayed reaction with each of her capable movements. She grunts and growls in frustration. Galen's eyes widen as she lifts her leg to kick. Her human legs are not powerful enough to do damage; water slows the movement, blunts the force of the blow. Still, she lands her mark on its eye, and the impact is enough to make the beast let go. It doesn't leave, just makes a wide circle around the girls. And then it swims directly at them.

Galen charges. Of his kind, he is the fastest. He can make it to her before the shark, snatch her away, and probably even change back to human form before she sees him. But why bother to change back at all? He's in blended form right now, his skin mimicking the water all around him. All she would see is a watery glob carrying her to shore. Even if he un-blended, if he let her see him, no one will believe her if she tells. They'll insist she lost consciousness, that she swallowed too much saltwater, that she was too traumatized to know what she saw.

But he wants her to know, wants her to see him. For some

reason beyond sense, he wants Emma to remember him. Because this will be the last time he ever sees her. There's no need to follow her, to watch her. After today he has no interest in her. A human cannot unite his people. Not even a breathtaking one.

Breathtaking? Rayna's right——you've lost your mind! He groans and speeds up. Emma's scream almost chokes him.

"Stop!" she yells.

Galen stops. But Emma's not talking to him. She's talking to the shark.

And the shark stops.

Emma wraps both arms around Chloe and hugs her to her chest, leaning her friend away from the attack. "You can't have her! Leave her alone! Leave us both alone!"

The shark turns, saunters away as if sulking.

Galen gasps. He watches until the smooth sway of its tail disappears in the distance. He tries to comprehend it. Because what he knows, *absolutely knows*, about bull sharks is that they don't back down. Aggressive and ruthless, they are one of the most feared creatures among Syrena and humans alike——the most likely to attack the young of either kind. And this one just surrendered his meal, his rightful kill.

Galen's attention whips back to Emma when he hears her strangled cry. She is still clutching Chloe, and they are sinking. Emma kicks her legs and flails with her free arm. Her face is not angry now but full of distress. Fear. Exhaustion. Emma looks like a real human.

Galen hears a noise approaching, the soft thrum of a boat

getting closer. *Rayna. But will she be in time?* Each passing second drains the spirit from Emma's fight. Her kicking becomes erratic, her arm thrashes without any clear purpose.

Galen is frozen in indecision. She isn't human—she can't be. Adrenaline might help a human hold her breath, but not for this long. Plus, humans don't talk underwater—especially when doing so sacrifices precious oxygen. And bull sharks do not back down from humans—especially one as puny as Emma. Still, they don't back down from Syrena either. Unless Dr. Milligan is right. Unless Emma has the gift of Poseidon.

But if she is Syrena, then why *didn't* she change? She could have saved her friend's life. Why doesn't she change now? Surely she knows her friend is dead. Why make a show of struggling in human form? *Can she sense me the way I sense her?* Galen shakes his head. There is not enough time to consider these things. For whatever reason, Emma is willing to drown to stay in human form.

And Galen will not allow it.

He launches toward her. The boat is visible a short distance away, breaking the waves on the surface. One way or the other, Emma will be saved. The boat stops overhead and Galen pauses. He can reach Emma if he needs to.

A white light strikes through the water, and the beam rests on Emma and Chloe; it is the first time Galen notices the absence of natural sunlight. The sun must be completely set. Two humans plunge in and swim directly to the girls. Galen knows Rayna must be on board, directing the light; without the Syrena's ability to see into the water, these helpless humans could never have found them, even with a spotlight.

Emma releases Chloe to the lifeguards, nodding to them in understanding as they pry her lifeless friend from her protective grip. The two exchange a surprised expression as they kick their way to the surface. They lift Chloe onto the boat, but not before Emma catches a glimpse of her leg—a dangling bone from knee to ankle. Her anguished cry siphons the last of her oxygen, the last of her will to fight. Her body falls limp, her eyes close.

Galen wraps his arms around her before she sinks an inch.

Ignoring the two splashes on the other side of the boat, he pushes Emma to the surface and into the waiting arms of his sister. Rayna heaves her over the rim of the craft.

When Galen falls back to the water, he spots the two lifeguards and rolls his eyes. They don't even realize Emma is already safe on board. They wade themselves stationary, not willing to search beyond an arm's length ahead of them. Without the spotlight, these pitiful creatures can see nothing. If Galen weren't here, Emma would be dead.

Infuriated, he torpedoes between them. The momentum spins them around like tiny whirlpools. He hears their startled cries as he swims away.

Galen dislodges his swimming trunks from under the rock; with a beach full of humans, he'd had to pull them off in the water. He slides them on, digs his feet in the muddy floor, and walks toward shore.

Rayna is waiting for him, sitting in the sand with her knees drawn to her chest. She wrings a piece of clothing in her hands until it resembles a rope; Galen recognizes it as the shirt Emma wore when he first saw her on the boardwalk. Even in the moon-light, he sees that his sister is crying.

He sighs and sits beside her. She accepts his arm around her shoulders without a fight, even leans her head on his chest when he draws her to him.

"Chloe's dead," she chokes out. For all her venom, his sister cares about life—human or not.

He nods. "I know. I didn't get there in time."

Rayna snorts. "Galen, this is one thing you can't take re-sponsibility for. I said she was dead. I didn't say you killed her. If *you* couldn't get to her, then nobody could have."

He pinches the bridge of his nose. "I waited too long to in-tervene."

"Galen—"

"Forget it. What about Emma?"

Rayna sighs. "She came to right when we got to shore. They let her ride in the white truck with Chloe."

"But how *is* she?"

She shrugs. "I don't know. She's breathing. And crying."

Galen nods, lets out a breath he didn't realize he'd been holding. "So she's okay." His sister pulls away and leans back. He lets his arm drop but doesn't look at her. "I think you should go home," he says quietly.

Rayna stands up and angles over him so that she's block-ing the moonlight. She plants her feet in the sand, hands on hips. Still, he doesn't expect her to yell like she does. "She isn't one of us! She's a pathetic human who couldn't even save her own friend. And you know what? Even if she *is* one of us, I don't want to know! Because then I'd have to kill her for letting her friend die!"

Galen is on his feet before she can finish the last sentence. "So if she's human, you hate her, and if she's Syrena, you hate her. Have I got that right?" He tries to keep the defensive edge out of his tone. His sister would probably have a different opinion if she'd just seen what he had. But she didn't. And since he's still not ready to tell her anything—not what Dr. Milligan said and not how the shark acted—he's going to have to be patient with her misconceptions about Emma. And he's going to have to do better than this.

"She's not Syrena! If she was, we would sense her, Galen."

This shuts him up. He'd assumed Rayna could sense Emma the way he could, since she is his twin. But who ever heard of sensing another Syrena on land? Did he just make it up? Could it be that he's just attracted to a human?

No. He knows what he felt when he touched her. *That* means *something, doesn't it?*

"Wait," Rayna says, jabbing her index into his bare chest. "Are . . . are you telling me you *did* sense her?"

He shrugs. "Did you get in the water?"

She tilts her head at him. "No. I was in the boat the whole time."

"So how do you know if you can sense her or not?"

She crosses her arms. "Stop answering my questions with questions. That only worked when we were young."

Galen cringes inwardly. There is no way to explain this to his sister without sounding foolish. And his answer would only lead to more questions—questions that weren't any of her business. For now, at least.

He crosses his arms, too. "It still works sometimes. Remember a few days ago when we came across that lionfish and—"

"Stop that! I swear by Triton's trident if you don't answer—"

Galen is saved by the faint sound of music coming from beneath their feet. They both step away and listen. Galen gently kicks the sand around, looking for the cell phone. He finds it on the last ring. He picks it up, brushes it off.

This phone doesn't look the same as the one Rachel—his self-appointed human assistant—bought him. It's pink with little jewels all over the cover. He presses a button, and a picture of Emma and Chloe lights up the screen.

"Oh," Rayna says, her brow wrinkled. "Whose . . . whose is it?"

"I don't know." He checks the missed call, but it only says, "Mom." He shakes his head. "I don't know how to tell who it belongs to."

"Would Rachel know?"

He shrugs. "Is there anything Rachel doesn't know?" Even Dr. Milligan admits that Rachel could likely be the most resourceful human alive. Galen has never told him her background, or how he found her, but if Dr. Milligan is impressed, then so is he. "Let's call her."

"She won't answer from this number, will she?"

"No, but I'll call the safe number and leave a message." He dials the 800 number she insisted on buying. It goes to a fake company, a "shell company" Rachel calls it, that's supposed to sell car warranties. She hardly ever gets a call, but when she does, she won't answer. And she only returns Galen's calls.

When he hears the voice prompt to leave a message, he says, "Rachel, call me back on this number, I don't have my cell phone. I need to know whose phone this is, both names if you can get it. Oh, and I need to know where Jersey is and if I have enough money to buy it."

When he hangs up, Rayna is staring at him. "*Both* names?"

Galen nods. "You know, like Dr. Milligan's names are Jerry and Milligan."

"Oh. Right. I forgot about that. Rachel said she has more names than a phone book. What does that mean?"

"It means she has so many names that no one can figure out who she is."

"Yeah, that makes perfect sense," Rayna mutters, kicking the sand. "Thanks for explaining."

The phone rings. The safe number lights up the screen.

"Hey, Rachel."

"Hiya, cutie. I can get you that name by morning," she says. She yawns.

"Did I wake you up? Sorry."

"Aw, you know I don't mind it, sweet pea."

"Thanks. What about Jersey?"

She laughs. "Sorry, hun, but Jersey's not for sale. If it was, my uncle Sylvester would already own it."

"Well then, I'll need a house there. Probably another car, too."

He turns away from his sister, who looks like she might eat

Emma's poor shirt. He prefers that she does—if it keeps her from biting *him*.

After a long silence, Rachel says, "A house? A car? What will you be doing in Jersey? Sounds pretty deep. Everything okay?"

He tries to put distance between him and his sister before he whispers, "I...I might be going to school there for a little while."

Silence. He checks the screen to make sure the signal is good. "Hello?" he whispers.

"I'm here, babe. You just, uh, surprised me, that's all." She clears her throat. "So umm...what kind of school? High school? College?"

He shakes his head into the phone. "I don't know yet. I don't exactly know how old she is—"

"*She?* You're buying a house and a car to impress a *girl*? Oh, swooooon!"

"No, it's not like that. Not exactly. Will you stop squealing, please?"

"Oh, no, no, no, I will *not* stop squealing. I'm going with you. This sort of thing is my specialty."

"Absolutely not," he says, running a hand through his hair. Rayna grabs his arm and mouths, "Get off the phone *now*." He shoos her away and is met with a growl.

"Oh, please, Galen," Rachel says, her voice syrupy sweet. "You've got to let me come. And besides, you're gonna need a mother if you want to register for school. And you don't know a thing about shopping for clothes. You *need* me, sweet pea."

He grits his teeth, partly because Rayna is twisting his arm to the point of snapping and partly because Rachel is right—he doesn't have a clue what he's doing. He flings off his sister and kicks sand on her for good measure before he walks farther down the beach.

"Fine," he says. "You can come."

Rachel squeals and then claps her hands. "Where are you? I'll come get you." Galen notes that she no longer sounds tired.

"Uh, Dr. Milligan said Destin."

"Okay. Where's Destin?"

"He said Destin and he said Florida."

"Okay, gotcha. Lemme see...." He hears clicking in the background. "Okay, it looks like I'll have to fly, but I can be there by tomorrow. Is Rayna coming, too?"

"Not in a million years."

The phone is snatched from his grasp. Rayna sprints away with it, yelling as she runs. "You bet I'm coming! And bring me some of those lemon-cookie things again, will you, Rachel? And some of that shiny stuff to put on my lips when they get too dry..."

Galen massages his temple with fingertips, contemplating what he's about to do.

And he considers kidnapping Emma instead.

5

DAWN BREAKS unwelcome and hazy against the bay windows of the living room. I groan and pull the quilt over my head, but not before I see the stoic face of the grandfather clock in the corner. I picked the living room to sleep in because it's the only room in the house with just one clock. All night I allowed myself to admire the driftwood clock, so long as I didn't look at the face. The last time I failed was two a.m. Now it is six a.m. Which means, for the first time since Chloe died, I have slept for four consecutive hours.

It also means the first day of my senior year will be starting in two. I am not ready for this.

I throw off the covers and sit up. The bay window shows me that it is not light, not dark, but gray outside. It looks cold, but I know it isn't. The wind whispers through the dune grass just off our back porch, making it look like a gathering of hula dancers. I wonder what the sea looks like this morning. For the first time since Chloe died, I decide to check.

I open the sliding glass door to a warm August breeze. A quick jump off the last step of the back porch and my bare feet sink in the cool sand. The beach is private, and I wrap my arms around myself, taking the path between the two huge dunes in front of our house. Past them is a miniature hill just big enough to block my view of the ocean from the living room. Had I slept in my room last night, I could already be soaking in the sunrise from my third-floor balcony.

But my room is full of all things Chloe. There is nothing on my shelves, on my desk, or in my closet that doesn't have something to do with her. Awards, pictures, makeup, clothes, shoes, stuffed animals. Even my bedding—a quilted collage of pictures from our childhood we made together for a school project. If I took everything out of my room connected to Chloe, my room would be pretty empty.

The same as I feel inside.

I stop a few feet from the wet sand and plop down, drawing my knees to my chest. Morning tide makes a great companion when you don't want to be around people. It soothes and comforts and doesn't ask for anything. But the sun does. The higher it gets, the more I am reminded that nothing stops time. There is no escaping it. It slips by no matter if you're looking at a driftwood grandfather clock or the sun.

My first day of school without Chloe has arrived.

I wipe the tears from my eyes and stand. I scrunch my toes in the sand with each step back to the house. Mom waits for me on the back-porch steps, smoothing out her robe with one hand and holding a travel mug of coffee in the other. Set against the gray-shingle beach house, she looks like an apparition in her white robe—except apparitions don't have long ebony hair, shockingly blue eyes, or drink espresso. She smiles the way a mother should smile at a daughter who is overwhelmed by loss. And it makes my tears spill bigger and faster.

"Morning," she says, patting the wood next to her.

I sit and lean into her, let her wrap her arms around me. "Morning," I rasp.

She hands me the mug and I sip. "Make you breakfast?" she squeezes my shoulder.

"Thanks, but I'm not hungry."

"You need some energy for your first day of school. I could make pancakes. French toast. I've got the stuff to make some good garbage eggs."

I smile. Garbage eggs are my favorite. She hunts down whatever she can find and puts it in my eggs—onions, bell peppers, mushrooms, hash browns, tomatoes, and whatever else might or might not have a place in an omelet. "Sure," I say, standing.

I smell the concoction from the bathroom and try to guess what's in it as I step out of the shower. Smells a lot like jalapeños, which brightens my mood a little. I fling my towel on the bed and pull a shirt off a hanger in the closet. I didn't feel like shopping for new school clothes, so my classmates will have to accept my old standby—T-shirt, jeans, and flip-flops. That's what everyone will be wearing in two weeks anyway, when the new wears off their carefully planned outfits. I twist my hair into a sloppy bun atop my head and secure it with a pencil. I reach for my makeup bag and stop. Mascara is not a good idea today. Maybe some foundation would be okay. I pick up the bottle— the shade is "porcelain." I slam it on my dresser in disgust. It's like putting Wite-Out on a blank sheet of paper—pointless. Besides, I can be porcelain all by myself. I'm practically *made* of porcelain these days.

Trudging down the stairs, a spicy aroma stings my nose. The garbage eggs are beautiful. They are piled high, steaming, and full of stuff. It is a shame that I mostly just push them around my plate. The glass of milk next to it sits untouched, unneeded.

I glance at my dad's old place setting at the head of the table. It's been two years since the cancer took him, but I can still remember the way he folded his newspaper beside his plate. The way he and Chloe fought over the sports page. The way the town's only funeral home smelled the same at his service as it did for hers.

I wonder how many empty place settings a person can look at before they begin to crack.

Across the table, Mom slides a key toward my plate, hiding her expression behind her coffee cup. "Feeling up to driving today?"

I'm surprised she doesn't wrap it up with "hint, hint." Or maybe a banner that reads, YOU NEED TO START DOING NORMAL THINGS, LIKE DRIVING YOURSELF AROUND.

I nod. Chew. Stare at the key. Chew some more. Grab the key, shove it in my pocket. Take another bite. My mouth should be on fire, but I taste nothing. The milk should be cold, but it's like tap water. The only thing that burns is the key in my pocket, daring me to touch it. I set the dishes in the sink, grab my backpack, and head for the garage. Alone.

As long as no one hugs me, I will be fine. I walk down a hall of Middle Point High School, nodding at the kids I've known since elementary school. Most of them have enough sense to just throw a sympathetic glance in my direction. Some talk to me anyway, but nothing too dangerous, just neutral things like "Good morning" and "I think we have third period together." Even Mark Baker, Middle Point's quarterback-slash-deity, gives me a supportive smile through the school-colored war paint smeared on his face. Any other day, I'd be texting Chloe to inform her that *the* Mark Baker acknowledged my existence. But the whole reason I don't is the same reason he acknowledged me in the first place: Chloe is dead.

They all lost their track star. Their bragging rights. In a few weeks, they won't even realize something's missing. They'll just move on. Forget about Chloe.

I shake my head but know it's true. A few years ago, a freshman riding on the back of her older brother's motorcycle died when he ran a stop sign and careened into a car. Flowers and cards were taped to her locker, the student body held a candlelit vigil in the football stadium, and the class president spoke at a special memorial the school arranged for her. Today, I can't for the life of me remember her name. She was in a few of the same clubs as me, some classes, too. I can see her face clearly. But I can't remember her name.

I test the combo to my new locker. It opens, third try. I stare into it, feeling as hollow as it looks. The hall takes awhile to clear out, but I wait until it does. When it is quiet, when the classroom doors ease closed, when the hall stops smelling like perfume and cologne, I slam the locker shut as hard as I can. And it feels good.

Because I am late to class, I'm forced to sit up front. The back row is ideal for spacing out or for texting, but I have no one to text. Today, I could space out on a roller coaster, so the front row is as good a seat as any. I glance around the room as Mr. Pinner passes out a class-rule sheet. Model airplanes hang by strings from the ceiling, timelines stripe the walls, and black-and-white pictures of the Egyptian pyramids adorn a nearby information board. History used to be my favorite class, but in view of my new vendetta against time, I'm just not feeling it.

Mr. Pinner is on Rule No. 3 when he looks up and to the back of the class. "Can I help you? Surely you're not already violating Rule Numero Uno! Anybody remember that one?"

"Arrive on time," chimes in a do-gooder from the back.

"Is this world history?" the presumable violator asks. His voice is even, confident, nothing like it should be, given that he's violated Numero Uno. I hear a few people shuffle in their chairs, probably to get a look at him.

"The one and only," says Mr. Pinner. "Unless, of course, you mean the one down the hall." He chuckles at his joke.

"Is this, or is this not, world history?" the student asks again.

A rash of whispers breaks out, and I smile at the timeline

I'm looking at. Mr. Pinner clears his throat. "Didn't you hear me the first time? I said this is world history."

"I did hear you the first time. You didn't make yourself clear."

Even the do-gooder snickers. Mr. Pinner fidgets with the leftover rule sheets in his hand and pushes his glasses up on his nose. The girl behind me whispers, "Gorgeous!" to her neighbor, and since she can't be talking about Mr. Pinner, I take the bait and turn around.

And my breath catches in my throat. *Galen.* He is standing in the doorway—no, he's filling up the doorway—holding nothing but a binder and an irritated expression. And he is already staring at me.

Mr. Pinner says, "Come have a seat up front, young man. And you can sit here for the remainder of the week as well. I don't tolerate tardiness. What is your name?"

"Galen Forza," he answers without taking his eyes off me. Then he strides to the desk next to me and seats himself. He dwarfs the chair meant for a normal adolescent male, and as he adjusts to get comfortable, a few feminine whispers erupt from the back. I want to tell them that he looks even better without a shirt on, but I have to admit that a tight T-shirt and worn jeans almost do him justice.

Even so, his presence sends me reeling. Galen has been a key player in my nightmares these past weeks, which have been nothing but a subconscious rehashing of the last day of Chloe's life. It doesn't matter if I sleep for forty minutes or two hours; I smack into him, hear Chloe approaching, feel embarrassed all over again. Sometimes she asks him to go to Baytowne with us and he agrees. We all leave together instead of getting in the water.

Sometimes the dream gets mixed up with a different one—the one where I'm drowning in Granny's backyard pond. The events run together like watercolors; Chloe and I fall in the water, and the school of catfish materialize out of nowhere and push us both to the surface. Dad's boat is waiting for us, but I taste saltwater instead of fresh.

I would rather have the dream with the real ending, though—it's horrible to see over and over, but it doesn't last very long, and when I wake up, I know Chloe is dead. When we take the alternate endings, I wake up thinking she's alive. And I lose her all over again.

But the tingles never show up in my dreams. I'd forgotten about them, in fact. So when they show up now, I blush. Deeply.

Galen gives me a quizzical look, and for the first time since he sat down, I notice his eyes. They're blue. Not violet like mine, as they were on the beach. Or were they? I could have sworn Chloe commented on his eyes, but my subconscious might have made that up, the same way it makes up alternate endings. One thing's for sure: I didn't make up Galen's habit of staring. Or the way it makes me blush.

I face forward in my desk, fold my hands on top of it, and train my eyes on Mr. Pinner. He says, "Well, Mr. Forza, don't forget where you're sitting because that's where you'll be until next week." He hands Galen a rule sheet.

"Thank you, I won't," Galen tells him. A few giggles sprinkle behind us. It is official. Galen has a fan club.

As Mr. Pinner talks about . . . well, really I have no idea what he's talking about. All I know is that the tingles give way to something else—fire. Like there's a stream of molten lava flowing between my desk and Galen's.

"Ms. McIntosh?" Mr. Pinner says. And if I remember correctly, Ms. McIntosh is me.

"Uh, sorry?" I say.

"The *Titanic*, Ms. McIntosh," he says, on the verge of exasperation. "Have any idea when it sank?"

Ohmysweetgoodness, I do. I became obsessed with the *Titanic* for a good six months after we studied it last year. Last year, before I had a vendetta against history, the passage of time. "April fifteen, 1912."

Mr. Pinner is instantly pleased. His thin lips open into a smile that makes him look toothless because his gums are so big. "Ah, we have a history buff. Very nice, Ms. McIntosh."

The bell rings. *The bell rings?* We've spent fifty minutes in this class already?

"Remember, people, study the rule sheet. Snuggle it at night, eat lunch with it, take it to the movies. It's the only way you're passing my class," Mr. Pinner calls over the bustle of students herding out the door.

I give Galen the opportunity to leave first. I open my binder, shuffle around some blank notebook paper, and make a show of tightening the straps of my backpack. He doesn't move. *Fine.* I stand, snatch up my things, and glide past him. The lava rallies at my wrist when he grabs it, like he's branding me with his touch.

"Emma, wait."

He remembers my name. Which means he remembers that I nearly knocked myself out on his bare chest. I wish I had applied the porcelain foundation this morning—it might have covered up at least some of my blush.

"Hi," I say. "I didn't think you'd remember me." I'm aware of a few stares coming from the back of the class—some of his fans have stayed behind and are patiently waiting their turn. "Well, welcome to Middle Point. You probably have to get to class, so I'll see you later."

He grips harder when I try to pull away. "Wait."

I glance down at his hold and he releases me. "Yes?" I say.

He looks down at his desk, runs a hand through his black hair. I remember that Galen's gift is not small talk. Finally, he looks up. The confidence has returned to his eyes. "Do you think you could help me find my next class?"

"Sure, but it's pretty simple. There are three halls here. The one hundred hall, the two hundred hall, and the three hundred hall. Let me see your schedule." He fishes it out of his pocket and hands it to me to unwad. Smoothing it out, I say, "Your next class is in room one twenty-three. That means you're going to the one hundred hall."

"But can you show me where it is?"

I check my schedule to see where I'm going, knowing even if my next class is in the complete opposite corner of the school from his, I will take him to room 123. Lucky for me, my next class is in room 123 as well—English lit.

"Uh, actually, we have the next class together, too," I tell him apologetically. He follows me out the door and keeps my slowish pace as I scan over our schedules to see how many more classes he will have to endure my awkward company—and how many more classes I can expect to be blushing in. The answer is all of them. I groan. Out loud.

"What?" he says. "Is something wrong?"

"Well, it's just that . . . it looks like we have the exact same schedule. Seven classes together."

"Is that a problem?"

Yes. "No. I mean, well it isn't for me, but . . . I just thought maybe you'd rather not have me around after what happened that day at the beach."

He stops and pulls me out of student traffic to a row of lockers. The intimacy of the move gets the attention of some passersby. Remnants of his fan club linger behind, still waiting for me to relinquish my turn.

"Maybe we should go somewhere private to discuss this," he says softly, leaning closer. He glances with meaning around us.

"Private?" I squeak.

He nods. "I'm glad you brought it up. I wasn't sure how to approach you about it, but this makes it easier for both of us, don't you think? And if you keep cooperating, I'm sure I can get you leniency."

I gulp. "Leniency?"

"Yes, Emma. Of course you realize I could arrest you right now. You understand that, right?"

Ohmysweetgoodness, he came all this way to press assault

charges against me! Is he going to sue me, sue my family? I'm eighteen now. I could legally be sued. The heat on my cheeks is part kill-me-now embarrassment and part where's-a-knife-when-you-need-one rage. "But it was an accident!" I hiss.

"*An accident?* You've got to be kidding me." He pinches the bridge of his nose.

"No, I am not kidding. Why would I ram into you on purpose? I don't even know you! And anyways, how do I know *you* didn't run into *me*, huh?" The idea is preposterous, but it leaves room for reasonable doubt. I can see by his expression he didn't think of that.

"What?" He is struggling to follow, but what did I expect? He can't even find his class in a school with only three halls. That he found me clear across the country seems more miraculous than a push-up bra.

"I said, you'll have to prove that I ran into you on purpose. That I meant to cause you harm. And besides, I checked with you at the time—"

"Emma."

"—and you said you didn't have injuries—"

"Emma."

"—but the only witness I have on my side is dead—"

"EM-MA."

"Did you hear me, Galen?" I turn around and yell at the remaining spectators in the hall as the bell rings. "CHLOE IS DEAD!"

Sprinting is not a good idea for me in the first place. Sprinting with tears blurring my vision, even worse. But sprinting with tears blurring my vision *and* while wearing flip-flops is a lack of respect for human life, starting with my own. So then, I am not surprised when the door to the cafeteria opens into my face. I am a little surprised when everything goes black.

6

HE PULLS into the driveway of the not-so-modest house he asked Rachel not to buy. Cutting the engine to the not-so-modest car, he throws his backpack full of books over his shoulder.

He finds Rachel in the kitchen, where she's pulling fish fillets from the oven. She wears an apron over her polka-dot dress, and her hair, a chaos of black curls, is pulled into a ponytail. She huffs up at her bangs to get them out of her face as she turns and smiles. "Hiya, cutie! How was your first day of school?" She pops the oven shut with her hip.

He shakes his head and pulls up a bar stool next to Rayna, who's sitting at the counter painting her nails the color of a red snapper. "This won't work. I don't know what I'm doing," he says.

"Sweet pea, what happened? Can't be *that* bad."

He nods. "It is. I knocked Emma unconscious."

Rachel spits the wine back in her glass. "Oh, sweetie, uh . . . that sort of thing's been frowned upon for years now."

"Good. You owed her one," Rayna snickers. "She shoved him at the beach," she explains to Rachel.

"Oh?" Rachel says. "That how she got your attention?"

"She didn't shove me; she tripped into me," he says. "And I didn't knock her out on purpose. She ran from me, so I chased her and—"

Rachel holds up her hand. "Okay. Stop right there. Are the cops coming by? You know that makes me nervous."

"No," Galen says, rolling his eyes. If the cops haven't found Rachel by now, they're not going to. Besides, after all this time, the cops wouldn't still be looking. And the other people who want to find her think she's dead.

"Okay, good. Now, back up there, sweet pea. Why did she run from you?"

"A misunderstanding."

Rachel clasps her hands together. "I know, sweet pea. I do. But in order for me to help you, I need to know the specifics. Us girls are tricky creatures."

He runs a hand through his hair. "Tell me about it. First she's being nice and cooperative, and then she's yelling in my face."

Rayna gasps. "She *yelled* at you?" She slams the polish bottle on the counter and points at Rachel. "I want you to be my mother, too. I want to be enrolled in school."

"No way. You step one foot outside this house, and I'll arrest you myself," Galen says. "And don't even think about getting in the water with that human paint on your fingers."

"Don't worry. I'm not getting in the water at all."

Galen opens his mouth to contradict that, to tell her to go home tomorrow and stay there, but then he sees her exasperated expression. He grins. "He found you."

Rayna crosses her arms and nods. "Why can't he just leave me alone? And why do you think it's so funny? You're my brother! You're supposed to protect me!"

He laughs. "From Toraf? Why would I do that?"

She shakes her head. "I was trying to catch some fish for Rachel, and I sensed him in the water. Close. I got out as fast as I could, but probably he knows that's what I did. *How does he always find me?*"

"Oops," Rachel says.

They both turn to her. She smiles apologetically at Rayna. "I didn't realize you two were at odds. He showed up on the back porch looking for you this morning and . . . I invited him to dinner. Sorry."

As Galen says, "Rachel, what if someone sees him?" Rayna is saying, "No. No, no, no, he is not coming to dinner."

Rachel clears her throat and nods behind them.

"Rayna, that's very hurtful. After all we've been through," Toraf says.

Rayna bristles on the stool, growling at the sound of his voice. She sends an icy glare to Rachel, who pretends not to notice as she squeezes a lemon slice over the fillets.

Galen hops down and greets his friend with a strong punch

to the arm. "Hey there, tadpole. I see you found a pair of my swimming trunks. Good to see your tracking skills are still intact after the accident and all."

Toraf stares at Rayna's back. "Accident, yes. Next time, I'll keep my eyes open when I kiss her. That way, I won't accidentally bust my nose on a rock again. Foolish me, right?"

Galen grins. Toraf is one of the best Trackers in Syrena history. His ability to sense others of his kind is acute, but more than that, he can home in on any one of them. He recognizes not only the presence of another Syrena, but after spending minimal time with them, can identify each one individually and from impossible distances. And the one he's most sensitive to is staring in an unhealthy way at a fillet knife across the counter.

"Rayna, your mate has come all this way to see you. You're being rude. Why don't you step away from the counter? Now?" Galen says, his tone hedged in warning. He's not in the mood to fight with either one of them. If Rayna makes a move, he'll be forced to subdue her. If he handles her too roughly, Toraf will take exception and handle *him* roughly. And besides, he's hungry and the fillets are almost cool enough to eat.

Rayna pushes back and whirls around. "He is *not* my mate."

Toraf clears his throat. Galen's eyes go wide, but Toraf cuts him a warning look, shakes his head almost indiscernibly.

"I was hoping your feelings would have changed by now, my princess. You know you won't find anyone else who would be more devoted to you than me. I've followed you around since you couldn't even swim straight," Toraf says. Although the words are tossed to her lightheartedly, Galen knows he means every one of them.

"Which is why I trusted you," Rayna snarls. "You knew me better than Galen. You knew I never wanted to mate. You let me think you agreed with my decision. But all that time, you were planning to take away my freedom yourself."

"Wow, shame on you Toraf," Rachel calls from the sink. "Anyone hungry?"

"Starving," Galen and Toraf say. Rayna rolls her eyes and stomps to the table.

They plop down on the moonlit beach. Toraf shakes the excess water from his hair onto Galen, who returns the favor by throwing a fistful of sand in his face. Galen leans back on his elbows and looks up at the star-freckled midnight sky. He shakes his head. "When are you going to tell her?"

Toraf stretches out beside his friend, resting his hands behind his head. "Tell her what?"

"That you're already mated."

Toraf grins. "You know me too well, I think, Highness."

"Don't call me that. When did my father agree to it?"

"Actually, he didn't. Grom sealed us."

Galen turns on his side, rests his head on his elbow. "She'll try to overturn it, you know. Grom's not technically king yet."

"Yeah, he technically is. And between you and me, I hope you have a fantastic excuse not to have been there. Oh, that reminds me." He reaches over and punches Galen square in the jaw. "That's for allowing your sister to hide out on land with you. I've spent the last two weeks thinking you were both dead."

Galen sits up and nods, rubbing his jaw. He can't argue with that. Rayna is breaking the law by staying in human form for more than a day. She doesn't have the immunity Galen has, but even *his* immunity doesn't extend this far, and he knows it. Toraf knows it, too. "So . . . you're saying you can't sense Rayna on land?"

"You know we can't sense each other on land, Galen."

"Yeah, I thought I knew. Wait, did you just say Grom is king? When did that happen?"

Toraf sits up. "First of all, I don't like your tone. I set out to find you, to bring you back for the ceremony. So don't act like you were accessible the whole time. *Two weeks ago,*" he reiterates. "And what do you mean you *thought*? I'm sitting right next to you. You can't sense me."

Galen shakes his head. "No. Not you, anyway."

"Right. You're saying you can sense someone. On land. I don't believe you."

Galen rubs his eyes. "I know. I can hardly believe it myself. I haven't told Rayna. She already said she can't sense her and—"

"*Her?* Her who?"

"Her name is Emma. Dr. Milligan found her." He tells Toraf everything—how Dr. Milligan left a message on Galen's cell phone, how Galen went to Florida to investigate the doctor's claim himself, how Emma ordered the shark away. How she has a habit of running into things.

Toraf is quiet for a long time. Then he says, "This doesn't make sense. How can she be one of us? If she is, then she would have done damage to the door, not the other way around. Her thick head would have left a dent in it."

"I know," Galen says, nodding. "At first, I thought she was faking it. But when I picked her up, she didn't blush. She was definitely unconscious."

"Even if she wasn't faking it, how can she be of Poseidon, Galen? King Antonis's only heir died in the explosion."

Galen shakes his head. "It doesn't make sense, does it?" No matter how many times he runs through the facts, he can't reconcile them with Emma. A long time ago, before Galen and Rayna were born, his brother, Grom, was engaged to King Antonis's daughter Nalia. As Galen heard tell of it, they were very much in love, a perfect match between the houses of Triton and Poseidon.

The law requires the firstborn heirs of each house to be mated, every third generation. To most, it is an obligation to fulfill, a motion to be carried out. It hardly ever happens that the firstborns actually *want* to be mated. But these two were different. Everyone insists these two had bonded the first time they saw each other. But right before their mating ceremony, they got into an argument—about what, either nobody remembers or nobody is saying—but several saw Nalia fleeing from Grom. Apparently, he gave chase—right into a mine set by the humans, who seemed to be at war all over the world at the time. Grom was badly injured. The best trackers from both kingdoms scoured everywhere. After days, they announced Nalia must have been blown to bits. Already widowed, the devastated Poseidon king accused Grom of killing his only daughter intentionally. Then Antonis vowed never to take another mate, to never sire an heir again—therefore eliminating any chance of their offspring inheriting the Gifts of the generals, Poseidon and Triton.

When he decreed the house of Triton an enemy, the two kingdoms split for good. Grom has never spoken of it, has never shown his feelings about any of it. Except that, he never chose another mate.

But now he doesn't have a choice. If Grom officially took the reigns of rulership from his father, the law requires him to select a mate. And if Emma is of Poseidon, then she is in line to fulfill that law.

"It doesn't make sense," Galen says again. "But I know what I saw. She talks to fish. And they listen. She's definitely of Poseidon."

Toraf exhales in a gust. "So, where has she been all this time? Why does she choose the company of humans over us?"

"That's what I'm trying to find out, idiot."

"Listen, minnow, not to be overly critical, but you don't really seem to know what you're doing. Threatening to arrest her? Chasing her down the hall? That's a little out of character for you, don't you think?"

"I was frustrated. Do you realize how . . . how . . . *sensual* female humans are? Within ten minutes of walking through those doors, a swarm of them followed me. *Everywhere.* Even the *adult* females in the office gave me mating signals! Rachel calls it hormones. She thinks hormones made Emma act so funny and run away like that, too."

"But if Emma has hormones, that means she's human."

"Are you listening to me? She can't be human. She has our eyes. And there's no way I could sense a human like that."

Toraf grins. "Like what? What does it feel like?"

"Stop smiling like you know something. It's not like that."

"Well, what's it like then? I'm a tracker remember? Maybe I can help you out on this one."

Galen nods. If anyone could help him figure out his sensing, it would be a Tracker. "It feels like . . . like . . . wrestling with an electric ray. And then when we touch, it's like swimming over a volcano vent. Hot, all over. But it's more than that. You know how you feel when one of our own is near? You feel their pulse, and you just know they're there?"

Toraf nods.

"Well, it's not like that with Emma, not exactly. I'm not just aware of her. I'm . . . I'm . . ."

"Drawn to her?"

Galen looks at his friend. "Yes. Exactly. How did you know that?"

"You remember the tracker who trained me?"

Galen nods. "Yudor. Why?"

"Well, he told me once that . . . you know what? Nevermind. It's stupid."

"I swear, Toraf, I'm going to knock every one of your teeth out if—"

"He said it means she's your mate," he blurts. "And not just any mate, your *special* mate. You feel the pull toward her, Galen."

Galen rolls his eyes. "I've heard that before. Romul says that's a myth. Nobody has a special mate." And as the oldest living Triton, Romul would know. Galen started visiting him years ago when he became ambassador to the humans. Romul taught him all the laws of the Syrena, the history of their kind, and the history of their relationship with humans. He also taught him about the ways of males and females—long before his parents ever intended him to know. Normally, when a Syrena male attains the age of eighteen, he becomes attracted to several match-worthy females at once. After spending time with each one, he is able to discern the most suitable for producing heirs and providing companionship. In cases of "the pull" though, he would only be attracted to one—and that one would be his perfect match in every way. It is thought that the pull also produces the strongest offspring possible, that it's something in the Syrena blood that ensures the survival of their kind. A few among the Syrena still believe in it. And Galen isn't one of them.

"Some think Grom felt the pull toward Nalia," Toraf says softly. "Maybe it's a family trait."

"Well, there's where you're wrong, Toraf. I'm not supposed to feel the pull toward Emma. She belongs to Grom. He's first-born, third generation Triton. And she's clearly of Poseidon." Galen runs his hand through his hair.

"I think that if Grom were her mate, he would have found Emma somehow instead of you."

"That's what you get for thinking. I didn't find Emma, Dr. Milligan did."

"Okay, answer me this," Toraf says, shaking a finger at Galen. "You're twenty years old. Why haven't you sifted for a mate?"

Galen blinks. He's never thought of it, actually. Not even when Toraf asked for Rayna. Shouldn't that have reminded him of his own single status? He shakes his head. He's letting Toraf's gossip get to him. He shrugs. "I've just been busy. It's not like I don't want to, if that's what you're saying."

"With who?"

"What?"

"Name someone, Galen. The first female that comes to mind."

He tries to block out her name, her face. But he doesn't stop it in time. *Emma.* He cringes. *It's just that we've been talking about her so much, she's naturally the freshest on my mind,* he tells himself. "There isn't anyone yet. But I'm sure there would be if I spent more time at home."

"Right. And why is it that you're always away? Maybe you're searching for something and don't even know it."

"I'm away because I'm watching the humans, as is my responsibility, you might remember. You also might remember they're the real reason our kingdoms are divided. If they never set that mine, none of this would have happened. And we both know it will happen again."

"Come on, Galen. If you can't tell me, who *can* you tell?"

"I don't know what you're talking about. And I don't think you do either."

"I understand if you don't want to talk about it. I wouldn't want to talk about it either. Finding my special mate and then turning her over to my own brother. Knowing that she's mating with him on the islands, holding him close—"

Galen lands a clean hook to Toraf's nose and blood spurts on his bare chest. Toraf falls back and holds his nostrils shut. Then he laughs. "I guess I know who taught Rayna how to hit."

Galen massages his temples. "Sorry. I don't know where that came from. I told you I was frustrated."

Toraf laughs. "You're so blind, minnow. I just hope you open your eyes before it's too late."

Galen scoffs. "Stop vomiting superstition at me. I told you. I'm just frustrated. There's nothing more to it than that."

Toraf cocks his head to the side, snorts some blood back into his nasal cavity. "So the humans followed you around, made you feel uncomfortable?"

"That's what I just said, isn't it?"

Toraf nods thoughtfully. Then he says, "Imagine how Emma must feel then."

"What?"

"Think about it. The humans followed you around a building and it made you uncomfortable. You followed Emma across the big land. Then Rachel makes sure you have every class with her. Then when she tries to get away, you chase her. Seems to me you're scaring her off."

"Kind of like what you're doing to Rayna."

"Huh. Didn't think of that."

"Idiot," Galen mutters. But there is some truth to Toraf's

observation. Maybe Emma feels smothered. And she's obviously still mourning Chloe. Maybe he has to take it slow with Emma. If he can earn her trust, maybe she'll open up to him about her gift, about her past. But the question is, how much time does she need? Grom's reluctance to mate will be overruled by his obligation to produce an heir. And that heir needs to come from Emma.

Toraf nudges him from his thoughts. "You know whose advice I need?" He nods toward the gigantic house behind them. "Rachel's."

"Actually, you don't," Galen says, standing. He reaches a hand down to help his friend.

"Why's that?"

"Rachel's expertise lies more along the lines of communication. You won't need to worry about communication when Rayna finds out you're already mated."

"We're *what*?" They both turn to Rayna who has stopped mid-stride in the sand. The emotions on her face change from surprise to full-blown murderous rage.

"You're gonna pay a special price for that, minnow!" Toraf calls before he hits the water.

Galen grins as Rayna slices through the waves in blood-thirsty pursuit. Then he heads for the house to talk to Rachel.

7

I PICK up the compact and smear porcelain all over my face. The pressure makes me wince and sends a shooting pain to my eye sockets. At least I don't have a bruise. Bruises—and zits—show up especially well on white skin. I glide on some sheer lip gloss and pucker in front of the mirror. Then wipe it off. Who am I kidding? That sticky stuff will bother me all day. The mascara tube mocks me from the sink in the bathroom, daring me to put some on. I accept the challenge—I'm not in any danger of crying today. I seize the tube, giving my lashes two good swipes. Funny how a little sleep, a little makeup, and a lot of contemplation can make you feel like a different person—a stronger version of yourself.

Mom wants me to stay out of school for one more day. But that's not going to happen. I spent all of yesterday in bed, alternating between crying and sleeping. Finally, at midnight, the waterworks stopped and my brain started working. This is what I decided:

Chloe is gone. She is never coming back. And the way I've been acting would hurt her. For at least an hour, I switch places with her in my mind—I am dead and Chloe is alive. How would she handle it? She would cry. She would be sad. She would miss me. But she wouldn't stop living. She would let people comfort her. She would sleep in her own room and smile at the memories as she drifted to sleep. And she would probably punch Galen Forza. Which brings me to what else I decided:

Galen Forza is a jerk. The details are hazy, but I'm pretty sure he had something to do with my accident Monday. Also, he's a bit weird. Staring habit aside, he keeps popping up everywhere. Every time he does, I handle it with the grace of a rhino on stilts. So I'm switching my schedule as soon as I get to school. There is no good reason I should humiliate myself for seven periods a day.

I smile with satisfaction at my plan as I pull up a chair at the table. Mom serves me garbage eggs again today, and this time I eat them. I even ask for seconds. She sets a glass of milk on the table for us to share. I accidentally guzzle it all. I don't even glance at Dad's place setting. Or Chloe's.

"You must be feeling better, then," Mom says. "But I wish you'd just stay home one more day. We could have a girls' day, you and me. Rent some chick flicks, eat chocolate and drink diet soda, exchange some small-town gossip. Whataya say?"

I laugh, which makes my head throb as if my brain is trying to escape. When she puts it like that, staying home is tempting and not just because of the chocolate. Watching Mom try to act girlie would be entertainment in itself. Our last attempt at a girls' day started with a pedicure and ended with a monster-truck rally. That was five years ago. And so was her last pedicure.

Still, I've already decided that today starts the rest of my normal life. Dragging a comforter and half gallon of ice cream to the couch feels like a cop-out, and risking another monster-truck rally is about as appealing as growing a third nostril. Picking up my dishes and walking them to the sink, I say, "Actually, I really want to go to school. Change of scenery, you know? How about a rain check?"

She smiles, but I know it's not real because it doesn't crinkle her eyes. "Sure. Some other time."

I nod and grab my car keys. Before I flip the light on in the garage, she's behind me, tugging on my backpack.

"You want to go to school? Fine. But you're not driving. Give me the key."

"I'm okay, Mom, really. I'll see you tonight." I plant a quick kiss on her cheek and turn to the door again.

"That's nice. Give it to me." She holds out her hand.

I clench the key in my fist. "You practically shoved that car down my throat Monday, and now you're taking the key. What did I do?"

"What did you do? Well, for starters, you used your face to stop a cafeteria door from swinging open." Foot tapping, *check.* Angry eyebrows, *check.* I'm-about-to-get-grounded tone, *check, check, check.* All the signs are there—I'm in trouble and I don't know why.

"Uh, I said I feel better. Dr. Morton said I could resume normal activities if I feel better. And I'm about to be late for school." Dr. Morton said no such thing. Since he was my dad's best friend though, he waited until Mom left the room to tell me I probably had a concussion. He knows how obsessive she can be. She has an affidavit on file at school not to call an ambulance for me in case of emergency, since Dr. Morton's office is across the street.

"School, huh? Are you sure that's where you're going?" Her hand is still outstretched, waiting for a key that she isn't getting. After a few empty seconds, she crosses her arms.

"Where *else* would I be going with my backpack and books?"

"Oh, I don't know. Maybe Galen Forza's house?"

Yep, didn't see that one coming. If I did, I might have stopped the blush sprouting on my cheeks. "Um. How do you know Galen?"

"Mrs. Strickland told me about him. Said you were arguing with him in the hall and that you were upset when you took off running from him. Said he carried you to the office himself when you ran into the door."

I *knew* he had something to do with my accident. And Mom talked to the principal about it. My lips turn so dry I expect to taste dust when I lick them. The blush spreads all over my body, even to my ears. "He *carried* me?"

"She said Galen wouldn't leave your side until Dr. Morton got there. Dr. Morton said he wouldn't go back to class until he assured him you would be okay." She taps her foot faster, then stops. "Well?"

I blink at her. "Well, what?"

Did my mother just growl? She throws her arms up and walks to the sink, leaning back and clutching the counter until her knuckles look like white beans. "I thought we were close, Emma. I always thought you would be open with me about this stuff, that you felt comfortable talking to me."

I roll my eyes. *You mean like the time I almost drowned and you laughed in my face when I told you how the fish saved me?* Who is she kidding? We both know Dad was my parental trash can, the fatherly receptacle on whom I dumped my emotions. Does she think because she offered me a blanket and chocolate-covered whatever that I'll just hand over the keys to my inner diary? Uh, no.

"I know you're eighteen now," she huffs. "I get it, okay? But you don't know everything. And you know what? I don't like secrets."

My head spins. The first day of the Rest of My Normal Life is not turning out as planned. I shake my head. "I guess I still don't understand what you're asking me."

She stomps her foot. "How long have you been dating him, Emma? How long have you and Galen been an item?"

Ohmysweetgoodness. "I'm not dating Galen," I whisper. "Why would you even think that?"

"Why would I think that? Maybe you should ask Mrs. Strickland. She's the one who told me how intimate you looked standing there in the hall. And she said Galen was beside himself when you wouldn't wake up. That he kept squeezing your hand."

Intimate? I let my backpack slide off my shoulder and onto the floor before I plod to the table and sit down. The room feels like a giant merry-go-round.

I am . . . embarrassed? No. Embarrassed is when you spill ketchup on your crotch and it leaves a red stain in a suspicious area.

Mortified? No. Mortified is when you experiment with tanning lotion and forget to put some on your feet, so it looks like you're wearing socks with your flip-flops and sundress.

Bewildered? Yep. That's it. Bewildered that after I screamed at him—oh yes, now I remember I screamed at him—he picked up my limp body, carried me all the way to the office, and stayed with me until help arrived. Oh, and he held my hand and sat beside me, too.

I cradle my face in my hands, imagining how close I came to going to school without knowing this. How close I came to walking up to Galen, telling him to take his tingles and shove them where every girl's thoughts have been since he got there. I groan into my laced fingers. "I can never face him again," I say to no one in particular.

Unfortunately, Mom thinks I'm talking to her. "Why? Did he break up with you?" She sits down next to me and pulls my hands from my face. "Is it because you wouldn't sleep with him?"

"Mom!" I screech. "No!"

She snatches her hand away. "You mean you *did* sleep with him?" Her lips quiver. This can't be happening.

"Mom, I told you, we're not dating!" Shouting *is* a dumb idea. My heartbeat ripples through my temples.

"You're not even *dating* him and you slept with him?" She's wringing her hands. Tears puddle in her eyes.

One Mississippi . . . two Mississippi . . . *Is she freaking serious?* . . . Three Mississippi . . . four Mississippi . . . *Because I swear I'm about to move out.* . . . Five Mississippi . . . six Mississippi . . . *I might as well sleep with him if I'm going to be accused of it anyway.* . . . Seven Mississippi . . . eight Mississippi . . . *Ohmysweetgoodness, did I really just think that?* . . . Nine Mississippi . . . ten Mississippi . . . *Talk to your mother—now.*

I keep my voice polite when I say, "Mom, I haven't slept with Galen, unless you count laying on the nurse's bed unconscious beside him. And we are not dating. We have never dated. Which is why he wouldn't need to break up with me. Have I missed anything?"

"What were you arguing about in the hall, then?"

"I actually don't remember. All I remember is being mad at him. Trust me, I'll find out. But right now, I'm late for school." I ease out of the chair and over to my backpack on the floor. Bending over is even stupider than shouting. I wish my head would just go ahead and fall off already.

"So, you don't remember what you talked about? You definitely should stay home and rest then. Emma? Emma, don't you walk away from me, young lady."

She doesn't come after me, which means this conversation is over.

I pull into my parking spot and check my makeup in the rearview. The porcelain foundation hides my blush as well as a magnifying glass. It's bound to get worse if I run into Galen. Taking a deep breath, I open the door as the bell rings.

The front office smells of fresh paint, crisp notebook paper, and coffee. I sign in as an unexcused tardy and wait for my hall pass. Mrs. Poindexter, a nice older lady who's worked in the front office since she was a nice younger lady, pulls a pad from a drawer and scribbles on it. She's recognizable in old faculty photos because, like then, she still stacks her white hair into an honest-to-goodness beehive, using enough hairspray to get the attention of the EPA. Oh, and she shows more cleavage than most prom dresses.

"We're all so happy you're feeling better, Miss McIntosh. Looks like you still have a good bump on your noggin, though," she says in her childlike voice.

Since there is no bump on my noggin, I take a little offense but decide to drop it. "Thanks, Mrs. Poindexter. It looks worse than it feels. Just a little tender."

"Yeah, I'd say the door got the worst of it," he says beside me. Galen signs himself in on the unexcused tardy sheet below my name. When his arm brushes against mine, it feels like my blood's turned into boiling water.

I turn to face him. My dreams really do not do him justice. Long black lashes, flawless olive skin, cut jaw like an Italian model, lips like—*for the love of God, have some dignity, nitwit. He just made fun of you.* I cross my arms and lift my chin. "You would know," I say.

He grins, yanks my backpack from me, and walks out. Trying to ignore the waft of his scent as the door shuts, I look to

Mrs. Poindexter, who giggles, shrugs, and pretends to sort some papers. The message is clear: *He's your problem, but what a great problem to have.* Has he charmed the sense out of the staff here, too? If he started stealing kids' lunch money, would they also giggle at that? I growl through clenched teeth and stomp out of the office.

Galen is waiting for me right outside the door, and I almost barrel into him. He chuckles and catches my arm. "This is becoming a habit for you, I think."

After I'm steady—after Galen steadies me, that is—I poke my finger into his chest and back him against the wall, which only makes him grin wider. "You . . . are . . . irritating . . . me," I tell him.

"I noticed. I'll work on it."

"You can start by giving me my backpack."

"Nope."

"*Nope?*"

"Right—nope. I'm carrying it for you. It's the least I can do."

"Well, can't argue with that, can I?" I reach around for it, but he moves to block me. "Galen, I don't want you to carry it. Now knock it off. I'm late for class."

"I'm late for it too, remember?"

Oh, that's right. I've let him distract me from my agenda. "Actually, I need to go back to the office."

"No problem. I'll wait for you here, then I'll walk you to class."

I pinch the bridge of my nose. "That's the thing. I'm changing my schedule. I won't be in your class anymore, so you really should just go. You're seriously violating Rule Numero Uno."

He crosses his arms. "Why are you changing your schedule? Is it because of me?"

"No."

"Liar."

"Sort of."

"Emma—"

"Look, I don't want you to take this personally. It's just that... well, something bad happens every time I'm around you."

He raises a brow. "Are you sure it's me? I mean, from where I stood, it looked like your flip-flops—"

"What were we arguing about anyway? We were arguing, right?"

"You... you don't remember?"

I shake my head. "Dr. Morton said I might have some short-term memory loss. I do remember being mad at you, though."

He looks at me like I'm a criminal. "You're saying you don't remember anything I said. Anything *you* said."

The way I cross my arms reminds me of my mother. "That's what I'm saying, yes."

"You swear?"

"If you're not going to tell me, then give me my backpack. I have a concussion, not broken arms. I'm not helpless."

His smile could land him a cover shoot for any magazine in the country. "We were arguing about which beach you wanted me to take you to. We were going swimming after school."

"Liar." With a capital L. Swimming—drowning—falls on my to-do list somewhere below giving birth to porcupines.

"Oh, wait. You're right. We were arguing about when the *Titanic* actually sank. We had already agreed to go to my house to swim."

Bells are going off in my head, but not the kind that should be ringing if this were true. I don't remember talking about the beach at all, but I *do* remember answering the question about the *Titanic* in Mr. Pinner's class. Even Galen, wielding his smile as a thought deterrent, couldn't have talked me into getting in the water, could he? "I . . . I don't believe you," I decide as I say it. "I wouldn't get that upset about a date. Historical or otherwise."

He shrugs. "It surprised me, too."

I raise a BS brow. "Why would you argue about the date anyway? You could Google it all over the place and get the same answer."

"True. You could look it up on the World Wide Web. Ever wonder whose web it is, exactly?"

"What?"

"What I mean is, have you ever considered that you only know the facts they *want* you to know?"

I shake my head. "Nope. Not falling for it. You're trying to distract me. What were we really arguing about?"

"What do you think we were arguing about?"

"Stop that. You're answering my questions with questions." He's pretty stinking good at it, too. I'm kind of impressed with myself for catching it, especially with a concussion.

He seems impressed, too. "Are you sure you don't remember? Your mind seems to be working fine to me."

"You know what? Just forget it. Whatever it was, I forgive you. Give me my backpack so I can go back to the office. We're about to get busted anyway, just standing here."

"If you really do forgive me, then you wouldn't still be going to the office." He tightens his hold on the strap of my backpack.

"Ohmysweetgoodness, Galen, why are we even having this conversation? You don't even know me. What do you care if I change my schedule?" I know I'm being rude. The guy offered to carry my things and walk me to class. And depending on which version of the story I believe, he either asked me out on Monday already, or he did it indirectly a few seconds ago. None of it makes any sense. Why me? Without any effort, I can think of at least ten girls who beat me out in looks, personality, and darker foundation. And Galen could pull any of them.

"What, you don't have a question for my question?" I ask after a few seconds.

"It just seems silly for you to change your schedule over a disagreement about when the *Titanic*—"

I throw my hands up at him. "Don't you see how weird this is for me?"

"I'm trying to, Emma. I really am. But I think you've had a rough couple of weeks, and it's taking a toll on you. You said every time you're around me something bad happens. But you can't really know for sure that's true, unless you spend more time with me. You should at least acknowledge that."

Something is wrong with me. Those cafeteria doors must

have really worked me over. Otherwise, I wouldn't be pushing Galen away like this. Not with him pleading, not with the way he's leaning toward me, not with the way he smells. "See? You're taking it personally, when there's really nothing personal about it," I whisper.

"It's personal to me, Emma. It's true, I don't know you well. But there are some things I do know about you. And I'd like to know more."

A glass full of ice water wouldn't cool my cheeks. "The only thing you know about me is that I'm life threatening in flip-flops."

That I won't meet his eyes obviously bothers him, because he lifts my chin with the crook of his finger. "That's not all I know," he says. "I know your biggest secret."

This time, unlike at the beach, I don't swat his hand away. The electric current in my feet prove that we're really standing so close to each other that our toes touch. "I don't have any secrets," I say, mesmerized.

He nods. "I finally figured that out. That you don't actually know about your secret."

"You're not making any sense." Or I just can't concentrate because I accidentally looked at his lips. *Maybe he did talk me into swimming. . . .*

The door to the front office swings open, and Galen grabs my arm and ushers me around the corner. He continues to drag me down the hall, toward world history.

"That's it?" I say, exasperated. "You're just going to leave it at that?"

He stops us in front of the door. "That depends on you," he says. "Come with me to the beach after school, and I'll tell you."

He reaches for the knob, but I grab his hand. "Tell me what? I already told you that I don't have any secrets. And I don't swim."

He grins and opens the door. "There's plenty to do at the beach besides swim." Then he pulls me by the hand so close I think he's going to kiss me. Instead, he whispers in my ear, "I'll tell you where your eye color comes from." As I gasp, he puts a gentle hand on the small of my back and propels me into the classroom. Then he ditches me.

8

THE FINAL bell rings and students leak from every crevice of the redbrick building. Bus brakes hiss in the distance and the lower classmen corral into the bus ramp, bottlenecking to board. The juniors and seniors herd to the parking lot in a steady stream, which seems to coagulate around Galen and his not-so-modest car. He leans against the trunk, nodding to the males admiring the vehicle and avoiding eye contact with the females admiring something else.

The wave of students turns into a traffic jam. The obligatory honking becomes less frequent as cars packed with human adolescents migrate to the highway. Behind him, Galen hears someone on a skateboard make the acquaintance of asphalt and the accompanying groan of pain.

He glances at the car parked beside his. *Where is she?*

When she appears at the double doors, the air between

them seems to crackle with energy. She locks eyes with him. Disappointed when she doesn't smile, he pushes away from the car, reaching her before she can take ten steps. "Let me carry your pack. You look tired. Are you okay?"

Emma doesn't fight about the backpack this time. Instead, she hands it over and pulls all her white hair to the side. "Just have a headache. And wow. You skipped an entire day of school after you *fought* with me about changing my schedule."

He grins. "I didn't think about it like that. I just knew you wouldn't concentrate on class if I stayed. You'd be bothering me all day about your secret, and you've missed enough school already."

"Thanks, Dad," she says, rolling her eyes. When they reach their cars, he throws her bag into the backseat of his convertible.

"What are you doing?" she says.

"I thought we made plans for the beach."

She crosses her arms. "You made plans. Then you left."

He crosses his arms, too. "You agreed to it Monday, before you hit your head."

"Yep, you keep saying that."

Without thinking, he takes her hand into his. Emma's eyes widen—she's as surprised as he is. *What am I doing?* "Fine, so you don't remember me asking you. But I'm asking now. Will you please come to the beach with me?"

She tugs her hand free, glancing at a few kids passing by who shield their whispers behind a yellow folder. "What does the beach have to do with my eyes? And why are you wearing contacts on yours?"

"Rach— Uh, my *mom* says they'll help me blend in better. She says the color would just draw attention to me."

Emma snorts. "Oh, she's definitely right. Blue eyes make you look so much more *average.* In fact, I almost didn't notice you standing there."

"That hurts my feelings, Emma." He grins.

She giggles.

He says, "I'd consider forgiving you—if you come with me to the beach."

She sighs. "I can't go with you, Galen."

He runs a hand through his hair. "Honestly, Emma, I don't know how much more rejection I can take," he blurts out. In fact, he doesn't remember *ever* being rejected, except by Emma. Of course, that could be due to the fact that he's a Royal. Or maybe it's because he doesn't spend a lot of time with his kind anyway, let alone the females. Actually, he doesn't spend a lot of time with anyone except Rachel. And Rachel would give him her beating heart if he asked for it.

"I'm sorry. It's not about you this time. Well, actually, it kind of is. My mom . . . well, she thinks we're dating." Her cheeks—and those lips—deepen to red.

"Dating?" *What is dating, again?* He tries to remember what Rachel told him. . . . She said it's easy to remember because it's almost the same as . . . *what is the rhyme for it?* And then he remembers. "It's easy to remember, because dating rhymes with mating, and they're almost the same," she'd said. He blinks at Emma. "Your mom thinks we're ma— Uh, dating?"

She nods, biting her lip.

For reasons he can't explain, this pleases him. He leans against the passenger door of her car. "Oh. Well. What does it matter if she thinks that?"

"I told her we weren't dating, though. Just this morning. Going to the beach with you makes me look like a liar."

He scratches the back of his neck. "I don't understand. If you told her we weren't dating, then why does she think we are?"

She relaxes against his driver-side door. "Well, this is all actually your fault, not mine."

"I'm obviously not asking the right questions—"

"The way you acted toward me when I hit my head, Galen. Some people saw that. And they told my mom. She thinks I've been hiding you from her, keeping you a secret. Because she thinks we've been . . . we've been . . ."

"Dating?" he offers. He can't understand why she'd have a difficult time discussing dating, if it means what he thinks it does—spending time with one human more than others to see if he or she would be a good mate.

The Syrena do the same, only they call it sifting—and sifting doesn't take nearly as long as dating. A Syrena can sift out a mate within a few days. He'd laughed when Rachel said some humans date for years. *So indecisive.* Then an echo of Toraf's voice whispers to him, calling him a hypocrite. *You're twenty years old. Why haven't you sifted for a mate?* But that doesn't make him indecisive. He just hasn't had *time* to sift and keep his responsibility watching the humans. If it weren't for that, he'd already be settled down. How can Toraf think Emma's the reason he hasn't sifted yet? Up until three weeks ago, he didn't even know she existed.

Emma nods, then shakes her head. "Dating, yes. But she thinks we're, uh, *more* than dating."

"Oh," he says, thoughtful. Then he grins. "*Oh.*" The reason her lips are turning his favorite color is because Emma's mom thinks they've been dating *and* mating. The blush extends down her neck and disappears into her T-shirt. He should probably say something to make her feel more comfortable. But teasing her seems so much more fun. "Well then, the least she could do is give us some privacy——"

"Ohmysweetgoodness!" She snatches her backpack from the seat and marches around her car to the driver's side. Before she can get the door unlocked, he plucks the key from her fingers and tucks it into his jeans' pocket. She moves to retrieve it, but stops when she realizes where she's about to go fishing.

He's never seen her this red. He laughs. "Calm down, Emma. I'm just kidding. Don't leave."

"Yeah, well, it's not funny. You should have seen her this morning. She almost cried. My mom doesn't cry." She crosses her arms again but relaxes against her door.

"She *cried*? That's pretty insulting."

She cracks a tiny grin. "Yeah, it's an insult to *me*. She thinks I would . . . would . . ."

"More than date me?"

She nods.

He steps toward her and puts his hand beside her on the car, leaning in. A live current seems to shimmy up his spine. *What are you doing?* "But she should know that you don't even think of me like that. That it would never even cross your mind," he murmurs. She looks away, satisfying his unspoken question—it *has* crossed her mind. The same way it crosses his. How often? Does she feel the voltage between them, too? *Who cares, idiot? She belongs to Grom. Or are you going to let a few sparks keep you from uniting the kingdoms?*

He pulls back, clenching his teeth. His pockets are the only safe place for his hands at the moment. "Why don't I meet her then? You think that would make her feel better?"

"Um." She swipes her hair to the other side of her face. Her expression falls somewhere between shock and expectation. And she had every right to expect it—he's been entertaining the idea of kissing her for over two weeks now. She fidgets the door handle. "Yeah, it might. She won't let me go anywhere— especially with you—if she doesn't meet you first."

"Should I be afraid?"

She sighs. "Normally I would say no. But after this morning..." She shrugs.

"How about I follow you to your house so you can drop off your car? Then she can interrogate me. When she sees how charming I am, she'll let you ride to the beach with me."

She rolls her eyes. "Just don't be *too* charming. If you're too smooth, she'll never believe—just don't overdo it, okay?"

"This is getting complicated," he says, unlocking her car.

"Just remember, this is your idea and your fault. Now would be the time to back out."

He chuckles and opens the door for her. "Don't lose me on the road."

~ ~ ~

Emma tosses her backpack on the counter and pokes her head up the stairwell. "Mom, could you come down a sec? We've got company."

"Sure, sweetie. Be right down. They just called me in, so I'm in a hurry though," is the answer from above.

He shoves his hands in his pockets. *Why am I nervous? It's just one more human to fool.* But everything hinges on this human liking him, accepting him. Winning over Emma's mother is just as important as winning over Emma. Her mother could make his task more difficult, cost him more time if she disapproves.

Self-doubt settles in. If he hadn't practiced with Rachel for those two weeks before school, he wouldn't even be trying this. But Rachel was thorough. She ran through what to expect in school and how to act, what certain phrases meant, what he should wear and when he should wear it. They brushed up on his driving skills. She even anticipated him meeting Emma's parents—just not under interrogation circumstances. Now he wishes he'd called her on the way here.

As he again contemplates kidnapping Emma, he glances around the room. From his vantage point in the kitchen, he can see the entire first floor. The only consistency in the decor is the theme of mismatching—mismatch appliances, furniture, paint. All the rooms open into each other without doors, as if in welcome. Beyond the living room, sand dunes tufted with grass peer into the huge window like they're eavesdropping.

All of this is already enough to make him covet this house—it makes the one Rachel bought seem cold, distant, impersonal. But what makes him downright jealous are the pictures smothering every wall of every room. Pictures of Emma. Her entire life hangs on these walls—and if he doesn't find a way to convince her mother of his good intentions, he might not ever get the chance to look at them.

Muffled footsteps plod down the stairs. Emma's mother emerges, clipping something to her shirt. When she sees Galen, she stops. "Oh."

Galen knows the shock on her face is mirrored in his own expression. *Is she Syrena?* All her features—dark hair and skin and lean muscular build—scream yes. Except those blue eyes. Blue eyes that rake over him with a familiarity, as if she knows who he is, knows why he's here. Then, with the next blink, those blue eyes change from guardian to hostess.

Emma transitions with grace. "Mom, this is my company. This is Galen Forza."

He smiles and holds out his hand to greet her, just as Rachel instructed him. "Hi, Mrs. McIntosh. It's nice to meet you."

She meets him halfway and accepts his hand. Her grip is confident but not overbearing, and without the slightest tingle. Not that he really expected electricity, but she *is* Emma's mother. Up close, he notices thin slithers of gray weaving through her hair. *Signs of aging; a human trait.* Her tone is the epitome of politeness, but her eyes—blue *without* contacts, as far as he can tell—are wide and her mouth never quite shuts. "Oh. Galen." She turns to Emma. "This is *Galen?*"

He can tell she's asking Emma a question within that question—one that has nothing to do with being Syrena. He shoves his hands in his pockets, abandoning his scrutiny of her in favor of memorizing each thread in the carpet. He can't meet her eyes, knowing what she, at this moment, is envisioning him and Emma doing. *Idiot! She's not worried why Galen the Syrena would be at her house. She's worried why Galen the human boy would.*

Emma clears her throat. "Yep. This is him."

"I see. Will you excuse us for a moment, Galen? Emma, can I talk with you privately please? Upstairs?"

She doesn't wait for a reply from either of them. Before Emma follows her up, she throws him an I-told-you-so smirk. He acknowledges with a nod.

Since he doesn't feel welcome to wander around the house and take in all the pictures, he trudges to the window, staring into the dune grass without seeing it. No noises—yelling, or otherwise—escape from upstairs, but he's not sure if that's good or bad. Humans resolve problems differently than Syrena, and even differently from each other. Sure, the Royals tend to have bad tempers. But most Syrena enlist the help of a third party, a mediator to keep things fair. Humans almost never do. They resort to yelling, fighting, sometimes even murder—how he found Rachel is proof enough of that. Tied to a cement block and thrown into the gulf. He was only thirteen years old at the time, but he still remembers how fast she sank, wriggling like live bait and screaming through the tape over her mouth. And the knots. He tore his fingers bloody and raw getting those knots loose.

When he took her to shore, she begged him not to leave her. He didn't want to stay, but she shook so hard he thought she might be dying anyway. Grom had just taught him how to build a fire—something most Syrena don't learn until it's time for them to mate on the islands—so he caught a few fish and cooked them for her. With guarded curiosity, he lingered while she ate. Any other adult human would have been rattled at seeing his fin. Not Rachel. In fact, she ignored it so well he thought she might not have noticed—until she told him she'd spent the last thirty years keeping secrets for people, and why should he be any different? So he stayed with her all night while she drifted in and out of sleep. In the morning, he announced it was time to part ways. She wouldn't accept that, said she wanted to pay him back. Reluctantly, he agreed.

In exchange for saving her life, he asked her to tell him about humans. He met her on the beach every night, in a place she called Miami, and she answered all the questions he could think of and questions he wouldn't know to ask. After he felt she'd repaid the debt, he insisted again on parting ways. That's when she offered to be his assistant. She said if he really wanted to learn about humans, to protect his kind from them, he would need her particular set of skills. When he asked her what skills she meant, she'd said simply, "I can do just about anything. That's why they tried to kill me, sweet pea. To humans, there's such a thing as knowing too much." And many times over, she's proved just what she can do. Their running joke is how he's the richest nonhuman on the planet.

Footsteps from the stairwell startle him out of the past. He turns around as Emma's mother takes the last step into the dining area, Emma right behind her.

Mrs. McIntosh glides over and puts her arm around him. The smile on her face is genuine, but Emma's smile is more like a straight line. And she's blushing.

"Galen, it's very nice to meet you," she says, ushering him into the kitchen. "Emma tells me you're taking her to the beach behind your house today. To swim?"

"Yes, ma'am." Her transformation makes him wary.

She smiles. "Well, good luck with getting her in the water. Since I'm a little pressed for time, I can't follow you over there, so I just need to see your driver's license while Emma runs outside to get your plate number."

Emma rolls her eyes as she shuffles through a drawer and pulls out a pen and paper. She slams the door behind her when she leaves, which shakes the dishes on the wall.

Galen nods, pulls out his wallet, and hands over the fake license. Mrs. McIntosh studies it and rummages through her purse until she produces a pen—which she uses to write on her hand. "Just need your license number in case we ever have any problems. But we're not going to have any problems, are we, Galen? Because you'll always have my daughter—my *only* daughter—home on time, isn't that right?"

He nods, then swallows. She holds out his license. When he accepts it, she grabs his wrist, pulling him close. She glances at the garage door and back to him. "Tell me right now, Galen Forza. Are you or are you not dating my daughter?"

Great. She still doesn't believe Emma. If she won't believe them anyway, why keep trying to convince her? If she thinks they're dating, the time he intends to spend with Emma will seem normal. But if they spend time together and tell her they're *not* dating, she'll be nothing but suspicious. Possibly even spy on them—which is less than ideal.

So, dating Emma is the only way to make sure she mates with Grom. Things just get better and better. "Yes," he says. "We're definitely dating."

She narrows her eyes. "Why would she tell me you're not?"

He shrugs. "Maybe she's ashamed of me."

To his surprise, she chuckles. "I seriously doubt that, Galen Forza." Her humor is short lived. She grabs a fistful of his T-shirt. "Are you sleeping with her?"

Sleeping . . . *Didn't Rachel say sleeping and mating are the same thing?* Dating and mating are similar. But sleeping and mating are the exact same. He shakes his head. "No, ma'am."

She raises a no-nonsense brow. "Why not? What's wrong with my daughter?"

That is unexpected. He suspects this woman can sense a lie like Toraf can track Rayna. All she's looking for is honesty, but the real truth would just get him arrested. *I'm crazy about your daughter—I'm just saving her for my brother.* So he seasons his answer with the frankness she seems to crave. "There's nothing wrong with your daughter, Mrs. McIntosh. I said we're not sleeping together. I didn't say I didn't want to."

She inhales sharply and releases him. Clearing her throat, she smoothes out his wrinkled shirt with her hand, then pats his chest. "Good answer, Galen. Good answer."

Emma flings open the garage door and stops short. "Mom, what are you doing?"

Mrs. McIntosh steps away and stalks to the counter. "Galen and I were just chitchatting. What took you so long?"

Galen guesses her ability to sense a lie probably has

something to do with her ability to tell one. Emma shoots him a quizzical look, but he returns a casual shrug. Her mother grabs a set of keys from a hook by the refrigerator and nudges her daughter out of the way, but not before snatching the paper out of her hand. She turns in the doorway. "Oh, and Galen?"

"Yes, ma'am?"

"Have your mother call me so I can get her number programmed into my phone."

"Yes, ma'am."

"You kids have a good time. I won't be home until late, Emma. But you'll be home by nine, sweetie. Won't she, Galen?"

"Yes, ma'am."

Neither Emma nor Galen say anything until they hear the car pull out of the driveway. Even then, they wait a few more seconds. Emma leans against the fridge. Galen is growing fond of hiding his hands in his pockets.

"So, what did you two chitchat about?" she asks as if uninterested.

"You first."

She shakes her head. "Uh-uh. I don't want to talk about it."

He nods. "Good. Me neither."

For a few seconds, they look at everything in the room but each other. Finally, Galen says, "So, did you want to go change—"

"That idea is fan-flipping-tastic. Be right down." She almost breaks into a run to get to the stairs.

9

WE PULL into his cobblestoned driveway, and I have to lean back in the seat to take in the whole thing. The beach house of my dreams. Four stories, maybe five—depending if that square on top is a room or not. All wood, painted sea green with white shutters. A huge front porch complete with white rocking chairs and matching wooden planters overflowing with red pansies. A wrought-iron gate leads to the back, which must overlook the beach—we drove so deep into the woods I thought we would hit water before we found his house.

"Nice shack," I tell him.

"Trade you."

"Any day."

"Really? You like it?" He seems genuinely pleased.

"What's not to like?"

He stands back and studies it as if for the first time. He nods. "Huh. Good to know."

We climb the three steps on the porch, but I grab his arm as he reaches for the door handle. The contact sends heat through my body, toasting me to the core. "Wait."

He pauses mid-motion and stares at my hand. "What? Is something wrong? You're not changing your mind are you?"

"No. I just . . . have to tell you something."

"What?"

I force a nervous laugh. "Well, the good news is, you don't have to worry about me rejecting you anymore."

He shakes his head. "That is good news. But you say it like it's not."

I take a deep breath. *Where is a good lightning bolt when you need one?* Because even if I take a hundred deep breaths, this will still be humiliating. . . .

"Emma?"

"I told my mom we were dating," I blurt. There. Doesn't that feel better? Nope. Nope, it doesn't.

While his smile surprises me, it mostly mesmerizes me beyond rational thought. "Are you kidding?" he says.

I shake my head. "It's the only thing she would believe. So now . . . now you have to pretend that we're dating if you come to my house. But don't worry, you don't ever have to go over there again. And in a few days, I'll pretend that we broke up."

He laughs. "No, you won't. I told her the same thing."

"Shut. Up."

"Why? What'd I say?"

"No, I mean, did you really tell her that? Why would you do that?"

He shrugs. "Same reason you did. She wouldn't take no for an answer."

The realization that we could have had the same conversation with my mother makes this pretty porch spin. Then this pretty porch gets black spots all over it. When we were little, Chloe and I used to spin each other around and around in my father's office chair. One time, she whirled me so fast and for so long that when I stood up, I walked in the exact opposite direction I meant to. As kids, we found that hilarious, like inhaling helium to talk like a chipmunk. Now though, it's just not as entertaining. Especially since Galen's face just disappeared behind a black spot. "Oh, no."

"Emma? What's wrong?"

The rest of the porch is sucked into the black hole of my vision. The welcome mat beneath me pitches like a rowboat during a hurricane. I reach for the door or the wall or Galen, but somehow I miss all three. Suddenly, my feet are swept out from under me, and my face smacks into his chest for the second time in my life. This time, my only option is to cling to him. I hear the door open and shut. The inferno of his touch is the only thing I'm sure of. Everything else—like up, down, left, and right—all seem to run together. "I . . . I might pass out. Sorry."

He squeezes me. "I'm laying you on the couch. Is that okay?"

I nod that it is, but I won't let go of his neck.

"Tell me what you need. You're scaring me."

I bury my face in his chest. "I can't see anything. I don't

want to lie down because . . . because I won't know where I am."
Already, the world has stopped spinning. I decide his arms are
the healthiest place to be right now.

Until I start to fall. I scream.

"Shhh. It's okay, Emma. I just sat down. You're on my lap."
He strokes my hair and rocks me back and forth. "Is it your
head? Tell me what I can do."

When I nod into his chest, the tears on my cheeks bleed onto
his shirt. "It's got to be my head. This never happens to me."

"Please don't cry, Emma."

He stiffens when I snicker into his shirt. As punishment,
my head throbs. "Bet you're regretting bringing me over here,"
I say.

He relaxes. "I wouldn't say that."

His tone is like a balm. Within the confines of his capable
arms, my body relaxes beyond my control. The panic flows away
from me like water from a shattered vase. My eyes refuse to
open. "I'm kind of tired."

"Should you sleep, though? Everything I read about head
injuries said you shouldn't go to sleep." Even as he says this, he
allows me to pull my legs closer, to nestle my shoulder into his
armpit and scoot higher on his lap. He secures my new position
with tight arms. The heat simmers between us and wraps around
me like a winter coat. Snuggling up to a sculpted block of gran-
ite just shouldn't be this comfortable.

"I think that's right after you hurt it. I'm pretty sure I'm
okay to sleep now. I mean, I slept last night, right? Actually, I'm
not sure I can even *stay* awake right now."

"But . . . you're not passing out, you're just sleeping? There's a difference."

I yawn again. "Just sleep. Maybe I just need a nap."

He nods into my hair. "You did look tired today after school."

"You can put me on the couch now."

He doesn't move, just keeps rocking me. Staying alert is a slippery slope right now.

"Galen?"

"Hmm?"

"You can put me down now."

"I'm not ready yet." He tightens his hold.

"You don't have to hold—"

"Emma? Can you hear me?"

"Uh, yes. I can hear fine. I just can't see—"

"That's a relief. Because for a minute there, I thought maybe you didn't hear me when I said I'm not ready yet."

"Jackass."

He chuckles into my hair. "Go to sleep."

It's the last thing I remember.

The bad thing is, he's not holding me anymore. The good thing is, I can see. I glance around the room but don't try to sit up yet. If I had to guess, I'd say I'm still at Galen's house. Everything about this room screams luxury. Art that you know is expensive because it's so ugly. Odd-shaped furniture made for looks instead of comfort. A huge flat-screen TV mounted on the wall over the fireplace. The cashmere blanket draped over me, so soft it wouldn't bother the worst sunburn. And yep, it overlooks the beach. The entire back wall of the house is a glass window. No dunes block the view. Even lying down, I see the waves rolling in, a storm percolating in the distance.

Sitting up is a big mistake for two reasons. First, it makes my head throb and my vision spotty. Second, it makes someone yell, "Gaaaaaa-len!"

Groaning, I cover my ears and retreat into a cave of cashmere.

"Triton's trident, Rayna, you're going to wake her up!"

Rayna? Fan-flipping-tastic. Galen's rude sister. But that voice wasn't Galen's. Does he have a brother, too?

"She's already awake, squid breath. Why else would I call for him?"

"Well he's not here, princess."

I hear shuffling and am almost curious enough to peek out from the blanket. Instead, the blanket is ripped from my face. Rayna stares down at me and points. "See? I told you she's awake."

The boy next to her shakes his head and leans toward me. "Emma?" I'm shocked to see yet another pair of violet eyes. And, of course, this boy is good-looking too—not as gorgeous as Galen, but really, who is?—with the same thick black hair and olive skin as Rayna and her brother.

In response to his question, I nod.

"Emma, I'm Toraf. I guess you already know Rayna?"

Toraf? His parents really named him Toraf? But I don't ask, just nod.

"Listen, you don't have to get up or anything. Galen just . . . uh . . . went for a swim. He'll be back real soon."

I look between them and past the beach. I shake my head.

"What? What's wrong, Emma?" he asks. I like Toraf. He seems genuinely concerned about me, without ever having met me. Rayna looks as if she might want to stomp on my head and finish the job I started with the cafeteria door.

"Storm," I say. The one syllable word polka-dots my vision.

Toraf smiles. "He'll be back before the storm. Can I get you anything? Something to eat? Something to drink?"

"A taxi?" Rayna pitches in.

"Go to the kitchen, Rayna," he says. "Unless you're ready to go find an island?"

I'm not sure how far away the kitchen is, but it seems like she stomps for a good five minutes. Finding an island doesn't really seem like a fitting punishment for being rude, but since I do have a head injury, I give them the benefit of the doubt. Plus, there's always the possibility that I imagined the whole thing.

"Do you mind if I sit?" Toraf says.

I shake my head. He eases onto the edge of the couch and pulls the blanket back over me. I hope he takes my nod for "Thanks."

He crouches down and whispers, "Listen, Emma. Before Galen gets back. There's something I want to ask you. Oh, don't worry, it's a yes or no question. No talking involved."

I hope he takes my nod for "Sure, why not? You're nice."

He glances around, as if he's about to rob me instead of ask a question. "Do you feel...uh...*tingly*...when you're around Galen?"

This time, I hope he takes my wide-eyed nod for "Ohymysweetgoodness, how did you know that?"

"I knew it!" he hisses. "Listen, I'd appreciate it if you didn't mention it to Galen. You'll both be better off if he figures it out on his own. Promise?"

I hope he takes my nod for "This is the strangest dream I've ever had."

Everything goes black.

I don't have to open my eyes to know the storm is here. Rain slaps the glass in waves and a constant rumble of thunder groans all around. *Or is that my stomach?* As I gravitate toward consciousness, flashes of lightning penetrate my eyelids like strobe lights. Peeking through tiny pores in the cashmere, I open my eyes. The lights in the living room are off, which makes my view of the storm like watching fireworks. I'd appreciate it more if the tantalizing smell of food weren't poking fun at my empty stomach.

When I sit up, the cashmere slithers to the floor. I hold still and clutch the couch, waiting for the room to pirouette around me or for my vision to evaporate. I turn my head side to side, up and down, all around. Nothing. No spinning, no blackouts, no throbbing. A flash of lightning ghosts into the room, and when it leaves again, my eyes follow it back out to sea. In the window's reflection, I glimpse a figure standing behind me. I don't need to turn around to see who creates such a big outline—or who makes my whole body turn into a goose-bump farm.

"How do you feel?" he says.

"Better," I say to his reflection.

He hops over the back of the couch and grabs my chin, turning my head side to side, up and down, all around, watching for my reaction. "I just did that," I tell him. "Nothing."

He nods and unhands me. "Rach— Uh, my *mom* called your mom and told her what happened. I guess your mom called your doctor, and he said it's pretty common, but that you should rest a few more days. My mom insisted you stay the night since no one needs to be driving in this weather."

"And my mother *agreed* to that?"

Even in the dark, I don't miss his little grin. "My mom can be pretty persuasive," he says. "By the end of the conversation, your mom even suggested we both stay home from school tomorrow and hang out here so you can relax—since my mom will be home supervising, of course. Your mom said you wouldn't stay home if *I* went to school."

A flash from the storm illuminates my blush. "Because we both told her we're dating."

He nods. "She said you should have stayed home today, but you threw a fit to go anyway. Honestly, I didn't realize you were so obsessed—ouch!"

I try to pinch him again, but he catches my wrist and pulls me over his lap like a child getting a spanking. "I was going to say, 'with history.'" He laughs.

"No you weren't. Let me up."

"I will." He doesn't.

"Galen, you let me up right now—"

"Sorry, not ready yet."

I gasp. "Oh, no! The room is spinning again." I hold still, tense up.

Then the room *does* spin when he snatches me up and grabs my chin again. The look of concern etched on his face makes me feel a little guilty, but not guilty enough to keep my mouth shut. "Works every time," I tell him, giving my best ha-ha-you're-a-sucker smirk.

A snicker from the entryway cuts off what I can tell is about to be a good scolding. I've never heard Galen curse, but his glower just looks like a four-letter word waiting to come out. We both turn to see Toraf watching us with crossed arms. He is also wearing a ha-ha-you're-a-sucker smirk. "Dinner's ready, children," he says.

Yep, I definitely like Toraf. Galen rolls his eyes and extracts me from his lap. He hops up and leaves me there, and in the reflection, I see him ram his fist into Toraf's gut as he passes. Toraf grunts, but the smirk never leaves his face. He nods his head for me to follow them.

As we pass through the rooms, I try to admire the rich, sophisticated atmosphere, the marble floors, the hideous paintings, but my stomach makes sounds better suited to a dog kennel at feeding time.

"I think your stomach is making mating calls," Toraf whispers to me as we enter the kitchen. My blush debuts the same time we enter the kitchen, and it's enough to make Toraf laugh out loud.

Rayna is at the counter, sitting Indian-style on a bar stool while trying to paint her toenails with the six different colors lined up in front of her. If she's trying to make them look like something other than M&M'S, she's got a long way to go. Mmm . . . M&M'S . . .

"Emma, I'd like you to meet my mother," Galen says. He puts his hand on his mother's back and launches her forward from the stove, where she's stirring a pot bigger than a tire. She extends an oven-mitted hand for me to shake. She giggles when I grasp it. Galen's mother is the most Italian person I've ever met. Big brown eyes, black curly hair piled like laundry on her head, and shocking red lipstick that matches the four-inch heels she's got to wear to reach the top of that pot.

"I'm so excited to meet you, Emma," she says. "Now I know why Galen won't shut up about you." Her smile seems to contradict the decades' worth of frown lines rippling from her mouth. In fact, it's so genuine and warm that I almost believe she *is* excited to meet me. But isn't that what all moms say when introduced to their son's girlfriend? *You're not his girlfriend, stupid. Or does she think we're dating, too?*

"Thanks, I think," I say generically. "I'm sure he's told you a million times how clumsy I am." Because how else am I supposed to take that?

"A million and one, actually. Wish you'd do something different for a change," Rayna drawls without looking up.

Rayna has outstayed her welcome on my nerves. "I could teach you how to color in the lines," I shoot back. The look she gives me could sour milk.

Toraf puts his hands on her shoulders and kisses the top of her head. "I think you're doing a great job, my princess."

She wiggles out of his grasp and shoves the polish brush back into its bottle. "If you're so good at it, why don't you paint your toes? They probably stay injured all the time from you running into stuff. Am I right?"

Yeah? And? I'm about to set her straight on a few things—like how wearing a skirt and sitting Indian-style ruins the effect of pretty toes anyway—when Galen's mom puts a gentle hand on my arm and clears her throat. "Emma, I'm so glad you're feeling better," she says. "I bet dinner would just about complete your recovery, don't you?"

I nod.

"Well, you're in luck, hon, because dinner is ready. Galen, can I get you to pull that pan out of the oven? And Rayna, you only set the table for four! Toraf, grab another place setting, will you? No, other cabinet. Thanks." While issuing orders, she walks me to the table and pulls out a chair. After she rams it into the back of my legs until I fall on it, she scampers in her heels back to the stove.

Toraf sets the dish in front of me so fast it warbles like a spun penny. "Oops, sorry," he says. I smile up at him. He slaps his hand on it to make it stop, then tosses a fork and knife on top. As he's lowering my drinking glass, Galen catches his forearm and snatches it from him.

"This is glass, idiot. Possibly you've heard of it?" Galen says. He sets it down as if it's a cracked egg, then winks at me. I'm glad he's taken the contacts out—his are the prettiest of all the violet eyes here. "Sorry, Emma. He's not used to company."

"Very true," Toraf says, sitting beside Rayna.

When everyone is seated, Galen uses a pot holder to remove the lid from the huge speckled pan in the center of the table. And I almost upchuck. Fish. Crabs. And . . . is that *squid* hair? Before I can think of a polite version of the truth—I'd rather eat my own pinky finger than seafood—Galen plops the biggest piece of fish on my plate, then scoops a mixture of crabmeat and scallops on top of it. As the steam wafts its way to my nose, my chances of staying polite dwindle. The only thing I can think of is to make it look like I'm hiccupping instead of gagging. *What did I smell earlier that almost had me salivating?* It couldn't have been this.

I fork the fillet and twist, but it feels like twisting my own gut. Mush it, dice it, mix it all up. No matter what I do, how it looks, I can't bring it near my mouth. A promise is a promise, dream or no dream. Even if *real* fish didn't save me in Granny's pond, the *fake* ones my imagination conjured up sure comforted me until help arrived. And now I'm expected to eat their cousins? *No can do.*

I set the fork down and sip some water. I sense Galen is watching. Out of my peripheral, I see the others shoveling the chum into their faces. But not Galen. He sits still, head tilted, waiting for me to take a bite first.

Of all the times to be a gentleman! What happened to the guy who sprawled me over his lap like a three-year-old just a few minutes ago? Still, I can't do it. And they don't even have a dog for me to feed under the table, which used to be my go-to plan at Chloe's grandmother's house. One time Chloe even started a food fight to get me out of it. I glance around the table, but Rayna's the only person I'd aim this slop at. Plus, I'd risk getting the stuff *on* me, which is almost as bad as *in* me.

Galen nudges me with his elbow. "Aren't you hungry? You're not feeling bad again, are you?"

This gets the others' attention. The commotion of eating stops. Everyone stares. Rayna, irritated that her gluttony has been interrupted. Toraf smirking like I've done something funny. Galen's mom wearing the same concerned look he is. Can I lie? *Should* I lie? What if I'm invited over again, and they fix seafood because I lied about it just this once? Telling Galen my head hurts doesn't get me out of future seafood buffets. And telling him I'm not hungry would be pointless since my stomach keeps gurgling like an emptying drain.

No, I can't lie. Not if I ever want to come back here. Which I do. I sigh and set the fork down. "I hate seafood," I tell him. Toraf's sudden cough startles me. The sound of him choking reminds me of a cat struggling with a hair ball.

I train my eyes on Galen, who has stiffened to a near statue. Jeez, is this all his mom knows how to make? Or have I just shunned the Forza family's prize-winning recipe for grouper?

"You . . . you mean you don't like this kind of fish, Emma?" Galen says diplomatically.

I desperately want to nod, to say, "Yes, that's it, not this kind of fish"—but that doesn't get me out of eating the crabmeat-and-scallop mountain on my plate. I shake my head. "No. Not just this kind of fish. I hate it all. I can't eat any of it. Can hardly stand to smell it."

Way to go for the jugular there, stupid! Couldn't I just say I don't *care* for it? Did I have to say I *hate* it? Hate even the *smell* of it? And why am I blushing? It's not a crime to gag on seafood. And for God's sakes, I won't eat *anything* that still has its eyeballs.

"You mean to tell me you don't eat fish?" Rayna barks. "I told you, Galen! How many times did I tell you?"

"Rayna, be quiet," he says without looking at her.

"We're wasting our time here!" She slams her fork down.

"Rayna, I said—"

"Oh, I heard what you said. And it's about time you listened to someone else for a change."

Now would be a good time to blackout. Or ten minutes ago, before they unveiled the seafood surprise. But I don't even feel remotely dizzy. Or tired. In fact, Rayna's ranting seems to be igniting a weird charge in the room, sparking some sort of hidden energy all around us. So when Galen stands so fast his chair falls over, I'm not surprised. I stand, too.

"Leave, Rayna. Right now," he grinds out.

When Rayna stands, Toraf does, too. He keeps his expression neutral. I get the feeling he's used to outbursts like these. "You're just using her as a distraction from your real responsibilities, Galen," she spits. "And now you've risked us all. For *her*."

"You were aware of the risks before you came, Rayna. If you feel exposed, leave," Galen says coolly.

Responsibilities? Exposed? I'm waiting for someone to admit they're part of some violet-eye cult, and I didn't make initiation. "I guess I don't understand," I say.

"Oh, well, that's a real shocker, isn't it?" Rayna says. Turning back to Galen she says, "Seems like you're always trying to send me away."

"Seems like you never listen," Galen returns.

"I'm your sister. My place is with you. Who is *she* to us?" she says, nodding toward me.

I move away from the table to put distance between Galen's sister and me. The energy in the room is no longer a spark, but a full-blown inferno.

"Are you okay?" he says. "You should sit down."

Rayna rounds the corner of the table and clutches the back of a chair. "Why are you still here, Galen? It's obvious she's just a pathetic human who couldn't even save her own friend. Course, we know how bloodthirsty they are, how little a reason they need to kill each other. Maybe she let her die on purpose."

I push away from the counter. "What did you just say?"

"Rayna!" Toraf bellows. "ENOUGH!"

"Emma, she doesn't know what she's talking about," Galen says, pulling my wrist to come back to him.

Rayna's smile is vicious when she says, "Oh, yes, I do, Emma. I know exactly what I'm talking about. You. Killed. Chloe."

I've never been in a fight before. Technically though, this won't count as a fight—this will be murder. For the first time in my life, precision replaces clumsiness. Even in bare feet, I run fast enough to knock the breath out of her. Ramming my shoulder into her gut, I pick up her legs and sprint her into the closest wall. She's more muscular than me. About two seconds ago, she thought she was angrier, too. But Rayna doesn't know what beyond-pissed-off really means—and I'm about to school her on it.

She clenches her teeth with the impact and grinds out, "See Galen? Her true colors are coming out!"

I punch her so hard my fist and her face should be broken. But both still work fine, because she head-butts me right between the eyes, and I use that same not-broken hand to box her ear. Somehow we scrap our way into the living room. I'm vaguely aware of Galen and Toraf scuffling. Galen's mom is screaming as if her leg's been amputated.

I've outstayed my welcome here. I will never be invited back. My chances with Galen ended when I tackled his sister. And when I punched her. And just now, when I kick her so hard she dry heaves.

So when she says, "Is this what you did to Chloe when you had her under the water?" I have nothing left to lose. Which is why I drive my shoulder into her rib cage, hoist her off the floor, and bulldoze us both through the glass wall, into the storm outside.

10

FOR THE five seconds it takes them to stir around in their bed of shattered glass, Galen tries to swallow his heart back down into his chest. When Emma moves—then growls when Rayna pulls herself up—he's able to breathe. Rayna shields herself when Emma kicks her legs out from under her. And it begins again.

Toraf shuffles up beside him in the living room and crosses his arms. "Rachel left," he says, sighing. "Says she's never coming back."

Galen nods. "She always says that. It's probably for the better tonight, though." They both wince as Rayna plants the ball of her foot in Emma's back, splaying her across the sea of shards.

"I taught her that," Toraf says.

"It's a good move."

Neither of the combatants seem to care about the rain, lightning, or the whereabouts of their hostess. The storm billows in, drenching the furniture, the TV, the strange art on the wall. No wonder Rachel didn't want to see this. She fussed over this stuff for days.

"So, it kind of threw me when she said she didn't like fish," Toraf says.

"I noticed. Surprised me too, but everything else is there."

"Bad temper."

"The eyes."

"That white hair is shocking though, isn't it?"

"Yeah. I like it. Shut up." Galen throws a sideways glare at his friend, whose grin makes him ball his fists.

"Hard bones and thick skin, obviously. There's no sign of blood. And she took some pretty hard hits from Rayna," Toraf continues neutrally.

Galen nods, relaxes his fists.

"Plus, you feel the pull—" Toraf is greeted with a forceful shove that sends him skidding on one foot across the slippery marble floor. Laughing, he comes back to stand beside Galen again.

"Jackass," Galen mutters.

"Jackass? What's a jackass?"

"Not sure. Emma called me that today when she was irritated with me."

"You're insulting me in human-talk now? I'm disappointed in you, minnow." Toraf nods toward the girls. "Shouldn't we break this up soon?"

"I don't think so. I think they need to work this out on their own."

"What about Emma's head?"

Galen shrugs. "Seems fine right now. Or she wouldn't have bashed the window into pieces with her forehead."

"Do you think she faked the whole thing?"

"No." Galen shakes his head. "You should have seen her on the porch. Terrified. More than terrified. She even let me carry her into the house. That's not like her. I mean, she wouldn't let me carry her *backpack* at school. She tried to snatch it out of my hands. No, something happened. I just don't know what."

"Maybe she knocked everything back into place then. Or maybe Rayna did."

"Could be."

After a few minutes of watching the gore, Galen pulls off his shirt. "What are you doing?" Toraf says.

"We should head toward shore. If Rayna's smart, she'll lure her to the water where she has the advantage." They can already see that Rayna is doing exactly that. She's made it past the pool, her arms roped around Emma's neck, dragging her as she kicks and bites.

"But what advantage does she have over Emma, if Emma's one of us *and* of Poseidon, on top of that?"

"Rayna knows what she is. Emma doesn't. But I think now's as good a time as any for her to know."

A bolt of lightning strikes close on the beach, startling the girls from the melee. Emma recovers first and fills Rayna's left eye with her knuckles, then slams a knee into her gut. When Rayna hunches over, Emma throws an uppercut to her chin, toppling her backward in the mud. Rayna rolls over and crawls toward the tide.

"What if Rayna gets her in the water and takes off with her?" Toraf says, peeling off his shirt in the rain.

Galen rolls his eyes. "She's almost as slow as you. I'll catch her."

They plod down the waterlogged beach. Emma thinks she has the upper hand by dragging Rayna by the hair to the water. "Looks like Emma's toying with the idea of drowning my fragile little princess," Toraf says, frowning.

"Why don't you ever call me my prince?" Galen says, feigning insult.

"Shut up, my prince. There, is that better?"

Galen laughs, but Toraf insists on defending his love. "I think everyone just misunderstands Rayna, you know? Sure, her passion sometimes comes off as—"

"Viciousness?" Galen offers.

"I was going to say, 'rude.'"

"So, accusing Emma of killing her best friend was *rude*?"

"Among other things, yes."

"It was evil and you know it."

"I admit she could have been more tactful. But she was just trying to goad Emma into telling the truth—" Toraf stops short when they hear a splash. The dark head surfaces first, then the white one. The girls struggle to find their footing, bracing themselves against waist-high waves in knee-deep water.

The look on Rayna's face is all he needs to see. Galen shakes his head. "Well, here we go."

"You *are* one of us!" Rayna screeches, pointing at Emma. But Emma doesn't notice the index inches from her eyeball. She stares into the water as if searching for something.

Toraf sticks his big toe in and nods to Galen. He can sense Emma.

Emma stays frozen as wave after wave smacks into her. She glances around her at the beach, past it to the house, then up at the storm. She wraps her arms around herself, settling her stare on Rayna as if she's seeing her for the first time. As if she doesn't know where she is or how she got there.

Rayna's lip quivers. She hugs herself like Emma. "But . . . but if you're one of us . . . that means you really *could* have saved . . ." Rayna shakes her head. "You didn't even try! You let her die!"

"I tried!" Emma sobs. "He wouldn't let go. It was just a game to him! He wasn't even hungry!"

Galen gasps. *She's right.* The way the shark writhed and pulled. The way it latched on to Chloe's leg, instead of going for more meat. That shark tried to *play* with Emma. Chloe was just a means to an end. A sea-grass rope in a game of tug. Did Emma realize it at the time? Could she read the shark's intentions, or did she think about it later? He shakes his head. These questions will have to wait—Emma is wavering like seaweed in high tide.

He sloshes into the water, wraps his arms around her. "It's okay, Emma. I've got you."

"What's happening to me? Is it my head?"

He presses her cheek against his chest. "Shhh. Calm down, Emma. It's not your head. This is your secret. What I know that you don't." He strokes her sopping hair, sets his chin on her head. When Rayna's mouth drops open, he flashes her a warning look. Her eyes go wide. "What are you *doing?*" she mouths. He rolls his eyes. *I wish I knew.*

"What secret? I don't understand. Not any of it," Emma whimpers into the sanctity of his chest. Her whole body wracks with the force of her sobs.

"Emma," he murmurs against her hair. "I'm sorry. This is a lot to take in. But this isn't half of it. I want to show you the rest. Will you let me?" He strokes her cheek with the back of his hand. After a few deep breaths, she nods. He turns her around, wraps his arms around her waist, moves them away from Rayna.

He's thought about this moment for days, trying to anticipate how Emma will react, how he should handle it. The possibility that she'll be disgusted is very real to him now and more painful than he could ever imagine. She said she wouldn't reject him anymore, but that was before he grew a fin. This could be the last time he holds her, the last time he feels the fire of her touch. He wants to savor the moment, to make the moment so much more, but Rayna is looking at him like he's grown an extra head. He sighs, tightens his hold on Emma. No turning back now.

"Hold your breath," he whispers in her ear.

"Hold my *breath*?" she gasps, peering down at the water.

He nods against her cheek, appreciating the silkiness of her skin, almost iridescent in the storm. "For now. But not always. Are you holding it?"

She nods.

He catapults backward—and under.

11

THIS CAN'T *be happening.* With his arms around my waist, I can't see his face as he pulls me deeper and deeper. We slice through the water so fast I shouldn't be able to keep my eyes open—but I can. We're too far down to see the storm on the surface anymore, to hear the thunder reverberate. I should be freaking out. But just like earlier on the couch, Galen's arms feel like a rope, a lifeline, all knotted with muscles wound tight around me.

The deeper we go, the darker it gets, but my eyes seem to adjust. In fact, they *more* than adjust—my vision sharpens down here. At first, it's like someone turned off the lights—everything is just a shadow. But the shadows take shape, turning into fish or rocks. Then everything appears plain as day, as if someone turned the light back *on.* But we're moving deeper, not closer to the surface. Where is the light coming from?

And where are we going? We pass schools of fish that dart

out of our way. Larger ones ease to the side as if we're driving a sports car on the interstate. How is Galen doing this? He's got his arms full of me, so he's not using them to swim. Even if he were, no one can swim this fast. I peer down to our feet—only, *our* feet aren't there. Just mine. And a fin.

"Shark!" I scream, gulping down water, hoping he understands through the garble. We stop so fast, my hair whips ahead of us.

"What?" He tightens his grip and whirls us around in place. "I don't see a shark, Emma. Where did you see it?"

"Down there—wait." I look behind us, but it's gone. Peering around Galen to see if it swam ahead of us—though I'm pretty sure a speedboat couldn't pass us—I begin to question the real strength of my vision down here. No shark. "I guess we scared it away—what the?...How are you doing that? How am *I* doing it?" This isn't how underwater sounds. Every word we say is clear, as if I'm sitting on his lap in his living room. It's not muffled, like when you're soaking in the bathtub and all you can hear is your heartbeat. There is no thrumming, no pressure in my ears. Just quiet.

"Doing what?" He faces me to him.

"I can hear you. You can hear me. And I *see* you, clear as day—but it's not day, not even on shore. What's happening, Galen?"

He sighs. *How can he sigh? We're underwater.* "This is the secret Emma." He nods toward our feet.

I follow his line of vision. And gasp. And gulp. And choke. The shark is back—and it has swallowed Galen's entire lower body, all the way to his waist! It flicks its fin, fighting to stay attached to him.

"Not you, too!" I scream. I kick it as hard as I can with bare feet. Galen grimaces and releases me.

"Emma, stop kicking me!" Galen says, grabbing my shoulders.

"I'm not kicking you, I'm kicking . . . I'm kicking . . . Ohmysweetgoodness." Galen is the shark. The shark is Galen. What I mean is, there is no shark. There's only Galen. His upper body is still there, big arms, chiseled abs, gorgeous face. But . . . his legs. Are. Gone. Not bit off, not swallowed. Nope, just *replaced* by a long silver fin. *Nofreakingway.*

I shake my head, wrench from his grasp. "Not happening. This is not happening." I propel away from him, but he follows.

"Emma," he says, reaching for me. "Calm down. Come here."

"Nope. You're not real. This isn't real. I'm ready to wake up now." I look to the surface. "I said, I'm ready to WAKE UP NOW!" I scream to myself, who must still be sleeping on Galen's couch. But myself doesn't wake up.

Galen glides closer without moving his arms. "Emma, you're awake. This is your secret. What makes your eyes that color."

"Stay right there." I point at him in warning. "In case you haven't noticed, *I* didn't turn into a fish, *you* did. That would be *your* secret then, don't you think?"

He smirks. "We have the same secret."

I shake my head. *Nope, nope, nope.*

He nods, thoughtful. "Well, I guess that's it then. The beach is that way," he says, pointing to the abyss behind me. "Well, it was nice to meet you, Emma."

My mouth drops open as he swims away. As his silhouette disappears from sight, I start to hyperventilate. He's leaving. He's leaving me. He's leaving me in the middle of the ocean. He's leaving me in the middle of the ocean because I'm not a fish. *No, no, no, no!* He can't leave me! I whirl around and around. How can I find the beach when I can't see the surface *or* the bottom? My breathing becomes more erratic—

But . . . but . . . how can I hyperventilate underwater? For the first time since leaving shore, I become aware of my oxygen. That I should have run out of it already. But I haven't. Not even close. During my meltdown, I just snorted air out of my nose— and not a lot of it. Like when I talked. Just enough air to make sound. Dad always said I had a good pair of lungs, but I doubt this is what he meant.

And now I've attracted an audience. There is nothing hazy or dream-like about the wreath of fish that surrounds me. As schizo as it sounds, I know this is real. None of these are fish I can name—except the monster of a swordfish lingering on the outskirt of the gathering. Textbook pictures are deceiving— swordfish are *much* scarier in person. Still, one big fish out of the hundred-or-so small ones is pretty good odds that I won't be eaten. They must realize that I would never, not ever, eat one of them because they move in on me like paparazzi on a celebrity. Some of them are brave enough to brush against me. One of the small red fish zips through my hair. I realize how not-normal it is, especially under these circumstances, for me to laugh. It's just that it tickles.

I reach out, my hand splayed open. Fish take turns darting in and out of my fingers. It reminds me of when Chloe and I visited the Gulfarium back in Destin. Chloe ditched me at the hands-on tank in favor of the cute guy working in the gift shop. Every time I put my hand in the water, the stingrays flitted to me, nuzzling against my fingers as if begging for me to pet them. They created a traffic jam in the tank to get to me. Even now, a stingray pushes through the halo and flits past my face, as if to play.

I shake my head. This is ridiculous. These creatures aren't here to play with me. They're just curious. And why shouldn't they be? I don't belong here any more than Galen does. *Galen.*

It's the first time I realize I can still . . . well, *feel* Galen. Not the goose bumps, or the pure lava running through my veins. No, this is different. An awareness, like when someone turns on a TV in a quiet room—even if it's on mute, a crackling sensation fills the air. Only, this sensation fills the water, and with Galen, it's much stronger, like a physical touch pulsating against me. Rayna's was noticeable, but Galen's is overwhelming. I knew the minute he stepped foot in the water, as if the pulse concentrated on the space between us. And I've felt it before today. This same feeling buzzed around me when I fought to free Chloe from the shark. *Was he there? Is he here now?*

I pivot in place, startling my spectators. Some scatter then return. Others keep going, not willing to take their chances with my skittish behavior. The swordfish eyes me, but still saunters at a distance. I check in every direction, pausing with each itty-bitty turn to squint into the underwater horizon. After circling twice, I give up. Maybe this pulse thing works over long distances. Galen could be swimming up to Ellis Island by now for all I know. But just in case, I give it another try.

"Galen?" I shout. This startles more of my neighbors. Fewer and fewer return. "Galen, can you hear me?"

"Yep," he answers, materializing right in front of me.

I gasp, my pulse spiking. "Ohmysweetgoodness! How did you do that?"

"It's called blending." He tilts his head. "Couldn't help but notice you're not dead yet. Kind of nonhuman of you."

I nod, a cocktail of relief and anger swirling in my stomach. "Then you will have also noticed that I don't have a big fin swallowing my butt either."

"But you do have violet eyes, like me."

"Huh. So . . . Rayna and Toraf?"

He nods.

"Huh. But what about your mom? She doesn't have the eyes."

"She's not really my mom. She's my assistant, Rachel. She's human."

"Of course. Your assistant. Makes perfect sense." As I try to process why a man-fish would need an assistant, I forget to tread and start sinking. Galen is a good sport and holds me up by the elbow. "But I can't change into a big blob of water. Blend, I mean."

He rolls his eyes. "I don't turn into water, my skin changes, so I can conceal myself. You'll eventually be able to, once you can shift into your fin."

"What makes you think I can? I don't look like you. Other than the eyes, I mean."

"I'm still trying to figure that out."

"And did I mention I don't have a big fin—"

"But, you do have everything else." He crosses his arms.

"Like what?"

"Well, you have bad temper."

"I do not!" Chloe had the bad temper. I earned the nickname Sugar our sophomore year because only *I* could sweet-talk her out of a fight. "In fact, they voted me Most Likely to Work for Hallmark in our middle school yearbook," I tell him as an afterthought.

"You realize I don't understand anything you just said."

"Basically, everyone thinks—*knows*—how sweet I am."

"Emma, you threw my sister through hurricane-proof glass."

"She started it! Did you just say hurricane-proof glass?"

He nods. "Which also means you have hard bones and thick skin like us. Otherwise, you would have died. Which we need to discuss. You threw yourself—and my sister—through a wall of glass when you thought you were both human. *What* were you thinking?"

I won't meet his glare. "I guess I didn't care." Telling him I meant to murder his sister probably wouldn't go over very well. It would definitely cancel out the Hallmark vote.

"Unacceptable. Don't *ever* risk your life like that again, do you understand?"

I snort, sending little air bubbles dancing upward. "Hey, you know what else I don't care about? You giving me orders. I acted stupid, but—"

"Actually, this is a good time to point out that I'm a Royal," he says, pointing to the small tattoo of a fork on his stomach, just above the border where his abs turn into fish. "And since you're obviously Syrena, you do have to obey me."

"I'm *what*?" I say, trying to figure out how an eating utensil could possibly validate his claim of seniority.

"Syrena. That's what we—including you—are called."

"Syrena? Not mermaids?"

Galen clears his throat. "Uh, mer*maid*?"

"Really? You're gonna go there *now*? Fine, mer*man*—wait, *I* wouldn't be a merman." Really though, what do I know about fish gender? Except that Galen is definitely male, no matter what species he is.

"Just for the record, we hate that word. And by we, I mean you also."

I roll my eyes. "Fine. But I'm not *Syrena*. Did I mention I don't have a big fin—"

"You're not trying hard enough."

"*Trying* hard enough? To grow a *fin*?"

He nods. "It's not natural to you yet. You've been in human form too long. But it will start to bother you, being in the water with legs. You'll get the urge to . . . stretch."

"Does it hurt?"

He laughs. "No. It feels good, the same way it feels good to stretch after you've been sitting a while. Your fin is one big muscle. When you separate it between two human legs, it's not as powerful. When you change into Syrena form, the muscles stretch and twist back together. Do you feel anything like that right now?"

I shake my head, eyes wide.

"It's just a matter of time," he says, nodding. "We'll figure it out."

"Galen, I'm not—"

"Emma, that you're talking to me half a mile underwater is proof enough of what you are. By the way, how do you feel?"

"Actually, my lungs feel kind of tight. What does that mean?"

Before more puny air bubbles escape, he wraps his arms around me and we shoot up. "It means you're running out of air now," he murmurs in my ear. My shiver isn't from the cold.

Wait. Isn't it supposed to be freezing half a mile deep in the Atlantic Ocean? I mean, as cold weather goes, I'm kind of a wuss. No one bundles up more than me in the winter. So why aren't my teeth chattering into bits? It's swimming-pool cold, not my-tear-ducts-have-ice-in-them cold. Is that thanks to the thick skin Galen mentioned? Does it work like insulation? Does it only work in water?

We break the surface. Galen nods in approval as I exhale the old air and take in the new. I gulp in a fresh lung-full and start to submerge, but he shakes his head, pulling me back up. "Let's not push it. I'm not sure how long you can hold your breath. I guess we'll have to keep an eye on that, at least until you figure out how to change."

He faces me forward and tucks me neatly under one arm,

which makes me feel like some sort of pet. The moon peers down at us as we ride the swells for a little while. In the distance, we can see the faint glow of occasional lightning, but not land.

When I can't stand the Chihuahua position anymore, I wriggle loose. He catches me before I go under and pulls me to him so that my nose just grazes his. Above water, it feels like we're exchanging kilowatts with our touch. Below, all I feel is Galen's "pulse," but it feels more like a magnetic force between us. When his fin rubs against my legs, it feels velvety, like the wings of a stingray instead of scaly like a fish.

He lets me squirm some distance between us, but doesn't let go. "If I'm Syrena, then where did I come from?" I say. "My mom doesn't have the eyes."

He nods. "I know. I looked for that."

"She hates the water, too. The only reason we live on the beach is because Dad loved it." In fact, Mom talks about moving farther into town all the time now that Dad's gone. I finally convinced her to wait until I left for college.

"And your father?"

"Blond. Blue eyes. Not as pale as me."

"Hmm." But he doesn't sound surprised. It sounds more like I confirmed what he already knew.

"What?"

"The only thing I can think of is that they're not your real parents. They can't be."

I gasp. "You think I'm *adopted*?"

"What does *adopted* mean again?"

· 117 ·

"That they raised me as their child, but I was born to someone else."

"Obviously."

I push away from him. The waves are a lot bigger when I try to negotiate them on my own. "Well, that's real easy for you to say, isn't it?" I decide to swallow the next wave instead of swim over it. I'm relieved when his arms encircle my waist again.

"Emma, I'm just exploring the options here. You've got to acknowledge that someone isn't telling the truth. And I don't think you can reasonably say *I'm* lying."

I shake my head. "No. You're not lying. But they are my parents, Galen. I have my dad's nose. And my mom's smile."

"Look, I don't want to argue with you. We'll just have to think harder about it, that's all."

I nod. "There's got to be some other explanation."

He offers a tight-lipped smile, his expression doubtful. In silence, we let the waves drift us toward shore. After a while, he pulls my legs up and lets me lean my head against his chest. We pick up speed as he propels us gently through the swells.

"Galen?"

"Hmm?"

"What happens when we get to shore?"

"Probably you should get some sleep."

He's already looking at me when I lift my chin. "You think I can sleep after all this? And anyway, that's not what I meant."

He nods. "I know it's not." He shrugs, adjusting me in his arms. "I was hoping you'd let me . . . help you."

"You want to help me turn into a fish."

"Something like that."

"Why?"

"*Why?* Why not?"

"Stop answering my questions with questions."

He grins. "It doesn't work, does it?"

"Stop that!" I give his jaw a little slap.

He laughs. "All right."

"But what I'm trying to say is, the reason you took such an interest in me since Chloe died . . . the reason you moved here, enrolled in my school, invited me to the beach . . . You were just trying to figure out if I'm one of you?"

Of course, stupid. When has anyone like Galen ever paid you any attention? When has there ever been anyone like Galen? Still, I'm surprised how much it hurts when he nods. I'm his little science project. All the time I thought he was flirting with me, he was really just trying to lure me out here to test his theory.

If stupid were a disease, I'd have died from it by now. But at least I know where he really stands—about his feelings for me anyway. But what his intentions for me *in general* are, I have no idea.

What happens if I *can* turn into a fish? Does he think I'll just kiss my mom good-bye, flush all my good grades—all those scholarships—down the toilet so I can go swim with the dolphins? He called himself a Royal. Of course, I don't know exactly what that means, but I can sure guess—that I'm another subject to him, someone to order around. He *did say* I had to obey him, after all. But if he's a Royal, why come out here himself? Why not send someone less important? I'm betting the U.S. President doesn't personally go to foreign countries looking for missing Americans who might not even be American.

But can I trust him enough to answer my questions? He already deceived me once, faking interest in me to get me out here. He lied to my face about having a mother. He even lied to my mom. What else would he lie about to get what he wants? No, I can't trust him.

Still, I want to know the truth, if only for myself. I'm not moving into some big seashell off the Jersey seashore or anything— but I can't deny that I'm different. What could it hurt to spend a little more time with Galen so he can help me figure this out? So what if he thinks I'm some sort of peasant fish who has to obey him? Why shouldn't I use him the way he used me—to get what *I* want?

It's just that what *I* want is holding me in his arms, acting like he's concerned that I'm not talking anymore.

12

FROM THE window seat, Galen watches Emma stir in the recliner. She mumbled all night, but he couldn't make out the words over Toraf's snoring. They stayed up late, Galen and Toraf, taking turns answering her questions. How did they find her, where do they live, how many are there? Emotion tampered with her expressions as they shifted from surprise to fascination to shock. Surprise when he told her how Dr. Milligan saw her at the Gulfarium—though Galen avoided the subject of her interaction with the animals. Fascination when he told her most Syrena live in plain sight on the bottom of the ocean—plain sight, that is, if humans could get deep enough—and that the Royals lived in the protection of the rock caverns. Captivation when he told her how Poseidon and Triton were flesh-and-blood Syrena, the first generals of their kind, not some gods that human lore made them out to be. Shock when Toraf estimated the combined population of the kingdoms to be over twenty thousand.

Galen clipped answers when the questions ventured too close to his purpose for being here—and once again, he thanked his good judgment for not telling Rayna. He wasn't—isn't—ready to tell Emma about Grom. Even Toraf steered the subject away from the big question buried inside all the little ones—why? Emma seemed to sense the conspiracy, sometimes asking the same questions in different ways. After a time, her expression surrendered to acceptance mostly, but her eyes still hinted at disbelief. And who could blame her? Her life changed last night. And he'd be a fool if he didn't admit that his did, too.

Watching her mingle with those fish sealed his fate. There is no chance that Emma is not a direct descendant of Poseidon. There is no chance that she can ever be his. And he better start getting used to it.

He glances at the bed meant for one person where Rayna is sleeping, oblivious to the fact that she's nestled into the crook of her mate's arm while he makes the sound of an injured leopard seal in her ear. Galen shakes his head. If Rayna wakes up, she'll make sure Toraf never breathes through his nose again.

"So last night really happened," Emma says, startling him. The only movement she makes is a groggy smile.

"Good morning," he whispers, inclining his head toward Rayna and Toraf.

Emma's eyes go wide as she nods. She eases the comforter off her body and onto the floor. Galen had rummaged through Rachel's drawers last night and found her a pair of pajamas to sleep in while her clothes dried. As she stretches in them now, Galen notes how much taller she is than Rachel—the tank top doesn't quite meet the rim of her pants—and how much curvier. The sight of Emma's flesh teasing the boundaries of that fabric makes him wonder how he's going to keep himself focused today. While female Syrena have strong, muscular builds, Emma's time spent in human form has made her soft in places—and he's surprised by how much he likes that.

Emma's stomach growls and she blushes. He's come to realize how much he likes that, too. Grinning, he points to the ladder leading to the hallway below. Since they stayed in the topmost floor last night, the only way in or out of the one room is to climb. She nods and descends without a word. Galen forces himself to look away from the tantalizing view as she takes the last step from the ladder. He follows with gritted teeth. Once in the hall, they exchange a knowing smile—Toraf is as good as dead.

By the smell of food wafting up the stairwell, Galen knows Rachel is already back. He can hear her high heels clicking around the kitchen, the oven opening and shutting, her loud curse, probably in response to burning herself on a pan. The morning breeze streams in through the remains of the living room, which now resembles an open patio. Emma winces as she assesses the damage again in daylight.

"I'm really sorry, Galen. I'll pay for all of it. Tell Rachel to send me a bill."

He laughs. "Do you think it would cost more or less than the medical bills you racked up when you knocked yourself out trying to get away from me?"

She grins. "Well, when you put it like that . . ."

Rachel is setting the table when they round the corner to the kitchen. "Good morning, my little lovebirds! I've got steamed fish and shrimp for you, sweet pea, and for Emma darling, the most magnificent omelet ever made. Juice Emma? I've got orange or pineapple."

"Orange, please," she says, taking a seat. "And you don't have to call us lovebirds anymore. Galen let me in on the secret last night. You know we're not really dating."

"Uh, actually Emma, I think we should keep that up for a while. For your mother's benefit," Galen says, handing her a glass. "She'll never believe we're spending so much time together and not dating."

Emma frowns as Rachel slaps a chubby omelet onto her plate with an oversize spatula. With her fork, Emma stabs into the belly of it and pulls out a steaming chunk of meat dripping with cheese. "I guess I didn't think of that," she says as she takes a bite. "I planned on telling her we broke up."

"He's right, Emma," Rachel calls from the stove. "You can't break up if you're going to be here all the time. She needs to think you're still a couple. And you'll need to be convincing about it, too. Lots of kissing and stuff in case your mother tries to spy on you."

Emma stops chewing. Galen drops his fork.

"Uh, I don't think we need to take it that far—" Emma starts.

"Oh, no? Teenagers don't kiss their sweethearts anymore?" Rachel crosses her arms, wagging the spatula to the beat of her tapping foot.

"They do, but—"

"No buts. Come on, sweetie. You think your mom's going to believe you keep your hands off *Galen*?"

"Probably not, but—"

"I said no buts. Look at you two. You're not even sitting next to each other! You need some practice, I'd say. Galen, go sit beside her. Hold her hand."

"Rachel," he says, shaking his head, "this can wait—"

"Fine," Emma grinds out. They both turn to her. Still frowning, she nods. "We'll make it a point to kiss and hold hands when she's around."

Galen almost drops his fork again. *No way. Kissing Emma is the last thing I need to do. Especially when her lips turn that red.* "Emma, we don't have to kiss. She already knows I want to sleep with you." He cringes as soon as he says it. He doesn't have to look up to know the sizzling sound in the kitchen is from Rachel spitting her pineapple juice into the hot skillet. "What I mean is, I already told her I want to sleep with you. I mean, I told her I wanted to sleep with you because she already thinks I do. Want to, I mean—" *If a Syrena could drown, this is what it would feel like.*

Emma holds up her hand. "I get it, Galen. It's fine. I told her the same thing."

Rachel plops down beside Emma, wiping the juice spittle from her face with a napkin. "So you're telling me your mom thinks you two want to *sleep* with each other, but you don't think she'll be expecting you to kiss."

Emma shakes her head and shovels a forkful of omelet into

her mouth, then chases it with some juice. She says, "You're right, Rachel. We'll let her catch us making out or something."

Rachel nods. "That should work."

"What does that mean? *Making out?*" Galen says between bites.

Emma puts her fork down. "It means, Galen, that you'll need to force yourself to kiss me. Like you mean it. For a long time. Think you can do that? Do Syrena kiss?"

He tries to swallow the bite he forgot to chew. *Force myself? I'll be lucky if I can* stop *myself.* It had never occurred to him to kiss anyone—*before* he met Emma. These days, it's all he can think about, her lips on his. He decides it was better for both of them when Emma kept rejecting him. Now she's ordering him to kiss her—for a long time. *Great.* "Yes, they kiss. I mean, *we* kiss. I mean, I can force myself, if I have to." He doesn't meet Rachel's eyes as she plunks more fish onto his plate, but he can almost feel her smirking down at him.

"We'll just have to plan it, that's all. Give you time to prepare," Emma tells him.

"Prepare for *what?*" Rachel scoffs. "Kissing isn't supposed to be planned. That's why it's so fun."

"Yeah, but this isn't for fun, remember?" Emma says. "This is just for show."

"You don't think kissing Galen would be fun?"

Emma sighs, putting her hands on her cheeks. "You know, I appreciate that you're trying to help us, Rachel. But I can't talk about this anymore. Seriously, I'm going to break out into hives. We'll make it work when the time comes."

Rachel laughs and removes Emma's empty plate after she

declines a second helping. "If you say so. But I still think you should practice." On her way to the sink, she says, "Where's Toraf and Rayna? Oh!" She gasps. "Did they find an island?"

Galen shakes his head and pours himself some water from a pitcher on the table, grateful for a topic change. "Nope. They're upstairs. He snuck into her bed. I've never seen anyone risk his life like that."

Rachel makes a tsking sound as she rinses some dishes.

"Why does everyone keep talking about finding an island?" Emma asks, finishing the rest of her juice.

"Who else is talking about it?" Galen frowns.

"In the living room, I heard Toraf give her a choice between going to the kitchen or finding an island."

Galen laughs. "And she picked the kitchen, right?"

Emma nods. "What? What's so funny?"

"Rayna and Toraf are mated. I guess humans call it married," he says. "Syrena find an island when they're ready to . . . mate in a physical sense. We can only do that in human form."

"Oh. *Oh.* Um, okay," she says, blushing anew. "I wondered about that. The physical part, I mean. So they're married? Seems like she hates him."

Galen hesitates. He remembers Rachel's outrage about this subject when he first told her all those years ago. *Emma will find out one way or another. Might as well be now.* "Toraf asked our brother for her, and he consented. I know humans do it a little differently, but—"

"*What?*" Emma eases out of her chair, leans over the table with arms crossed.

Here we go. "Toraf asked—"

"You're telling me your brother forced her to marry Toraf?" Speaking while her jaw is clenched makes her words difficult to understand.

"Well, it's not like she was there—"

"*What?* She wasn't at her own wedding?"

"Emma, you need to calm down. Syrena don't call it a wedding. They call it—"

"I don't care what you call it," she shouts. "And I don't care if she's human or not. You don't force someone to marry someone else!"

"I agree!" Rayna calls from the living room. Toraf follows her into the kitchen grinning, despite his split lip. Rayna plants herself beside Emma, crosses her arms the same way.

Emma nods to her. "You see? She doesn't like it. She shouldn't have to be married if she doesn't like it."

"Exactly my point," Rayna says, elbowing Emma in a show of camaraderie. Galen shakes his head. Emma doesn't seem to remember that just last night, Rayna used that same elbow to try to puncture her left eye.

"Morning," Toraf says pleasantly, taking the seat next to Galen. "I trust everyone slept well?" Rachel silently serves him breakfast and pours him some water.

Galen sighs. "Emma, please sit down. This isn't some new law she didn't know about. She did have a choice at first. If Rayna had picked a mate sooner, this wouldn't have—"

"There's a time limit to picking a mate? Really? This just gets better and better. So tell me, Galen, if I turn out to be one of you, will I be expected to mate? Do you already have someone in mind for me, Your Highness?"

There she goes again. All night she called him Your Highness and Majesty. And by the face she makes, she considers it an insult. Which is why he's dying to tell her she's a Royal too, but that would create more trouble than eradicating that smug expression would be worth. And it would make her think she could pick her mate, like most female Royals can. But Emma isn't like most female Royals. She's the last living proof of the Poseidon line—which dwindles her choices of a mate to one.

"*Do* you have someone in mind, Galen?" Toraf asks, popping a shrimp into his mouth. "Is it someone I know?"

"Shut up, Toraf," Galen growls. He closes his eyes, massages his temples. This could have gone a lot better in so many ways.

"Oh," Toraf says. "It must be someone I know, then."

"Toraf, I swear by Triton's trident—"

"These are the best shrimp you've ever made, Rachel," Toraf continues. "I can't wait to cook shrimp on our island. I'll get the seasoning for us, Rayna."

"She's not going to any island with you, Toraf!" Emma yells.

"Oh, but she is, Emma. Rayna wants to be my mate. Don't you, princess?" he smiles.

Rayna shakes her head. "It's no use, Emma. I really don't have a choice."

She resigns herself to the seat next to Emma, who peers down at her, incredulous. "You *do* have a choice. You can come live with me at my house. I'll make sure he can't get near you."

Toraf's expression indicates he didn't consider that possibility before goading Emma. Galen laughs. "It's not so funny any-more is it, tadpole?" he says, nudging him.

Toraf shakes his head. "She's not staying with you, Emma."

"We'll see about that, *tadpole*," she returns.

"Galen, do something," Toraf says, not taking his eyes off Emma.

Galen grins. "Such as?"

"I don't know, arrest her or something," Toraf says, crossing his arms.

Emma locks eyes with Galen, stealing his breath. "Yeah, Galen. Come arrest me if you're feeling up to it. But I'm telling you right now, the second you lay a hand on me, I'm busting this glass over your head and using it to split your lip like Toraf's." She picks up her heavy drinking glass and splashes the last drops of orange juice onto the table.

Everyone gasps except Galen—who laughs so hard he al-most upturns his chair.

Emma's nostrils flare. "You don't think I'll do it? There's only one way to find out, isn't there, Highness?"

The whole airy house echoes Galen's deep-throated howls. Wiping the tears from his eyes, he elbows Toraf, who's looking at him like he drank too much saltwater. "Do you know those foolish humans at her school voted her the sweetest out of all of them?"

Toraf's expression softens as he looks up at Emma, chuck-ling. Galen's guffaws prove contagious—Toraf is soon pounding the table to catch his breath. Even Rachel snickers from behind her oven mitt.

The bluster leaves Emma's expression. Galen can tell she's in danger of smiling. She places the glass on the table as if it's still full and she doesn't want to spill it. "Well, that *was* a couple of years ago."

This time Galen's chair does turn back, and he sprawls onto the floor. When Rayna starts giggling, Emma gives in, too. "I guess . . . I guess I do have sort of a temper," she says, smiling sheepishly.

She walks around the table to stand over Galen. Peering down, she offers her hand. He grins up at her. "Show me your other hand."

She laughs and shows him it's empty. "No weapons."

"Pretty resourceful," he says, accepting her hand. "I'll never look at a drinking glass the same way." He does most of the work of pulling himself up but can't resist the opportunity to touch her.

She shrugs. "Survival instinct, maybe?"

He nods. "Or you're trying to cut my lips off so you won't have to kiss me." He's pleased when she looks away, pink restaining her cheeks.

"Rayna tries that all time," Toraf chimes in. "Sometimes when her aim is good, it works, but most of the time kissing her is my reward for the pain."

"You're trying to kiss Emma?" Rayna says, incredulous. "But you haven't even sifted yet, Galen."

"Sifted?" Emma asks.

Toraf laughs. "Princess, why don't we go for a swim? You know that storm probably dredged up all sorts of things for your collection." Galen nods a silent thank you to Toraf as he ushers his sister into the living room. For once, he's thankful for Rayna's hoard of human relics. He almost had to drag her to shore by her fin to get past all the old shipwrecks along this coast.

"We'll split up, cover more ground," Rayna's saying as they leave.

Galen feels Emma looking at him, but he doesn't acknowledge her. Instead, he watches the beach as Toraf and Rayna disappear in the waves, hand in hand. Galen shakes his head. No one should feel sorry for Toraf. He knows just exactly what he's doing. Something Galen wishes he could say of himself.

Emma puts a hand on his arm—she won't be ignored. "What is that? *Sifted?*"

Finally he turns, meets her gaze. "It's like dating to humans. Only, it goes a lot faster. And it has more of a purpose than humans sometimes do when they date."

"What purpose?"

"Sifting is our way of choosing a life mate. When a male turns eighteen, he usually starts sifting to find himself a companion. For a female whose company he will enjoy and who will be suitable for producing offspring."

"Oh," she says, thoughtful. "And . . . you haven't sifted yet?"

He shakes his head, painfully aware of her hand still on his arm. She must realize it at the same time, because she snatches it away. "Why not?" she says, clearing her throat. "Are you not old enough to sift?"

"I'm old enough," he says softly.

"How old are you, exactly?"

"Twenty." He doesn't mean to lean closer to her—*or does he?*

"Is that normal? That you haven't sifted yet?"

He shakes his head. "It's pretty much standard for males to be mated by the time they turn nineteen. But my responsibilities as ambassador would take me away from my mate too much. It wouldn't be fair to her."

"Oh, right. Keeping a watch on the humans," she says quickly. "You're right. That wouldn't be fair, would it?"

He expects another debate. For her to point out, as she did last night, that if there were more ambassadors, he wouldn't have to shoulder the responsibility alone—and she would be right. But she doesn't debate. In fact, she drops the subject altogether.

Backing away from him, she seems intent on widening the space he'd closed between them. She fixes her expression into nonchalance. "Well, are you ready to help me turn into a fish?" she says, as if they'd been talking about this the whole time.

He blinks. "That's it?"

"What?"

"No more questions about sifting? No lectures about appointing more ambassadors?"

"It's not my business," she says with an indifferent shrug. "Why should I care whether or not you mate? And it's not like *I'll* be sifting—or sifted. After you teach me to sprout a fin, we'll be going our separate ways. Besides, you wouldn't care if I dated any humans, right?" With that, she leaves him there staring after her, mouth hanging open. At the door, she calls over her shoulder, "I'll meet you on the beach in fifteen minutes. I just have to call my mom and check in and change back into my swimsuit." She flips her hair to the side before disappearing up the stairs.

He turns to Rachel, who's hand-drying a pan to death, eyebrows reaching for her hairline. He shrugs to her in askance, mouth still ajar. She sighs. "Sweet pea, what did you expect?"

"Something other than that."

"Well, you shouldn't have. We human girls are a bit feistier than your Syrena females—Rayna being the exception of course."

"But Emma's not human."

Rachel shakes her head at him as if he's a child. "She's been human all her life. It's all she knows. The good news is, she can't date anyone right now."

"Why's that?" Because to him, it sounded like maybe Emma thought she could.

"Because she's *supposed* to be dating you. And if I were you, I'd mark my territory as soon as I got back to school—if you know what I mean."

He scowls. He hadn't planned on staying in school after Emma learned the truth—the whole purpose for going was to eventually get Emma to the beach. He didn't anticipate having to teach her how to become Syrena. And he didn't anticipate that up until yesterday she actually thought she was human. In fact, there's a list the length of his fin of things he didn't anticipate.

Like how thick the school books are. Rachel had taught him to read and write over their years together, but he doesn't have a need for math or gym. Human geography is virtually useless to him. What does he care where the humans draw their invisible land boundaries? Still, science could be interesting. And if Emma likes history, it wouldn't hurt to look into that either.

Galen isn't above admitting that learning more about humans could be advantageous to him—but not in the way Emma hopes. The idea of revealing his kind to them, of negotiating terms of peace, is laughable. Humans can't even be peaceable with their *own* kind. And he's seen how much they care about the masses living below sea level—devastating entire communities of life with a single careless accident. Or ruthlessly hunting some species into nonexistence. Even in the days of Triton and Poseidon, when humans and Syrena coexisted in friendship, some humans still showed a disregard for their dependence on the oceans surrounding them—which led the two generals to pass the Law of Gifts. Their foresight proved to be invaluable over the centuries as the humans developed technology enabling them to cross the oceans in their big ships and, eventually, to invade the depths with their death machines.

But Emma's just as naive as Rachel. They both maintain that the more you know about humans, the more you'll like them. It's at least partly why Rachel's encouraging him to go back to school, even if she hides it behind the *other* good reason he should attend—to keep some adolescent human male from getting himself killed. Just the thought of Emma walking the halls without him makes him ball his fists.

"You're right," he says with finality. "I need to stay in school." He peels off his shirt and tosses it over a chair. "Tell Emma I'm waiting for her."

13

WHEN MY feet touch bottom, Galen releases me. I tiptoe toward shore, jumping with the waves like a toddler. Reaching the beach, I deposit myself in the sand just far enough in for the tide to tickle my feet. "Aren't you coming in?" I call to him.

"I need you to throw me my shorts," he says, pointing behind me.

"Oh. *Oh.* You're naked?" I squeak, bordering on dolphin pitch. Of course, I should have realized that fins don't come with a cubby for carry-on luggage, and most Syrena wouldn't have a need to stash something like swimming shorts. It doesn't matter much when he's in fish form, but seeing Galen—no, *thinking about Galen*—naked in human form would be detrimental to my plan to use him. Could be my undoing.

"Guess that means you can't see into the water yet," he says. When I shake my head, he says, "I took them off before you came out this morning. I'd prefer not to ruin them if I don't have to."

Clearing my throat, I hoist myself up and trudge through the sand, finding them a few feet away. I toss them to him and take my seat again, in case my vision suddenly gives me an unhealthy view of the briny deep. Thankfully, he keeps everything submerged as he makes his way to the floating trunks and pulls them on. Tying them as he walks ashore, he kicks water on me before sitting beside me.

"Why can't I change, Galen?" I draw my knees to my chest.

He leans back on his elbows and stares out to sea, as if deciding on how to answer. We've been out here all day, and I haven't felt so much as an itch in my legs, let alone the twisting sensation he'd promised. "I don't know," he says. "Maybe you're too self-conscious about it. Maybe if you could relax, it would just happen."

"Is that how it happens for you? Like, accidentally?"

"No, it's never an accident. What I mean is, if you'd stop watching for it and just try to have a good time, maybe it will come to you how to change."

"I'm having a good time," I say without looking at him.

"I am, too."

"At least tomorrow is Friday. We'll have the whole weekend to practice. Plus, we can practice after school tomorrow—oh, I guess you wouldn't need to come to school anymore," I say. "You already accomplished your purpose for going, right?" I ignore the tiny pang in my gut.

"Actually, I was going to keep at it for a while. Your mom

probably wouldn't be too happy if you're dating someone who quit school."

I laugh. "Nope, don't think so. But I do think she likes you."

"Why do you say that?" he says, cocking his head at me.

"When I called her, she told me to tell you good morning. And then she told me you were 'a keeper.'" She also said he was hot, which is a ten and a half on the creep-o-meter.

"She won't think that when I start failing out of all my classes. I've missed too much school to give a convincing performance in that aspect."

"Maybe you and I could do an exchange," I say, cringing at how many different ways that could sound.

"You mean besides swapping spit?"

I'm hyperaware of the tickle in my stomach, but I say, "Gross! Did Rachel teach you that?"

He nods, still grinning. "I laughed for days."

"*Anyway,* since you're helping me try to change, I could help you with your schoolwork. You know, tutor you. We're in all the same classes together, and I could really use the volunteer hours for my college applications."

His smile disappears as if I had slapped him. "Galen, is something wrong?"

He unclenches his jaw. "No."

"It was just a suggestion. I don't have to tutor you. I mean, we'll already be spending all day together in school and then practicing at night. You'll probably get sick of me." I toss in a soft laugh to keep it chit-chatty, but my innards feel as though they're cartwheeling.

"Not likely."

Our eyes lock. Searching his expression, my breath catches as the setting sun makes his hair shine almost purple. But it's the way each dying ray draws out silver flecks in his eyes that makes me look away—and accidentally glance at his mouth.

He leans in. I raise my chin, meeting his gaze. The sunset probably deepens the heat on my cheeks to a strawberry red, but he might not notice since he can't seem to decide if he wants to look at my eyes or my mouth. I can smell the salt on his skin, feel the warmth of his breath. He's so close, the wind wafts the same strand of my hair onto both our cheeks.

So when he eases away, it's me who feels slapped. He uproots the hand he buried in the sand beside me. "It's getting dark. I should take you home," he says. "We can do this again—I mean, we can *practice* again—tomorrow after school."

I pull my hair to one side, shielding my disappointment from him. "Sure." So much for using *him*.

"Actually, you can't go to school tomorrow, minnow." We both look up at Toraf and Rayna walking toward us on the beach. Plodding through the sand jostles the armful of human junk Rayna carries, but the satisfied smile spread across her face hints she wishes she could carry more.

"Why can't he?" I say.

"Because he needs to check in with his family. Everyone is wondering where the Royal twins are, since they happened to miss Grom's kingship ceremony. At least I had the good sense to hold a private mating ceremony—in view of Rayna's absence and all."

Galen scowls. "He's right. We need to go home for a few days. Our father isn't as protective as your mother, but he likes to see us once in a while. Especially Rayna. She's spoiled."

Rayna nods. "It's true. I am. Besides, I need to get our mating-seal overturned."

"Aw, princess, I thought we had a good time today. You know I'll make sure you're still spoiled. Why would you want to unseal us?" Toraf says. She lets him take some of her load but turns up her nose at his attempt to kiss her cheek.

Galen ignores their marriage meltdown. Looking at me, he says, "It won't take long, I promise. When I get back, maybe we could visit Dr. Milligan. He might be able to help us."

"In Florida?" The idea of sunny white beaches makes me nauseous. In my dreams, they're always stained red with Chloe's blood.

Galen nods. "He could run a few tests. You know, see if we're missing something."

A feeling of failure waylays me. "So, you think I should have changed already. What am I doing wrong?"

"It's nothing you're doing," he says. "Water triggers our natural instinct to change. It takes more effort *not* to change than it does *to* change. Maybe Dr. Milligan can help us figure out how to make your instinct stronger."

I nod. "Maybe. But I'm pretty sure Mom won't consent to a field trip across the country with my hot boyfriend. Especially not back to Florida." I clamp my mouth shut so fast my teeth should be chipped.

He grins. "You think I'm hot?"

"My mom thinks you are." Except, Mom's not the one blushing right now.

"Hmm," he says, giving me a you're-busted look. "As hot as I am, I don't think she'd buy into my charm on this one. We'll have to call in a professional." Then that fish prince actually winks at me.

"You mean Rachel," I say, toeing the sand. "I guess it's worth a shot. Don't expect much, though. I've already missed too much school."

"We could fly down on the weekend. Be back before school on Monday."

I nod. "She might go for that. If Rachel plays her cards right." Yeah, she might go for that. She might also pierce her tongue, dye her hair cherry red and spike it peacock-style. *Ain't happening.* I shrug. "I'll just keep practicing while you're gone. Maybe we don't have to go—"

"No!" Galen and Toraf shout, startling me.

"Why not? I won't go too deep—"

"Out of the question," Galen says, standing. "You will not get in the water while I'm gone."

I stomp a hole in the sand. "I already told you that you're not ordering me around, didn't I? Now you've pretty much *guaranteed* that I'm getting in the water, Your Highness."

Galen runs a hand through his hair and utters a string of cuss words, courtesy of Rachel, no doubt. He paces in the sand a few seconds, pinching the bridge of his nose. Suddenly he stops. Relaxes. Smiles even. He walks over to his friend, slaps him on the back. "Toraf, I need a favor."

14

GALEN KNOWS where to find his brother. Intruding on Grom's solitude in the remnant of the human mines is the last thing he wants to do, but he's pressed for time. Emma's specialty is not obedience. Toraf's specialty is not supervision—he'll cave to her will at the first sign of a tantrum. He already pointed out to Galen that technically she'll be their queen one day, so he wants to stay on good terms with her. And it took a Royal order to get Toraf to stay behind, unable to plead his case to Grom when Rayna demands the dissolution of their seal. As he approaches the edge of the old minefield, Galen resolves to speak on Toraf's behalf. Rayna will be furious—and so will Emma, for that matter—but he owes his friend that much.

The mines make him nervous, always have. Fish and plants have long abandoned this part of the Triton territory. In fact, as far as Galen knows, Grom is the only visitor this place hosts.

Holes big enough to swallow a fishing boat pock the seafloor from the blasts. The mud around each pit is stained a darker color, as if the explosion left its shadow behind. Just two of the hundreds of bombs remain intact, defective and impotent, as if a silent monument to what was lost here. And with Nalia's death, the Syrena lost more than a future queen. They lost unity. They lost trust. They lost legacy. And they might have lost their ability to survive.

Galen shudders as he passes one of the decrepit bombs. Anchored to the floor by a chain, the metal ball floats undisturbed, consumed by rust, left behind by the humans after they finished investigating the sudden activity. As if the scars in the mud weren't enough.

When he sees his brother, he calls out to him, though he knows Grom sensed him before he entered the minefield. Grom hovers on the precipice of the deep canyon beyond the mines, arms crossed. "It seems I've missed your kingship ceremony, Your Majesty," Galen says.

The corner of Grom's mouth curves into an almost-grin. "Pity Father didn't make good on his promise to remove your tongue, little brother. I thought he might do it this time."

Galen laughs. "I did, too. But Rayna insisted I keep my tongue for just a little while longer."

"You'd do well to keep that one happy. If it weren't for her, you'd be dead, disinherited, or both by now. I think she deserves a special trip to the tropics for her efforts."

Galen chuckles. Rayna's favorite place to scavenge for human rubble is along the commercial cruise routes in the Gulf of

Mexico. She insists people on the ships intentionally throw their belongings overboard, to leave a small part of themselves behind. At least that's what Rachel told her. "I just might. If she stays mated to Toraf."

Grom whips his head toward his brother. "She accepted Toraf?"

"No. That's what I'm talking about. She wants to ask you for a dissolution."

"A dissolution of what?"

"Of their sealing."

"Rayna and Toraf are *sealed*?" Grom asks. "When did this happen?"

"Very funny."

Grom smirks. Galen tries to picture his brother as an eighty-year-old human. Gray hair, more wrinkles than a shell has ridges, and that boyish grin would probably be toothless. But as an eighty-year-old Syrena, he looks as young as Galen. Has more teeth too, thanks to Toraf. Despite it all, he's still all wrong for Emma. Too calm, too composed, too set in his ways to deal with a hurricane like Emma Stubborn McIntosh.

"I've been waiting for the day I could make Rayna someone else's problem," Grom says. "I do feel bad about it though. I always did like Toraf."

"So you won't dissolve it?"

"Not even if Toraf asks me to. It's been so peaceful around here without her. Where have you two been anyway?"

Galen shrugs. "The usual." Guilt nips at his conscience like baby crabs. "The usual" is visiting Dr. Milligan to get caught up on the latest marine news. Or spending a few days with Rachel moving her most recent purchases around one of his many houses. "The usual" is *not* living as a human, going to their schools, driving their cars, or wearing their clothes.

"Did Dr. Milligan have anything interesting for you?"

"A few things. Nothing to worry about, though."

Grom nods. "Good. The last thing I need is something else to worry about."

Finally, Galen notices his brother's tense profile. Clenched jaw, taut biceps from tightly crossed arms. White knuckles where his hands grip impressions into his shoulders.

Galen stiffens. "What? What is it?"

Grom shakes his head, hoarding his misery to himself behind a scowl.

"Tell me."

"It could be nothing," Grom says.

"It could be, but I can tell it isn't."

His brother sighs. He faces Galen, eyes hard. "I'll tell you, little brother. But first, promise me a few things."

"What things?"

"Promise me that whatever happens, you'll get Rayna to safety. I don't care if you have to live as humans for the rest of your lives, you keep our sister safe. Promise."

"Grom—"

"Promise!" Grom bellows, uncrossing his arms.

"You already know I will." In fact, he's insulted his brother would doubt it.

Grom nods, relaxes. "I know. But I needed to hear it." He looks away when he says, "I had a private meeting with Jagen."

"You *what*? Have you lost your mind?" A distant cousin of King Antonis, Jagen is the bluster behind the storm of conspiracy brewing in the Poseidon territory. Anyone can see he's making a play for the throne, but over the decades, Antonis's inflexibility has bloated the ranks of Jagen's followers.

A good reason for Grom to be concerned with his siblings' safety. If Jagen is truly ambitious enough to plot against his own king, he can't be trusted not to try to overthrow the house of Triton. Plus, if anyone saw Grom meet with him, they might assume Jagen gained the support of the new Triton king. Or worse, King Antonis might assume that. The question is, *should* they?

"I know what I'm doing, Galen," Grom growls.

"Apparently not. What does Father say?"

"You know I didn't tell him."

Galen nods. Grom would be a fool to tell their father. King Herof and King Antonis were friends long before they were enemies. And now King Grom would widen the chasm between them? "What did Jagen want?"

Grom sighs. "He requested permission to use Toraf. He needs him to Track someone. Someone the other Trackers can't find."

Nothing extraordinary. Because of their value, trackers are the only Syrena able to cross kingdom borders without fear of arrest. Of course, Jagen would want Toraf—he's the best Tracker in the history of their kind. Out of respect for Galen's family, though, Toraf never crosses the borders. And he would never agree to do Jagen's bidding without royal permission from the house of Triton. Even then, he might not do it. "That's it? Who does he need to track?"

"I wish that were it. It's not so much *who* he needs to track, but *why*."

"I swear by Triton's trident if you don't start talking—"

"His daughter Paca is missing. He thinks Antonis took her."

Galen rolls his eyes. "Why would Antonis take her? If Antonis cared about Jagen's treason, he would have done something about it years ago." But Antonis didn't seem to care about anything these days. Since Nalia died, he's holed himself up in the Royal caverns. Some Poseidon Trackers told Toraf he hasn't come out since he declared the house of Triton an enemy.

"According to Jagen, Paca has the gift of Poseidon."

The words knock the breath out of Galen. "That's not possible."

Slowly, Grom shakes his head. "It's not likely. But it's possible. She's got Royal blood in her, no matter how diluted. And if she is of Poseidon, I can't ignore the ramifications of her ability."

"But that's not how it works. The Gift has never shown up in anyone but a direct descendant." *What am I saying? Won't I be trying to convince Grom of the same thing about Emma, with even less proof than this? At least Paca can prove some royal blood. But Emma's father isn't trying to claim the throne. In fact, Galen found Emma by accident. Which makes Paca's Gift seem suspicious, at best.*

·148·

"I spoke to the Archives. Of course, I didn't tell them about Jagen's accusation. They believe I'm just a new eager king, exploring our legacy." The Archives are the collection of ten of the eldest among their kind—five from each house—entrusted with remembering the history of the Syrena. Galen agrees it would be natural for Grom to seek their counsel.

"And?"

"In their collective memory, they don't recall it ever happening. But one of the Archives, your friend Romul, believes it would be possible. He reminded us that the Gifts were to ensure the survival of our kind, not just the survival of Royal lineage. He said he wouldn't be surprised if Triton and Poseidon thought of this beforehand, that a Royal might abuse his power. He thinks they might have made a provision somehow."

Galen crosses his arms. "Huh."

Grom chuckles. "That's what I said."

"But you said you didn't tell them about Jagen."

"I didn't. I'm a new king without a mate inheriting a bloodless war against the only other kingdom of our kind. It's only natural for me to be asking creative questions."

Galen nods. "But if the Gifts can be transferred to someone else, why even bother forcing the Royals to mate? The Law of Gifts has always been strictly enforced. Romul's theory renders that law—and the Royals—pointless." And it doesn't sit well with Galen. Especially that Romul gave his opinion at all. The Archives are bound to tell the facts—nothing more, nothing less. Romul had told him that himself when Galen first visited him as a youth. But Romul is more than just an Archive to

Galen, he's his mentor. No, more than that, he's his friend. Friends share opinions with each other.

But Archives have no place speculating before kings.

"Well, it's like you said, it's just a theory. But it's one I can't ignore. I've decided to let him use Toraf. If Paca's alive, Toraf will find her."

Galen nods. *And if Paca has the Gift of Poseidon, there won't be a need for Emma . . . at least not for Grom.* His heart races with an emotion he can't name. "If this gets out—"

"It won't."

"Grom—"

"But just in case it does, keep Rayna with you, wherever you've been. I don't want to see your faces again until this is resolved."

"We're not fingerlings. Rayna's even mated."

"No, but you're what's left of the Triton Royals, little brother."

The words hover between them, prodding them with the gravity of the situation. So much at stake, so much dependant on *if.* Does Antonis have Paca? And if he does, will he turn her over peaceably? And if he *doesn't* have her, will Grom's investigation incite Antonis to make a bloodless war bloody?

But it's worth the risk. If Paca does have the Gift, mating with Grom will ensure the survival of the Syrena. And Galen will be free and clear to chase after a certain white-haired angelfish.

But is anything ever that simple?

Grom stares out over the canyon, entombed in his thoughts,

emotions absent from his face. Galen clears his throat, but it doesn't pull his brother out of his trance. He considers dropping the subject altogether. Opening old wounds is the last thing he wants to do, but he has to know. There will never be a good time to talk about it, but this might be the only *appropriate* time. "Grom, I need to ask you something."

Hesitant, Grom tears his gaze from the abyss and settles it on his brother, but his eyes still hold a distance. "Hmm?"

"Do you believe in the pull?"

The question visibly jolts Grom, replacing the detachment in his eyes with pain. "What kind of question is that?"

Galen shrugs, guilt stabbing him like a trident. "Some say you felt the pull for Nalia."

Grom massages his eyes with fingertips, but not before Galen sees the torment deepen. "I didn't realize you listened to gossip, little brother."

"If I listened to gossip, I wouldn't bother to ask."

"Do you believe in the pull, Galen?"

"I don't know."

Grom nods, sighing. "I don't know either. But if there *is* such a thing, I guess it would be safe to say I felt it toward Nalia." With a flit of his tail, he swims forward, turning away from his brother. "Sometimes I swear I can still sense her. It's faint, and it comes and goes. Some days it's so real, I think I'm losing my mind."

"What . . . what does it feel like?" Galen almost can't ask. He'd already determined to never have this conversation with Grom. But things have changed.

To his surprise, Grom chuckles. "Is there something I need to know, little brother? Has someone finally hooked you?"

Galen doesn't quite get his mouth closed before his brother turns around. Grom's laugh seems foreign in this dismal place. "Looks like she's got you hooked *and* reeled. Who is she?"

"None of your business." *At least not yet.*

Grom grins. "So that's where you've been. Chasing after a female."

"You could say that." In fact, his brother can say anything he wants. He's not telling Grom about Emma. Not while Paca is out there somewhere, just waiting to be mated with a Triton king.

"If you won't tell me, I'll just ask Rayna."

"If Rayna knew, there would have already been a public announcement."

"True," Grom says, smirking. "You're smarter than I give you credit for, tadpole. So smart, in fact, that I know I don't have to tell you to keep her away from here, whoever she is. Just until things settle down."

Galen nods. "You don't have to worry about that."

15

THE SMELL of blueberry muffins usually sweetens my mood, but after the lukewarm shower I just took, blueberry muffins don't stand a chance at making my mood any sweeter than vinegar. Mom's pulling the pan from the oven as I take the last step down the stairs.

"Is the water heater broken?" I say, pulling a bowl from the cabinet.

"Good morning to you, too," she says, forking a muffin onto wax paper to cool.

"Sorry. Good morning. Is the water heater broken?" I scoop a mound of oatmeal from the pot on the stove and slop it into my bowl. A muffin hits my foot—we always have at least one casualty because the pan sticks.

"Not that I know of, sweetie. I showered this morning and didn't notice anything different."

"Probably broke on my shift," I grumble, grabbing a muffin and sauntering to the table. My legs are too sore to lower myself with any kind of dignity, so I drop into the chair and spoon oatmeal into my mouth to keep from complaining more. Mom worked all night, then cooked me breakfast. She doesn't deserve vinegar.

"Galen picking you up for school?"

"No, I'm driving myself." Vinegar turns to acid. Sure, it's irritating to take a lukewarm shower when you intended to scald the flesh from your body. But not being able to see Galen today is more disappointing than not having hot water all winter. And I hate it.

Spending all of yesterday with him slaughtered my intention of keeping him at a distance. Even if he weren't worthy of his own billboard underwear ad, he's just too likeable. Except for his habit of almost-kissing me. But his obsession with trying to order me around is too cute. Especially the way his mouth gets all pouty when I don't listen.

"You two fighting already?"

She's fishing, but for what I don't know. Shrugging seems safe until I can figure out what she wants to hear.

"Do you fight often?"

Shrugging again, I ladle enough oatmeal into my mouth to make talking impossible for at least a minute, which is more than enough time for her to drop it. It doesn't work. After the exaggerated minute, I reach for my glass of milk.

"You know, if he ever hit you—"

The glass in mid-tilt, I swallow before the milk can escape through my nose. "Mom, he would never hit me!"

"I didn't say he would."

"Good, because he wouldn't. Ever. What's with you? Do you have to interrogate me about Galen every time you see me?"

This time she shrugs. "Seems like the right thing to do. When you have children, you'll understand."

"I'm not stupid. If Galen acts up, I'll either dump him or kill him. You have my word."

Mom laughs and butters my muffin. "I guess I can't ask for more than that."

Accepting the muffin—and the truce—I say, "Nope. Anything more would be unreasonable."

"Just remember, I'm watching you like a hawk. Except for right now, because I'm going to bed. Soak your bowl in the sink before you leave." She kisses the top of my head and yawns before she shuffles up the stairs.

I'm exhausted when I get home, even though the school day was the equivalent of a seven-hour yawn without Galen or Chloe. Mom is darting around the house like an agitated wasp. "Hi, sweetie, how was your day? Have you seen my keys?"

"Nope, sorry. Did you check yesterday's pockets?" I say, opening the fridge door to pull out some strawberries.

"Good idea!" The carpet on the stairs muffles her stomping. She reappears a few seconds later as I pop a strawberry in my mouth and hoist myself onto the counter. "I didn't have pockets yesterday," she says, tugging on her hair to tighten her ponytail.

"Why don't you just take the Honda? I'll keep looking for your keys."

Mom nods. "You don't need to go anywhere this afternoon? Still fighting with Galen?"

"The only plans I made for tonight is make-up work." That is, after I step out back and try to turn into a fish.

When Mom's doubtful frown doesn't escalate into another interrogation, I know she's trying to uphold our truce from this morning. "Okay. There's leftover stew in the fridge. If Julie doesn't show up again tonight, I'll be working another double so I might not see you until later tomorrow. Don't forget to lock up before you go to bed."

When I hear the Honda's gears grinding in the driveway, I pick up my cell phone. Galen said Rachel never answers, but she calls back if you leave a message. After an automated woman from Trans-Atlantic Warranty Company gives me the option of leaving a message or calling back during normal business hours, I wait for the beep. "Hey, Rachel, it's Emma. Tell Toraf he's off the hook for tonight. I can't make it over there for practice today. Maybe I'll see him tomorrow." NOT. I don't need a babysitter. Galen needs to get it through his thicker-than-most head that I'm not one of his royal subjects. Besides, Toraf earned a place on my equivalent-to-zoo-dirt list, forcing Rayna to marry him and all.

After a few minutes, Rachel makes good on Galen's promise.

When I answer the phone, she says, "Hey there, cutie pie. You're not feeling bad again, are you?"

"No, I'm fine. Just a little sore from yesterday, I guess. But Mom had to take my car to work, so I don't have a way to get over there."

Contemplation hovers in the silence that follows. I'm surprised when she doesn't offer to come get me. Maybe she doesn't like me as much as she lets on. "Give me a call tomorrow, okay? Galen wants me to check in with you."

"That's so sweet of him," I drawl.

She chuckles. "Give the guy a break. His intentions are good. He hasn't figured out how to handle you yet."

"I don't need to be handled."

"Apparently, he thinks you do. And until he doesn't, I'm afraid you'll have to put up with me."

I try not to sound curt when I say, "Do you always do what he says?"

"Not always."

"Yeah, right."

"Emma, if I always did what I'm told, you'd be locked in a hotel room somewhere while I secured us a private jet to a place of Galen's choosing. Now get some rest. I'll be expecting your call tomorrow."

Tossing my towel in the sand, I get a running start and make a clean dive into the waves. I expect the first plunge to be refreshing, an exhilarating rush of breath-stealing cold, the kind of frigid any self-respecting New Jersey autumn would produce. But when I surface, I feel gross. The water is lukewarm. Just like my shower. Just like my love life.

I wade against the swells, and then force myself below the influence of the surf. I hold my breath and drift, pressing the start button on Dad's old stopwatch. And I find one more reason to hate the passage of time: It's boring. To keep from staring at the minutes dragging by, I recite the alphabet. Then I recite the statistics of the *Titanic*, just as any obsessed person would do. A few crabs side-wind beneath me, listening to me compare the number of lifeboats to passengers while the waves wash me to shore.

After fifteen minutes, my lungs start to tighten. At seventeen minutes, they feel like a rubberband stretched to max capacity. At twenty minutes, it's an all-out emergency. I surface and stop the watch.

Twenty minutes, fourteen seconds. Not bad for a human—the world record is set at thirteen minutes, thirty-two seconds. But as far as fish go, it pretty much sucks. Not that fish hold their breath or anything, but I don't exactly have gills to work with. According to Galen, he doesn't hold his breath either. Syrena fill their lungs with water and apparently absorb the oxygen they need from it. My faith isn't strong enough to try. In fact, growing a tail of my own is the only way to make me a believer. Even breaking a human world record on my first trial run isn't enough to convince me to inhale seawater. Not gonna happen.

I traipse back to neck-deep and clear the time on the watch.

Drawing in a lung-packing breath, I press the start button. And then I feel it. It saturates the water around me, thrumming without rhythm. The pulse. Someone is close. Someone I don't recognize. Slowly, I tiptoe backward, careful not to splash or slosh. After a few seconds, tiptoeing doesn't make a whole lot of sense. If I can sense them, they can sense me. The pulse is getting stronger. They're heading straight toward me. Fast.

Leaving caution, etiquette, and Dad's stopwatch behind, I scramble like a lunatic to shallower water. Suddenly, Galen's order to stay on dry land doesn't seem so unreasonable. *What was I thinking?* The little I know about Syrena is what we crammed into the last twenty-four hours at his house. They have a social structure like humans. Government, laws, family, friendship. Do they have outcasts, too? The same way humans have rapists and serial killers? If so, I've just done the human equivalent of wandering into a dark parking lot alone. Stupid, stupid, stupid.

Gasping into a wave lets me know my lungs aren't prepped for water just yet. Sputtering and coughing slows me down a little, but the shore is close, and I've got my eye on a stick thicker than my arm just beyond the wet sand. That it will break like a twig over the head of any Syrena is not important.

I'm knee-deep when the hand grabs my ankle. I look down, but my attacker is obviously in Blended form, barely making an outline through the waves. The water doesn't interrupt my scream, but it does shut it off from the human world. The hand is strong and big, pulling me from safety like a rip current. I'm wasting precious air by kicking and screaming at the Blended blob, but going without a fight just won't do.

The ocean bottom is a steep hill. Only a few fingers of sunlight splay through to the deep. Those fingers disappear as my eyes adjust, casting an afternoon-like glow on everything. The more I struggle, the faster we torpedo through the water—and the tighter my abductor strengthens his hold.

"You're hurting me!" I wail. We stop fast enough to give me whiplash.

"Oops, sorry," the blob says, materializing as Toraf. He releases my ankle.

"You!"

"Of course it's me. Who else would it be?"

We surface against the night sky. Stars fill my vision, but I'm not sure if they're real or the result of running out of oxygen. Toraf shows off by shooting his body out of the water, slicing through the waves on the tip of his tale like a dolphin at Seaworld. "Stop messing around," I tell him. "How did I do that time? Give me the watch.'"

"Twenty-seven minutes, nineteen seconds," he says, placing it in my outstretched hand. He gasps. "Whoa. What's wrong with your hands?"

"What do you mean?" I turn them over and over, straining to see in the moonlight. No blood, cuts, scrapes. Wiggling all ten fingers, I tell him, "There's nothing wrong with them, see?"

His widened eyes make me check again. Still nothing. "Toraf, if this is another joke—"

"Emma, it's not a joke. *Look* at your hands! They're . . . they're . . . wrinkled!"

"Yes. That's because—"

"No way. I'm not going down for this. This isn't my fault."

"Toraf—"

"Galen will find some way to blame me though. He always does. 'You wouldn't have gotten caught if you didn't swim so close to that boat, tadpole.' No, it couldn't be the human's fault for fishing in the first place—"

"Toraf."

"Or how about, 'Maybe if you'd stop trying to kiss my sister, she'd stop bashing your head with a rock.' How does my kissing her have anything to do with her bashing my head with a rock? If you ask me, it's just a result of poor parenting—"

"*Toraf.*"

"Oh, and my favorite: 'If you play with a lionfish, you're going to get pricked.' I wasn't *playing* with it! I was just helping it swim faster by grabbing its fins—"

"TOR-AF."

He stops pacing along the water, even seems to remember that I exist. "Yes, Emma? What were you saying?"

I inhale as if I'm about to submerge for the next half hour. Letting it out slowly, I say, "This isn't anybody's fault. My skin gets all wrinkled like that when I stay in the water too long. Always has."

"There's no such thing as staying in the water too long. Not for Syrena. Besides, if your skin wrinkles like that, you'll never be able to blend." He holds his hand out to me, shows me his palm, smooth as a statue. Then he submerges his hand and it disappears. Blended. He crosses his arms, triumphant. The accusation is clear.

"Oh, you're right. I'm just a human with thick skin, purple eyes, and hard bones. Which means you can go home. Tell Galen I said hi."

Toraf opens and shuts his mouth twice. Both times it seems like he wants to say something, but his expression tells me his brain isn't cooperating. When his mouth snaps shut a third time, I splash water in his face. "Are you going to say something, or are you trying to catch wind and sail?"

A grin the size of the horizon spreads across his face. "He likes that, you know. Your temper."

Yeahfreakingright. Galen's a classic type A personality—and type A's hate smartass-ism. Just ask my mom. "No offense, but you're not exactly an expert at judging people's emotions."

"I'm not sure what you mean by that."

"Sure you do."

"If you're talking about Rayna, then you're wrong. She loves me. She just won't admit it."

I roll my eyes. "Right. She's playing hard to get, is that it? Bashing your head with a rock, splitting your lip, calling you squid breath all the time."

"What does that mean? Hard to get?"

"It means she's trying to make you think she doesn't like you, so that you end up liking her more. So you work harder to get her attention."

He nods. "Exactly. That's exactly what she's doing."

Pinching the bridge of my nose, I say, "I don't think so. As we speak, she's getting your mating seal dissolved. That's not playing hard to get. That's playing impossible to get."

"Even if she does get it dissolved, it's not because she doesn't care about me. She just likes to play games."

The pain in Toraf's voice guts me like the catch of the day. She might like playing games, but his feelings are real. And can't I relate to that? "There's only one way to find out," I say softly.

"Find out?"

"If all she wants is games."

"How?"

"*You* play hard to get. You know how they say, 'If you love someone, set them free. If they return to you, it was meant to be?'"

"I've never heard that."

"Right. No, you wouldn't have." I sigh. "Basically, what I'm trying to say is, you need to stop giving Rayna attention. Push her away. Treat her like she treats you."

He shakes his head. "I don't think I can do that."

"You'll get your answer that way," I say, shrugging. "But it sounds like you don't really want to know."

"I do want to know. But what if the answer isn't good?" His face scrunches as if the words taste like lemon juice.

"You've got to be ready to deal with it, no matter what."

Toraf nods, his jaw tight. The choices he has to consider will make this night long enough for him. I decide not to intrude on his time anymore. "I'm pretty tired, so I'm heading back. I'll meet you at Galen's in the morning. Maybe I can break thirty minutes tomorrow, huh?" I nudge his shoulder with my fist, but a weak smile is all I get in return.

I'm surprised when he grabs my hand and starts pulling me through the water. At least it's better than dragging me by the ankle. I can't help but think how Galen could have done the same thing. *Why does he wrap his arms around me instead?*

By Saturday night, I can stay under for thirty-five minutes. By Sunday afternoon, I'm up to forty-seven. There's something to be said about practice—even if I'm not actually practicing anything. Just hanging out in the water, holding my breath, withering my skin to grandma-like wrinkles.

I pull off the flippers Toraf brought me and chuck them onto shore. I keep my back turned while he maneuvers his shorts into place. "Are you decent?" I call after a few seconds. No matter how many times I tell him I can't see into the water yet, he insists I'm just trying to look at his "eel." *For crying out loud.*

"Oh, I'm more than decent. I'm actually quite a catch."

I couldn't agree more. Toraf is good-looking, funny, and considerate—which makes me question Rayna's attitude. I'm beginning to understand why Grom sealed her to him. Who could be better for her than Toraf?

But mentioning that to Toraf would break our silent pact not to talk about Rayna or Galen. Since Friday night, we've talked about everything but them. About Grom and Nalia. About the peace treaty General Triton and General Poseidon made after the Great War. About how seafood tastes—well, we argued about that one.

But mostly we just practice, me holding my breath, Toraf timing me. He can't explain any better than Galen how to change into a fish. He agrees it feels like an almost overwhelming need to stretch.

Toraf wades to where I stand in the tide. "I can't believe it's already sunset," I tell him.

"I can. I'm starving."

"I am, too." Must be all the extra calories I'm burning in the water.

He shrugs. "All I know is—" His head jerks toward the water and back at me. He grabs my shoulders, pulls me close. And then he breaks our silent agreement. "Remember what you said about Rayna? About playing hard to get?" He darts a glance toward the open sea, whips his head back to me again. His eyebrows melt together as he scowls.

I nod, startled by his about-face.

"Well, I've been thinking about it. A lot. And I'm going to do it. But . . . but I need your help."

"Of course I'll help you. Whatever you need," I say. But something feels off when he pulls me closer.

"Good," he says, peeking again at the sunset. "Galen and Rayna are close."

I gasp. "How do you know that? I can't feel them." My heart turns traitor, beating like I just ran five miles uphill. It has nothing to do with sensing and everything to do with the mention of Galen's name.

"I'm a Tracker, Emma. I can sense them from almost across the world. Especially Rayna. And from the feel of things, Galen is flittering that cute little fin of his like crazy to get back to you. Rayna must be riding on his back."

"You can tell what she's doing?"

"I can tell how fast she's moving. No one can swim as fast as Galen, Rayna included. He must be pretty impatient to see you."

"Yeah. Impatient for me to change so he can have another royal subject to order around."

Toraf's laughter startles me, not because it's loud, but because his mood seems to swing around on an axis. "Is that what you think?" he says.

Suddenly, Galen's pulse hits my legs like a physical blow. Toraf drags me out of the water and hauls us toward the house. "He's had plenty of chances to show me something different," I say, my words bouncing with each hurried step chunking into the sand. Behind us, I hear Galen and Rayna laughing about something. The way they slosh makes me think they're splashing each other.

Toraf stops us at the little picket fence, an apathetic boundary separating Galen's beach sand from the county's beach sand. "Well, I'm about to teach those spoiled Royals a lesson. Do you trust me, Emma?"

I nod, but something tells me I shouldn't have. My instinct is confirmed when Toraf pulls me against his chest and lowers his mouth to mine. When I try to pull away, he grabs a handful of my hair and uses it to hold my face in place. The sudden silence behind us is louder than the laughter ever could have been.

I can tell Toraf is a good kisser. He moves his mouth just

the right way, gentle and firm at the same time. And for all the seafood he eats, he doesn't taste like it one bit.

But everything about this kiss is wrong, wrong, wrong. If I had a brother, this is what kissing him would feel like. And then I feel something else. Hair-raising prickles all over. Like I'm about to be struck by lightning.

Then Galen—not a lightning bolt—slams into Toraf, wrenching our lips apart. To his good credit, Toraf releases me immediately instead of taking me down with him. They crash into the sand, Galen launching punches like bullets from a machine gun. But I'm too stunned to move.

16

BETWEEN PUNCHES, Galen bellows his rage. "I trusted you! I said to keep an eye on her, not your filthy lips!"

Toraf's laugh makes him hit harder. Galen is aware of Emma screaming for him to stop. Now that she's snapped out of the trance Toraf kissed her into.

Fire sears into his biceps where Emma struggles to restrain the next blow with both hands. "Stop it, Galen! Right now!"

His head whips toward her, her concern for Toraf almost driving him beyond sense. "Why? Why should I stop?"

"Because he's your friend. Because he's your sister's mate," she shouts.

"But those are the same reasons I should *kill* him, Emma. You're not making any sense."

"Rayna, help me!" Emma throws herself at Galen, ramming her shoulder into his chest.

With his arms full of Emma, it's difficult to keep hammering Toraf. Emma is soft and sweet-smelling, which would distract him even if she wasn't wrapping herself around him like an octopus. He can't tell whose limbs are whose when they tumble off of Toraf and spill into the sand beside him.

Landing on top, Galen uses his hand to cushion the back of Emma's head from hitting a piece of driftwood. Worrying about her last head injury already shortened his life span. "Triton's trident, Emma, you can't just throw yourself in the middle of a fight. You could get hurt," he says, out of breath.

She pushes against him, fists balled. "A fight is two-sided, Highness. You didn't notice Toraf wouldn't hit back?"

Actually, no. And he didn't care. He eases off her. She refuses the hand he offers to help her up. He shrugs, irritated at her small rejection. "His loss. Now go to the house. Toraf and I aren't finished."

By now Toraf is standing up, slapping the sand off his body. It takes a few moments for Galen to realize that Rayna didn't help disentangle him from her mate. In fact, she hasn't said a word.

She's still standing on the beach where he left her, her face contorted into a jumble of shock, anger, and pain. The anger dissipates when Toraf straightens his swimming trunks and walks right past her. In fact, the shock goes away, too. Only pain stays behind, crumbling her expression.

Her mate is knee-deep in the water when she finally calls out to him. "Toraf?" The way her voice cracks takes Galen off guard. Toraf doesn't notice. That, or he doesn't care. "Hmm?" Toraf says, as if she doesn't deserve the effort of a whole word.

"You . . . you kissed Emma."

"Yes?" he says, glancing impatiently out to sea.

"But . . . but you're mated to *me.*"

He shrugs. "Am I? Last time I checked, you were hurrying back to Grom to get us unsealed. I figured I wouldn't waste any more of your time—or mine. And you have to admit, Emma's not a bad catch." He turns, winks at Emma. Galen launches toward him, but Emma latches onto his arm. Galen grinds his teeth.

Rayna takes small slow steps toward Toraf as if she's approaching a feeding shark. "But I didn't unseal us. We're still mated."

Toraf crosses his arms. "Really? Grom wouldn't unseal us then?"

Rayna stops, arms hanging limply from rounded shoulders. "I didn't ask him to." Galen can't see her face, but by the way the words waver, she's fighting to stay in control, and for once it's not of her temper.

What's gotten into everyone? Toraf dallies on the edge of indifference. Rayna wraps her arms around herself in insecurity. And Emma . . . Emma hasn't changed at all. Still beautiful and still stubborn as ever.

"I don't know why," Toraf says, sloshing into deeper water. "We both know it won't work between us."

Rayna wades in, too. "What's not working? You said you loved me."

His laugh is sharp. "And you split my lip for it."

"You shouldn't hold grudges," she says. "Besides, you caught me off guard."

"Off guard? I've been chasing you since we were fingerlings. No," he says, shaking his head. "You were right all along. We don't belong together. In fact, I'm going to ask Grom to unseal us myself." Without another word, he dives in, a small piece of his tail peeking through the waves.

Rayna turns to Galen, her expression incredulous. "Is he serious?"

"He looked serious," Galen says, just as shocked as his sister.

"Toraf, wait!" Rayna calls before throwing herself into the surf after him.

Galen and Emma stare after them as the last bit of sun sets. Galen's not sure any of this just happened—or that he'll ever be able to close his mouth again. *How could he betray me like that?* Toraf has more loyalty than a beach has sand. *Or so I thought.* If he was wrong about that, what else was he wrong about?

Did he misjudge Toraf's devotion to Rayna? How could he? Toraf refused to sift, insisting Rayna was the one for him all along. He got physically sick when she turned him down the first time. No, Toraf would never treat Rayna like that. And Rayna would never chase after Toraf. Ever.

Then there's Emma. She obviously bonded with Toraf in the three days he's been gone. *This is my fault. I should have kissed her. Should have left her with that memory instead of fighting with her to stay on shore.* But what would that solve? The possibility that she'll be kissing his brother one day is still very real. Shouldn't he get used to her kissing someone else? *But that's different. I never planned to see her kissing Grom.* In fact, he never planned to see her at all after turning her over to his brother.

Grom. Toraf also betrayed Grom. Technically, he could have just kissed his future queen. When Toraf said he wanted to get on her good side, Galen had no idea he would take it this far. But Toraf can't expect to mate with Emma. She's already spoken for—one way or the other.

Out of the corner of his eye, he shifts his gaze to her. Arms crossed, eyes wide. Lips and cheeks as red as a cooked lobster. He clears his throat. "How . . . how long has this been going on?" he asks softly.

She turns to him. "How long has what been going on?"

"You and Toraf. Kissing."

"Oh. About ten minutes."

Better than he'd hoped for. Relief hits him like a tsunami. If it happened the entire time he was gone . . . he can't even think about it. Toraf broke Syrena law when he kissed Emma. To kiss someone other than your mate gets you ten cycles of the moon in the ice caverns. It's considered one of the most serious offenses. If he'd kissed her all weekend, each kiss could count as an individual violation.

Still, Toraf thought Rayna unsealed them. He thought he was free to kiss anyone he wanted. *But why did it have to be Emma?* She's the worst possible choice for him for more reasons than Galen can name.

As if I didn't have enough to worry about. My kingdom is threatened by war, extinction, or both, and the only way to solve it is to give up the only thing I've ever really wanted. Then Toraf pulls something like this. Betrays me and my sister. Galen can't imagine how things could get worse. So he's not expecting it when Emma giggles.

He turns on her. "What could be funny?"

She laughs so hard she has to lean into him for support. He stiffens against the urge to wrap his arms around her. Wiping tears from her eyes, she says, "He kissed me!" The confession makes her crack up all over again.

"And you think that's *funny*?"

"You don't understand, Galen," she says, the beginnings of hiccups robbing her of breath.

"Obviously."

"Don't you see? It worked!"

"All I saw was Toraf, my sister's mate, my *best friend*, kissing my . . . my . . ."

"Your what?"

"Student." *Obsession.*

"Your student. Wow." Emma shakes her head then hiccups. "Well, I know you're mad about what he did to Rayna, but he did it to make her jealous."

Galen tries to let that sink in, but it stays on the surface like a bobber. "You're saying he kissed you to make *Rayna* jealous?"

She nods, laughter bubbling up again. "And it worked! Did you see her face?"

"You're saying he set Rayna up." *Instead of me?* Galen shakes his head. "Where would he get an idea like that?"

"I told him to do it."

Galen's fists ball against his will. "You told him to kiss you?"

"No! Sort of. Not really though."

"Emma—"

"I told him to play hard to get. You know, act uninterested. He came up with kissing me all on his own. I'm so proud of him!"

She thinks Toraf is a genius for kissing her. Great. "Did . . . did you like it?"

"I just told you I did, Galen."

"Not his plan. The kiss."

The delight leaves her face like a receding tide. "That's none of your business, Highness."

He runs a hand through his hair to keep from shaking her. And kissing her.

"Triton's trident, Emma. Did you like it or not?"

Taking several steps back, she throws her hands on her hips. "Do you remember Mr. Pinner, Galen? World history?"

"What does that have to do with anything?"

"Tomorrow is Monday. When I walk into Mr. Pinner's class, he won't ask me how I liked Toraf's kiss. In fact, he won't care what I did for the entire weekend. Because I'm his student. Just like I'm *your* student, remember?" Her hair whips to the side as she turns and walks away with that intoxicating saunter of hers. She picks up her towel and steps into her flip-flops before heading up the hill to the house.

"Emma, wait."

"I'm tired of waiting, Galen. Good night."

The beach used to soothe him. Like the minefields soothe Grom. Now, the moon reminds Galen of the color of Emma's hair. The sand, of how she likes to anchor her feet into the ocean floor.

Even the dune grass imitates the sway of her hips. Tonight, the beach tortures him. Like the minefields must torture Grom. And just like Grom, he can't bring himself to leave it.

Toraf emerges from the shallow water, wearing a pair of Galen's shorts. Galen doesn't get up. Toraf sits beside him. Just out of reach. "You should get some sleep, minnow. Don't you have school tomorrow?"

Galen nods without looking at him. "In about three hours. Where's my sister?"

"She's setting up the island we found tonight."

Galen shakes his head. "You slithering eel. You might have told me what you were up to."

Toraf laughs. "Oh sure. 'Hey, Galen, I need to borrow Emma for a few minutes so I can kiss her, okay?' Didn't see that going over very well."

"You think your surprise attack went over better?"

Toraf shrugs. "I'm satisfied."

"I could have killed you today."

"Yeah."

"Don't ever do that again."

"Wasn't planning on it. Thought it was real sweet of you to defend your sister's honor. Very brotherly." Toraf snickers.

"Shut up."

"I'm just saying."

Galen runs a hand through his hair. "I only saw Emma. I forgot all about Rayna."

"I know, idiot. That's why I let you hit me fifty-eight times. That's what I would do if someone kissed Rayna."

"Fifty-nine times."

"Don't get carried away, minnow. By the way, was Emma boiling mad or just a little heated? Should I keep my distance for a while?"

Galen snorts. "She laughed so hard I thought she'd pass out. I'm the one in trouble."

"Shocker. What'd you do?"

"The usual." Hiding his feelings. Blurting out the wrong thing. Acting like a territorial bull shark.

Toraf shakes his head. "She won't put up with that forever. She already thinks you only want to change her so she can become another of your royal subjects."

"She said that?" Galen scowls. "I don't know what's worse. Letting her think that, or telling her the truth about why I'm helping her to change."

"In my opinion, there's nothing to tell her unless she can actually change. And so far, she can't."

"You don't think she's one of us?"

Toraf shrugs. "Her skin wrinkles. It's kind of gross. Maybe she's some sort of superhuman. You know, like Batman."

Galen laughs. "How do you know about Batman?"

"I saw him on that black square in your living room. He can do all sorts of things other humans can't do. Maybe Emma is like him."

"Batman isn't real. He's just a human acting like that so other humans will watch him."

"Looked real to me."

"They're good at making it look real. Some humans spend

their whole lives making something that isn't real look like something that is."

"Humans are creepier than I thought. Why pretend to be something you're not?"

Galen nods. *To take over a kingdom, maybe?* "Actually, that reminds me. Grom needs you."

Toraf groans. "Can it wait? Rayna's getting all cozy on our island right about now."

"Seriously. I don't want to know."

Toraf grins. "Right. Sorry. But you can see my point, right? I mean, if Emma were waiting for you—"

"Emma wouldn't be waiting for me. I wouldn't have left."

"Rayna made me. You've never hit me that hard before. She wants us to get along. Plus, there's something I need to tell you, but I didn't exactly get a chance to."

"What?"

"Yesterday when we were practicing in front of your house, I sensed someone. Someone I don't know. I made Emma get out of the water while I went to investigate."

"And she *listened* to you?"

Toraf nods. "Turns out, you're the only one she disobeys. Anyway, I followed the pulse."

"Who was it?"

"The pulse disappeared before I got there."

"Got where?"

"Emma's house, Galen. Fresh footsteps marked the sand from the water to the house. That's why the pulse disappeared— it left the water."

"You're a Tracker. You've been introduced to every Syrena from both houses. How can there be someone you can't identify?"

"Obviously, I haven't been introduced to *everyone*. I'm telling you, I've never felt that pulse before. Emma didn't recognize it either. Not that I'd expect her to."

Galen pinches the bridge of his nose. Emma wouldn't recognize it because she has held a grudge against water all these years. If there were Syrena living nearby, they wouldn't have sensed her until now. He shakes his head. "Someone must know about her. I need to go over there right now. She's alone. Her mom works at night." The dread he feels all over bottlenecks like a dam in his throat. "Toraf, you need to go to Grom. Tonight. Right now. You need to find Paca before this stranger gets to Emma."

"Jagen's daughter? What does she have to do with Emma?"

Galen stands. "Jagen claims Paca has the Gift of Poseidon. If that's true, I'm going to make sure she's Grom's mate, instead of Emma. But that won't happen if someone—whoever this is—gets to Emma before you get to Paca."

"Galen—"

"I know, it's a long shot. But it's no more unbelievable than Emma having the Gift. And it's the only hope I have."

Toraf nods as understanding takes hold. "Okay. If she's alive, I'll find her, Galen. I swear I will."

"If there's anyone who can do it, it's you. And send Rayna to me while you're gone."

17

BEING A straight-A student doesn't guarantee anyone common sense. I'm no exception. By the time I figure out the steam in the bathroom means the shower *is* getting hot—I just can't feel it because of my Syrena flesh—Mom has called a repairman. Making up a story even a kindergartner wouldn't believe is my only option. Somehow Mom buys it—along with the service-fee repairmen charge when teenage girls waste their time and gas.

This all lends to my new theory—hitting my head triggered my Syrena instincts. All the changes in my life seem to center around that. More than hitting my head. Whatever happened to me at Galen's house—seeing spots, getting dizzy—seemed to seal the deal. That night symbolizes the firsts and lasts of a lot of things.

The first time I held my breath longer than an Olympic

swimmer. The last time I took a hot shower. The first time I could see in pitch-black water. The last time I trusted Galen. The first time I sensed another Syrena. The last time I hated Rayna. The first and the last time I put my head through hurricane-proof glass. The list of correlations to that night is as long as the Jersey coast.

And so is the list of reasons I shouldn't be looking forward to seeing him at school. But I can't help it. He's already texted me three times this morning: Can I pick u up for school? and Do u want 2 have breakfast? and R u getting my texts? My thumbs want to answer "yes" to all of the above, but my dignity demands that I don't answer at all. He called me his *student.* He stood there alone with me on the beach and told me he thinks of me as a pupil. That our relationship is platonic. And everyone knows what platonic means—*rejected.*

Well, I might be his student, but I'm about to school *him* on a few things. The first lesson of the day is Silent Treatment 101.

So when I see him in the hall, I give him a polite nod and brush right by him. The zap from the slight contact never quite fades, which means he's following me. I make it to my locker before his hand is on my arm. "Emma." The way he whispers my name sends goose bumps all the way to my baby toes. But I'm still in control.

I nod to him, dial the combination to my locker, then open it in his face. He moves back before contact. Stepping around me, he leans his hand against the locker door and turns me around to face him. "That's not very nice."

I raise my best you-started-this brow.

He sighs. "I guess that means you didn't miss me."

There are so many things I could pop off right now. Things like, "But at least I had Toraf to keep me company" or "You were gone"? Or "Don't feel bad, I didn't miss my calculus teacher either." But the goal is to say nothing. So I turn around.

I transfer books and papers between my locker and backpack. As I stab a pencil into my updo, his breath pushes against my earlobe when he chuckles. "So your phone's not broken; you just didn't respond to my texts."

Since rolling my eyes doesn't make a sound, it's still within the boundaries of Silent Treatment 101. So I do this while I shut my locker. As I push past him, he grabs my arm. And I figure if stomping on his toe doesn't make a sound . . .

"My grandmother's dying," he blurts.

Commence with the catching-Emma-off-guard crap. How can I continue Silent Treatment 101 after that? He never mentioned his grandmother before, but then again, I never mentioned mine either. "I'm sorry, Galen." I put my hand on his, give it a gentle squeeze.

He laughs. Complete jackass. "Conveniently, she lives in a condo in Destin and her dying request is to meet you. Rachel called your mom. We're flying out Saturday afternoon, coming back Sunday night. I already called Dr. Milligan."

"Un-freaking-believable."

I stare at the Gulf of Mexico from our hotel-room window. Today's storm made the white beach look like sugared oatmeal, the rain dimpling the sand and making it clumpy. The freakish turbulence from that same storm also made Galen sick on the plane.

I glance to the hideous love seat, where he's sleeping off the nausea. Judging by his rhythmic snores, the tiny couch isn't as uncomfortable as it looks. That, or projectile puking takes so much energy, you don't care where you collapse afterward.

The sun is setting, but we still have a while before we meet up with Dr. Milligan at the Gulfarium. He wants us to come after closing to make sure we have plenty of privacy for the tests. That's another five hours.

With time to kill, I change into my bathing suit and head to the beach, careful not to wake Galen. He needs his rest, and besides, I need some time to think. Plus, the rain scattered the remnants of tourists, so there won't be any witnesses in case I grow a fin at an inopportune time.

Peeling off my shirt, I wade in. I don't know how close I am to where Chloe died. I didn't recognize the hotels around us, but the place Rachel booked for us is more luxurious than the affordable-enough room Chloe's parents reserved. It doesn't matter. Chloe isn't here.

And neither am I, not really. At least, I'm not the same Emma she brought down here. The one who followed her around the halls at school like a white shadow. The one who stayed a few feet behind her while she flitted around like a bee, pollinating each of her social groups. A wispy, forgettable phantom.

I wonder if Chloe's bigger-than-life personality would have room for the upgraded Emma. An Emma who lied to her mother to jump a plane with a strange boy-fish. An Emma who's already

waist-deep in the water without an ounce of terror splinter-
ing her nerves. An Emma who's more prone to pick a fight than
stop one. Maybe *upgraded* isn't the right word for the new me.
Maybe it's more in the neighborhood of *different*. Possibly even
indifferent.

The humidity is almost thick enough to drown in. Any
second I expect rain to mingle with the tears as they slide down
my cheeks. So much for indifferent.

I dive in.

The gulf is nothing like I remember it. Of course, that's
because last time, the salt hurt my eyes. Also, the water felt cool
and refreshing against the suffocating Florida heat. Now, like
the hotel Jacuzzi, the Atlantic, and every puddle between here
and there, the water feels lukewarm.

It's almost as frustrating as Galen's game of hot and cold.
Thing is, I'm not sure it's a game. From his expression, there's
out-and-out war going on behind the scenes. He leans in, pulls
away. Leans in, pulls away. It's like a battle between good and
evil. I'm just not sure which one he thinks kissing me is.

Probably evil.

Which is pathetic. For the next twenty-four hours, I'm going
to be stuck in a hotel room, unsupervised, with a guy who's trying his hardest not to kiss me. *Lovely.*

I swim my grouchy self along the sloping bottom, making a
game out of how many crabs I can irritate into snapping at me.
Most are good sports and have a go at it. Even if one actually
latches on to my finger, it won't hurt anymore than a clothes-
pin. But my strategy only works for so long before Galen and

his succulent lips creep back into my thoughts. He's like the club remix of a song I already hated, one I couldn't get out of my head the first time around. One that plays over and over and over.

I wonder what Chloe would tell me to do. *God, I miss her.* Unlike me, she was a connoisseur of all things male. She knew when they were cheating. She knew when they were talking trash to their friends. She knew when they wanted her number even when all they asked for was a pencil. She would be able to take one look at Galen and tell me why he won't kiss me, how to make him, and where to hold our wedding reception.

Too irritated to go farther, I turn around. The smell of metal hits me like a wave. *Smell? Is that even possible?* Then I see it. A cloud of blood. The ripple of a struggle. A fin. Two fins. I scream. It hears me. *They* hear me. They stop thrashing, pieces of a dead something falling around them like confetti. Bloody confetti.

Turning back around, I already know I'm dead. The good news is, two sharks will kill me faster than one. Two sets of jaws have a better chance of slicing an important artery right away. It should be quick. Part of me wants to stop and get it over with. The other part, the bigger part, wants me to swim like mad. Fight and kick and gouge. Make this their hardest kill ever. Hope they choke on my thick Syrena bones.

I hear the swish of their approach and tense up. One of them rams into me, knocking air bubbles from my lungs. I cry out and scrunch my eyes shut. No one wants to see their own death. A jaw clamps around my waist, powerful and tight. It lunges us forward so fast my head snaps back. *This is it.* I wait for the penetration of teeth. It doesn't come. Just keeps swimming. I've heard of alligators doing this, of snatching its prey and taking it somewhere else. Saving the meal for later. Saltwater is probably a great preservative for keeping a corpse like me fresh.

I force one eye open. And gasp. Not a jaw around my waist, so powerful and tight. A pair of arms. Arms I've memorized every contour of.

Galen. And he's so burning mad the water around us should be boiling. Maybe it is. Maybe we're just moving too fast to see it. By the look on his face, he's thinking about killing me himself. Maybe I was better off with the sharks.

Galen swims for a long time. He won't look at me, won't talk to me. I know better than to talk to him. After a while, jet lag, near death, and the security of Galen's arms all team up against me. If I weren't underwater, I'd yawn. Instead, I close my eyes. . . .

"Emma! Emma, can you hear me?"

The slap to my cheek startles me awake. "Huh?" Not my most attractive moment. I rub my eyes. I'm cradled in his arms, princess-style. The stars come into focus. *When did we surface?* Billions of beautiful stars on a clear night. Fish Prince Charming holding me. It's probably the most romantic moment of my life.

Galen ruins it by growling. "I thought you were dead. Twice."

"Sorry." It's all I can think of. Oh yeah, and, "Thanks for saving me."

He shakes his head. Obviously it's not my turn to talk.

"I wake up and you're gone," he says, his jaw tight. "Then you don't answer your cell phone."

I open my mouth, but his eyes widen. *Still not my turn then.*

"I told you to never get in the water alone—"

And that's my cue. "I don't take orders, Highness." Oops. I can tell by his glower that I'm the opposite of smart.

He takes several breaths. Then several more. I wait for him to start hyperventilating. He doesn't. Instead, he grabs my chin. Hard. Eyeing my mouth, his expression softens. Releasing my chin, he peers down into the water beside us.

Then he pulls us under.

Still holding me like a bride over the threshold, we descend faster than a free-falling elevator. But it's the I-know-something-you-don't-know smirk on his face that has me almost squirming.

Finally we stop. He nods behind me, then changes to blended form. By default, I dread turning around. And I'm right. I press myself into Galen, but he won't let me get behind him. A whale. A ginormous one. And since Galen's blended, I'm the only one it can see. "What are you doing, Galen? Get us out of here."

"You're the one who wanted to go swimming. Alone. Change your mind?"

"I said I was sorry."

"You also said you don't take orders—"

"I was just kidding." Ha ha.

He snickers, materializing. "He won't hurt you, Emma."

"He's getting closer. Galen."

"He's curious about you."

"You mean about how I taste?" And why isn't Galen speed-ing us away yet? Lesson learned already!

"No." He laughs. "Although, I'm dying to know that myself."

I whirl on him. "That's not funny. At least *you* can Blend. Get us away from him. Please."

He shakes his head. "He won't hurt us. He's a Knobby. Hu-mans call them sperm whales. They eat squid mostly. I've never heard of one attacking our kind. He's just coming over here to investigate—I swear it." With one hand, he turns me around in his arms. The gigantic fish is so close I can see his eyes, which are about the size of my whole head. "Talk to him," Galen whispers.

I gasp. "Have you lost your mind?" The trembling in my voice matches the trembling of my body. Galen's nose nudging my neck calms me—a little.

"Emma, talk sweet to him. Tell him we won't hurt him."

We won't hurt *him*? "You tell him. You're the fish."

"Emma, he understands you. He doesn't understand me."

"Galen, let's go. Please. I'll do anything you want. I'll never step foot in the water again without your permission. Ever."

He turns me around again and lifts my chin with his thumb. "Listen to me, Emma. I would never let anything happen to you. I'm trying to show you how special you are. But I need you to calm down."

He grabs my face, doesn't let me turn away. Locking eyes with me, he strokes my hair. Brushes his fingers against my cheek. Presses his forehead against mine. After about a minute, I do calm down. He smiles. "You stopped shaking."

I nod.

"Are you ready to turn around?"

My gulp is involuntary. "Is he close?"

Galen nods. "He's right behind you. Emma, if he wanted to eat you, he would have done it already. You're only afraid of him because he's so big. Once you get past that, it's like talking to a goldfish." I don't get a chance to mull over the comparison because he whirls me around so fast, it startles both me and Goliath. "Talk to him, Emma."

"What do I say to a whale, Galen?" I hiss.

"Tell him to come closer."

"No way."

"Fine. Tell him to back up."

I nod. "Right. Okay." I lace my fingers together to keep from wringing my hands raw. Even more than terror, I feel the insanity of the situation. I'm about to ask a fish the size of my house to make a U-turn. Because Galen, the man-fish behind me, doesn't speak humpback. "Uh, can you please back away from me?" I say. I sound polite, like I'm asking him to buy some Girl Scout cookies.

I feel better in the few moments afterward because Goliath doesn't move. It proves Galen doesn't know what he's talking about. It proves this whale can't understand me, that I'm not some Snow White of the ocean. Except that, Goliath *does* start to turn away.

I look back at Galen. "That's just a coincidence."

Galen sighs. "You're right. He probably mistook us for a relative or something. Tell him to do something else, Emma."

"Galen, can't we just—"

"Tell him."

Goliath has put some distance between us. Now he only looks as big as a single school bus instead of three. The little movement it takes his enormous tail to fan him away reminds me of a flag swaying lazily in a gentle breeze. "Wait," I call out. "Come back. You don't have to leave."

When that whale stops, when he turns around, when he lumbers toward us again, the doubt leaves my body like water from a busted hydrant. Goliath comes so close that if he opens his mouth we'll be sucked in. He's ugly. His giant noggin makes him look like a bobble head. And he forgot to floss; there's a squid tentacle the size of my arm flapping out the side of his mouth. Hopefully it's not still alive.

But I'm not afraid anymore. Galen is right. If Goliath wanted to eat us, he would have done it already. Those huge eyes seem gentle, not like the feral emptiness I expected to find. Not like the blank, mechanical stare of a shark.

"Talk to him," Galen murmurs again, tightening his hold on my waist.

I do more than that. Galen lets me ease from his arms but holds my wrist for safekeeping. With my free hand, I reach out and touch Goliath's nose—or at least, the vicinity of his nose. "I was afraid of you, because I thought you would eat us," I tell him. "But you won't eat us, will you?"

While I'm not expecting Goliath to start speaking with a French accent or anything, a small part of me expects him to communicate back to me somehow. Still, the way he shifts quietly with the current speaks decibels. He's not tense or still, like a cobra ready to strike out. He's calm, curious, serene.

"Listen. If you can understand what I'm saying, I want you to swim away in that direction," I say, pointing to my right, "and then come back here." Goliath does exactly what I tell him to. *Nofreakingway.*

My new friend follows us to the surface when my lungs get tight. On the way, Galen points to different fish to see if they all understand. As we pass, I call out my instructions. "Swim that way, swim in a circle. You swim fast, you swim slow, you swim straight down." They all obey.

By the time I—and Goliath—refuel on oxygen, enough fish surround us to fill a swimming pool from top to bottom. Some jump out of the water. Some nibble at my toes. Some swim through my legs or between me and Galen.

They follow us until we reach shore. There are so many fish flitting in the shallow water that the surface looks like it's getting pelted with rain. We sit on the beach and watch them play. When the seagulls start to take notice though, self-preservation wins over curiosity, and my fan club dwindles.

"So," I say, turning to Galen.

"So," he returns.

"You said I'm special. How special am I?"

He takes in a breath and lets it out slowly. "Very."

"How long have you known I'm a fish whisperer?" He doesn't get my joke. But at least he understands what I'm asking.

"Remember when I told you Dr. Milligan saw you at the Gulfarium?"

I nod. "You said he recognized my eye color and thought I might be one of you."

Galen rubs his neck, won't look me in the eyes. "That's pretty much true. Your eye color was significant. Especially since Syrena aren't supposed to be consorting with humans." He grins. "But he really got excited about the way you interacted with the animals there. He said you bonded with them. All of them."

I gasp. Not just my imagination then. Not a fluke. I'd convinced myself the animals were trained to be friendly to visitors. But didn't I notice they weren't friendly to everyone? Didn't I notice they seemed to single me out, pay me exclusive attention? Yes, I noticed. I just didn't acknowledge that it meant anything. Why would I? What *does* it mean? And why didn't Galen tell me this before? "You kept it from me. Why? Does Toraf know? And Rayna? And how can I talk to fish, Galen? Especially when you can't? And if Dr. Milligan saw me doing it at the Gulfarium, then I could do it *before* I hit my head. What does that mean? What does any of it mean?"

He chuckles. "Which question do you want me to answer first?"

"Why did you keep it from me?"

"Because I wanted to let you adjust to the fact that you're not human. You have to admit, it would be a lot to try to absorb all at one time."

I nibble on that for a minute. I detect some BS in there somewhere, but what can I say to that? He's right, even if he is lying. I nod. "I guess that makes sense. So what about Toraf and Rayna. Do they know?"

"Toraf does. Rayna doesn't. And by the way, if you want everyone to know your personal business, just tell Rayna."

"Why don't you want her to tell other Syrena about me?"

"Because what you have is a gift of the Generals. The Gift of Poseidon. So technically, you're my enemy."

I nod without understanding. "Yeah. No."

He laughs. "When the generals made their peace agreement all those millennia ago, they made provisions for the Syrena in the form of certain gifts that would ensure their survival. Each house has a different gift. Yours shows that you're of the house of Poseidon."

"Is that why you make me get out of the water when you sense someone close? Because you could get in trouble for hanging out with me?"

He nods, thoughtful. "You could get into trouble, too. Don't forget, your house sits on the shore of Triton territory."

So we're enemies. The battle in his mind isn't between good and evil. It's between the house of Triton and the house of Poseidon. Which I couldn't possibly care about. But I can't change who I am and neither can he. If he won't kiss me because I'm of the Poseidon house, do I really want him to anyway? *Yep, yep, I do.*

Since I've inched myself to the verge of blushing with thoughts of kissing Galen, I decide on more neutral questions to keep the heat at bay. "But how does talking to fish ensure our survival?" *Did I just say "our"?*

Galen clears his throat. "Well . . . whoever has the Gift of Poseidon can ensure that we always have something to eat."

Swallowing the instant bile, I shake my head. "You're saying that I can talk to fish ... to kill them ... and eat them. ..."

Galen nods. "I mean, you might not have to ever use your gift for that. Right now, we've got plenty to eat. But I think the generals must have anticipated the humans overstepping their boundaries and invading the waters. I think eventually, maybe as soon as decades from now, we'll need the Gift of Poseidon in order to feed ourselves."

I hope I don't look as sick as I feel. "The generals couldn't have picked a worse candidate for *that* Gift!" Holding my stomach doesn't stop it from churning. I can't imagine befriending Goliath and then leading him to the Syrena to be eaten. But I also can't imagine letting Galen or Toraf starve. Probably not Rayna either. *It's time to introduce my new friends to the world of pizza. . . .*

"The generals are dead, Emma. They didn't pick you. It's a gift passed through bloodlines. Dr. Milligan calls it genetics."

Genetics means that my parents really aren't my parents. I know Galen has thought this all along, but I still can't accept it. I also can't completely shun the possibility either. Especially after I just conducted a symphony of fish. How would I even start that conversation with my mom? "So, Galen thinks you've been lying to me for the past eighteen years." Even if I didn't say it directly, that's what it amounts to. And when she asks where I'd get an idea like that? "Well, I recently discovered I can hold my breath for almost two hours and tell fish what to do. I couldn't help but notice that you can't." Yeah, not happening. There's got to be some other way. . . . "Hey!" I almost shout, startling Galen. "Isn't that Rachel's specialty? Finding out stuff? She could investigate where I came from."

"She's already done that."

"What do you mean? She did a background check or something? I'm talking about digging deep—"

"Your birth certificate says you were born in a hospital. Both your parents signed it, and so did the attending physician. He happens to be a college professor now who teaches aspiring doctors how to birth humans. Rachel also found a picture in a newspaper of your father and mother celebrating an award he received. Your mother was pregnant in the picture. From the date of the article, it looked reasonable to assume she carried you in her womb."

My mouth hangs open but no words come out. Galen doesn't notice. He says, "Your school records showed attendance since kindergarten to present, and your address never changed. Your medical records can pass as human, though you've never had the chicken pox. You broke your arm when you were four years old, you've never had surgery, and all your immunizations are up to date—"

"Ohmysweetgoodness!" I yell, standing up. I kick as much sand on him as I can. "That's none of her business! And none of yours! She had no right to—"

"You just said you wanted her to dig deep," he says, standing, too. "I thought you'd be pleased that we already did that."

"You invaded my privacy!" I say as I step into my flip-flops and stomp toward the hotel. Heat wraps around my wrist as he jerks me back.

"Emma, calm down. I had to know—"

I point my finger in his face, almost touching his eyeball. "It's one thing for me to give you permission to look into it. But I'm pretty sure looking into it without my consent is illegal. In fact, I'm pretty sure everything that woman does is illegal. Do you even know what the Mafia is, Galen?"

His eyebrows lift in surprise. "She told you who she is? I mean, who she used to be?"

I nod. "While you were checking in with Grom. Once in the Mob, always in the Mob, if you ask me. How else would she get all her money? But I guess you wouldn't care about that, since she buys you houses and cars and fake IDs." I snatch my wrist away and turn back toward our hotel. At least, I hope it's our hotel.

Galen laughs. "Emma, it's not Rachel's money; it's mine."

I whirl on him. "You are a fish. You don't have a job. And I don't think Syrena currency has any of our presidents on it." Now "our" means I'm human again. I wish I could make up my mind.

He crosses his arms. "I earn it another way. Walk to the Gulfarium with me, and I'll tell you how."

The temptation divides me like a cleaver. I'm one part hissy fit and one part swoon. I have a right to be mad, to press charges, to cut Rachel's hair while she's sleeping. But do I really want to risk the chance that she keeps a gun under her pillow? Do I want to miss the opportunity to scrunch my toes in the sand and listen to Galen's rich voice tell me how a fish came to be wealthy? Nope, I don't.

Taking care to ram my shoulder into him, I march past him and hopefully in the right direction. When he catches up to me, his grin threatens the rest of my hissy fit side, so I turn away, fixing my glare on the waves.

"I sell stuff to humans," he says.

I glance at him. He's looking at me, his expression every bit as expectant as I feel. I hate this little game of ours. Maybe because I'm no good at it. He won't tell me more unless I ask. Curiosity is one of my most incurable flaws—and Galen knows it.

Still, I already gave up a perfectly good tantrum for him, so I feel like he owes me. Never mind that he saved my life today. That was *so* two hours ago. I lift my chin.

"Rachel says I'm a millionaire," he says, his little knowing smirk scrubbing my nerves like a Brillo pad. "But for me, it's not about the money. Like you, I have a soft spot for history."

Crap, crap, crap. How can he already know me this well? I must be as readable as the alphabet. What's the use? He's going to win, every time. "What stuff? What history?"

There he goes again, wielding his smile as a thought-preventative. "I recover things lost at sea and sell them to humans," he says, folding his hands behind his back. "When it's too big to handle myself, like old war submarines or planes, I give the human governments the location—for a price. Rachel handles the legal stuff, of course."

I blink at him. "Really?"

He shrugs, uneasy, as if my full attention suddenly makes him nervous. "I have some private buyers, too. We give them first pick, since they tend to pay more than most nations."

"What about shipwrecks? Pirate treasure?" The possibilities are endless—or at least, only restricted by the boundaries of the Triton territory, which spans from the Gulf of Mexico to dead-center Indian Ocean.

He nods. "Plenty. My biggest was an entire Spanish fleet carrying gold."

I gasp. He shifts his weight from one foot to the other. It occurs to me that I might be the only other person he's told, besides Rachel. "How much gold? Did they question how you found it? Where was it?" My questions bubble up like a shaken soda.

He pinches the bridge of his nose, then laughs. "Rachel has everything saved on the computer, including pictures. You can go through it all you want when we get home."

I clap like a trained seal. I also ignore the flutter in my stomach at hearing him say, "When we get home." As if home could be on dry land.

18

THE SECURITY guard lets them into the Gulfarium and ushers them inside The Living Sea exhibit to wait for Dr. Milligan. In awe, Emma shuffles to the floor-to-ceiling tank and taps on the glass. Galen stands back, leans against the wall. He watches her coo at the tropical fish grappling for her attention. A sea turtle lazily treads over to investigate.

She paces back and forth in front of the glass, tracing her hand along the surface. The tank transforms into one giant multispecies school of fish. Stingrays, sea turtles, eels. More kinds of fish than Rachel puts in her seafood-surprise casserole. Even a small shark joins the parade.

"She's amazing."

Galen turns to Dr. Milligan, who's standing beside him and staring at Emma as if she were floating in midair. "Yes, she is," Galen says.

Dr. Milligan looks at Galen, a knowing smile plastered on his face. "Looks like she's enchanted more than just the *little* fish. In fact, looks like you're worse off than any of them, my boy."

Galen shrugs. He's got nothing to hide from Dr. Milligan.

Dr. Milligan lets out his breath in a whistle. "What does Rayna say?"

"She likes her." The good doctor raises a thin gray brow. Galen sighs. "She likes her *enough*."

"Well, can't ask for more than that, I suppose. Shall we, then?"

Galen nods. "Emma. Dr. Milligan is here."

Emma turns. And freezes. "You!" she chokes out. "*You're* Dr. Milligan?"

The older man bows his head. "Yes, young lady, I am. You remember me, then."

She nods, walking slowly toward them as if she smells a trap. "You tried to give me free season passes. You talked to me at the petting tank."

"Yes," he says. "*Of course* I offered you season passes. How else could I study your fascinating interaction with the specimens?"

She crosses her arms. "I didn't know I could talk to fish at the time. How did you?"

"At first I didn't," he says, closing the distance between them and gently taking her hand. "But when I saw your eye color, I knew you had to be Syrena. I remembered Galen telling me about that gift, but I never really believed it. Which is silly, I suppose. I mean, if I believe in mermaids—ahem, excuse me Galen, *Syrena*—then why not a gift like that?"

"And what do you think now, Dr. Milligan?" Galen says, a

little perturbed at the revelation that his friend thought he lied. Also, "mermaids" was uncalled for.

Dr. Milligan chuckles softly, rubbing Emma's hand. "I think I stand corrected, as usual. Emma, how about a private tour?"

She nods, excitement dancing in her eyes.

They follow Dr. Milligan into the hallway and to a set of stairs. He shepherds them to each exhibit, spouting off facts and statistics about each animal. Every one of the creatures remembers Emma. The sea lions bob their heads and make a noise only Emma could find charming. The otters do the same. Even the alligators respond to her commands, rotating in a circle like synchronized swimmers.

The doctor leads Galen and Emma into an exhibit called Dune Lagoon. He explains it's a sanctuary for injured birds cared for at the Gulfarium. Emma walks around, talking and murmuring to the winged creatures. None of them care. In fact, they seem more excited to see Dr. Milligan. A duck walks right past Emma and quacks at Dr. Milligan's feet. "Fascinating," he says.

Emma laughs. "There's nothing fascinating about getting rejected."

Dr. Milligan smiles and pulls some brown pellets from his pocket, scattering them on the floor for the impatient duck. "This fellow just knows about my treats. Listen, how about we visit the penguins?"

"Aren't penguins birds?" she says. "I mean, I know they can't fly or anything, but they're still birds. They wouldn't respond to my Gift, would they?"

Dr. Milligan nods. "Aquatic birds. And there's only one way to find out, isn't there?"

The penguins love Emma. They waddle around, dive in and out of their pool, call out to her. She laughs. "They sound like donkeys!"

"Maybe you can talk to donkeys, too," Dr. Milligan smiles.

Emma nods. "I can. Sometimes Galen can be a jackass."

"That hurts my feelings, Emma," Galen says, trying to look hurt. She throws him a saucy grin.

Dr. Milligan laughs and leads them back into the hallway. The square windows punctuating the interior wall reveal three dolphins keeping pace with them. They shriek at Emma, eager to meet her acquaintance. Next to a sign that says DOLPHIN SHOW, Dr. Milligan points up a set of stairs. "Shall we?"

The top level is an open deck. Galen's seen the show before. The wooden bleachers facing the tank aren't quite far enough away that the front row won't get wet. Which delights the nose-picking miniature humans, especially in the heat of summer. Galen's glad they came after closing.

Emma walks to the edge of the tank and peers down. She tickles the water with her fingers. Three gray heads poke up and shrill their enthusiasm. Giggling, Emma leans over, cupping her hand over her mouth. The animals draw closer, as if to hear a secret.

The heads disappear. When they emerge again, there's a toy in each mouth. They bring their treasures to Emma. A black ring the size of a hula hoop and two soccer balls. She hands the balls to Galen, then accepts the ring from the smallest dolphin.

"Throw the balls in the middle, Galen. Let's see if they're good at basketball."

Chuckling, Galen complies. Emma holds the ring over the edge of the pool. The dolphins shriek in anticipation. "Shhh," she tells them. They quiet down, hold still. "Try to put the ball through the hoop."

Two of the heads disappear. The third one stays behind and squeals at Emma. She quiets him down again, just as one of the balls pops off the surface of the water and through the hoop she's holding. Then the second one pops up, but this one misses the mark, grazing Emma's hair instead. "I almost got a black eye out of the deal!" But she laughs and rewards the animals with a nose rub.

"It's your turn," she tells the smallest dolphin. Retrieving both soccer balls from the bleachers, she tosses them back in the center of the pool. "Go on," she says, making a shooing motion with her hand. The animal stays put, it's mouth slightly ajar as if smiling.

She turns to Dr. Milligan. "Looks like he doesn't understand," she says.

He snorts. "Oh, he understands, all right. He just doesn't listen."

This doesn't seem to sit well with Emma. She splashes water at him. "Go on! What's the matter? You too chicken-of-the-sea to play?"

Still, he stays, thrashing his head around like he's arguing. His squeals sound contrary even to Galen's untrained ears. The poor creature doesn't realize how close to foot tapping Emma is, but Galen recognizes that stiff stance of impatience. It's the same one she directed at him when they first met on this very beach. The same one she directed at Toraf when she informed him that Rayna could live with her. The same one she directed at Rachel when she booked the honeymoon suite for the two of them.

Just as Galen decides to intervene, the tension leaves Emma's shoulders. "Oh," she says softly. She steps out of her flip-flops and hoists herself onto the cool blue edge of the concrete tank.

"Emma," Galen warns, though unsure of what exactly he's warning against. He and Dr. Milligan exchange a look.

"I'm fine, Galen," she says without looking back. She dangles her legs in the water, kicking in a slow, soothing rhythm. The two biggest dolphins come to her immediately, nudging her feet and creating choppy waves around her. But it's the smallest dolphin who hoards her attention from across the tank by doing nothing at all. Hesitant, he inches toward her. When she reaches out to him, he submerges and shoots to the other side of the tank. Turning back to Galen and Dr. Milligan, Emma says, "He doesn't trust us. Humans, I mean."

"Hmm," Dr. Milligan says. "What makes you say that?"

"His behavior." Emma tilts her head. "See how he keeps his nose below the water? The other two poke their entire heads out. But he doesn't, as if he's thinking about jetting or something. And his eyes. They're not as perky as the others. They look dull, out of focus. Not disinterest, not exactly." She thumps water toward him, flicking droplets onto his nose. He doesn't flinch. "No, he's definitely curious about me. He's just . . . well, he's sad, I think."

"Do you know, I think you're right," Dr. Milligan says, his expression somewhere between admiration and disbelief. "I'm not sure if you remember, but he wasn't here this summer when you visited. He was beached on shore over in Panama City a few weeks ago. He's the only one not born in captivity. We named him Lucky. I guess he would disagree."

Emma nods. "He doesn't like it here. Why was he beached?" By now Lucky has eased himself to within reach of Emma. She extends a hand to him, not to pet him, but in invitation for him to touch her first. After a few indecisive seconds, he nestles his nose into her palm.

"We don't know. He wasn't sick or injured, and he's relatively young. How he got separated from his pod, we don't know."

"I think humans had something to do with him getting beached," she says. Galen is surprised by the bitterness in her tone. "Will he ever get to go home?" Emma asks, not looking up. The way she caresses Lucky's head reminds Galen of how his mother used to comb her fingers through Rayna's hair trying to get her to sleep. The simple touch was a lullaby in itself. It looks like Lucky thinks so, too.

"Usually not, my dear. But I'll see what I can do," Dr. Milligan says.

Emma gives him a rueful smile. "That would be good."

Galen stops short of shaking his head. If Dr. Milligan feels as rewarded by her smile as Galen does, then Lucky will be free in no time.

After a few more minutes, Dr. Milligan says, "My dear, I hate to draw you away, but perhaps we could make our way to the examination room."

"Well, she's definitely got the thick skin, doesn't she?" Dr. Milligan says, inspecting the second needle he's bent trying to penetrate her vein. "I guess I should break out the big guns." He tosses the needle in the trash to dig around the top drawer of a stainless steel cabinet. "Ah-ha. This should be sufficient."

Emma's eyes go as round as sand dollars. Her legs press into the metal tabletop she's sitting on. "That's not a needle, that's a straw!"

Galen stifles the reflex to take her hand in his. "He uses it on me, too. It doesn't hurt, just pinches a little."

She turns huge violet eyes to him. "You let him take *your* blood? Why?"

He shrugs. "It's kind of an exchange. I give him samples to study, and he keeps me informed of what his colleagues are up to."

"What do you mean, 'his colleagues'?"

Galen hoists himself on the counter across from her. "Dr. Milligan happens to be a well-known marine biologist. He keeps track of news that could affect our kind. You know, new exploration devices, treasure hunters, stuff like that."

"To protect you? Or to make sure you get to the treasure first?"

Galen grins. "Both."

"Has anyone else ever seen—OUCH!" She whips her scrutiny from Galen to her arm, where Dr. Milligan is drawing blood and smiling apologetically while doing it. Emma returns her glare to Galen. "Pinch, huh?"

"It was for the greater good, angelfish. The worst part is over. You still want his help, right?" Galen's reasonable tone wins him no love.

"Don't you 'angelfish' me. I agreed to have these tests done, so I'm not going to punk out! OUCH!"

"Sorry, just one more tube," Dr. Milligan whispers.

Emma nods.

When Dr. Milligan finishes, he hands her a cotton ball to press against the hole already scabbing over. "Galen's blood clots fast, too. You probably don't even need to hold it." He puts the half dozen tubes of blood into the shaking machine and flips the switch. Retrieving a small white box from a shelf, he says, "Emma, do you mind if I take your blood pressure?"

She shakes her head, but says, "Why do you have a human blood pressure machine in an animal hospital?"

He chuckles. "Because *my* doctor says I need to keep an eye on mine." Dr. Milligan taps Emma's knee. "Okay, now uncross your legs so I can get a good reading." She does, then holds out her arm. Dr. Milligan shakes his head. "No, my dear, I always get the best reading on your calf. I've found that the main artery of the fin divides in two when Galen changes into human form, one in each leg."

Again, Emma's eyes go wide. "You said it doesn't hurt to change, just like you said it wouldn't hurt when he stabbed me with that straw," she says, glowering at Galen. "I'll just bet it doesn't hurt," she grumbles. "Arteries splitting in half."

As Galen opens his mouth to answer, Dr. Milligan says, "Huh. That's strange."

"What?" they ask in unison. Emma bites her lip. Galen crosses him arms. Neither of them like the sound of "Huh."

The blood pressure cuff releases, and Dr. Milligan stands up. "Your heartbeat isn't quite as slow as Galen's. And your blood pressure isn't as low. Galen, why don't you hop up on the table and let me check yours again?"

Without effort he plunks off the counter and onto the table. As the doctor trades the small cuff for a larger one to accommodate his more muscular calf, Emma leans into Galen. "What does that mean?" she whispers.

He shrugs, trying not to enjoy her scent. "I don't know. Maybe nothing."

As the cuff squeezes, Galen feels an occasional thud in his leg. The cuff hisses its release and Dr. Milligan stands again. The look on his face is far from comforting.

"What is it?" Galen says, ready to shake the doctor into a coma for not sharing. "Is something wrong?" At Emma's sharp intake of breath, Galen grabs her hand, unable to stop himself.

"Oh, no. I wouldn't say something is *wrong*, necessarily. Emma's heartbeat is definitely slower than any human's. It's just not as slow as yours." Dr. Milligan stalks to a tall rectangular cabinet full of drawers. He pulls out a note pad and begins sifting through the pages. "Ah," he says, more to himself than his guests. "It seems your heartbeat is faster since last time, my boy. That or I can't read my own scribble." He flips the page. "No,

I'm sure that's right. Your pulse was consistently lower for the last ten readings. Interesting."

"Which means?" Galen says through clenched teeth.

"Well, traditionally, Galen, every heart has a finite number of beats until it will one day *stop* beating. Animals with slower heartbeats live longer. Say, sea turtles, for instance. While they have the same number of beats as any other heart, it takes them longer to reach that number. That's why sea turtles can live to be well over a hundred years old. A human heart averages about two point five billion heartbeats. At seventy-two beats per minute, that puts the normal human lifespan at eighty years. From the tests I've run on you and Rayna, the average Syrena heart only beats nineteen times per minute. So theoretically, it will take you about three hundred years to reach two point five billion heartbeats. But according to this last reading, Galen, you're at twenty-three beats per minute right now. Something has your heart rate up, my boy."

"Three hundred years is about right," Galen says, ignoring Dr. Milligan's meaningful glance at Emma. "In fact, some of the Archives are over three hundred and twenty years old."

"So, how many beats per minute do *I* clock?" Emma says.

Then Galen understands. *Emma's heart beats faster than mine. . . . She'll die before I do.* Every muscle in his body seems to team up against him and spasm. He can't stop it from coming. Lurching off the table, he barely makes it to the sink before the vomit explodes everywhere. The drain can't handle the volume, even with the water running full blast. Of course, the unidentifiable chunks from lunch don't help either.

"Don't worry about it, Galen," Dr. Milligan whispers, handing him a paper towel. "I'll take care of that later."

Galen nods and pools water from the faucet into his mouth to rinse out the leftovers. Drying his face and hands with the paper towel, he stalks back to the table, but leans against it instead of hoisting himself back up. Just in case he has to make a run for it again.

"Still sick from the flight?" Emma whispers.

He nods. "Dr. Milligan, you were saying?"

The doctor sighs. "Thirty-two beats per minute."

"And in years?" Galen says, his stomach tightening again.

"Roughly? Right around one hundred and seventy-five years, I think."

Galen pinches the bridge of his nose. "Why? Why does her heart beat faster than other Syrena?"

"I wish I could tell you, Galen. But we both know Emma is different than you in other ways, too. Her hair and skin, for instance. Maybe these differences have something to do with her inability to change into Syrena form."

"Do you think it has anything to do with her head injury?" Galen says.

Emma shakes her head. "Can't be."

"Why is that, Emma?" Dr. Milligan says, crossing his arms thoughtfully. "Galen said you hit it pretty hard. I'd say it's at least reasonable to consider the possibility that you may have damaged something."

"You don't understand, Dr. Milligan," she says. "I didn't have *any* Syrena abilities before I hit my head. Hitting my head is what changed everything. Besides, I've been white as the moon all my life. That's got nothing to do with a concussion."

"That's true," Galen says. "But you could hold your breath for a long time *before* you hit your head. And you had the Gift before that, too. Maybe the abilities were always there, you just never knew to test them." *Stupid, stupid.* The hurt on her face confirms his mistake.

"You're talking about the day Chloe died," she says quietly.

Slowly, he nods. No point in lying about it. Even if he wasn't talking about Chloe, she's already thinking about it, already traveling back in time to that day, torturing herself with *if only.* If only she had known about her Syrena blood, if only she had known about her Gift of Poseidon. Chloe would be alive. She doesn't need to say it. It's all over her face.

"Everyone wrote it off as adrenaline," she says. "I should have known better."

Dr. Milligan clears his throat. "Just to be thorough, let's take some X-rays before you go tomorrow. Is that all right with you, Emma?"

She nods, but Galen can tell it's just a reflex.

Galen calls for a cab to drive them back to the hotel; he can't subject Emma to another walk on the beach where her best friend died. Especially since he's not sure how long he can stay in the same room with her without using his arms—or his lips—to comfort her.

It's going to be a long night.

19

DR. MILLIGAN taps the X-ray lit up on the screen. "See here, Galen, this is where your bones thicken to protect your organs. Where people have ribs, you have an enclosure of bone plating, like a shell, really. And this is Emma's X-ray," he says, flipping on the light behind the other image on the white box. "See how hers looks like ribs at first? It barely shows up, but if you look closer, you can see that thin layer of bone plating connecting the ribs. Not quite as thick as yours, though. In fact, none of her bones hold the same density."

"But what does that mean?" Galen says, frowning. I'm glad Galen's not the only one having a difficult time following Dr. Milligan. My thoughts keep vacillating between the draft that feels more like a gust in this sizes-too-big hospital gown, and Dr. Milligan's proposal that I'll live to be 175 years old. This is getting a little weird, even under the circumstances. I'm hundreds of miles from home, half naked in a room with two guys I barely know. Taken out of context, I'd have to question my common sense. *Heck, even in context.*

Dr. Milligan shrugs. "I'm not sure. Could be a few different things, I guess. There's still so much about your kind I don't know, Galen. Growth patterns, for instance. Maybe since Emma spent her life on land, her bones didn't develop fully. Like her coloring. Maybe the Syrena body reacts to something in the water that triggers pigmentation development. That's just a guess though. Really, I have no idea."

Galen looks at me, concern lurking in every crevice of his expression. I know it bothers him when I'm quiet. He'd probably be surprised to find that I'm usually quiet, just not around him. "Emma, do you have any questions for Dr. Milligan?"

I bite my lip and pull the hospital gown tighter around myself. "How can I talk to fish? Why do they all understand English? And don't say it's magic." It's not the question I want to ask, but it's a good one nonetheless, and the answer will give me more time to sponge up the confidence I've been hemorrhaging since changing into this gown.

Dr. Milligan smiles and takes off his glasses. Wiping them with his lab coat, he says, "Well, my dear, Galen is convinced that's genetic as well. If it *is* genetic, I hardly think it could be magic. And I'm not convinced they could understand a language as complex as English. If they did, there'd be no point in baiting a hook ever again, right? A fisherman would simply drop a bucket in the water and tell his catch of the day to swim into it." He chuckles. "If I had to guess, I'd say it has to do with the sound of your voice. We already know that many species of marine life communicate between each other with sound. Whales and dolphins, for example. It's possible your voice has a one-size-fits-all frequency, or some special inflection that they understand. It's possible that what you want them to do translates not in *what* you say but in *how* you say it. Unfortunately, I don't have the equipment to test that theory, or even the ability to get my hands on it right now."

I nod, unsure how I'm supposed to react to that. To any of this.

"Is there anything else bothering you, Emma?" Galen says, surprising me. I wonder why we bothered with the X-rays at all, when Galen can apparently see straight through me, into my deepest parts. Like last night, in the hotel room. When I got dressed after my forty-five-minute cry-a-thon in the shower, I found a box of chocolate-covered strawberries on my pillow and Galen folded up on the ugly love seat, sound asleep.

I clear my throat. "Dr. Milligan, I'm not sure if Galen told you or not, but my father was an MD. He took care of my runny noses, my scrapes, my immunizations. When he died, his friend Dr. Morton took over. How could they miss my bone structure, my slow pulse? You'd think they'd notice my heart is on the opposite side of my chest. I mean, are you sure you're reading this right? You're not a *human* doctor, you're basically a veterinarian, right? You could be wrong."

Galen seems antsy, shifting in his chair. While metal and

polyester aren't exactly the ingredients for coziness, I get the feeling it's my question unsettling him instead of any physical discomfort.

Dr. Milligan pulls the rolling stool up to where I sit on the exam table. Reflexively, I lean toward him, crinkling the thin strip of paper separating me from the vinyl. He reaches out to pat my hand. "Emma, my dear, it's natural to feel that way. And you're right, I'm definitely not a human doctor, like your dad was. But it doesn't take a human doctor to see the differences between my X-ray, Galen's X-ray, and yours." For emphasis, he inclines his head toward the wall where our bones are illuminated on the screen. Then he double-takes. "Good grief." Jumping to his feet, he sends the metal stool toppling behind him.

Galen and I watch as Dr. Milligan rearranges the images in a whirlwind of warbling plastic: Dr. Milligan's X-rays of himself, mine, then Galen's. "Is this really possible?" he says, peering over the rim of his glasses at us, concentration knitting his brows together like kissing caterpillars.

Galen stands and crosses his arms, cocking his head at the lighted screen. Finally, he says, "I guess I'm not following, Dr. Milligan. What do you see?"

Dr. Milligan looks at me, his excitement making him appear years younger. I shake my head, unable to offer an intelligent guess. Dr. Milligan doesn't miss a beat. "The first one, mine, is human. The last one, Galen's, is Syrena. This is Emma's, here in the middle. It's obvious. So obvious, I'm ashamed. She's definitely not human. But she isn't Syrena either."

I'm not liking the sound of this. I can tell Dr. Milligan

thinks he's already explained himself clearly; he's looking at both of us like we're opening a gift he gave us, and he can't wait to see our reactions.

Galen saves us. "Dr. Milligan, you know as far as these things go, I'm pretty ignorant. For my sake, could you just give us the idiot version?"

I don't like being impressed with Galen. Just when I had him sculpted as a snobby Royal in my head, he turns all humble on me, smashing the image.

Dr. Milligan chuckles. "Of course, my boy. Emma is neither human nor Syrena. She appears to be *both*. Though I'm not sure if that's even possible. Syrena DNA is very different from human DNA."

Galen steps back and takes his seat again. I'd do the same, if I weren't already sitting. We both scowl at the lighted screen. As I stare at it, playing musical X-rays with my eyes, I see it. The three sharp images become a single blurry one. Human and Syrena bones melt together until there's only one image on the entire screen: mine. A combination of the two.

"It's possible," Galen says quietly.

Dr. Milligan leans against the wall, curiosity lighting up his face. "It's happened before," he says, lacing his fingers together, probably to keep from fidgeting. "You've heard of it, haven't you?"

Galen nods. He turns to me. "It's the main reason for the Great War. The reason we have two territories," he tells me. "Thousands of years ago, Poseidon decided to live on land with the humans. Interaction wasn't outlawed then, just sort of frowned upon. The humans revered him as one of their gods, sacrificing animals to him, making ridiculous flattering statues of him. They even built a city for him, and the Syrena who joined him on land. Tartessos, they called it."

"Atlantis?" Dr. Milligan breathes, a hand over his chest.

Galen nods. "Some humans called it that at first." He turns back to me. "Poseidon enjoyed living with the humans. He permitted his followers to mate with them. Even Poseidon chose a human mate, against his brother Triton's wishes. Triton believed the humans were poisonous and destructive, and that mating with them was unnatural. As a show of his disapproval, he divided the territories; the Triton territory became home for those who didn't approve of humans, the Poseidon territory for those of the opposite opinion. Poseidon ignored his brother and continued as he saw fit, using his gift to feed the growing population of Tartessos. Unfortunately, the human mate he chose belonged to someone else, a human king."

"What human king?" Dr. Milligan asks, picking up his discarded metal stool and brushing it off as if it accumulated dust balls since his last sitting.

Galen shrugs. "I don't know." He turns to me again, a wry smile on his face. "Don't care either. We Tritons tend to dislike humans."

"Not a very good attitude for an ambassador," I tell him. "But don't worry. I won't tell Dr. Milligan. Or Rachel."

Galen grins. "Anyway, the human king sent something like half his army to collect his 'belongings.' He gained support from other human kingdoms by telling stories of enslavement and unnatural breeding of humans. When the armies arrived, they killed everyone in sight, even some of Poseidon's own half-human children. To stop the carnage, Poseidon appealed to Triton for help against the humans. Triton agreed to help, with one stipulation: Poseidon had to abandon his city and promise to live as Syrena from then on. He agreed. Triton used his gift to create great waves that destroyed the city, the half-breeds, and the human armies. There were no survivors. After that, the generals agreed to help each other against the humans. Breeding with them became outlawed, the offspring of such a union viewed as an abomination." Galen hesitates on the last word, probably because he knows it's a direct insult to me, assuming I'm really a Half-Breed. Somehow, though, I'm not insulted. The way he told the story was more a formal recital than telling it in his own words. It makes me think he doesn't believe it or, at least, doesn't believe parts of it. Also, the way he's looking at me right now hardly makes me feel like an "abomination."

"I thought the war was between the kingdoms," I tell him. "Not against the humans."

Galen shakes his head. "We've never warred against each other. Not physically anyway." An unfamiliar emotion flickers across his face, then disappears like the flash of a camera.

"So, that's Triton's Gift? To control the sea?" I ask.

"No," Galen says, scratching his neck. "At least, not exactly. We don't know how he did it. Some say strength, that he cracked the earth and that caused the waves. Some say he did it with speed.

We don't know. It's been a long time since a Royal inherited the Gift of Triton. So long that the Archives disagree on what that Gift is."

For a few moments we sit in silence, engrossed in the ghost of Galen's story, of everything said and of things unsaid. And the more I think about it, the angrier I get. "So, I don't belong anywhere?" I say, jolting them from wakeful slumber.

"What's that?" Dr. Milligan says, his eyes still glazed with the past.

"Basically, we're all in agreement that I'm a freak. Is that right?"

"You're not a freak," Galen says.

"I'm not Syrena and I'm not human. The Syrena think I'm an abomination. Humans will treat me like a science experiment if they find out. Which still leaves that big question wide open, Dr. Milligan. How has no one found out?"

Dr. Milligan sighs. He pulls out a handkerchief from his pocket and cleans imaginary fog from his glasses' lens. His movements are so deliberate, so meticulous, that even I recognize he's trying to calm me. "Emma, my dear, you haven't known me for a long time, as Galen has. Yet I consider you my friend and hope you consider me yours. So if we're friends, then I can be honest with you, right?"

I nod, chewing my lip as if it's filled with cheesecake.

Dr. Milligan smiles in a generic, obligatory way. "Good. Now then, I believe that your father knew of your condition all along."

The tears well up instantly, and I don't know why. Galen looks away.

"That's not possible," I whisper. "It's just not. My mom could tell if he was hiding something. She's the bloodhound of lies."

"I'm sure she knew about it, too," Dr. Milligan sighs. "Like you said, you're a medical *anomaly*," he says, even as I mouth the word "freak" at him. "I don't have any children myself, but if I did, I wouldn't want to publicize it either. Scientists from all over the world would be stalking your family, begging for the chance to run a few tests. Your life would be chaos. Your father knew that."

I take a deep breath. "I guess that could be true. But the thing is, if they're not my parents, then where did I come from?"

"Could you ask your mother directly?" Dr. Milligan says.

"She'd commit me to a nuthouse. No, wait. She'd laugh in my face, *then* commit me to a nuthouse." Memories of the day I almost drowned make the words taste rancid in my mouth. The way I crawled into her lap, so trusting and confident, to tell her about the catfish. The way she laughed so hard she could hardly catch her breath. It was the first time I realized I couldn't trust my mother with myself. Not my whole self, anyway.

Dr. Milligan nods. "But you don't have to mention anything about being Syrena do you? She may not even know that part. She may just know you're different."

"I guess," I say doubtfully. If she knew about me, about my Gift, she wouldn't have laughed at me all those years ago. She would have comforted me and told me what I was then and there. *Wouldn't she?* Suddenly, I'm too overwhelmed to think. My world keeps shattering and putting itself back together, but every time it does I'm presented with a different mosaic of reality. Maybe I do belong in a nuthouse.

I hop from the exam table, the linoleum slapping my bare feet. "I'm ready to go home," I say to neither of them. I almost choke on the word "home." It sounds foreign on my tongue, like I've just made it up. As if it doesn't exist. "You're done with your tests, right Dr. Milligan?"

The doctor stands, extending his hand to me. "Yes, I won't poke and prod you anymore, my dear." There is nothing generic about his smile now. "It was certainly a pleasure to meet you, young lady."

But I'm already down the hall, my clothes tucked tight under my arm.

20

GALEN SLIDES into his desk, unsettled by the way the sturdy blond boy talking to Emma casually rests his arm on the back of her seat.

"Good morning," Galen says, leaning over to wrap his arms around her, nearly pulling her from the chair. He even rests his cheek against hers for good measure. "Good morning . . . er, Mark, isn't it?" he says, careful to keep his voice pleasant. Still, he glances meaningfully at the masculine arm still lining the back of Emma's seat, almost touching her.

To his credit—and safety—Mark eases the offending limb back to his own desk, offering Emma a lazy smile full of strikingly white teeth. "You and Forza, huh? Did you clear that with his groupies?"

She laughs and gently pries Galen's arms off her. Out of the corner of his eye, he sees the eruption of pink spreading like spilled paint over her face. She's not used to dating him yet. Until about ten minutes ago, he wasn't used to it either. Now though, with the way Mark eyes her like a tasty shellfish, playing the role of Emma's boyfriend feels all too natural.

The bell rings, saving Emma from a reply and saving Mark thousands of dollars in hospital bills. Emma shoots Galen a withering look, which he deflects with what he hopes is an enchanting grin. He measures his success by the way her blush deepens but stops short when he notices the dark circles under her eyes.

She didn't sleep last night. Not that he thought she would. She'd been quiet on the flight home from Destin two nights ago. He didn't pressure her to talk about it with him, mostly because he didn't know what to say once the conversation got started. So many times, he's started to assure her that he doesn't see her as an abomination, but it seems wrong to say it out loud. Like he's willfully disagreeing with the law. But how could those delicious-looking lips and those huge violet eyes be considered an abomination?

What's even crazier is that not only does he *not* consider her an abomination, the fact that she could be a Half-Breed ignited a hope in him he's got no right to feel: *Grom would never mate with a half human.* At least, Galen doesn't *think* he would.

He glances at Emma, whose silky eyelids don't even flutter in her state of light sleep. When he clears his throat, she startles. "Thank you," she mouths to him as she picks her pencil back up, using the eraser to trace the lines in her textbook as she reads. He acknowledges with a nod. He doesn't want to leave her like this, anxious and tense and out of place in her own beautiful skin.

But he needs to go to Romul. Romul will be able to tell him more about the half-humans, about why Triton hated them. It's not something Galen ever thought he'd ask; it's always been easy enough to find reasons to hate the humans. Still, his handful of human friends makes it impossible for him to hate the species as a whole. And one day, he might need the law to side with him on that point.

The bell rings, startling him from his thoughts and Emma from another mini nap. He grabs her backpack and holds it open while she shovels her book and paper into it. Before she can get away, he grabs her hand, entwining their fingers the way Rachel showed him. He's surprised when Emma leans into him, resting her head on his biceps. Maybe she's more used to dating him than he thought.

She yawns. "Let's skip the rest of the day and take a nap at your house."

He squeezes her hand. Spending the rest of the day with her alone at his house is the best and worst thing he can think of. "Your mom will kill me and ground you."

"I didn't sleep last night."

"I can tell."

"I look that bad?"

"You look that tired."

They stop in front of the door to their next class. He reaches to open it for her. "Galen," she says, looking up at him. "Please."

He sighs. "I can't miss school today. I might miss tomorrow."

The curiosity perks her right up. "Why?"

He pulls her out of the way as some of their classmates dawdle into the room. The tardy bell rings. "I'm going to talk to the Archives tonight. To see what else I can find out about the half-breeds. I thought maybe that would make you feel better about . . ." He shrugs, unable to finish the half truth. "Besides, I have to get back here before Friday. Rachel thinks we need to go on a date Friday night. You know, for show."

"Oh," she says, her lashes tangling together in the world's longest blink. She yawns again. "Like the movies or something?"

"She said a few things. Movies was one of them, I think. Something about roller-skating and bowling, too."

Emma gives a drowsy laugh. "If you think I'm deadly in flip-flops, you should see me in roller skates."

"Movies it is, then. I'm not willing to risk another concussion." He ushers her to the door, and she lets him open it for her. Tyler, a junior with an Adam's apple the size of his nose, subtly waves them to the seats he saved in the back row. Galen slips him a twenty dollar bill as Tyler shuffles his things to an open desk up front.

While Emma sleeps through physics, Galen dutifully takes notes on thermodynamics for her. On a separate sheet of paper, he lists questions he wants to ask Romul. Still, even after he's checked and rechecked the list, there's a question he's forgetting. It gnaws at him, teasing him from the edge of his brain, not quite getting close enough to grasp.

Beside him, Emma sighs in her sleep. Galen stiffens. *Emma. Who will watch Emma while I'm gone?* Toraf hasn't returned from searching for Paca. Rachel can watch her on land, but if Emma gets in the water, she's as good as gone. Not that she looks up to practicing any time soon, exhausted as she is. But Emma is practically made of defiance and stubbornness and resilience, and everything else that could possibly make his life difficult. If she wants to get in the water, she will.

That only leaves one person. *Rayna*.

21

THE CHANNELS on the TV continue to change even after Rayna stops pressing the button on the remote. She slides down the front of the couch, planting herself on the floor. "Four hundred channels and nothing worth watching. Unbelievable," she mutters.

I glance up from where I'm sitting in the recliner and fold the page of my book. "You could help me practice. They wouldn't have to know." I don't even feel like practicing. It just seems I should get in the water on principal, since Galen told me not to. And especially since he left me with a babysitter.

She throws me a sideways glare. "Fat Lips would know. He can sense me from anywhere, remember? And he'd snitch to Galen. He would know something's wrong if you and me got in without my brother."

I shrug. "Since when do you care about getting in trouble?"

"Since never. But Galen said if I kept you out of the water, he'd teach me how to drive his car."

Jackpot. "I happen to know how to drive. I could teach you."

"Galen said I wasn't allowed to ask you, or the deal's off."

"You didn't ask me. I offered."

She nods, biting her lip. "That's true. You did."

I set the book on the ugly glass coffee table and squat next to her. "I'll teach you how to drive if you let me get in the water. You don't even have to get in."

The way she raises her brow reminds me of Galen. "You're wasting your time trying to change if you ask me. You're half human. You probably don't even have a fin in there."

"What do you know about the half-breeds?"

She shrugs. "Not much. Enough to know that if you're one of them, there's no point in trying to change. No one is going to accept you. At least, no Syrena will."

I decide not to take offense. I don't put much stock in her opinion anyway, and she won't care if she offended me or not. Rayna can be counted on to say what she's thinking. Taking offense would waste everyone's time. Besides, she's still here. If *she* thought of me as an abomination, she wouldn't have anything to do with me, would she?

"That might be true. But if it were you, wouldn't you want to know if you could change?"

She considers, then shrugs again. "Probably."

"So we have a deal?" I say, holding my hand out for a shake. She eyes it and crosses her arms. I set my hand on the couch, feeling awkward, wondering if she even knows what a hand shake is.

"You'll teach me to drive your car if I let you get in the water?"

"Uh, no. I'll teach you how to drive *Galen's* car if you let me get in the water. You're not touching my car without a license. A real one, not some shiny plastic thing Rachel made between afternoon talk shows." Even if Galen doesn't have insurance, he's got enough in his wallet to buy a new one. I, on the other hand, have just enough in savings to cover my deductible.

Her eyes go round. "You'll let me drive his little red one? The combustible?"

Why not? I nod. "Yep. The convertible. Deal?"

She grabs my hand from the couch to pull us both up. Then she shakes it. "Deal! I'll go get the keys from Rachel."

I pull over on the dirt shoulder of the most abandoned road in the farthest hem of the farthest outskirt of Middlepoint. The rearview shows me nothing but our dusty trail disappearing like phantoms into the trees on either side. Ahead of us, a mail truck stops with flashing lights at the only mailbox on the whole stretch. When it passes us, the driver tips his cap our way, eyeing us as if he thinks we're up to no good—the kind of no good he might call the cops on. I wave to him and smile, wondering if I look as guilty as I feel. Better make this the quickest lesson in driving history. It's not like she needs to pass the state exam. If she can keep the car straight for ten seconds in a row, I've upheld my end of the deal.

I turn off the ignition and look at her. "So, how are you and Toraf doing?"

She cocks her head at me. "What does that have to do with driving?"

Aside from delaying it? "Nothing," I say, shrugging. "Just wondering."

She pulls down the visor and flips open the mirror. Using her index finger, she unsmudges the mascara Rachel put on her. "Not that it's your business, but we're fine. We were always fine."

"He didn't seem to think so."

She shoots me a look. "He can be oversensitive sometimes. I explained that to him."

Oversensitive? No way. She's not getting off that easy. "He's a good kisser," I tell her, bracing myself.

She turns in her seat, eyes narrowed to slits. "You might as well forget about that kiss, Emma. He's mine, and if you put your nasty Half-Breed lips on him again—"

"Now who's being oversensitive?" I say, grinning. *She does love him.*

"Switch places with me," she snarls. But I'm too happy for Toraf to return the animosity.

Once she's in the driver's seat, her attitude changes. She bounces up and down like she's mattress shopping, getting so much air that she'd puncture the top if I hadn't put it down already. She reaches for the keys in the ignition. I grab her hand. "Nope. Buckle up first."

It's almost cliché for her to roll her eyes now, but she does.

When she's finished dramatizing the act of buckling her seat belt—complete with tugging on it to make sure it won't unclick—she turns to me in pouty expectation. I nod.

She wrenches the key and the engine fires up. The distant look in her eyes makes me nervous. Or maybe it's the guilt swirling around in my stomach. Galen might not like this car, but it still feels like sacrilege to put the fate of a BMW in Rayna's novice hands. As she grips the gear stick so hard her knuckles turn white, I thank God this is an automatic.

"*D* is for *drive*, right?" she says.

"Yes. The right pedal is to go. The left pedal is to stop. You have to step on the left one to change into drive."

"I know. I saw you do it." She mashes down on the brake, then throws us into drive. But we don't move.

"Okay, now you'll want to step on the right pedal, which is the gas—"

The tires start spinning—and so do we. Rayna stares at me wide-eyed and mouth ajar, which isn't a good thing since her hands are on the wheel. It occurs to me that she's screaming, but I can't hear her over my own screeching. The dust wall we've created whirls around us, blocking our view of the trees and the road and life as we knew it.

"Take your foot off the right one!" I yell. We stop so hard my teeth feel rattled.

"Are you trying to get us killed?" she howls, holding her hand to her cheek as if I've slapped her. Her eyes are wild and glassy; she just might cry.

"Are you freaking kidding me? You're the one driving!"

"You said to step on the brake to put us into drive, then to step on the right one to—"

"Not at the same time!"

"Well, you should have told me that. How was I supposed to know?"

I snort. "You acted like the freaking Dalai Lama when I tried to tell you how to shift gears. I told you, one was for go and one was for stop. You can't stop and go at the same time! You have to make up your mind."

From the expression on her face, she's either about to punch me or call me something really bad. She opens her mouth, but the really bad something doesn't come out; she shuts it again. Then she giggles. *Now I've seen everything.*

"Galen tells me that all the time," she chortles. "That I can never make up my mind." Then she bursts out laughing so hard she spits all over the steering wheel. She keeps laughing until I'm convinced an unknown force is tickling her senseless.

What? As far as I can tell, her indecisiveness almost got us killed. Killed isn't funny.

"You should have seen your face," she says, between gulps of breaths. "You were all, like—" And she makes the face of a drunk clown. "I bet you wet yourself, didn't you?" She cracks herself up so much she clutches her side as if she's holding in her own guts.

I feel my lips fracture into a smile before I can stop them. "You were more scared than me. You swallowed like ten flies while you were screaming."

She spits all over the steering wheel again. And I spew

laughter onto the dash. It takes a good five minutes for us to sober up enough for another driving lesson. My throat is dry, and my eyes are wet when I say, "Okay, now. Let's concentrate. The sun is going down. These woods probably get pretty creepy at night."

She clears her throat, still giggling a little. "Okay. Concentrate. Right."

"So, this time, when you take your foot off the brake, the car will go on its own. There, see?" We slink along the road at an idle two miles per hour.

She huffs up at her bangs. "This is boring. I want to go faster."

I start to say, "Not too fast," but she squashes the gas under her foot, and my words are snatched away by the wind. She gives a startled shout, which I find hypocritical because after all, *I'm* the one helpless in the passenger seat, and *she's* the one screaming like a teapot, turning the wheel back and forth like the road isn't straight as a pencil.

"Brake, brake, brake!" I shout, hoping repetition will somehow penetrate the small part of her brain that actually thinks.

Everything happens fast. We stop. There's a crunching sound. My face slams into the dash. No wait, the dash becomes an airbag. Rayna's scream is cut off by her airbag. I open my eyes. A tree. A freaking tree. The metal frame groans, and something under the hood lets out a mechanical hiss. Smoke billows up from the front, the universal symbol for "you're screwed."

I turn to the rustling sound beside me. Rayna is wrestling with the airbag like it has attacked her instead of saved her life.

"What is this thing?" she wails, pushing it out of her way and opening the door.

One Mississippi . . . two Mississippi . . .

"Well, are you just going to sit there? We have a long walk home. You're not hurt are you? Because I can't carry you."

Three Mississippi . . . four Mississippi . . .

"What are those flashing blue lights down there?"

22

IT'S ALMOST a straight shot from the Jersey Shore to the Cave of Memories, where the Archives live. Galen reaches it within hours. Above him, the thick Arctic ice serves as a first defense against the prying eyes of the humans.

For centuries stacked on centuries, the miles-thick layers of frozen past was the only defense needed. Now, though, humans have figured out how to send down their robotic cameras. Many of the ancient Syrena relics, which once sat out on the seafloor in plain view, were moved to chambers of the cave. Which is a shame, since access to the cave is restricted to Royals and Archives.

He passes a site where huge Roman columns used to loom over Syrena visitors, as if in welcome. Now it's just an abandoned plot of ocean floor, gray and cold for more reasons than the temperature. Galen shakes his head. Humans really do ruin everything. *No*, he tells himself. Most *humans ruin everything. Not all.*

He reaches the portal of the cavern. Two Syrena trackers allow him entry without question. No doubt they sensed him before he even made it as far as Greenland. The narrow portal opens into a wide corridor that looks like a giant jaw full of thin, sharp teeth. The rocks growing down from the top almost touch the growths from the bottom. Galen hopes that if humans ever do infiltrate this site, they'll feel like a meal.

Even if they dared to travel past the mouth and into the belly, they'd be hard-pressed to find anything foreign that hadn't been a natural part of this place for thousands of years. The Cave of Memories spans for hundreds of miles, a maze of passages and tunnels and chambers. Some are too narrow for even an eel to slip through. Others could accommodate an army of humans. The relics, the history of Galen's kind, are hidden away in the deepest parts, through the most complicated passageways. Finding the way out would be impossible, even with the most advanced human technology.

But the Syrena have a natural tool to guide them: sensing. The Archives no longer need sensing in the cave; having exercised and stretched their memories to full capacity, they can find their way without it. Galen grins, thinking of Emma's irritated expression at learning Syrena have photographic memories, according to Dr. Milligan. She'd almost fallen out of her chair when Galen scored higher than her on their first calculus test.

As he rounds a narrow bend, Galen picks up on Romul's pulse and follows it through another convoluted mess of passages.

Romul is waiting for him in the ceremony chamber, the place where mating records are kept. Galen has never found Romul here before. He wonders if it might have something to do with Paca's lineage. *Is he trying to prove she has Royal blood?*

Romul bows before Galen, but it's Galen who feels humble. "Ah, my favorite of the Royals," Romul says. "How do things go with you, young Galen?"

"I'm well, Romul. Thank you."

"What brings you to this distant part of existence, my prince? More importantly, how may I be of service to you?"

"I need some information about the humans again, Romul," Galen says without hesitation. He's still wary of Romul's involvement in Grom's search for Paca, but asking about the humans is one of Galen's most common requests. Romul isn't likely to suspect anything unusual, especially since Galen is ambassador to the humans.

Romul smiles and nods, his black hair long and wispy. "Of course, my prince. What can I do for you?"

"I'd like to view the Tartessos remains. I have questions about the half-breeds."

Romul raises a surprised brow. "As you wish, young prince. This way, please."

Galen follows his mentor deeper into the cave. They pass the Scroll Room, which is an inaccurate title for what's contained there. The fragile papyrus scrolls of mankind's lost civilizations have long since disintegrated, but the freezing waters of the Arctic keep the other records—tablets, pottery, jewelry, and sometimes whole walls of hieroglyphics—well-preserved.

The freezing temperatures also keep the Tomb Chamber—the giant catacomb of Syrena dead—intact. Galen has never been in the tomb himself, but Rayna used to visit their mother in the first few years after she died. The tomb ensures that Syrena remains will never fall into human hands. Galen shudders as he thinks of the worldwide search that would surely ensue if a Syrena body—or even a bone—were to wash up on a beach somewhere.

They reach the Civic Chamber, the biggest of all the chambers where the ruins of cities are kept. Galen has been here before, many times, but never with a human eye, so to speak. Or rather, the eye of a Half-Breed. Emma could get lost in here for days, maybe months. And he'd love to bring her here to do just that.

Romul leads him past the large remnants of Alexandria, Egypt, and artifacts from Cleopatra's quarters. Past some ancient temples of Thailand, painstakingly removed from their underwater site and rebuilt here in the Cave of Memories. Past a towering pyramid deconstructed centuries ago off the coast of the island called Japan and reestablished here for a well-deserved eternity. Finally, they reach Tartessos, perhaps the most important of all the cities here, because of its connection to their kind.

Out of them all, Tartessos is the most intact city. Built like an enormous target, the metropolis would have been circular, with streets curving around the central structures. Romul and Galen cross the first salvaged bridge, whose water now flows over it instead of under it. They swim past statue after statue of

Poseidon himself—or at least, the humans' version of him. Even fractured and chipped, missing pieces of tails and parts of his trident, the statues are striking.

The Syrena commissioned for the task of re-creating the roads proved meticulous in placing each recovered cobblestone paver into a perfect sphere of winding paths leading to the palace in the middle. Though gliding through the water above it, Galen and Romul follow the fragmented road as they pass buildings and fountains and public baths. Galen can easily imagine an ancient population bringing life to this desolate, inanimate place, exchanging their abundance of gold, silver, and copper for food, clothing, and services. *But what about people who look like Emma?*

Galen gets his answer as they round the last bend to the palace. His breath catches as they approach a wall he's seen a thousand times before but never really looked at. Images of humans sacrificing large bulls in honor of Poseidon. Most of them have black hair, olive skin, violet eyes. Rigid lines are drawn on their torsos, probably to emphasize their physiques. But in the corner of the panorama, there are other humans. Humans he's never noticed before because their outlines almost blend in with the wall. White skin. White hair. Violet eyes. Humans who look like Emma.

Galen clears his throat. "These humans here," he says, running his finger over one whose soft curves remind him of her. "Who are they?"

"My prince, none of the images on this wall are of humans. These are our Syrena brethren in their human forms. And these," he says, his voice filled with disdain, "are the half-breeds. These in particular, sired of Poseidon himself."

Galen stiffens against the bitterness in Romul's tone. "Right. I think you mentioned them before. Something about abominations . . . I can't remember exactly. Why were they hated?"

Romul shakes his head. "They themselves were not hated. No, my young friend. In fact, Poseidon loved his half-human offspring very much. That was part of the problem. Many of our brethren sacrificed themselves for their human mates."

"Sacrificed themselves? What do you mean?"

"It is in our collective memory that many of our ancestors chose to spend most of their time on land," another voice calls from behind them. Galen and Romul turn to see Atta, an Archive of the house of Poseidon.

Romul smiles warmly at her. In the Cave of Memories, there is no division of houses. "Atta, welcome." He turns back to Galen. "Yes, she is correct, young friend."

"But what's wrong with that? Spending time on land?" Galen wishes he would have phrased the question better; it sounds a little like questioning the law. Like treason.

"Our bodies are not suited for land, my prince," Atta says, skimming her small hand along the wall in a sort of reverential way. "The . . . heaviness . . . on land makes our bodies work harder than they do in the water. It makes us age faster."

"Heaviness?" Galen says, mulling over what she could mean. He turns to Romul. "Is she talking about gravity?" *Of course.* That's why he's so tired at the end of a school day. It takes more energy to move his body around on land than floating, almost weightless, in the water. Much more energy. A small flick of his fin gets him triple the distance than using the same effort to move his human legs.

Romul nods. "Yes, gravity, very good, Galen. The Syrena population began to decrease very rapidly, because many of our brethren chose to stay on land with their human mates and die a human death. Triton knew if that continued, our kind would eventually disappear."

It makes us age faster. Galen remembers what Dr. Milligan said about heart rates. The faster the heart rate, the shorter the life. During this last visit, Dr. Milligan had said Galen's heart rate was faster than when he'd checked it just months before. *Because I've been spending so much time on land.*

His throat constricts. "These half-breeds. What were they like?"

Atta and Romul exchange a look. Romul says, "I'm afraid we don't understand the question, my prince."

"What I mean is, were they able to change into Syrena form? Did any of Poseidon's half-human offspring inherit his gift?"

Romul knits his brows. Atta folds her hands in front of her. She says, "Not that we recall, Highness. It is our shared understanding that the half-breeds were never able to change into form. It is thought that none inherited Poseidon's Gift."

"It's thought? You're not sure?" Galen says, his frustration growing.

"My prince," Romul says, "it is possible that they inherited his Gift. The Law of the Generals requiring the two houses to mate was not put in place until after Tartessos was besieged by humans. We cannot confirm if any of Poseidon's half-human offspring inherited the Gift, as they were all destroyed in the great waves of Triton."

Emma can hold her breath for a long time but not indefinitely. Depending on how long Triton pounded the shore, the Half-Breeds very well could have been wiped out. *Still, some could have lived, couldn't they?* He stares at the Half-Breed on the wall, the one who reminds him of Emma. It turns his stomach to think she drowned.

Lost in his self-torment, he stares at the image long enough to bore his archive companions. "Highness, may we be of further use to you at this time?" Atta gently coaxes him from his trance.

Galen nods. "I have one more question, Atta, if you don't mind."

"Of course not, Highness," she says graciously.

"The Half-Breeds. Were they very bad? Did they turn against us? Is that why Triton destroyed them with the humans?"

"No," she says. "Triton felt they should be destroyed because of what they stood for. He did not want Poseidon to be reminded of his human mate or his half-human offspring. He did not want any more of our kind to be tempted to live—to die—on land. He believed our survival depended on our staying below the surface, away from humans."

"May we help you with anything else, young friend?" Romul asks, after a few moments.

Galen shakes his head. "No. Thank you for your time today, both of you."

"It's our pleasure to serve you, Highness," Atta says, bowing away from him in her retreat. Her long hair undulates behind her like a piece of fabric.

Galen turns to leave as well, but something catches his eye on the wall. He scans it again, searching for a glimpse of it. He finds it a few feet away. Swimming up to an image of a Syrena male, he traces his finger around the shape of his eye. "Blue?" he asks Romul. "Are his eyes blue?"

Romul shakes his head. "No, my prince. Some of the paint the humans used to depict our brethren was apparently inferior. Over the years, the color seems to have faded."

"Of course. Purple is made from blue." Galen nods at the picture, then at Romul. "Well, thanks again, Romul. I'll see you later."

Romul inclines his head toward him. "Always an honor, young friend. Be well."

Galen follows the pulse of the two Trackers to find his way out of the cave. Traveling home seems to take longer than getting there. He suspects the weights burdening his mind are responsible for slowing him down physically as well.

Dr. Milligan is right. Emma is definitely a Half-Breed. But she still possesses the Gift of Poseidon. The law requiring the two houses to mate every third generation must be for show—Royals aren't the only ones who can inherit the Gift. Galen suspects it must be another reminder from Triton to stay loyal to each other instead of to the humans. *That makes Paca as good a candidate as any, Royal blood or not.* If she has the Gift, she'll pass it on to her offspring. And so will Emma.

Could it be possible that some of Poseidon's half-human

children did survive and reproduced? Could Emma somehow be a descendant of those offspring? She says her father had fair skin, light hair. Could he be the link they're looking for?

And what if he is? Which would be more important to Grom—upholding the law by not mating with a Half-Breed, or mating with one to ensure the survival of the Gifts? Galen doesn't know. But even if Grom chooses not to reproduce with Emma, will he allow Galen to take her as his mate? Because if Romul and Atta are right, Emma will never sprout a fin. Which means Galen will have to live with her on land.

Is it worth it? To give up years of my life to be with her? Galen thinks of the curve of her hips, the fullness of her lips, the way she blushes when he catches her looking at him. And he remembers how sick he felt when Dr. Milligan indicated Emma would die before him.

Oh, yes. It's absolutely worth it.

23

OFFICER DOWNING pulls into the driveway next to Mom's car. *Of course* she's home. I don't know why I even wasted hope that she wouldn't be. Maybe because I'm eighteen, which means they don't bother calling your parents to the scene. But even if I'm not a victim of the law, I'm a victim of the small-town grapevine. A victim of flashing blue lights, whispered scorn, and heads shaking in disapproval. And, boy, do I feel like a victim, because not only is she home, she's standing on the front porch, arms crossed. Waiting.

Officer Downing opens the back door to the low-budget cop car that smells like vinyl, BO, and humiliation. I step out. He hands me my backpack, which Rachel was so kind to bring out when we dropped Rayna off at Galen's house. She was also kind enough not to kill me for showing up at her house with a cop.

"You get some rest, young lady," Officer Downing says.

"You'll likely be sore tomorrow. It usually takes a day or two to feel the effects of an accident."

"Thanks for the ride home, Officer Downing. I appreciate the help," I say sheepishly.

"You're certainly welcome, Miss McIntosh. Have a good evening." He waves to my mom in sort of a clipped salute, then gets in the car and backs out.

I trudge toward the porch, entertaining the idea of running the other way. But technically, I shouldn't be in any trouble. It wasn't my car. I'm not the one who got a ticket. Samantha Forza did. And the picture on Samantha Forza's driver's license looks a lot like Rayna. She told Officer Downing that she swerved to keep from hitting a camel, which Officer Downing graciously interpreted as a deer after she described it as "a hairy animal with four legs and a horn."

Since no one formed a search party to look for either a camel or a unicorn, I figured we were in the clear. But from Mom's expression, I'm miles from clear.

"Hi," I say as I reach the steps.

"We'll see about that," she says, grabbing my face and shining a pen light in my eyes.

I slap it away. "Really? You're checking my pupils? Really?"

"Hal said you looked hazy," she says, clipping the pen back on the neckline of her scrubs.

"Hal? Who's Hal?"

"Hal is the paramedic who took your signature when you declined medical treatment. He radioed in to the hospital after he left you."

"Oh. Well, then Hal would have noticed I was just in an accident, so I might have been a little out of it. Doesn't mean I was high." So it wasn't small-town gossip, it was small-*county* gossip. Good ole Hal's probably transported hundreds of patients to my mom in the ER two towns over.

She scowls. "Why didn't you call me? Who is Samantha?"

I sigh and push past her. There's no reason to have this conversation on the porch. She follows me into the house. "She's Galen's sister. I didn't call because I didn't have a signal on my cell. We were on a dead road."

"Where was Galen? Why were you driving his car?"

"He was home. We were just taking it for a drive. He didn't want to come." Technically, all these statements are true, so they sound believable when I say them.

Mom snorts and secures the dead bolt on the front door. "Probably because he knows his sister is life threatening behind the wheel."

"Probably." I stalk to the kitchen and set my backpack on the counter. After grabbing a bottle of water from the fridge, I sit at the dining-room table to unlace my tennis shoes.

She pulls up a chair beside me. "You're not hurt? Hal said you hit your head. I was worried."

"I did hit it, on the airbag. But I'm fine. Not even dizzy."

Mom's tone morphs from motherly concern to all business. "So, you want to tell me what really happened? Because I'm not buying the whole we-decided-to-take-a-BMW-down-a-dirt-road crap. A deer? You're kidding, right?"

I hate when she pulls this. The whole good cop/bad cop

thing. She doesn't get that she's supposed to pick one, not be both. "I'll tell you if you tell me," I say, washing my hands of maturity. I'm tired of the double standard—she keeps secrets, but I'm not allowed. Also, I'm tired, period. I need sleep. Which means I need answers.

"What do you mean? Tell you what?"

"I'll tell you what we were really doing out there. After you tell me who my real parents are." There, I opened it. A chunky can of wiggling worms.

She laughs, just like I expect her to. "Are you serious?"

I nod. "I know I'm adopted. I want to know how. Why. When."

She laughs again, but there's something false in it, as if it wasn't her first reaction. "So that's what this is about? You're rebelling because you think you're adopted? Why on earth would you think that?"

I fold my hands in front of me on the table. "Look at me. We both know I'm different. I don't look like you or Dad."

"That's not true. You have my chin and mouth. And there's no disinheriting the McIntosh nose."

"What about my skin? And my hair?"

"What about it?"

"Oh, never mind," I say, waving my hand at her. I stand to walk away. She's not going to budge, just like I knew she wouldn't. "I don't feel like getting laughed at. I'm getting in the shower and going to bed."

She grabs my arm. "What do you mean laughed at? Why would I laugh?"

Aside from the fact that she's already laughed twice in this conversation? I raise a skeptical brow but sit back down. After a deep breath, I blurt, "Because that's what you do every time I try to talk to you."

She blinks. "Since when do you ever try to talk to me?" she says quietly.

Huh. She has a good point. When she puts it like that, it doesn't really sound fair of me. I open and shut my mouth a couple times. What, am I supposed to say, "Since I was four"? After all, she's the reason I don't talk to her, right? "When those fish saved me—"

She throws her hands up, startling me. "For God's sakes, I thought you wanted to have a real conversation, Emma. You're bringing that up? You were four years old. How could you even remember that?"

"I don't know, I just do. I remember those fish saving me. I remember you laughing at me when I tried to tell you. But Dad didn't. Dad believed me."

She sighs. "Look, I know you miss Dad. But what in the world does that have to do with you being adopted?"

I stand up, almost knocking over the chair. "Just forget it, okay? You're my real mom. Dad's my real dad. And Ra— *Samantha*—swerved to hit a deer. There. Now life can go on. I'm going to bed." I stomp up the stairs and start peeling off my clothes. Now is one of those times when a hot bath would reincarnate me into a pleasant Emma. But I'm doomed to lukewarm everything for the rest of my freakish life.

Deep down, I know I'm punking out. I should keep talking

to her, keep questioning her. But somehow *I* ended up in the hot seat instead of her. Somehow it's suddenly *my* fault that we don't have an open relationship.

I jerk the shower curtain open and step into the steaming water. It feels like I'm bathing in spit. Dumping shampoo into my hand, I work up a good lather. I stiffen when I hear Mom's voice on the other side of the curtain.

"You're right. Dad did believe you," she says without emotion. "But that man would believe anything you said. Emma, you were so distraught about it and so emotional. Of course you thought it was real. I'm sure it was very real to you. I'm sorry I laughed. I don't know if I ever said that before. But I am. I didn't realize it hurt you."

My lip quivers. I can't say anything. It would be a simple thing to tell her it's okay. To accept her apology. But I've held on to this bitterness for so long that I can't just let it go. Not yet. So I don't. She doesn't say anything else. I never hear her leave.

When I step out of the shower, my birth certificate is on the bathroom sink, along with a few baby pictures I've never seen. A picture of Dad posing for the camera as he cuts an umbilical cord. A picture of Mom, hours of labor etched into her face, but still smiling while she cradles a pale baby with almost-see-through skin and a cap of white hair crusted in blood. Me.

Could it all have been staged? The birth certificate forged? And if so, then WHY? It doesn't make any sense. But that could have a lot to do with how tired I am. Maybe in the morning I can look at these pictures with fresh eyes. I'll even take the birth certificate to Rachel to see if she can tell if it's real.

Satisfied with my plan, I wrap a towel around my head genie-style, then wrap another one around my body. I open the bathroom door. And almost jump out of my skin. Galen is sitting on my bed. *I've really got to start locking my balcony doors.*

He looks mad and happy at the same time. It's only been twenty-four hours since I've seen him, but even sleep deprived and grouchy, I'm excited that he's back.

"I think your dad was a Half-Breed," he says. He frowns. "And I never told Rayna I would teach her how to drive."

24

FRIDAY NIGHT *is finally here.*

Galen makes the turn down Emma's road, mentally review-
ing the must-do list Rachel gave him for their date tonight. He's
determined to keep Emma engaged all evening; she needs a
distraction even more than *he* does. She's been hounding him
with questions about her father. Galen told her everything the
Archives said. She showed him the birth certificate—which
Rachel confirmed was either authentic or the best fake she'd
ever seen—and her baby pictures. It all just confirms what he'd
already concluded—Emma's father was a descendant of the
half-breeds. He had the blond hair and the light skin. Plus, he
wore contacts. Emma swears they weren't color-enhanced, but
Galen's sure they were. They had to be.

There are other coincidences, too. Her father loved the
ocean. He adored seafood. He believed Emma when she told

him about the catfish saving her. Why would he believe her unless he knew what she was? And as a physician, he had to have known about all her physical abnormalities. How could he not be a Half-Breed?

But Emma resists all of Galen's reasonings, based on the fact that it doesn't "feel right."

Speaking of things that don't feel right ... He pulls his new SUV into her driveway, the excitement sloshing in his stomach like high tide. As he steps out, he notices how much he likes sliding down instead of hoisting himself up from a little compact death trap. He's almost glad Rayna tied the red car around a tree— except that she and Emma could have gotten hurt. He shakes his head, crunching across the gravel of Emma's driveway in his suede Timberlands.

Even over that, he hears the thud of his heart. *Is it faster than usual?* He's never noticed it before, so he can't tell. Shrugging it off as paranoia, he knocks on the door then folds his hands in front of him. *I shouldn't be doing this. This is wrong. She could still belong to Grom.*

But when Emma answers the door, everything seems right again. Her little purple dress makes the violet in her eyes jump out at him. "Sorry," she says. "Mom threw a fit when I tried to leave the house in jeans. She's old-school I guess. You know, 'Thou must dress up for the movies,' says the woman who doesn't even own a dress."

"She did me a favor," he says, then shoves his hands in his pockets. *More like she did me in.*

~ ~ ~

After they buy their tickets, Emma pulls him to the concession line. "Galen, do you mind?" she says, drawing a distracting circle on his arm with her finger, sending fire pretty much everywhere inside him. He recognizes the mischief in her eyes but not the particular game she's playing.

"Get whatever you want, Emma," he tells her. With a coy smile, she orders seventy-five dollars worth of candy, soda, and popcorn. By the cashier's expression, seventy-five dollars must be a lot. If the game is to spend all his money, she'll be disappointed. He brought enough cash for five more armfuls of this junk. He helps Emma carry two large fountain drinks, two buckets of popcorn and four boxes of candy to the top row of the half-full theater.

When she's situated in her seat, she tears into a box and dumps the contents in her hand. "Look, sweet lips, I got your favorite, Lemonheads!" *Sweet lips? What the—* Before he can turn away, she forces three of them in his mouth.

His instant pucker elicits an evil snicker from her. She pops a straw into one of the cups and hands it to him. "Better drink this," she whispers. "To take the bite out of the candy."

He should have known better. The drink is so full of bubbles it burns clear up to his nostrils. Pride keeps him from coughing. Pride, and the Lemonhead lodged in his throat. Several more heaping gulps and he gets it down.

After a few minutes, a sample of greasy popcorn, and the rest of the soda, the lights finally dim, giving Galen a reprieve.

While Emma is engrossed in what she calls "stupid previews," Galen excuses himself to vomit in the bathroom. Emma wins this round.

When he returns to his seat, Emma is gone, her arsenal of food left behind. *Doesn't matter. She already started a war.* Since his eyes only adjust to darkness in water, he has to rely on the tingles to find her. She's sitting a few rows down, on the opposite end of the theater. He takes the empty seat next to her and gives her a quizzical look. The screen brightens enough for him to see her roll her eyes. "We were sitting in front of a bunch of kids," she whispers. "They talked too much."

He sighs and wiggles around in his chair to get comfortable— it's going to be a long night. Watching humans play pretend for two hours doesn't exactly flip his fin. But he can tell Emma's getting restless. And so is he.

Just as he nods off, a loud noise pops from the screen. Emma latches onto his arm as if he's dangling her over a cliff. She presses her face into his biceps and moans. "Is it over yet?" she whispers.

"The movie?"

"No. The thing that jumped out at her. Is it gone?"

Galen chuckles and pries his arm from her grasp, then wraps it around her. "No. You should definitely stay there until I tell you it's clear."

She whips her head up, but there's an almost-smile in her eyes. "I might take you up on that, pretend date or no. I hate scary movies."

"Why didn't you tell me that? Everyone at school was practically salivating over this movie."

The lady next to her leans over. "Shhh!" she whisper-yells.

Emma nestles into the crook of his arm and buries her face in his chest, where she returns frequently as the movie goes on. Galen admits to himself that humans can make everything look pretty real. Still, he can't understand how Emma can be afraid when she knows they're only actors on the screen getting paid to scream like boiling lobsters. But who is he to complain? Their convincing performance keeps Emma in his arms for almost two solid hours.

When the movie is over, he pulls the car to the curb and opens the door for her just as Rachel instructed. Emma accepts his hand as he helps her in.

"What should we call our new little game?" he says on the way home.

"Game?"

"You know, 'Have some Lemonheads, sweet lips!'"

"Oh, right." She laughs. "How about . . . Upchuck?"

"Sounds appropriate. You realize it's your turn, right? I was thinking of making you eat a live crab."

She leans over to him. He almost swerves off the road when her lips brush his ear. "Where will you get a live crab? All I have to do is poke my head in the water and tell them to scatter."

He grins. She's been getting more comfortable with her Gift. Yesterday, she sent some dolphins chasing after him. The day before, she directed every living thing in the immediate area to retreat when a fishing boat passed overhead.

They pull into her driveway and he shuts off the car. It seems like every force in the universe is pushing him toward her—just like a magnet. Or maybe every force in the universe is *pulling* her to him. Just like Toraf said. Either way, he's getting tired of fighting it. Something's got to give. And it needs to happen soon.

He opens his door, but she stops him, putting her hand on his. "You don't have to walk me to the door," she says. "Mom's not home now, so no need for a show, right? Thanks for the movie. I'll see you tomorrow."

And that's it. She gets out, walks to the front door, lets herself in. After a few seconds, her front porch lights shut off. Galen backs out of the driveway. When he turns onto the main road, his feeling of emptiness has nothing to do with losing the game of Upchuck.

Out of the corner of his eye, he sees Emma glance at the pink gift bag on the island in the kitchen. He knows it's cruel to play havoc with her curiosity, but he can't help himself. She's still on problem two of her calculus homework. She's been on problem two for close to an hour.

She scowls and slams her pencil down on the counter. "I despise doing homework on Saturdays," she says. "This is all your fault. You need to stop skipping school. Then I wouldn't feel obligated to be productive while you're doing your catch-up work." She snatches his pencil from his hand and launches it across the kitchen, narrowly missing Rachel by the fridge. Rachel shoots them a quizzical look but keeps cleaning.

Galen grins. "We could just chill if you want."

Emma raises a brow at Rachel. Rachel shrugs her innocence. "Nuh-uh. Don't look at me. I didn't teach him that."

"Picked it up all on my own," he says, retrieving his pencil from the floor.

"Figures," Emma sneers.

"Aww, don't hate on me, boo."

"Okay, I'm drawing the line at 'boo.' And don't call me 'shorty' either," Emma says.

He laughs. "That was next."

"No doubt. So, did anyone explain how you chill?"

Galen shrugs. "As far as I can tell, chillin' is the equivalent of being in a coma, only awake."

"That's about right."

"Yeah. Doesn't sound that appealing. Are all humans lazy?"

"Don't push it, Highness." But she's smirking.

"If I'm Highness, then you're 'boo.' Period."

Emma growls, but it doesn't sound as fierce as she intends. In fact, it's adorable. "Jeez! I won't call you Majesty either. And you Will. Not. Ever. Call me 'boo' again."

His grin feels like it reaches all the way to his ears as he nods. "Did . . . did I just win an argument?"

She rolls her eyes. "Don't be stupid. We tied."

He laughs. "If you say I won, I'll let you open your present."

She glances at the gift bag and bites her lip—also adorable. She looks back at him. "Maybe I don't care about the present."

"Oh, you definitely care," he says, confident.

"No, I definitely do NOT," she says, crossing her arms.

He runs a hand through his hair. If she makes it any more difficult, he'll have to tell her where they're going. He gives his best nonchalant shrug. "That changes everything. I just figured since you like history . . . Anyway, just forget it. I won't bother you about it anymore." He stands and walks over to the bag, fingering the polka-dot tissue paper Rachel engorged it with.

"Even if I say you win, it's still a lie, you know." Emma huffs.

Galen won't take the bait. Not today. "Fine. It's a lie. I just want to hear you say it."

With an expression mixing surprise and suspicion in equal parts, she says it. And it sounds so sweet coming from those lips. "You won."

As he walks the bag over to her, he feels giddy, like he were the one getting a gift. In a way, he is. When he passed the wreck on his way back from the Cave of Memories, he knew he had to take her there. "Here. Go change. You don't need the mask and flippers, but I want you to wear the suit. It's designed to retain your body heat. It can keep a human alive in freezing temperatures for a few hours, so you should be nice and cozy in it."

She peers into the bag. "A diving suit? Why would I need this?"

He rolls his eyes. "Go change."

When she emerges from the bathroom, he almost falls off the bar stool. The suit hugs every curve of her body. The only thing he doesn't like is the way she's scowling. "I look like a seal in this thing," she says, pointing to the hoodie.

He grins. "Keep it on. If you're warm enough when we get there, you can take it off, I promise."

She gives an impatient nod. "This better be good."

To preserve her air, they stay surfaced. Occasionally, he dives to check their location. This last time, he grins. "We're here."

She smiles. "Finally. For a while I thought we might be going to Europe."

"Before we go down, are you okay? Cold?"

She shakes her head. "Not at all. Actually, I'm kind of hot. This thing really works."

"Good. Deep breath, okay? Dr. Milligan told me to pull you down slowly to make sure your body can handle it. If you feel tightness in your chest or anything uncomfortable, you need to tell me right away. We're going deeper than ten Empire State Buildings."

She nods, eyes wide. Her cheeks flush with either excitement or the heat she complained about. He smiles as his arms encircle her waist. As they descend, she talks to the curious fish flitting about. But the farther they go, the fewer and fewer fish there are until Galen would be surprised to see any that didn't glow.

"How did you meet Dr. Milligan, anyway?" she says, almost as an afterthought.

"I saved his life. Well, we saved each other's lives."

She rests her head against his chin. "Says the guy who hates humans."

"I don't hate humans." *At least, not anymore.*

After a few minutes, she wiggles in his arms. "Well?" she says.

He turns her around to face him. "Well what?"

"Are you going to tell me *how* you saved Dr. Milligan's life?"

"You really are the most curious person I know. It worries me."

"It should."

He chuckles. When she arches a stubborn brow, he sighs. "Toraf, Rayna, and I were playing around some reefs off the coast of the Bridge Land—er, Mexico, is what you call it. We were about ten years old, I think. Anyway, Dr. Milligan was snorkeling with two of his friends on the other side of it. We were careful to stay away from them, but Dr. Milligan had strayed from the rest of the party. I found him on our side, lying on the bottom and clutching his leg; he had a cramp. I could tell he was about to pass out. I pulled him to the surface. His friends saw us and pulled him into the boat. They saw my fin; I wasn't very good at changing into human form yet. Or blending. They tried to pull me into the boat."

Emma gasps. Galen gives her a crooked smile. "This won't give you nightmares, will it? You know how it ends. The good guys get away."

She pinches him. "Get on with the story."

"Dr. Milligan put the boat in gear, full-speed. They lost their balance and dropped me. The end."

"Nooooo. Not the end. How did you find each other again? That was before you met Rachel, right?"

He nods. "I didn't see him again for another year. I kept going back to the reef, because I thought he might, too. And one day, he did."

"What about his friends? Did they ever try to find you again?"

Galen laughs. "They still do. And they're not his friends anymore."

"Aren't you worried they told someone about you?"

He shrugs. "No one believes them. Dr. Milligan denied the whole thing to the human authorities. It's his word against theirs."

"Hmm," she says, thoughtful.

They spend the next few minutes in silence. Just when he thinks he can't take it anymore, she talks again.

"I'm definitely not hot anymore," Emma says. Galen stops. "No," she says quickly. "It feels good. Keep going."

She would tell him anything at this point to see the surprise. And he would give her the benefit of the doubt. The truth is, he's excited this moment is here.

When they get close, he faces her to him again. "Close your eyes. I want this to be a real surprise."

She laughs. "You think I even know where we are? We could be in the North Pole for all I know. I don't have a sense of direction on land, Galen."

"Well, just the same, close your eyes."

When she complies, he picks up speed, skirting them along the ocean floor until he sees it looming ahead of them. He turns her around. "Open your eyes, Emma," he whispers.

He knows the exact moment she opens them. She gasps. He knew she would recognize it. "The *Titanic*," she breathes. "Ohmysweetgoodness."

He swims them to the hull. She reaches out to brush her fingers along the rail made so famous in movies. "Careful of the rust," he warns.

"It looks so lonely. Just like in the pictures."

He heaves them over the rail and supports her body weight so she can touch her feet on the deck. The stirred-up muck floats around them like an apparition. Emma laughs. "Wouldn't it be funny to leave fresh footprints here? I bet they'd come up with all sorts of ghost stories. It would make headlines."

"It would only increase the traffic down here. They're already selling trips to the *Titanic* to tourists who can afford it."

She giggles.

"What?" he says, smiling.

"There's this big glass jug in the back of my closet. Last year when we studied this in school, I started throwing all my change in it to save up for one of those tours."

He chuckles and lifts her from the deck to move forward. "What will you spend it on now?"

"Probably some of that chocolate Rachel keeps around the house. I hope I have enough."

Everywhere she wants to go, he takes her. To the port-side deck, to the anchor, to the giant propeller. He pushes them inside and shows her the officer's quarters, dilapidated halls, frames of windows with no glass. "We can go deeper in if your eyes are adjusting."

She nods. "It's like looking at things in the moonlight on a clear night. I can see almost everything if I really focus."

"Good." He reaches a hole in the hall floor and points into

the darkness. "No human has been down there since the ship sank. You up for it?"

He can see the hesitation in her eyes. "What?" he asks. "You feel bad? Are you low on air? Is the pressure too much?" He clutches her tight, ready to spring up if she answers yes to any of it. Instead, she shakes her head and bites her lip.

"No, it's not that," she says, her voice cracking.

He stops. "Triton's trident, Emma, what is it? Are . . . are you crying?"

"I can't help it. Do you realize what this is? It's a steel coffin for over fifteen hundred people. Mothers drowned with their children here. People who once walked down these halls got trapped underneath them. They ate off the dishes broken everywhere. Someone actually wore that boot we passed. Crew members kissed their families for the last time the day this ship left port. When we studied it in school, it made me sad for all these people. But it never felt as real as this. This is heartbreaking."

He brushes her cheek with the back of his hand, imagining the tear that would be there if they weren't twelve miles deep. "I shouldn't have brought you here. I'm sorry."

She grabs his hand but doesn't move it away from her. "Are you kidding? This is the best surprise you could have planned. I can't think of anything else that could top this. Seriously."

"Do you want to keep going then? Or have you seen enough?"

"No, I want to keep going. I just felt I should acknowledge what happened here all those years ago. To be a respectful visitor, not just a mindless tourist."

He nods. "We'll explore a few more minutes below, then I need to take you up. We need to surface slowly, so your lungs can adjust if they need to. But I promise, I'll bring you back if you want."

She laughs. "Sorry, but I think this is my new favorite hangout. We might as well pack a lunch next time."

Together, they swim deeper.

A warm glow from inside her house illuminates the doorstep. He shuts off the engine, fighting off the urge to back them out of the driveway and go somewhere, anywhere else. As long as they go together.

"Mom's home," Emma says softly.

He smiles. Her hair is still damp from the shower she took at his house, and her spare change of clothes—jeans and a paint-splattered T-shirt—are a bit wrinkled from their time spent shoved in a travel bag in the bottom of Rachel's closet. This cozy look is just as inviting to him as the little purple dress she wore on their human date. He's about to tell her so when she opens her door.

"Well, I'm sure she heard the car pull up so I'd better get inside," she says.

He laughs, trying to swallow the disappointment as he walks her to the door. She fidgets with the keys as if she's trying to decide which one will unlock the dead bolt. Since there are only three keys on the ring—and the other two are car keys—Galen takes delight in the fact that she's stalling. She doesn't want this day to end any more than he does.

She looks up then, meeting his eyes. "I can't even tell you what a great time I had today. The best time, honest to goodness."

"You know what my favorite part was?" he says, stepping closer.

"Hmm?"

"We didn't fight. Not once. I hate fighting with you."

"I do, too. It seems like a waste of time when . . ."

He leans impossibly closer, holding her gaze. "When?"

"When we could be enjoying each other's company instead," she whispers. "But you probably don't enjoy my company here lately. I haven't been very nice—"

He brushes his lips against hers, cutting her off. They're softer than he ever imagined. And it's not enough. Moving his hand from her jawline to entwine it in her damp locks, he pulls her to him. She tips up on her toes to meet him and as he lifts her from the ground, she folds her arms around his neck. Just as hungry for him as he is for her, she opens her mouth for a deeper kiss, pressing her soft curves into him. And Galen decides there is nothing better than kissing Emma.

Everything about her seems made for him. The way her mouth moves in perfect rhythm with his. The way she combs her fingers through his hair, sending a stirring jolt down his spine. The way her cool lips ignite heat through his whole being. She fits in his arms, as if her every curve fills a place on his own body. . . .

Neither of them realize when the door opens, but their lips break apart when Emma's mom clears her throat. "Oh, excuse me," her mom blurts. "I thought I heard a car pull up. . . . Uh, well, I'll just be inside then." She disappears behind an almost slammed door.

Galen grins down at Emma, still in his arms. The contentment he feels is shattered when he sees pain in her eyes.

She tugs free of his grasp and steps back. "All this time, I worried *you* wouldn't be able to perform, but *I* almost dropped the ball."

"Dropped the ball?" he asks, alarmed by the way her swollen lips quiver. *Is she about to cry?* "Did I do something wrong?" he whispers. She moves away when he reaches for her.

Giving a forced smile, she says, "No, it was perfect. I didn't even hear her coming. Now she won't have any doubts about us dating, will she?"

Understanding hits him like a rogue wave. *Emma thinks I kissed her for her mom's benefit.* "Emma—"

"I mean, for a minute there, you almost had *me* convinced that we . . . Anyway, I'd better go inside before she checks on us again."

"Have you *lost your mind?*" someone hisses from the bushes beside the porch. Galen doesn't have to turn around to know it's Rayna. She marches up the stairs, already pointing at Galen.

Oh, no.

Rayna pokes Galen's chest. "You've got a lot of nerve, you know that? Following her all over the world, pretending to have the kingdom's interest in mind. You slimy eel! You kissed her. I can't believe you kissed her."

Emma gives a nervous laugh. "You knew he was going to do that, Rayna. We told you, remember?"

Rayna gives her a horrified scowl. "Oooooh, no. He was going to *pretend* to kiss you. That kiss was real. Trust me on this one, Emma. I've known him a lot longer than you have."

"Maybe we should take this out back to the beach?" Emma says, glancing at the front door.

Rayna nods, but Galen shakes his head. "No, you can go in, Emma. Rayna and I can talk about it on the drive home."

"Uh-uh. No way, Galen. You're telling her the truth." If Rayna keeps raising her voice, Emma's mom will hear. Galen grabs Rayna's arm and pulls her from the porch. When she struggles, he throws her over his shoulder.

"Emma!" Rayna shouts, wiggling around like a hooked fish. "You need to hear this! Tell her, Galen! Tell her why you shouldn't be kissing her at all."

Emma walks to the edge of the porch and leans on it. "I already know I'm of the Poseidon house, Rayna. I won't tell if you won't," she says, smiling at Galen.

"Stop being dumb, Emma," Rayna yells back as they round the corner of the house, disappearing from sight. "You're supposed to mate with Grom. Galen is supposed to take you to Grom!"

Galen stops. It's too late. She's said too much. The conversation could have been salvaged up until now. He sets his sister down. She won't look up at him, just keeps her eyes focused behind them.

"Did you think I wouldn't notice?" Rayna says without looking up. A tear glistens in the moonlight as it slides down her cheek. "How the fish follow her around? You thought I was too stupid to figure out why we tracked her across the big land, then stayed with her after you found out she was a half-breed? It's not right what you did. She belongs to Grom. The decision to breed with her or not is his. It's not fair to Emma either. She likes you. The way she should like Grom."

It's kind of bittersweet in a way. His sister just ruined the best night of his life and possibly any chance of getting what he wants. But she did it out of respect for Grom. And for Emma. How can he be mad about that?

Galen hears the front door open. Rayna stiffens. "What's going on out here?" Mrs. McIntosh says.

"Oh, um. Nothing, Mom. We're just talking, that's all," Emma says, from the corner of the house. Galen wonders how long Emma's been standing there, looking at his back. Listening to Rayna accuse him of all sorts of nasty, true things.

"I heard yelling," her mother says in a no-nonsense sort of way.

"Sorry. I'll be quieter." Emma clears her throat. "Galen and I are going to walk on the beach."

"Don't go too far," her mom says. "And don't make me come look for you."

"Mom," Emma groans at the shutting door.

Rayna visibly relaxes when they hear the dead bolt slide into place. Emma pushes past them both and heads toward the sand dunes behind her house. Exchanging a look, Galen and Rayna follow.

At the edge of the water, the moon seems to shine down on them like a spotlight, as if somehow the universe knew tonight would be one of enlightenment. Emma turns and faces them, her face stricken.

She looks at Rayna. "Spill it."

"I just did," Rayna says. "I just told you everything I know." She wraps her arms around herself as if she's freezing.

"Why am I supposed to mate with Grom? I'm of the house of Poseidon. I'm Grom's enemy."

Rayna opens her mouth, but Galen cuts her off. "Wait. I'll tell her." His sister stares at him, doubtful. He sighs. "You can stay if you want. In case I miss anything."

She juts her chin out and nods once, ready for him to begin.

Galen turns back to Emma. "Remember when I told you that Grom was supposed to mate with Nalia, but that she died?"

Emma nods. "In the mine blast."

"Right. They were supposed to mate with each other because they were third generation, firstborn of each house. Anyway, the reason they needed to mate was to perpetuate the Gifts of the Generals. To make sure the Gifts—"

"I know what *perpetuate* means," she says. "Get on with it."

Galen shoves his hands in his pocket to keep from moving toward her. "I told you that King Antonis refused to sire an heir after Nalia's death. Without an heir for Grom to mate with, the Gifts could disappear. At least, that's what the law says. When Dr. Milligan told me about you, when I saw you, I knew you had to be a direct descendant of Poseidon. So I—"

She holds up her hand. "Stop right there. Like you said before, I know how the story ends, don't I?" She doesn't try to wipe the tears streaming down her face. She laughs, a sharp sound, full of venom. "I knew it," she whispers. "Deep down, I knew you had some ulterior motive here. That you weren't trying to help me out of the kindness of your heart. Geez, I really fell for that, didn't I? No, I fell for *you*. Lesson learned, right?"

"Emma, wait—" He reaches for her, but she backs away.

"No. Don't you touch me. Don't you ever touch me again." She keeps backing away as if he's going to attack her or something. His gut twists.

Galen and Rayna watch as Emma disappears between the sand dunes in front of her house, taking double-size steps like she was late for something.

"You hurt her," Rayna says quietly.

"You didn't help."

"I didn't do anything wrong."

He sighs. "I know."

"I like Emma."

"I do, too."

"Liar. You love her. That kiss was real."

"It was real."

"I knew it. What are you going to do?"

"I don't know," he says, watching the light flick on in Emma's third-floor bedroom. He scratches the back of his neck. "In a way, I'm glad she knows. I didn't like hiding it. But she probably wouldn't cooperate if I told her the truth."

Rayna snorts. "You think?" She tucks a short tendril behind her ear. "Besides, everything turned out *sooo* much better now because you hid it."

"What are you doing here anyway?"

She shrugs. "You might remember that you sent my mate on some sort of secret mission. I was bored."

"Glad we could entertain you."

"Look, I wanted to see Emma's house. Maybe meet her mom. Do something girlie. I didn't come over here to ruin your life." Her voice is quivering.

He puts his arm around her. "Don't cry again. Come on. I'll take you home," he says quietly.

Rayna pinches the snot from her nose. Then she backs away from him, too, just as Emma had, only she's moving toward the water. "I know the way home," she says, before turning and diving in.

It's only second period, and the whole school knows Emma broke up with him. So far, he's collected eight phone numbers, one kiss on the cheek, and one pinch to the back of his jeans. His attempts to talk to Emma between classes are thwarted by a hurricane of teenage females whose main goal seems to be keeping him and his ex-girlfriend separated.

When the third period bell rings, Emma has already chosen a seat where she'll be barricaded from him by other students. Throughout class, she pays attention as if the teacher were giving instructions on how to survive a life-threatening catastrophe in the next twenty-four hours. About midway through class, he receives a text from a number he doesn't recognize:

If u let me, I can do things to u to make u forget her.

As soon as he clears it, another one pops up from a different number:

Hit me back if u want to chat. I'll treat u better than E.

How did they get my number? Tucking his phone back into his pocket, he hovers over his notebook protectively, as if it's the only thing left that hasn't been invaded. Then he notices the foreign handwriting scribbled on it by a girl named Shena who encircled her name and phone number with a heart. Not throwing it across the room takes almost as much effort as not kissing Emma.

At lunch, Emma once again blocks his access to her by sitting between people at a full picnic table outside. He chooses the table directly across from her, but she seems oblivious, absently soaking up the grease from the pizza on her plate until she's got at least fifteen orange napkins in front of her. She won't acknowledge that he's staring at her, waiting to wave her over as soon as she looks up.

Ignoring the text message explosion in his vibrating pocket, he opens the container of tuna fish Rachel packed for him. Forking it violently, he heaves a mound into his mouth, chewing without savoring it. Mark with the Teeth is telling Emma something she thinks is funny, because she covers her mouth with a napkin and giggles. Galen almost launches from his bench when Mark brushes a strand of hair from her face. Now he knows what Rachel meant when she told him to mark his territory early on. But what can he do if his territory is unmarking herself? News of their breakup has spread like an oil spill, and it seems as though Emma is making a huge effort to help it along.

With his thumb and index finger, Galen snaps his plastic fork in half as Emma gently wipes Mark's mouth with her napkin. He rolls his eyes as Mark "accidentally" gets another splotch of JELL-O on the corner of his lips. Emma wipes that clean too, smiling like she's tending to a child.

It doesn't help that Galen's table is filling up with more of his admirers—touching him, giggling at him, smiling at him for no reason, and distracting him from his fantasy of breaking Mark's pretty jaw. But that would only give Emma a genuine reason to assist the idiot in managing his JELL-O.

When he can't take anymore, Galen plucks his phone from his pocket and dials, then hangs up. When the call is returned, he says, "Hey, sweet lips." The females at the table hush each other to get a better listen. A few of them whip their heads toward Emma to see if she's on the other end of the conversation. Satisfied she's not, they lean closer.

Rachel snorts. "If only you liked sweets."

"I can't wait to see you tonight. Wear that pink skirt I like."

Rachel laughs. "Sounds like you're in what we humans like to call a pickle. My poor, drop-dead-gorgeous sweet pea. Emma still not talking to you, leaving you alone with all those hormonal girls?"

"Eight-thirty? That's so far away. Can't I meet you sooner?"

One of the females actually gets up and takes her tray and her attitude to another table. Galen tries not to get too excited.

"Do you need to be checked out of school, son? Are you feeling ill?"

Galen tosses a glance at Emma, who's picking a pepperoni

off her pizza and eyeing it as if it were dolphin dung. "I can't skip school to meet you again, boo. But I'll be thinking about you. *No one* but you."

A few more females get up and stalk their trays to the trash. The cheerleader in front of him rolls her eyes and starts a conversation with the chubby brunette beside her—the same chubby brunette she pushed into a locker to get to him two hours ago.

"Be still my heart," Rachel drawls. "But seriously, I can't read your signals. I don't know what you're asking me to do."

"Right now, nothing. But I might change my mind about skipping. I really miss you."

Rachel clears her throat. "All right, sweet pea. You just let your mama know, and she'll come get her wittle boy from school, okay?"

Galen hangs up. *Why is Emma laughing again?* Mark can't be *that* funny.

The girl beside him clues him in: "Mark Baker. All the girls love him. But not as much as they love you. Except maybe Emma, I guess."

"Speaking of all these girls, how did they get my phone number?"

She giggles. "It's written on the wall in the girls' bathroom. One hundred hall." She holds her cell phone up to his face. An image of his number scrawled onto a stall door lights up the screen. In Emma's handwriting.

Dividing waves as he tears through the water, his path leaves a frothy white line on the surface. Submerging when he sees a boat on the horizon, he pushes so hard he might not even appear on their fishing radar if they have one.

This is his second swim to Europe and back this week. Since tomorrow's Friday, he'll probably be doing it again. But no matter how far he swims, no matter how fast, it doesn't relieve him of his tension. And it doesn't change the fact that Emma has a date with someone else.

He senses other Syrena as he goes, but he doesn't recognize them, and besides, he's not in the mood to chat. In fact, solitude is more important to him right now than his next five meals. Trying to navigate the halls at school has been like wading through high tide wearing hiking boots filled with rocks—the human females have lost their minds. They locked around him in waves, grasping at him, shouting over each other, calling each other names that Rachel later clarified meant mating with more than one male—a lot. They only displayed unity when he tried to escape into the men's restroom—or when he attempted to head in Emma's general direction.

But he isn't just tired of humans—it would be unfortunate for any Syrena to press him into a conversation at this point. And any passerby would inevitably be curious as to what brings a Royal this far from the caverns. His response right now wouldn't win his brother the support he needs as a new king—and it just might push his father to cut out his tongue after all. And groveling at Emma's feet without a tongue would be inconvenient.

Gritting his teeth, he pushes even harder, ripping through the water faster than any man-made torpedo. Only when he reaches what the humans call the English Channel does he slow and surface. As he approaches a patch of land he recognizes, he can't even muster a half smile for the new personal record. *From New Jersey to Jersey Island in less than five hours.* The three thousand miles in distance he put between himself and Emma tonight is nothing compared with the enormous chasm separating them when they sit next to each other in calculus.

Emma's ability to overlook his existence is a gift—but not one that Poseidon handed down. Rachel insists this gift is uniquely a feminine trait, regardless of the species. Since their breakup, Emma seems to be the only female utilizing this particular gift. Even Rayna could learn a few lessons from Emma in the art of torturing a smitten male. *Smitten? More like fanatical.*

He shakes his head in disgust. *Why couldn't I just sift when I turned of age? Why couldn't I find a suitable mild-tempered female to mate with? Live a peaceful life, produce offspring, grow old, and watch my own fingerlings have fingerlings someday?* He searches through his mind for someone he might have missed in the past. For a face he overlooked before but could now look forward to every day. For a docile female who would be honored to mate with a Triton prince—instead of a temperamental siren who mocks his title at every opportunity. He scours his memory for a sweet-natured Syrena who would take care of him, who would do whatever he asked, who would never argue with him.

Not some human-raised snippet who stomps her foot when she doesn't get her way, listens to him only when it suits some secret purpose she has, or shoves a handful of chocolate mints down his throat if he lets his guard down. Not some white-haired angelfish whose eyes melt him into a puddle, whose blush is more beautiful than sunrise, and whose lips send heat ripping through him like a mine explosion.

He sighs as Emma's face eclipses hundreds of more mate-worthy Syrena. *That's just one more quality I'll have to add to the list: someone who won't mind being second best.* His jaw locks as he catches a glimpse of his shadow beneath him, cast by slithers of sterling moonlight. Since it's close to three a.m. here, he's comfortable walking around without the inconvenience of clothes, but sitting on the rocky shore in the raw is less than appealing. And it doesn't matter which Jersey shore he sits on, he can't escape the moon that connects them both—and reminds him of Emma's hair.

Hovering in the shallows, he stares up at it in resentment, knowing the moon reminds him of something else he can't escape—his conscience. If only he could shirk his responsibilities, his loyalty to his family, his loyalty to his people. If only he could change everything about himself, he could steal Emma away and never look back—that is, if she'll ever talk to him again.

Tired of floating, he changes into human form and stands in the knee-deep water, squinting into the horizon as if he could see her if he just looked long enough. He should be getting back. Though he hasn't sensed the stalker in front of Emma's house for an entire week, it still makes him nervous to leave her un-attended. But lingering around her balcony makes him just as uneasy—Mark has called her three times this week, according to Rachel's phone-tap records. And she's never mentioned Galen to him once.

As he shakes his head at himself for being a lovesick seal pup, he finally senses a Syrena he recognizes. Toraf. He waits for him a good ten minutes before his friend eventually surfaces.

Giving him a stout punch to the shoulder, Toraf says, "So, you decided to hold still for more than two seconds, minnow. I've been tracking you for the last five hours, but you were moving too fast. Where are we?"

"England." Galen grins. He needs a good diversion, and distraction happens to be one of Toraf's many talents.

Toraf shrugs. "Wherever that is."

"So," Galen says, crossing his arms. "What brings you across Triton territory this fine morning? You miss me?"

Toraf glances up at the moon and raises a brow. "I was going to ask you the same thing."

Galen shrugs. "It's a lot quieter without all the obnoxious background noise."

"Aw. You *did* miss me. That means a lot, minnow. I missed you, too." He glances around the shore. "Where's Emma? She doesn't like Eggland?"

"Eng-land. She's at home, probably sleeping peacefully. You didn't sense her did you?" For a half second, his pulse spikes. She's been getting in the water without him. Every time he gets close enough to sense, she gets out. Which is just fine with him.

"Oops. Was it my turn to keep an eye on Emma? I kind of thought you'd give me a break since you sent me to look for Paca and all."

"Did you find her?"

Toraf nods.

"And?"

Crossing his arms, Toraf smirks. "Are you sure you want to know?" When Galen clenches his fists, Toraf laughs. "All right, all right, minnow. I can see you're in a fighting mood, but I would rather save my energy for your sister."

"I swear by—"

"She has the Gift, Galen."

Instead of spiking, Galen's pulse sputters. "Paca has the Gift of Poseidon? Are you sure?"

Nodding, Toraf says, "I saw it myself. She can communicate with fish. They do what she says. She demonstrated it to me and Grom and her father. She made a dolphin do tricks for us."

"What kind of tricks?"

Toraf shrugs. "Anything she wants, I guess. After the first few, we were all satisfied. Amazed, actually."

Galen crosses his arms. "Where has she been all this time?"

"Triton territory, staying on the coast of the long land. Said she hid out of the water in case King Antonis sent trackers after her. I only found her after she submerged to hide from some humans who caught sight of her camp on the beach. She seemed happy to see me."

The Syrena know it as the long land. Humans know it as Florida. *Where we found Emma.* Galen is beginning to think Florida has some sort of power to create Poseidon's Gift. "What does Grom say?"

"Grom says he hopes you won't miss his mating ceremony. It would hurt his feelings."

"He's going to mate with Paca? You're sure?"

"I wouldn't have followed you across the world if I wasn't sure."

Galen ignores the twist of excitement in his gut. "She's not a Royal."

"And Emma is?"

"Good point." If Grom would be willing to mate with Paca, who's not a Royal, would he be willing to mate with Emma? *It doesn't matter, stupid. He's mating with Paca.*

"Anyway, the ceremony will be in two moon cycles. Grom wants to keep it a secret for now while he thinks of a way to present it to everyone else. The only thing he can think of is to have her demonstrate the Gift to an audience. Otherwise, he'll have blood on his hands."

"That's a good idea." Grom's already treading in icy waters by taking a Poseidon mate against Antonis's wishes. But because of who Grom is—firstborn, third-generation Triton Royal— he's basically rendering the law obsolete by mating with Paca, who is, by the law's standards, a Common. Which isn't fair, since King Antonis's refusal to produce more offspring forced him to this decision. But would the kingdoms see that? Would they see it as a self-sacrificing effort on Grom's part to keep the benefit of the Gifts? Or would they view it as a power-hungry move to rule both kingdoms—especially given Jagen's reputation for treasonous talk?

"He wants you and Rayna both to stay away until he

announces the ceremony. I told him you had plenty to keep you occupied until then."

"What do you mean?"

"Are you brainless as a reef, minnow? You can have Emma now. Why you're wasting your time here in Eggland—Galen? Galen, wait for me!"

25

I'M NOT sure if all Syrena have bulletproof endurance or if Galen is particularly blessed with it. Even now, as I lock the front dead bolt while Mark holds his car door open for me, Galen is blowing up my cell. I slide into the passenger seat of the pickup truck and try to organize my face into a convincing expression of relaxed, even though my insides are twisting faster than a whirlpool.

I thought Galen had given up trying to talk to me. I mean, what else is there to say? He played me like an Xbox. A broom and dustpan couldn't clean up all the pieces of my heart he shattered. I've been so stupid. But not anymore.

Keeping distance between us at school hasn't been easy, but I've managed. And when I sense him in the water in front of my house, I get out. By Wednesday, he stopped calling me. He even skipped school today. *So what's his deal now? Doesn't he see that I need to get away from him?*

And why can't I have an ignore button like my phone? As I hit it, his calls disappear from the screen and the ringing stops. But the tingles are still at my fingertips, as if he sent them through the phone to grab me. Shoving it in my purse—the pockets on skinny jeans must just be for show 'cause nothing else is fitting in there—I smile at Mark.

Ah, Mark. The blue-eyed, blond-haired, all-American quarterback. Who knew he had a crush on me all these years? Not Emma McIntosh, that's for dang sure. And not Chloe. Which is weird, because Chloe was a collector of this kind of information. Maybe it's not true. Maybe Mark's only interested in me because Galen was—who *wouldn't* want to date the girl who dated the hottest guy in school? But that's just fine with me. Mark is . . . well, Mark isn't as fantabulous as I always imagined he would be.

Still, he's good-looking, a star quarterback, and he's not trying to hook me up with his brother. *So why am I not excited?*

The question must be all over my face because Mark's got his eyebrow raised. Not in a judgmental arch, more like an arch of expectation. If he's waiting for an explanation, his puny human lungs can't hold their breath long enough for an answer.

Aside from not being his business, I can't exactly *explain* the details of my relationship with Galen—fake or otherwise. The truth is, I don't know where we can go from here. He ripped holes in my pride like buckshot. And did I mention he broke my heart?

He's not just a crush. Not just a physical attraction, someone who can make me forget my own name by *pretending* to kiss me. Not just a teacher or a snobby fish with Royal blood. Sure, he's all of those things. But he's more than that. He's who I want. Possibly forever.

But I'm not in danger of becoming "that girl." The one who throws away her college education in favor of marrying some guy right out of high school. The one who sacrifices everything she wants in order to make *his* dreams come true, to make *him* happy. The one who hangs on his every smile, his every word, bears his children, cooks his dinner, and snuggles up to him at night. Nope, definitely not in danger of becoming *her*.

Because Galen doesn't want me. If that kiss were real, I might have thrown scholarships to the wind and followed him to our own private island or his underwater kingdom. I might have even cooked him fish.

Sure, Galen would love for me to do all those things. *With his brother.*

So it's a good thing I'm being proactive about my own recovery by going on a date, even if it is a rebound—and even if I'm rebounding from a relationship that didn't actually exist. *My* feelings were real. That's all that matters, isn't it? There's no stipulation in the broken-heart rule book that states the relationship had to actually be authentic, right? Sure, I'm gray-shading the line that separates stable and crazy, but the point is, there *is* a line. And I haven't completely crossed over to lunatic.

Mark sitting next to me proves it. I'm moving on. Getting on with my life. Staying in school. Enrolling in college. Cooking chicken instead of fish. Dating other people. And with enough luck, I'll be kissing other people by the end of this date. Even if it doesn't mean anything.

"Is everything okay?" Mark asks as we turn onto the interstate.

"Sure. Why?" But we both know why he'd ask.

Mark's obviously too much of a gentleman to point out that I'm getting more space time than an astronaut. He says, "You just seem quiet tonight. I hope I didn't already do something to screw this up."

I laugh. "That's exactly what I was just thinking. That I didn't want to screw it up, I mean."

He nods, gives a knowing smile.

"What?" I say.

He shrugs.

"No. You gave me a look," I say, crossing my arms.

"No I didn't."

"I don't date liars." *Anymore.*

He laughs. "Fine. If you must know, I don't think there's anything you could possibly do to screw this up."

I can't help but smile. "Oh, you shouldn't have said that out loud." Good-looking, smart, funny. And now sweet. *So quit waiting for your purse to ring, stupid.*

"You might remember that you forced me to say it out loud. But don't worry. I'm not superstitious."

"I'm not either."

The drive to Atlantic City is just over an hour, and we pass it by playing Twenty Questions. Mark is the youngest of four brothers, wants to be either a physicist or an animator at Disney World—he promises to decide before he graduates college on his football scholarship—and his most embarrassing moment was when he walked in on his parents while they were doing the deed. Last week.

His questions for me are almost the same, word for word. Except the one he asks when we pull into the parking lot along the boardwalk strip. "Question number nineteen is, Who keeps texting you tonight?'"

Here we go again. Since Mark seems to saturate the air with easygoing, the whirlpool in my stomach had turned into no more than a swirl, as powerless as a flushed toilet, even when my purse beeped. But now that swirl is more like an island-swallowing vortex. Things are going too well tonight to ruin it with the truth, but since this could be the first of many dates with Mark, a lie would ruin it, too. "It's Galen."

Mark takes a sharp breath. "Okay. So I'm ditching my original question number twenty for a new question number twenty: Should I be worried about Galen?"

I laugh. "In what way?"

"Well, in any way, I guess. For instance, he's a big guy. Does he know how to fight? Does he know how to shoot a gun? And did you tell him where we were going tonight?"

"No. Why?"

"Because he's standing outside your window."

My gaze whips around to settle on Galen standing inches

from the truck, arms crossed. Mark is courteous enough to roll down the window for me, since I'm too stunned to move, talk, or breathe.

"Emma, can you please come talk to me for a minute?" Galen says, eyes hard.

"Hey, Galen. How's it going, man?" Mark adds a little edge to his normally friendly tone.

"Mark." Galen nods, jaw tight.

"Kind of surprised to see you, man. Are you here with anyone?" Mark is good at BS.

"In fact, I am. I'm here with Emma."

"Really? How's that?"

"She's my girlfriend. I thought I'd made that clear before, Mark."

Mark chuckles. "Well, I'm not sure where you're from, but in this country, when one party breaks up, they both do. Learned that one the hard way myself, so I feel your pain, man."

"Not yet," Galen mutters.

"I'm sorry? What did you say?" By the sound of it, Mark really didn't hear him. By the look on Galen's face, he wasn't really meant to. But I heard it. And I know what he meant.

"He didn't say anything," I tell Mark, finally able to move my mouth other than in the direction of hanging open.

"Yes, he did, Emma," Mark whispers to me, patting my leg. "Don't worry, I'll handle this." Leaving his hand there, he calls around me to Galen, "Now what did you just say? Or is it not worth repeating?"

It feels like hot lava is oozing over me. That, along with a sense of dread. When I turn back, I'm not surprised when my nose almost touches Galen's through the truck window. But he's not looking at me. Mark seems unaffected by the glower. Galen talks through clenched teeth. "I said not yet. You haven't even begun to feel pain. Yet. But if you don't take your hand off her leg—"

I open the truck door. Galen steps back to let me out.

"Emma, this is insane. You don't have to talk to him. I can hold my own in a fight if he wants to push it that far," Mark says for Galen to hear.

Football player that he is, I doubt Mark has ever been beaten with a steel pipe, which is exactly what Galen's Syrena fists will feel like on his face. I give him an apologetic smile. "It will only take a second. I'll be right back, okay?"

As I step away from the truck, Galen slams the door shut. "Actually, Mark, it will take more than a second. She's coming with me."

Mark swings his own door open and meets us by the tailgate. "Why don't we ask Emma who she's coming with? I mean, it's her choice, right?"

The look Galen gives me is clear: *Take care of this, or I will.* Or maybe it's more like, *It would be my pleasure to take care of this.* Either way, I don't want Mark taken care of.

Standing between them, the testosterone-to-air ratio is almost suffocating. If I pick Galen, the chances of Mark ever calling me again are as good as Galen eating a whole cheesecake by himself. If I choose Mark, the chances of Galen not wielding his built-in

brass knuckles are as good as Rayna giving someone a compli-
ment.

My desire to salvage this date with Mark is almost as strong
as my desire to salvage his face from certain disfigurement. But
salvaging the date as opposed to his face would be selfish in the
long run. I sigh in defeat. "I'm sorry, Mark."

Mark lets out a gust of air. "Ouch." Scratching the back of
his neck, he chuckles. "I guess I should be more superstitious,
huh?"

He's right. I screwed this up. I should have salvaged the
date, his pride. And I should have broken Galen's Royal nose
with my own Syrena fist. I turn to His Highness. "Galen, could
you give me a minute please? You'll have the next hour to talk to
me since you're taking me straight home."

Without a word, Galen nods and walks away.

I can't quite meet Mark's eyes when I say, "I'm so sorry. I
don't know what his deal is. He never acts like this." Except that
time he beat Toraf like a stepchild on the beach when he kissed
me. But only because Toraf betrayed Rayna. *Right?*

Mark smiles, but it doesn't reach his eyes. "Can't say I blame
him. I can already tell you're worth it. I just never had the guts
to ask you out. Chloe threatened my life. You know that chick
could hit like a man, right? She said you were too good for me.
I think she was right."

"Wh . . . what? Chloe knew you liked me?"

"Yeah. She never told you? Course not. She thought I was a
player."

I nod, still too stunned that my best friend also acted as my bodyguard without me knowing. "She did think you were a player. And she could definitely hit like a man."

"That's what my friend Jax says anyway." Then a little lower, "Geez, Galen's watching me like a hawk right now. He has serial-killer eyes, you know that?"

I giggle.

"What do you think he'd do if I kissed you good-bye on the cheek?" he whispers conspiratorially.

"Don't worry, I'll protect you." He has no idea how serious I am. As he leans in, I brace myself. At the slightest spark of electricity, I'm prepared to turn around with my fists up. But the lightning doesn't strike. Galen is behaving for now.

As Mark pulls away from his barely there peck, he sighs. "Do me a favor," he whispers.

"Mmm?"

"Keep my number. Give me a call if he screws up again."

I smile. "I will, I promise. I had a good time tonight." *Did the date* and *Mark's face get salvaged? Do I have a chance to redeem myself with him?*

He chuckles. "Yeah, glad we got to drive here from Middle Point together. Next time, we'll make it a real adventure and take the bus. See you at school, Emma."

"Bye."

I turn on my high heel, which is no easy feat in a gravel parking lot. Not losing eye contact with Galen, I stare him down until I get to the door he's opened for me. He seems unconcerned. In fact, he seems downright emotionless. "This better be good," I tell him as I plop down.

"You should have returned my calls. Or my texts," he says, his voice tight.

As he backs out of the parking space, I yank my cell out of my purse, perusing the texts. "Well, doesn't look like anyone died, so why the hell did you ruin my date?" It's the first time I've ever cursed at royalty and it's liberating. "Or is this a kidnapping? Is Grom in the trunk? Are you taking us on our honeymoon?"

You're supposed to be hurting him, *not yourself, moron.* My lip trembles like the traitor it is. Even though I'm looking away, I can tell Galen's impassive expression has softened because of the way he says, "Emma."

"Leave me alone, Galen." He pulls my chin to face him. I knock his hand away. "You can't go forty miles an hour on the interstate, Galen. You need to speed up."

He sighs and presses the gas. By the time we reach a less-embarrassing speed, I've abandoned my hurt for rage-o-plenty, struck by the realization that I've turned into "that girl." Not the one who exchanges her doctorate for some kids and a three-bedroom two-bath, but the *other* kind. That girl who exchanges her dignity and chances for happiness for some possessive loser who beats her when she makes eye contact with some random guy working the hot dog stand.

Not that Galen beats me, but after his little show, what will people think? He acted like a lunatic tonight, stalking me to Atlantic City, blowing up my phone, and threatening my date with physical violence. He made serial-killer eyes, for crying out loud. That might be acceptable in the watery grave, but by dry-land standards, it's the ingredients for a restraining order. *And why are we getting off the interstate?*

"Where are you taking me? I told you I want to go home."

"We need to talk," he says quietly, taking a dark road just off the exit. "I'll take you home after I feel you understand."

"I don't want to talk. You might have realized that when I didn't answer your calls."

He pulls over on the shoulder of Where-Freaking-Are-We Street. Shutting off the engine, he turns to me, putting his arm around the back of my seat. "I don't want to break up."

One Mississippi . . . two Mississippi . . . "You followed me like a crazy person to tell me that? You ruined my date for *that*? Mark is a nice guy. I deserve a nice guy, don't I, Galen?"

"Absolutely. But I happen to be a nice guy, too."

Three Mississippi . . . four Mississippi . . . "Don't you mean Grom? And you're not a nice guy. You threatened Mark with physical pain."

"You threw Rayna through a window. Call it even?"

"When are you going to get over that? Besides, she provoked me!"

"Mark provoked me, too. He put his hand on your leg. We won't even talk about the kiss on your cheek. Don't think I didn't hear you give him permission either."

"Oh, now that's rich," I snort, getting out of the car. Slamming the door, I scream at him. "Now you're acting jealous on behalf of your brother," I say, spinning in place. "Can Grom do anything without the almighty Galen helping him?" Having a few half fish in my family tree keeps my vision from blurring through the pudgy tears—I can perfectly see the solid yellow line on the road as I walk it. When I hear him following, I rip off my heels and start sprinting. Two months ago, this kind of abuse to my bare feet would leave them bleeding and with who-knows-what embedded in them. But with the convenience of my new thick skin, running barefoot is like running in Nike's latest kicks.

Galen is apparently a flying fish though—his hand wraps around my arm, braking my own sad attempt at flight. He whirls me around. Pulling me to him, he lifts my chin with the pad of his thumb. When I jerk away, he grasps it tight, forcing me to look at him. The old Emma would be bruised within the next ten minutes. The new one is just pissed off.

"Let go!" I screech, pushing against his chest. Somehow this just gets me closer to him.

"Emma," he growls as I stomp his foot. "What would you have done?"

Okay, that's unexpected. I stop flailing. "What?"

"Tell me what you would have done if you were me. Tell me what you would do if you had to choose between the survival of mankind—and I'm talking babies and grandmothers and all your human relatives," he says, breathless. I realize I've never seen that before. Galen low on air. "Tell me how easy it would be to abandon them, if it meant you could have the only thing you've ever wanted in your whole life? Tell me, Emma. Which would you pick?"

"I . . . I don't . . . under—"

He shakes me, his grip inflexible. "Yes, you do, Emma. You

know exactly what I'm saying. Answer me. Think of what you want the most. The one thing you might not be able to live without."

Well, that's a no-brainer. It's Galen, hands-down. "Okay."

"Now imagine how you'd feel if you were asked to trade that one thing you love so that the human race could go on. People you don't even know. People who aren't even born yet. Would you do it? *Could* you? Even if almost no one ever knew the huge sacrifice you made for them and would never appreciate what you gave up?"

Gently, I shake free from his grasp. He lets me step away from him. The intensity in his eyes sends chills down the length of me. "It would be selfish not to trade," I say quietly. "It's not even a choice, really."

"Exactly. I didn't have a choice."

"Are you saying . . . What are you saying?" Is he . . . *could* he be talking about me?

He runs a hand through his hair. I've never seen him this emotional before. He's always so controlled, so sure of himself. "I'm saying you're what I want, Emma. I'm saying I'm in love with you."

He steps forward and lifts his hand to my cheek, blazing a line of fire with his fingertips as they trace down to my mouth. "How do you think it would make me feel to see you with Grom?" he whispers. "Like someone ripped my heart out and put it through Rachel's meat grinder, that's how. Probably worse. It would probably kill me. Emma, please don't cry."

I throw my hands in the air. "Don't cry? Are you serious?

Why did you come here, Galen? Did you think it would make me feel better to know that you do love me, but that it still won't work out? That I still have to mate with Grom for the greater good? Don't you tell me not to cry, Galen! I . . . c . . . c . . . can't h . . . h . . . help—" The waterworks soak me. Galen looks at me, hands by his side, helpless as a trapped crab. I'm bordering on hyperventilation, and pretty soon I'll start hiccupping. This is too much.

His expression is so severe, it looks like he's in physical pain. "Emma," he breathes. "Emma, does this mean you feel the same way? Do you care for me at all?"

I laugh, but it sounds sharper than I intended, because of a hiccup. "What does it matter how I feel, Galen? I think we pretty much covered why. No need to rehash things, right?"

"It matters, Emma." He grabs my hand and pulls me to him again. "Tell me right now. Do you care for me?"

"If you can't tell that I'm stupid in love with you, Galen, then you aren't a very good ambassador for the hum—"

His mouth covers mine, cutting me off. This kiss isn't gentle like the first one. It's definitely not sweet. It's rough, demanding, searching. And disorienting. There's not a part of me that isn't melting against Galen, not a part that isn't combusting with his fevered touch.

I accidentally moan into his lips. He takes it for his cue to lift me off my feet, to pull me up to his height for more leverage. I take his groan for my cue to kiss him harder.

He ignores his cell phone ringing in his pocket. I ignore the rest of the universe. Even when headlights approach, I'm willing to overlook their intrusion and keep kissing. But, prince that he is, Galen is a little more refined than me at this moment. He gently pries his lips from mine and sets me down. His smile is both intoxicated and intoxicating. "We still need to talk."

"Right," I say, but I'm shaking my head.

He laughs. "I didn't come all the way to Atlantic City to make you cry."

"I'm not crying." I lean into him again. He doesn't refuse my lips, but he doesn't do them justice either, planting a measly little kiss on them before stepping back.

"Emma, I came out here to tell you that you don't have to mate with Grom."

I raise a brow. "Uh, I was never going to mate with Grom."

"What I mean is, Grom is mating with someone else who has the gift of Poseidon. Which means that—"

"I don't have to mate with Grom," I finish for him.

"That's what I just said."

"I mean, I don't have to feel like I've let the entire species of Syrena go extinct because I *won't* mate with Grom."

He grins. "Exactly."

"But that doesn't change what I am—a Half-Breed. You still can't be with me, can you?"

He rubs his thumb over my bottom lip, thoughtful. "The law forbids it right now. But I think if we give it time, we could get it overturned somehow. And I'm not going anywhere until I do."

He turns us toward the SUV, stopping to retrieve my heels from the side of the road. He helps me in the passenger seat of the Escalade, then hands me my shoes.

"Thank you," I tell him as he walks around to the driver's side.

"It's a little late to blush," he says, strapping in.

"I don't think I'll ever stop blushing."

"I really hope not," he says, shutting his door. Taking my face into both hands, he pulls me to him again. His lips brush mine, but I want more. Sensing my intention, he puts his hand over mine and the seat belt I'm trying to unstrap. "Emma," he says against my lips. "I've missed you so much. But we can't. Not yet."

I'm not trying to do *that*, I just want to get in a better position to accept his lips. Telling him so would just embarrass us both. But he said yet. What does that mean? That he wants to wait until he can get the law overturned? Or will he give it time, and if it doesn't work out, break Syrena law to be with me?

For some reason, I don't want the answer bad enough to ask. Images of "that girl" flare up in my head. I don't want Galen to break his laws—it's a big part of why I love him so much. His loyalty to his people, his commitment to them. It's the kind of devotion almost nonexistent among humans. But I don't want to be "that girl" either. Syrena or not, I want to go to college. I want to experience the world above *and* below sea level.

But it's not like any decisions need to be made right now, do they? I mean, life-changing decisions take time to make. Time and meditation. And physical space between my lips and his.

I pull back. "Right. Sorry."

He seizes a few tendrils of my hair and runs them along his face, grinning. "Not as sorry as I am. You'll have to help me keep my hands off you."

I laugh, even as a charge runs through my veins. "Yeah. No."

He laughs too and turns to start the car, then stops. Letting go of the keys, he says, "So. About breaking up."

"Let me think about it some more," I tell him on the brink of giggling at his expression.

"I'll see what I can do to help you make up your mind."

We stay parked for another fifteen minutes. But at least we're not broken up anymore.

Digging my feet into the sand, I hold my hand down to Rayna, who just got comfortable on a towel. "Come on," I tell her. "Let's go inside and I'll give you a pedicure."

She peers up at me, the moonlight catching the violet in her eyes. "That's not a good idea," she says, even though she takes my hand. "They said they'll be right back."

I sigh. "Rayna, you know the routine. They scurry to my house, don't find anyone, then spend an hour swimming the shore to see if they sense him again. We both know Galen won't let me get in the water for the rest of the night. And anyway, since when did you start taking orders?"

She nods. "But I want you to do it the French way, with the white stuff on the tips." I smile at the back of her head as she passes me on the beach and jogs to the house. She's no Chloe, but she's not Mom either. She's bonafide female companionship.

Rachel greets me at the sliding glass door. "Hiya, cutie. Your mom called. She's home and would like to know why you're not."

I lift my chin, ready to fire off a few different reasons, beginning with the fact that I'm eighteen years old and ending with the fact that even if I weren't of legal age, I'm still within my curfew. Then I realize Mom's home early—which means she came home about the same time Toraf and Galen sensed the Syrena stalker. Whether it's just a coincidence or a mother's intuition working in overdrive is a toss-up. I didn't believe in either until just now—but this is the third time it's happened this week. Trying not to snatch her cell when Rachel hands it to me, I press the EMMA'S MOM icon on the touch screen.

"Hello?" she says, her voice tight.

"Mom, it's me. You called?" Sounding casual is difficult when it feels like your heart's river-dancing in your rib cage.

"Yes, I just wondered where you were. You didn't answer your cell. Is everything okay?" She sighs, but I can't tell if it's in relief or parental aggravation.

"Everything's fine. My battery is dead, but Galen bought me a charger to keep over here, so it's charging."

"How sweet of him," she says, knowing good and well she instructed him to do so. "Well, just wanted to check in. Should I wait up for you? I don't appreciate you missing curfew the last few nights. Technically, staying over there until four in the morning is a coed sleepover, which I don't allow, or had you forgotten? Your trip to Florida with Galen's family was a special circumstance."

"I stayed the night at Chloe's all the time with JJ there." JJ is Chloe's eight-year-old brother. Not a great comeback, but it will have to do.

"You know what I mean, Emma," she snaps.

"Why are you so grouchy? And why are you home early again?"

"I don't know. I'm tired, I guess. Listen, I noticed you haven't brought your swimsuit home yet. I hope you're not still getting in the water. It's too cold for swimming, Emma."

I do my own laundry. Digging around in my drawers is the only way she could have "noticed" anything missing. Does she also look for condoms or other incriminating evidence moms usually scavenge for? Does she come home *to* scavenge? The thought tickles my temper. Making a mental note to buy a new bathing suit strictly for Galen's house, I say, "You're telling *me* this? You know how cold-natured I am." My laugh is loud enough to be suspicious, but Mom doesn't seem to notice. Rachel smirks though.

"Don't try to tell me you and Galen haven't figured out how to stay warm in the water."

"Mom!"

"Just promise you won't get in the water," she says, her voice tight again. "I don't need you getting sick."

"Fine. I promise."

"And be home before dawn this time. I dare you to bring home anything less than an A on your report card after this. I double dog dare you."

I mouth the words into the phone as she says them; you'd think she'd at least change the wording after all these years. It's her go-to threat for just about everything. But somehow, it doesn't work this time. There's no bluster behind it. She's getting soft lately, and I think it has to do with the night I accused her of adopting me. "Okay. Before dawn."

"Good night, sweetie. I love you."

"Loveyoutoo, good night."

I hang up the phone and hand it back to Rachel, who exchanges it for a mug of hot chocolate with three gargantuan marshmallows floating on top. "Thanks," I tell her, shuffling to the kitchen behind her.

Rayna is sitting at the table, pulling enough polish, clippers, and buffers out of her kit to open her own nail salon. "I know I said I wanted the French kind, but I really like this color," she says, holding up a cantaloupe shade.

Rachel shakes her head. "That'll look tourist tacky against your olive skin, honey bunches."

Hoping to get a different opinion, Rayna jiggles the bottle at me. I shake my head. Pouting, she slams it on the table, then dumps the entire contents of the kit on top of it. "Well, is there *any* color that would look good?"

I take the seat next to her. "What's Toraf's favorite color?"

She shrugs. "Whatever I tell him it is."

I raise a brow at her. "Don't know, huh?"

She crosses her arms. "Who cares anyway? We're not painting *his* toenails."

"I think what's she's trying to say, honey bunches, is that maybe you should paint your nails his favorite color, to show him you're thinking about him," Rachel says, seasoning her words with tact.

Rayna sets her chin. "Emma doesn't paint her nails Galen's favorite color."

Startled that Galen has a favorite color and I don't know it, I say, "Uh, well, he doesn't like nail polish." That is to say, he's never mentioned it before.

When a brilliant smile lights up her whole face, I know I've been busted. "You don't know his favorite color!" she says, actually pointing at me.

"Yes, I do," I say, searching Rachel's face for the answer. She shrugs.

Rayna's smirk is the epitome of *I know something you don't know.* Smacking it off her face is my first reflex, but I hold back, as I always do, because of the kiss I shared with Toraf and the way it hurt her. Sometimes I catch her looking at me with that same expression she had on the beach, and I feel like fungus, even though she deserved it at the time.

Refusing to fold, I eye the buffet of nail polish scattered before me. Letting my fingers roam over the bottles, I shop the paints, hoping one of them stands out to me. To save my life, I can't think of any one color he wears more often. He doesn't have a favorite sport, so team colors are a no-go. Rachel picked his cars for him, so that's no help either. Biting my lip, I decide on an ocean blue.

"Emma! Now I'm just ashamed of myself," he says from the doorway. "How could you not know my favorite color?"

Startled, I drop the bottle back on the table. Since he's back so soon, I have to assume he didn't find what or who he wanted—and that he didn't hunt them for very long. Toraf materializes behind him, but Galen's shoulders are too broad to allow them both to stand in the doorway. Clearing my throat, I say, "I was just moving that bottle to get to the color I wanted."

Rayna is all but doing a victory dance with her eyes. "Which is?" she asks, full of vicious glee. Toraf pushes past Galen and plops down next to his tiny mate. She leans into him, eager for his kiss. "I missed you," she whispers.

"Not as much as I missed you," he tells her.

Galen and I exchange eye rolls as he walks around to prop himself on the table beside me, his wet shorts making a butt-shaped puddle on the expensive wood. "Go ahead, angelfish," he says, nodding toward the pile of polish.

If he's trying to give me a clue, he sucks at it. "Go" could mean green, I guess. "Ahead" could mean . . . I have no idea what that could mean. And angelfish come in all sorts of colors. Deciding he didn't encode any messages for me, I sigh and push away from the table to stand. "I don't know. We've never talked about it before."

Rayna slaps her knee in triumph. "Ha!"

Before I can pass by him, Galen grabs my wrist and pulls me to him, corralling me between his legs. Crushing his mouth to mine, he moves his hand to the small of my back and presses me into him. Since he's still shirtless and I'm in my bikini, there's a lot of bare flesh touching, which is a little more intimate than I'm used to with an audience. Still, the fire sears through me, scorching a path to the furthest, deepest parts of me. It takes every bit of grit I have not to wrap my arms around his neck.

Gently, I push my hands against his chest to end the kiss, which is something I never thought I'd do. Giving him a look that I hope conveys "inappropriate," I step back. I've spent enough time in their company to know without looking that Rayna's eyes are bugging out of their sockets and Toraf is grinning like a nutcracker doll. With any luck, Rachel didn't even see the kiss. Stealing a peek at her, she meets my gaze with open-mouthed shock.

Okay, it looked as bad as I thought it did. Like a child, I close my eyes as if they can't see me either. The fire from the kiss broadcasts itself all over me in the form of a full-body blush.

Galen laughs. "There it is," he says, running his thumb over my bottom lip. "*That* is my favorite color. Wow."

I'm going to kill him. "Galen. Please. Come. With. Me," I choke out. Gliding past him, my bare feet slap against the tile until I'm stomping on carpet in the hallway, then up the stairs.

I can tell by the prickles on my skin that he's following like a good dead fish. As I reach the ladder to the uppermost level, I nod to him to keep following before I hoist myself up. Pacing the room until he gets through the trap door, I count more Mississippis than I've ever counted in my whole life.

He closes the door and locks it shut but makes no move to come closer. Still, for a person who's about to die, he seems more amused than he should. I point my finger at him, but can't decide what to accuse him of first, so I put it back down.

After several minutes of this, he breaks the silence. "Emma, calm down."

"Don't tell me what to do, Highness." I dare him with my eyes to call me "boo."

Instead of the apology I'm looking for, his eyes tell me he's considering kissing me again, right now.

Which is meant to distract me. Tearing my gaze from his mouth, I stride to the window seat and move the mountains of pillows on it. Making myself comfortable, I lean my head against the window. He knows as well as I do that if we had a special spot, this would be it. For me to sit here without him is the worst kind of snub. In the reflection, I see him run his hand through his hair and cross his arms. After a few more minutes, he shifts his weight to the other leg.

He knows what I want. He knows what will earn him entrance to the window seat and my good graces. I don't know if it's Royal blood or manly pride that keeps him from apologizing, but his extended delay just makes me madder. Now I won't accept an apology. No, now he must grovel.

I toss a satisfied smirk into the reflection only to find he's not there anymore. His hand closes around my arm and he jerks me up against him. His eyes are stormy, intense. "You think I'm going to apologize for kissing you?" he murmurs.

"I. Yes. Uh-huh." *Don't look at his mouth! Say something intelligent.* "We don't have any clothes on." Fan-flipping-tastic. I meant to say he shouldn't kiss me in front of everyone, especially half naked.

"Mmm," he says, pulling me closer. Brushing his lips against my ear, he says, "I did happen to notice that. Which is why I shouldn't have followed you up here."

His cell phone vibrates on the nightstand, almost startling

my hair off my head. He grins and walks over to pick it up, leaving me there to stare after him. "It's Dr. Milligan," he says. "Hello? Hold on, Dr. Milligan, let me put you on speaker. Emma's here." Galen presses the button on the screen. "Okay, Dr. Milligan," he says. "Go ahead."

"Well, my boy, I just wanted to let you know that I received the results back for the DNA tests. Emma is definitely half human."

Galen winks at me. "You don't say?"

I cover my mouth to stifle a giggle. Rudeness should never be contagious.

"Yes, I'm afraid so. That said, I'm not sure if she even has the capability of forming a fin."

Galen laughs. "We sort of already went along with that assumption, Dr. Milligan. Then the Archives confirmed it. There's a painting of people who look just like Emma in Tartessos."

Dr. Milligan sighs. "You could have called me."

"I'm sorry, Dr. Milligan. I've been . . . busy."

"Did Emma figure out her lineage, then?"

Galen shakes his head, though the reaction is lost on Dr. Milligan in Florida. "As far as we can tell, Emma's father was a Half-Breed. He's got the coloring, he wore contacts, he loved seafood and the ocean. He obviously knew about Emma's physical issues." He tells Dr. Milligan about his theory that some of the half-breeds survived the destruction of Tartessos.

Dr. Milligan is quiet for a few seconds. "What else?"

Galen gives me a quizzical look. I return a shrug. "What do you mean?" he says.

"I mean, my boy, what other evidence do you have to go on?

The man you just described could be me. I used to have blond hair before the gray took over. I wear contacts. I happen to love seafood and the beach, if where I live is any indication. I also know about Emma's physical issues. Emma could be my daughter then. Is that what you're saying? If that's all you're basing it on, Emma could be almost any man's daughter in the Panhandle here. Not very scientific."

Galen frowns.

"You there, Galen?" Dr. Milligan says. I sit beside Galen on the bed, not liking the turn of the conversation.

"I'm still here."

"Good. There's something else to consider. If Emma's father was a descendant of the Half-Breeds, like you say, then he wouldn't really be a Half-Breed anymore, would he? He'd be more like a quarter-breed, or who-knows-how-many-fractions-of-a-breed? Which would dilute Emma's blood even more. Really, how likely is it that Emma's father was an actual Half-Breed? There'd have to be some naughty Syrena out there to produce a full-blooded Half-Breed, don't you think? And if Emma is just a descendant from these long-ago half-humans, well, then she'd mostly be human. But that's not what my test results show, my boy. She's exactly half."

"What are you saying Dr. Milligan?" Galen says, flustered.

"I'm saying, Galen, that I don't think you've found the answer. I think you need to keep looking. I do wish you would have called me. I could have helped you reason it out and saved you some time. But there is one more thing I wanted to mention before we disconnect."

"What's that?" Galen says, almost in a daze.

"Didn't you tell me once that Syrena young develop into full maturity at nine years old?"

"Yes. Nine or ten. Some even earlier than that."

"And that includes the ability to sense?"

"Yes. And their bones are matured already. They don't grow anymore."

"But you see, my boy, since Emma is half human, she matured at a slower pace. Precisely half the pace, I'd say. Which, if I'm correct, means she wouldn't hit maturity until age eighteen."

My mouth drops open. Hitting my head had nothing to do with my Syrena abilities. I had just finished maturing. Right before Chloe died.

"I see," Galen says, wrapping his arm around me and pulling me to him. "Well, thank you, Dr. Milligan. I'm sorry we didn't call you before. You have no idea how sorry."

"Yes, well, I'm just trying to help." But he sounds upset. As if he was left out of the loop. Technically, he was.

But I'm betting my bikini bottoms he never will be again.

26

CAREFUL NOT to wake her, Galen brushes Emma's hair from her face, her cheeks pink from the glow of sunrise. Her sundress is ruined, the Atlantic leaving stains on it resembling a mountain range. She managed to tear the hem of it while hunting for her other shoe in the moonlight. Then she spread her dress out like a fan for him to lay on instead of the sand. And that's where he stayed all night. *This is why I never sifted. No one else could fit as perfectly in my arms as she does.* Leaning down, he grazes her lips with his. She sighs, as if she felt it.

Gulls squawk in the distance, eager for breakfast. Morning tide sloshes against the shore. The wind laces through the dune grass, like it's whispering a secret he's not meant to hear. And Emma sleeps. *This is the definition of peace.*

The definition is interrupted by Toraf's ringtone. *Why did Rachel get Toraf a phone? Does she hate me?* Fumbling behind him in the sand, Galen puts a hand on it right before it stops ringing. He waits five seconds and . . . Yep, he's calling again.

"Hello?" he whispers.

"Galen, it's Toraf."

Galen snorts. "You think?"

"Rayna's ready to leave. Where are you?"

Galen sighs. "We're on the beach. Emma's still sleeping. We'll walk back in a few minutes." Emma braved her mom's wrath by skipping curfew again last night to be with him. Grom's mating ceremony is tomorrow, and Galen and Rayna's attendance is required. He'll have to leave her in Toraf's care until he gets back.

"Sorry, Highness. I told you, Rayna's ready to go. You have about two minutes of privacy. She's heading your way." The phone disconnects.

Galen leans down and sweeps his lips over her sweet neck. "Emma," he whispers.

She sighs. "I heard him," she groans drowsily. "You should tell Toraf that he doesn't have to yell into the phone. And if he keeps doing it, I'm going to accidentally break it."

Galen grins. "He'll get the hang of it soon. He's not a complete idiot."

At this, Emma opens one eye.

He shrugs. "Well, three quarters maybe. But not a complete one."

"Are you sure you don't want me to come with you?" she says, sitting up and stretching.

"You know I do. But I think this mating ceremony will be

interesting enough without introducing my Half-Breed girl-friend, don't you think?"

Emma laughs and pulls her hair to one side, draping it over her shoulder. "This is our first time away from each other. You know, as a couple. We've only been really dating for two weeks now. What will I do without you?"

He pulls her to him, leaning her back against his chest. "Well, I'm hoping that this time when I come back, it won't be to the sight of you kissing Toraf."

The snickers beside them let them know their two minutes of privacy are up. "Yeah. Or someone's gonna die," Rayna says cordially.

Galen helps Emma up and swats the leftover sand out of her sundress. He takes her hands into his. "Could I please just ask one thing without you getting all mad about it?"

She scowls. "Let me guess. You don't want me to get in the water while you're gone."

"But I'm not *ordering* you to stay out of it. I'm asking, no begging, very politely, and with all my heart for you not to get it in. It's your choice. But it would make me the happiest man-fish on the coast if you wouldn't." They sense the stalker almost daily now. That and the fact that Dr. Milligan blew his theory about Emma's dad being a Half-Breed out of the water makes Galen more nervous than he can say. It means they still don't have any answers about who could know about Emma. Or why they keep hanging around.

Emma rewards him with a breathtaking smile. "I won't. Because you asked."

Toraf was right. I just had to ask. He shakes his head. "Now I can sleep tonight."

"That makes one of us. Don't stay gone too long. Or Mark will sit by me at lunch."

He grimaces. "I'll hurry." He leans down to kiss her. Behind them, he hears Rayna's initial splash.

"She's leaving without you," Emma whispers on his lips.

"She could have left hours ago and I'd still catch her. Good-bye, angelfish. Be good." He places a forceful kiss on her forehead, then gets a running start and dives in.

And he misses her already.

Galen finds Grom exactly where he shouldn't be—the minefield. Hours before his mating ceremony, he still sulks for his lost love. But who is Galen to judge? His brother is mating with someone he doesn't love—which enables Galen to be with someone he does.

Grom greets him with a smile full of nausea. "I'm not ready for this, little brother," he confesses.

"Sure you are," Galen laughs, slapping his brother's back.

Grom shakes his head. "It feels like . . . like I'm betraying her. Nalia."

Galen stiffens. *Oh.* He doesn't feel qualified to talk Grom out of this kind of mood. "I'm sure she would understand," he offers.

Grom studies him thoughtfully. "I'd like to think she would. But you didn't know Nalia. She had an amazing temper."

He chuckles. "I keep looking over my shoulder, expecting to see her ready to bludgeon me with something for mating with someone else."

Galen frowns, unsure of what to say.

Grom chuckles. "I'm joking, of course." Then he shrugs. "Well, half joking, anyway. I swear I've been sensing her lately, Galen. It feels so real. It takes all I've got not to follow the pulse. Do you think I'm losing my mind?"

Galen shakes his head out of obligation. Secretly though, he thinks he might be. "I'm sure you're just feeling guilty. Er . . . not that you have a reason to feel guilty. Uh, it's just natural that you feel that way before your mating ceremony. Nerves and all." Galen runs a hand through his hair. "I'm sorry. I'm not very good at this sort of thing."

"What sort of thing? Being mature?" Grom smirks.

"Funny."

"Maybe you should spend some more time on land, then come back and talk to me. Being on land ages you, you know. Might do you some good."

Galen snorts. *Now you tell me.* "I heard."

Out of nowhere, Grom grabs Galen's face and wrestles him into a hold. Galen hates it when he does this. "Let me see that cute little face of yours, minnow. Yep, just like I thought. Your eyes are turning blue. How much time have you been spending on land? Please tell me you're not head over fin for a human!" Then he laughs and releases him just as suddenly.

Galen stares at him. "What do you mean?"

"I was just teasing, minnow. Giving you a hard time."

"I know but . . . why did you say my eyes are turning blue? What does that have to do with the humans?"

Grom waves a dismissive hand at him. "Forget it. I think you might be more uptight than me right now. I said I was just kidding."

"Grom, if it's something about the humans, I need to know. I'm ambassador. You're keeping me from doing my job." Galen's voice is more calm than he feels. He remembers the painting on the wall in Tartessos. The Syrena whose eyes looked blue instead of violet.

"Triton's trident, Galen. It's got nothing to do with your responsibility as ambassador. It's just a rumor. In fact, I'm surprised you haven't heard of it before."

Galen crosses his arms. "Well, I haven't."

Grom rolls his eyes. "You're right. You're not very good at this sort of thing. The legend is that sometimes when Syrena spend a lot of time on land, their eyes fade to blue. It's just a myth, minnow. Calm down. Your eyes aren't turning blue."

Maybe I do spend too much time on land. I know more about human history than Syrena history.

"What are you two up to?" a feminine voice calls from behind them. They turn to see Paca.

Galen cringes on the inside. Paca shouldn't be here. She might be Grom's mate in a few hours, but this place is sacred. He sees his brother stiffen by his side. Then he feels Rayna's pulse approaching. Jagen's pulse is close behind her. Something feels off.

"Hello, Paca," Galen says politely. "We were just about to come see you, weren't we, Grom?" Paca is not ugly, but she's not pretty either. *Plain* would be a good word to describe her. But not just plain. There's something about the look in her eyes that makes her less innocent, less deserving than plain. Plain could be pitied. But Paca doesn't incite pity from Galen.

"I hope you were going to come pry your sister off my back," Paca clips as Rayna swims up. "She's quite rude."

Galen throws Rayna a look, to which she lifts her chin. "Paca and her pudgy father over there are full of whale dung," Rayna informs her brothers.

"Rayna," Grom barks. "Mind your manners."

Rayna lifts her chin even higher. *Here we go.* "Paca is a fraud, Grom," she says. "You can't mate with her. Sorry to ruin your ceremony. Let's go, Galen."

Paca gasps as Jagen swims up to the party, almost stuttering in his fury. "You little . . . little stonefish! How dare you insult my daughter?"

Galen grabs Rayna's arm. "What did you do?" he hisses.

She jerks her arm away and gives him a superior look. "If Paca has the Gift of Poseidon, I have the Gift of Triton. Don't ask me what it is though, because I don't have a clue."

"Rayna, enough!" Grom says, grabbing her other arm. "Apologize. Right now."

"Apologize for what? Telling the truth? Sorry, not feeling it." She shrugs, but doesn't struggle to free herself from Grom's grasp.

"How can you say she's a fraud? She just showed you her

Gift!" Jagen says, slicing a hand through the water in frustration.

Rayna snorts. "She didn't show Galen the Gift. Galen, have you seen her demonstrate the Gift? Let her show you the Gift." She turns to Paca. "Did you hear what I said, Princess Cheater-Cheater-Whale-Dung-Eater? Show my brother your pathetic Gift."

Paca's eyes are full of murder. She looks at Grom. "*Do* something about your sister. You're going to let her insult me right in front of you? Is this how I can expect to be treated when I'm mated to you?"

Rayna laughs. "You bet your sweet—"

"Rayna!" Galen says. "Enough!"

She rolls her eyes but doesn't say anything else. Galen turns to Paca. Trying to sound apologetic, he says, "Please excuse my sister's lack of . . ."

"Sanity?" Paca offers icily.

Galen smiles. Sort of. "Paca, of course, I would love to see you demonstrate the Gift of Poseidon. Would you be so kind as to show me? We've heard such amazing things about it already from Toraf."

This seems to placate Paca and Jagen. A little. Grom even loosens his grip on Rayna.

Paca bows low, a sign of deep respect for Galen. It takes all he has not to roll his eyes. "Of course, young prince. Please follow me." She leads them a considerable distance from the minefield, which surprises Galen.

They pass all sorts of fish she could have demonstrated the

Gift on. After each one they pass, Rayna's expression gets smugger and smugger, if that's even possible.

"What's gotten into you?" Galen whispers for her ears only. She winks at him, of all things. "You'll see," she mouths back.

They swim far enough to reach the shelf that leads to shallow water. This all seems like a lot of trouble for just a tiny demonstration, but Galen goes along with it because it doesn't seem fair that Grom should frown on the day of his mating ceremony.

"Paca, maybe we could stop here for the demonstration. We'll need to get back soon; you don't want to keep everyone waiting for the ceremony," Galen says.

"We're almost there," she calls over her shoulder. Galen looks at Rayna, but she's not saying anything. She's just smiling like she really has misplaced her sanity.

When they pass the shelf into shallow water, she stops. Finally. "Just a moment," she says. "I'm going to call them."

She shoots up to the surface.

Galen looks at Jagen. "Call who?"

Jagen smiles. "The dolphins, young prince."

Rayna still won't make eye contact with Galen, so he's forced to wait—impatiently—for Paca to return with her pod. After a few minutes, she comes back, three dolphins flanking her.

"I can make them jump out of the water, swim in circles, or swim at each other," she says to Galen. "Take your pick."

What? He throws an incredulous glare at Rayna, who returns a rare, humongous smile full of teeth.

"Grom likes to see them swim in circles, my dear," Jagen says. "Why don't you make them do that? Our young prince obviously can't make up his mind."

Paca turns to her dolphin friends and says, "Circles!" Then she draws a huge circle with her hands, over and over. The dolphins comply.

Galen gasps. *Oh, no. Hand signals.* She's using hand signals like the trainers at the Gulfarium. Rayna must have recognized it.

Jagen apparently mistakes Galen's gasp for awe. "It's quite astonishing, isn't it, my prince?" he says with a knowing smile.

"Very," he chokes out. He clears his throat. "Paca, what about these flounder here on the bottom? What can you make them do?"

Paca sulks. "I thought you wanted to see the dolphins."

"You've done well with them. Very well. But I'd like to see the flounders do something funny. Can you make them swim in circles, too?"

"My prince, that's not how the Gift of Poseidon works," Jagen cuts in. "It's limited to certain—"

"Liar!" Rayna yells, startling everyone. The dolphins get skittish and dart.

"Rayna," Grom says.

"Ow," she wails. "You're hurting me."

Galen sighs, his heart sinking. "Let her go, Grom. She's telling the truth. Paca doesn't have the Gift of Poseidon." Grom releases her and scowls at his brother. Rayna swims to the sanctity of Galen's back.

"Don't tell me she's talked you into her little game," Grom tells him.

"This is outrageous!" Jagen bellows. "Grom, you need to get your siblings under control before I do it myself."

Galen rolls his eyes. Jagen is over 150 years old. If he wants to tussle with Galen, he's more than welcome to come closer. "Grom, the Gift of Poseidon isn't limited to a few species of fish. The Gift was meant to feed all of us. What about the Cave of Memories? There are no dolphins that deep. How would she feed the Archives if she needed to?"

Grom crosses his arms, his face like stone. "I think you need to stick to what you know best, little brother. The humans. And take your sister with you. I can't look at her."

"What?" Galen says, swimming closer to his brother. "You're telling me to leave?"

"You've both caused enough hard feelings today. We'll have a long talk about it after the ceremony."

"That's what we're trying to tell you!" Rayna says. "There shouldn't *be* a mating ceremony."

"Rayna," Galen says gently. "I'll handle this. Please."

"No, you won't, Galen," Grom says. "You've insulted my future queen—*your* future queen—all over your own narrow-minded opinion."

"My opinion?" Galen says, irate.

"Watch your tone, brother. Don't make me expel you. It's just your opinion unless you can prove otherwise. There's no evidence to say Paca doesn't have the Gift of Poseidon."

Expel me? "She's using her hands!" Galen shouts. "She's

trained those dolphins to respond to hand signals. The real
Gift of Poseidon is by voice alone."

Grom raises a brow. "Really? Can you prove it?"

Galen opens his mouth, then shuts it again. *Not without
Emma.* "Well—"

"No, he can't prove it," Rayna blurts. She won't look at
Galen, even though he's staring her down. *What is she doing?*

She swims over to him. "He'll never believe you about Emma,
Galen," she whispers. "Don't even tell them. He won't stop the
ceremony to wait for you to go get her. Look at him. He's made
up his mind," she whispers.

"I know he can't prove it," Grom growls. "And if he could,
then he should have brought it to everyone's attention sooner.
It's a little late to take an interest in it now, don't you think?"

"Why are you doing this? Why are you being so hardheaded?"
Galen says. "Is this about Nalia? Taking a mate won't make you
forget about her. I hope that's not what you're trying to do."

It's Rayna's turn to gasp. Galen crossed the line, but he
doesn't care. Grom is being very unreasonable. Grom is being
very un-Grom.

Grom becomes stiff and cold as an iceberg. "Leave. Both of
you. Now."

"That's it then?" Galen says lacing his hands behind his
head. "We're expelled?"

Grom nods slowly.

"Let's go, Rayna." Galen says, still looking at Grom. "Let's
go home."

~ ~ ~

By the time they reach shore, Galen's exhausted. In a hurry to see Emma, he'd carried Rayna on his back the whole way home for the sake of speed. He finds a pair of trunks he'd anchored under a rock and pulls them on. Rayna finds her own pair of bottoms a few yards down.

He didn't sense Emma or Toraf in the water, so he makes his way for the house, hoping against hope Emma is there for some reason, waiting for him. She isn't. But Toraf is. And he doesn't look happy.

"How'd it go? We need to talk," Toraf blurts.

Galen stops cold. "Where's Emma? Is she okay?"

"She's home with her mom. She's fine. But there's a problem."

"In case you didn't notice, I'm not interrupting you," Galen says, his jaw clenched so tight it might lock up. "Feel free to keep talking."

Toraf wrings his hands. "Don't get too upset."

"Too late."

"Fine, be upset then. But I did it for your own good."

"Triton's trident, Toraf!" Rayna shouts. "What did you do? We've had a long day!"

Toraf lets his breath out in a gust. "I asked Yudor to come and help me. I explained that I either didn't recognize the stalker, or that I was getting the stalker's pulse mixed up with someone else's. I didn't tell him anything else."

"You what?" Galen's already balling his fists.

Toraf holds up his palms in a show of peace. "Galen, he recognized her immediately."

"Emma?" Galen breathes. *This can't be happening.*

"No. The stalker."

"Wait," Rayna says. "*Her?* Her who?"

"Galen," Toraf says. "It's Nalia. Yudor swears on Triton's memory it is. She's not dead. He's on his way back to stop the mating ceremony."

Nalia. It all comes together as if the pieces of the puzzle were suddenly jarred into place.

Galen tears through the living room and to the beach, Toraf and Rayna close behind him.

Emma's house illuminates the top of the sand dunes in front of it. That usually means Emma and her mother are both home, living separate lives in separate rooms.

Galen sprints to the back sliding-glass door and bangs on it. There's no time for etiquette. He motions for Rayna and Toraf to stay back. He can tell Rayna would rather eat her own ear than obey, but Toraf restrains her.

Emma comes to the door, a brilliant smile on her face. "You in a hurry for some reason?" she says, excitement lighting up those huge violet eyes.

"He must have missed me," Emma's mom calls from the kitchen. She winks at Galen, completely oblivious to how her world is about to shift.

"Mom. Ew," Emma says, handing Galen a towel and shutting the door.

"Thanks," he tells her. "For the towel, I mean."

"Something wrong?" From her expression, he must look as anxious as he feels.

He brushes her cheek with the back of his hand. "I love you. More than you know. No matter what happens."

She turns to kiss his palm. "Uh-oh. No matter what happens? That's kind of morbid, don't you think?" she whispers. "But no matter how morbid, I love you, too. God, I missed you so much. And it's only been twenty-four hours!"

He leans down, sweeps his lips across hers, cherishing the softness. Normally, he wouldn't kiss her in front of her mother out of respect, but he considers this a special circumstance.

He'll always remember this moment. The moment before everything changed. He gives her one last kiss, then turns toward the kitchen.

"Let me help you with that, Mrs. McIntosh."

She smiles and shakes her head. "Oh, that's okay, Galen. I'm almost done. Besides, you're still dripping wet."

Still, Galen approaches the sink. The fragmented clues line up with each step he takes, forming the complete picture.

He's wasted all this time suspecting Emma's dad. *How could I be so stupid?*

Her Syrena coloring, only with blue eyes. Blue eyes without contacts, blue eyes that faded from violet from her years on land. *It's not a legend. The painting in Tartessos was right.* And those same years on land are responsible for her gray streaks of hair—a sign of aging faster.

The way she had an eerie habit of calling every time the stalker showed up. She probably sensed them all in the water and wanted to make sure Emma was safe. If Dr. Milligan was right, if

Emma didn't mature until recently, she may not have ever sensed her before. She may not even realize Emma's gift.

Sensed. Grom swears he'd been sensing her again. *Could he really sense her from that far away after all this time?* Maybe all the myths are true. Maybe there is such a thing as the pull.

Still, pull or none, she's been breaking the law—and his brother's heart—by staying on land all this time. Not to mention the widening chasm she gouged between the two kingdoms when she left. As much as he loves Emma, Galen can't ignore her mother's actions.

And he can't let Grom mate with the wrong person.

Mrs. McIntosh gives him a quizzical look but doesn't say anything when he reaches her side. He plunges his hands into the dishwater. And senses her immediately. The stalker. The look in her eyes, the way her mouth hangs open, the way she glances down at the trident on his stomach, is all the confirmation he needs. "You've got a lot of explaining to do, Nalia."

ACKNOWLEDGMENTS

In case you were wondering, yes, the acknowledgments are the hardest part of a book to write. So many people contributed an ingredient to the recipe that turned into *Of Poseidon*, that I just know I'm going to forget someone, and when that happens, please, pretty please, forgive me! That said, I've decided that the fair (obsessive-compulsive) way to thank everyone is to start in chronological order, as they appeared in my writing life:

Thanks to my sister-in-law, Amanda, who gave me tinder for the fire that got this whole thing started. Thanks to my friend, Elayne, who was always my guinea but never my pig. Thanks to my friend and cheerleader, Cathy B., and she knows exactly why!

Thanks to the ECW critique group, but most especially to Sheryl and Vance, who gently ripped apart my manuscript and forced me to put it back together the RIGHT way. And did you know *Of Poseidon* has an Auntie Heather? Well, it does, and like any good aunt, she loved it and fed it and spanked it when necessary. Thanks, Auntie Heather!

Thanks to my sisters, Beatrice Thomas, Beatrice Garrett, and Beatrice Lyons, who did not laugh in my face when I finally admitted I was writing a book, and who kept a close watch on my daughter as I floated around the cruise ship after receiving "the call." And very, very special thanks to Maia, who listened as I read aloud and laughed when I meant to be funny and gasped when I meant to shock and grimaced when a character upchucked.

Honestly, I can't even describe how grateful I am to my fantabulous agent, Lucy Carson, whose many talents include selling the snot out of manuscripts, talking insane writers away from ledges, and turning hermits into social butterflies.

Ginormous thanks to my editors, Jean and Liz, whose experience and guidance made this project the very best it could be. Also, thanks to The Other Anna, for not telling anyone about my copyediting scandal. And thanks to Holly, who did so much behind the scenes on my behalf.

If I've missed anyone—and I'm certain I have—it's not a reflection on you, it's a reflection on me, and more specifically on my ability (or lack thereof) to remember things now that I've turned thirty.

Okay, wait. What were we talking about again?

Turn the page for

OF

POSEIDON

bonus materials. . . .

GOFISH

questions for the author

ANNA BANKS

What did you want to be when you grew up?

A writer. Or a doctor. Or an oceanographer. Or a hobo. Still kind of want to be a hobo . . .

When did you realize you wanted to be a writer?

I hate this question, because the answer makes me look like a jerk. The answer *exposes* me as a jerk. But here it is: The first time I read *Twilight*, I thought to myself, "If this chick can write a book, then you can!"

One day, Stephenie Meyer is going to give me a bloody nose. I accept that like I accept that I will one day get wrinkles.

To Stephenie Meyer: Could you come at me from the right side? That side of my face could use adjusting. . . .

What's your most embarrassing childhood memory?

Unfortunately, I was too nerdy to feel embarrassed about much. I did however, fall asleep once in class. (Just joking. I always fell asleep in this particular class.) The teacher was fed up. He sent another student to get a cup of water. They gently poured it onto my desk, soaking my sleeves, hair, face, etc. Then my teacher made a loud noise.

In my very realistic dream, the sound almost toppled me from the dragon I'd been riding and all I could think of was that I needed to get back to the castle to help the villagers. (In my defense, the class was economics.) The loud explosion sounded more like a yardstick slapping a desk, and that's when I knew those villagers would be safe.

I was startled awake, utterly dragonless, to face a class full of grinning juniors. My delighted teacher asked if I always drooled so much in my sleep.

Humiliating? Indeed. Brilliant? Oh, heck yes.

What's your favorite childhood memory?

Occasionally, my cousin would stay the night and when all the grownups were asleep, we'd open my older sister's box of tampons—we had no idea what they were yet—engorge them with tap water, and wage silent wars with them all over the house in the dark. We twirled them in the air like lassos before flinging them at each other. There would be tampons stuck to walls, the ceiling, the fridge. We tried to clean up all the evidence before morning. We failed.

So, there's that.

As a young person, who did you look up to most?

Look, I was a budding writer, so you have to understand I was always in Fruit Cup Land, m'kay? Therefore, the person I looked up to wasn't real. It was Scarlett O'Hara.

Oops?

What was your favorite thing about school?

Usually a boy. If I was between crushes, I used to find history class entertaining. And I stinking loved the rolls the cafeteria served at lunch. Not that I didn't make good grades. I did. I just . . . had ulterior motives for attending school.

What was your least favorite thing about school?

I hated dressing for physical education. Yeah, I get it. You change your clothes to avoid sweaty B.O., blah blah blah. But let's face it: I'm not going to *purposely* exert the energy it would take to make me red and sweaty—right in time for my next class—so just give me a B and move on, m'kay?

What were your hobbies as a kid? What are your hobbies now?
As a kid, I loved to read. Romance novels, no less. I also played softball and was in a bowling league for like fifty years or something.

Now my favorite thing in the world is to scare people. Unsuspecting people. Unsuspecting people who trust me. And unsuspecting people who are strangers. Strangers who don't think other strangers will honk at them as they cross the street or load their eggs and milk into the trunk of their car.

What was your first job, and what was your "worst" job?
I got my first job at sixteen as a hostess at a restaurant called PoFolks. I greeted people like so: "Howdy y'all! Smokin' or non-smokin'? Table or booth?" My black vest had vegetables on it, and a piece of wood with my name carved on it served as a name tag. I had a blast.

My worst job was waitressing at this busy, uppity breakfast restaurant. The customers were soooo snooty. One customer asked for his jelly "on the left side of my plate," and he said it as if I would contract a horrible disease if it weren't served exactly that way. Of course—OF COURSE—it was served incorrectly. Alas, he called me over to the table, face red with a rich-person temper tantrum, and said, "The jelly is on the *right* side of the place. I made it very, very clear that I wanted it on the *left* side." Quickly, I turned his plate around so that the jelly was on the left side. . . . Yeah, he didn't appreciate the wisdom in that.

I still have nightmares about that place.

What book is on your nightstand now?
Outpost by Ann Aguirre. AM LOVING IT.

How did you celebrate publishing your first book?

I threw a book launch party at a bookstore, which included a cake with the cover of *Of Poseidon* on it, and a bunch of swag bags for my partiers. Plus, I threw a blog party with lots of giveaways.

Oh, and I bought myself a fabulous pair of red heels that I'm hoping to be able to walk in soon. ☺

Where do you write your books?

At home in my office, usually in my polka dot writing pajamas. Lately though, I've had this weird yearning to sit at Starbucks with my laptop and a peppermint mocha latte. Which is not good, since I talk to myself while I write, and I also crack myself up. Out loud.

What sparked your imagination for *Of Poseidon*?

It was while I was watching this documentary about the ocean. For centuries, the colossal squid had been a legend, the stuff of fishermen's lore. The science community was doubtful of its existence—until an intact specimen washed ashore in 2005.

I thought to myself, "If a colossal squid is out there, what *else* could be?" After all, we spend more money on space exploration than we do digging around our own planet. I was all, *Why couldn't mermaids exist?* So I set out to propose how they could. And I made sure to add the very real possibility of hot mermen with delicious abs. . . .

Are mermaids and Syrena the same thing?

For the most part, but there are some important differences between mermaids and Syrena. For instance, traditionally, most mermaids depicted have scaly fins and wispy, fancy tails.

Syrena have fins that look and function like a shark's: velvety gray and very powerful. None of this fancy schmancy goldfish stuff.

What's your favorite thing to do at the beach?

Parking my beach chair under an umbrella, scrunching my toes in the sand, and letting the sound of the waves lull me into a nap.

Have you ever seen a shark?

Oh, heck yes. When I was younger, my brother took me on a helicopter ride along the shore of the Gulf of Mexico. Oh. Em. Gee. From our height, we could see hundreds of sharks swimming in between groups of people. Hundreds. And they didn't even know!

It took me a long time to get in the water after that.

What's your favorite water-dwelling creature?

There are too many to name. I do know I never miss Shark Week. And I'm saving my pennies to buy a Megalodon tooth. So there seems to be an underlying crush on sharks?

Do you have a favorite mermaid-related movie?

Of course, I loved Disney's *The Little Mermaid*, hands down. *Splash* was good, but left a lot of unanswered questions. . . .

What challenges do you face in the writing process, and how do you overcome them?

I have this irritating habit of editing while I write. Don't get me wrong, editing is essential. But for the first draft, editing while you write is like trying to sprint through water instead of swimming.

The words need to spew forth, you need to barf it on the screen. *Next* comes the editing. But noooooo. I have to edit a sentence or phrase while I'm writing the first draft, and if I don't, then I get an eye twitch and have dreams about red pens and I start craving fried chicken.

I overcome it by . . . Well, I haven't overcome it yet. Sorry.

Which of your characters is most like you?

Emma. I'm told she gets a lot of her sarcasm from me. Which is weird, because we're not even related.

What makes you laugh out loud?

Scaring people. While they're coming out of the bathroom. While they're sitting in the library. While they're in the crosswalk. While they're talking to me about something serious.

What do you do on a rainy day?

Sleep. Read. Rinse and repeat.

What's your idea of fun?

I'm not sure if I mentioned this, but I love to scare the snot out of people. Also, going on a book tour with a bunch of other crazy authors was pretty fantabulous, too.

What's your favorite song?

"The Promise" by When in Rome.

That song was whispering in the background while I wrote a lot of the scenes between Galen and Emma.

Who is your favorite fictional character?

Scarlett O'Hara, Elizabeth Bennet, and Anne Shirley. Don't ask me to pick between them.

What was your favorite book when you were a kid? Do you have a favorite book now?

I really loved The Babysitters Club series. LOVED. Now, it's so difficult to pick between from among the awesomeness that is YA right now. I'd have to say *Shadow and Bone* by Leigh Bardugo is my fave. Not sure what could top that.

What's your favorite TV show or movie?

I love *The Walking Dead* on AMC. That show scares me so hard, but I can't stop watching it! Favorite movie would have to be *The Avengers* because holy crap.

If you were stranded on a desert island, who would you want for company?

Bear Grylls. A girl's gotta eat.

If you could travel anywhere in the world, where would you go and what would you do?

I would go to Egypt, burden a camel with my generous body weight, and force it to take me to the Valley of the Kings and keep me there until the brilliant plot of an Egyptian-based YA novel unraveled in my head.

If you could travel in time, where would you go and what would you do?

I would definitely go back to the 1700s. Women with pale skin and flabulous curves were all the rage back then. I could marry into royalty, people. I feel so cheated.

What's the best advice you have ever received about writing?

I've received so much good advice about writing! Here are a few gems:

1.) Lay off the –ly words. No, seriously.

2.) End each chapter with a cliffie. The reader will come to loathe you. But the reader will turn the page, nonetheless.

3.) Write. Don't talk about writing, or think about it, or gossip about it behind its back. WRITE.

What advice do you wish someone had given you when you were younger?

Don't let your mom give you a Dutch Boy haircut. It really isn't in style, and even if it were, the lady at the beauty school wouldn't know how to do it anyway.

Do you ever get writer's block? What do you do to get back on track?

I call this writer's constipation. And reading is the laxative. Read and read and read until you can't bear to read anyone else's words, until all you long to do is make your own words.

What do you want readers to remember about your books?

That I made them laugh out loud. Admit it: You laughed.

What should people know about you?

That sometime during our relationship, no matter how brief it may be, I will try to scare you.

What do you like best about yourself?

Not to brag, but I'm pretty good at eating beef jerky. I also handle stress well. I don't throw up until AFTER the stressful situation.

Do you have any strange or funny habits? Did you when you were a kid?

When I was a kid, I never watched TV shows. I would only stop what I was doing to watch the commercials.

Now that I'm older, I don't do anything strange, except for everything.

What do you consider to be your greatest accomplishment?

Getting published. It's hard! (But worth it.)

What do you wish you could do better?

Write, cook, whistle, apply eyeliner, pick outfits, uppercut, the splits, be tactful, refrain from snickering, respect speed-limit signs.

What would you do if you ever stopped writing?

I would learn to walk in high heels, get braces, and try out for *Saturday Night Live*. (Do they have tryouts for that?)

What would your readers be most surprised to learn about you?

That I broke my ankle by falling off a toilet. Then again, they probably wouldn't be surprised by that.

Emma has just learned a shocking secret about her family.
But this secret won't just hurt Emma's family—it could turn
the two Syrena kingdoms against each other.

ANNA BANKS

OF TRITON

"A refreshing story filled with vibrant characters, feisty humor, and an irresistible romance."
—**Marissa Meyer**, *New York Times*-bestselling author of *Cinder*, on *Of Poseidon*

Find out what happens in . . .

OF TRITON

1

MY EYES won't open. It's like my lashes are coated with iron instead of mascara, pulling down my lids with a heaviness I can't fight. A medicated kind of heaviness.

I'm disoriented. Part of me feels awake, as if I'm swimming from the bottom of the ocean to the surface, but my body feels floaty, like I'm already there rolling with the lull of the waves.

I run a groggy diagnostics on my other senses.

Hearing. The hushed roar of tires negotiating a road beneath. The repetition of a cheesy chorus on an eighties radio station. The wheeze of an air conditioner that has long needed attention.

Smell. The wispy scent of Mom's perfume. The pine-tree air freshener forever dangling from the rearview. The conditioned leather of her car.

Touch. The seat belt cutting into my neck at an angle I'll pay for later. The sweat on the back of my legs, pasting me to the leather.

Road trip.

I used to love this about my parents. I'd come home from school and the car would already be packed. We'd take off without a destination, me and Mom and Dad and sometimes my best friend, Chloe. Just driving and seeing and stopping when we wanted to see more. Museums and national parks and little specialty stores that sold things like plaster castings of Sasquatch footprints. We fell victim to Dad's hobby as an amateur photographer, forced to hold touristy poses for the camera and the sake of memories. To this day, our house is practically wallpapered with past road trips—pictures of us giving one another bunny ears or crossing our eyes and sticking out our tongues like asylum patients.

The car jolts, sending my thoughts chasing after each other in a hazy race. Memories churn in a kind of mental whirlwind, and a few clear images pause and magnify themselves, like still life photos of a normal day. Mom, doing dishes. Chloe, smiling at me. Dad, sitting at the kitchen table. Galen, leaving through the back door.

Wait. Galen . . .

All the images line up, filing themselves in order, speeding up, animating the still shots into a movie of my life. A movie that shows how I came to be buckled in Mom's car, groggy and confused. That's when I realize that this is not a McIntosh family road trip. It couldn't be.

Two and a half years have passed since my dad died of cancer.

Three months have passed since the shark killed Chloe in

the waters of Destin. Which means that three months have passed since I met Galen on that beach.

And I'm not sure how much time has passed since Galen and his best friend Toraf left my house to retrieve Grom. Grom, the Triton king, Galen's older brother. Grom, who was supposed to mate with my mother. Grom, who is a Syrena, a man-fish. A man-fish who was supposed to mate with my mother. My mother, who is also Nalia, the long-lost supposed-to-be-dead Poseidon princess who's been living on land all these years because _____.

Speaking of Her Esteemed Majesty Mom . . . she's lost her freaking mind.

And I've been kidnapped.

2

GALEN STEALS glances at Grom as they approach the Jersey shore. He looks for emotion on Grom's face, maybe a glint of happiness or gratitude or excitement. Some hint of reassurance that he made the right decision in bringing his brother here. Some sign of encouragement that he didn't completely unravel the cord of his life by telling Grom where he's been. Who he's been with. And why.

But as usual, Grom is like a stingy oyster, all rigid exterior and sealed shut, protecting everything inside. And as usual, Galen has no idea how to shuck him. Even now, as they reach the shallow water, Grom floats like an emotionless piece of driftwood making its inevitable journey toward shore.

Galen retrieves a pair of swimming trunks bunched up under a familiar rock—one of the many hiding places he has around Emma's house—and hands them to Grom. He leaves his brother to stare at the Hawaiian-style fabric while he and

Toraf find their own pairs of shorts and slide them on. Before Galen switches to human form, he takes the time to stretch his fin, kneading his fists into the length of it. Ever since they left Triton territory, his fin has ached nonstop because of all the tension leading up to this, up to Grom reuniting with Nalia.

Up to the answers they've all been waiting for.

Finally, Grom changes to human form and eases the trunks up as if the leg holes were lined with shark teeth. Galen wants to tell him that putting on a pair of shorts is the easy part. Instead, Galen says, "The house is just a short walk up the beach."

Grom nods, tight-lipped, and plucks a piece of seaweed off his nose as his head emerges from the water. Toraf is already on shore, shaking off the excess water like a polar bear. Galen wouldn't be surprised if Toraf broke into a run to get to the house; Galen had insisted on leaving Rayna behind. Given their current standing as outcasts to both kingdoms, Grom was more likely to believe Toraf than either of his own siblings at the moment. Luckily, Yudor had reached him first, had already informed the Triton king that he himself had sensed Nalia's pulse. Yudor is the trainer of all Trackers, and Toraf's mentor. There is no arguing with Yudor.

Still, it would have been a lot easier if Nalia would have just accompanied Galen and Toraf to Triton territory. Convincing Grom she was alive was almost as difficult as convincing him to come ashore. But just like Grom, Nalia had closed herself off, unwilling to offer even the slightest explanation for what happened all those years ago. The only words they could finally extract from her were a strangled, "Bring Grom to me, then."

Short of dragging her to the water kicking and screaming—and destroying Emma's trust in him—Galen made the snap decision to leave them both in Rayna's care. And the word "care" can be very subjective where his sister is concerned.

But they couldn't waste any more time; with Yudor's head start on them, a search party might have already been dispatched, and if not, then Galen knew it was coming. And he couldn't—wouldn't—risk them finding Emma. Beautiful, stubborn Half-Breed Emma.

And he's a little perturbed that Nalia would.

The three of them plod holes in the sand reaching up to Emma's back porch, alongside a recent trail of someone else's—probably Emma's—footsteps leading from the beach. Galen knows this moment will always be burned into his memory. The moment when his brother, the Triton king, put on human clothes and walked up to a house built by humans, squinting in the broad daylight with eyes unaccustomed to the sun.

What will he say to Nalia? What will he do?

The steps creak under their bare feet. Toraf slides open the glass door and ushers Galen and Grom in. And Galen's heart plummets to his stomach.

Whoever tied Rayna to the barstool—the same barstool occupied by Nalia last time he'd seen it—made sure it would be a painful fall if she tried to move too much. Both of her hands are bound behind her with an electrical cord, and each of her ankles are cinched to the stool with a belt. A broad piece of silver tape over her mouth muzzles all the fury bulging in her eyes.

Toraf runs to his mate. "My poor princess, who did this to

you?" he says, tugging gently at a corner of the tape. She snatches her face away from him and chastises him in muffled outrage.

Galen strides to them and promptly rips the tape from Rayna's mouth. She yelps, raking him over with a scalding look. "You did that on purpose!"

Galen wads the tape into a sticky ball then drops it to the floor. "What happened?"

Rayna squares her shoulders. "I'm going to kill Nalia for good this time."

"Okay. But what *happened*?"

"She poisoned me. Or something."

"Triton's trident, Rayna. Just tell me what hap—"

"Nalia kept saying she needed to go to the restroom, so I let her use the downstairs bathroom. I figured it would be okay because she seemed to have calmed down since you left, so I untied her. Anyway, she was taking a long time in there." Rayna points to the bathroom below the stairwell. "So I checked on her. I knocked and knocked but she didn't answer. I opened the door—I should've known something was off since it wasn't locked—and the bathroom was dark. Then she grabs me from behind and puts something over my face. The last thing I remember is Emma standing in the doorway screaming at Nalia. Next thing I know, I wake up in this chair, tied up like some common human."

Toraf finally frees her. She examines the red lines embedded into her wrists. Rubbing them, she winces. "I'm going to do something bad to her. I can be creative, you know." Rayna clutches her stomach. "Uh-oh. I think . . . I think I'm gonna—"

To her credit, she does try to turn away from Toraf, who's now squatting on his haunches to unstrap her feet. But it's as if he were the target all along, as if Rayna's upchuck was attracted to him somehow. "Oh!" she says, vomit dripping down her chin. "I'm sorry." Then she growls, baring her teeth like a piranha. "I hate her."

Toraf wipes the wet chunks from his shoulder and gently lifts Rayna. "Come on, princess," he murmurs. "Let's get you cleaned up." Shifting her in his arms, he turns to Galen in askance.

"Are you serious?" Galen says, incredulous. "We don't have time for that. Did you not hear what she just said? Emma and Nalia are gone."

Toraf scowls. "I know." He turns to Grom. "Just so you know, Highness, I'm upset with Princess Nalia for tying Rayna up like that."

Galen runs a hand through his hair. He knows how this works. Toraf will be useless until Rayna is sufficiently calmed down and happy again. Trying to convince his best friend of doing anything otherwise is a waste of time they don't have. *Unbelievable.* "There's a shower on the third floor," Galen says, nodding toward the stairs. "In Emma's room."

Galen and Grom watch as Toraf disappears up the stairwell with their sister. "Don't worry, princess," they hear him coo. "Emma has all those nice-smelling soaps, remember? And all those pretty dresses you like to wear. . . ."

Grom cocks his head at Galen.

Galen knows this looks bad. He brings his brother to land

to reunite him with his long-lost love and the long-lost love has tied up his sister and run away.

Not to mention how else this looks: illegal. Rayna wearing human dresses and taking showers with human soaps and up-chucking human food. All evidence that Rayna is much more familiar with the human way of life than she should be.

But Galen can't worry about how anything looks. Emma is missing.

It feels like every nerve in his body is braided around his heart, squeezing until it aches incessantly. He stalks to the kitchen and flings open the garage door. Nalia's car is gone. He grabs the house phone on the wall and dials Emma's cell. It vibrates on the counter—right next to her mother's cell phone. Dread knots in his stomach as he dials Rachel, his human assistant. Loyal, devoted, resourceful Rachel. At the beep he says, "Emma and her mother are gone and I need you to find them." He hangs up and leans against the refrigerator, waiting with the patience of a tsunami. When the phone rings, he snatches at it, almost dropping it. "Hello?"

"Hiya, sweet pea. When you say Emma and her mother are 'gone,' do you mean—"

"I mean we found Rayna tied up in their house and her mother's car is gone."

Rachel sighs. "You should have let me put a GPS tracker on it when I wanted to."

"That's not important right now. Can you find them?"

"I'll be there in ten minutes. Don't do anything stupid."

"Like what?" he says, but she's already hung up.

He turns to Grom, who is holding a picture frame in his hands. His brother traces the outline of Nalia's face with his finger. "How is this possible?" he says softly.

"It's called a photograph," Galen says. "Humans can capture any moment of time in this thing they call a—"

Grom shakes his head. "No. That's not what I mean."

"Oh. What do you mean?"

Grom holds up the picture. It's an up-close black-and-white photo of Nalia's face, probably taken by a professional photographer. "This is Nalia." He runs a hand through his hair, a trait he and Galen inherited from their father. "How is it possible that she's still alive and I'm just now learning of it?"

Galen lets out a breath. He doesn't have an answer. Even if he did, it's not his place to tell his brother. It's Nalia's place. Nalia's responsibility. *And good luck getting it out of her.* "I'm sorry, Grom. But she wouldn't tell us anything."

LEGACY LOST

ANNA BANKS

Grom's fin gives an occasional thrust, a reflex really, to maintain a forward motion if only at the speed of driftwood. But comparing himself to driftwood would be unfair—to the driftwood. *At least driftwood doesn't have to mate with the hideous Poseidon heir.*

He keeps his back to the abyss below and his face upturned to the ceiling of ice above him. A ceiling to the Syrena, a floor to the humans, but most importantly, a divider of the worlds. Even when the humans had begun to submerge their steel death ships—long, ugly things that breathed fire underwater and hurled chunks of metal at one another—none of them dared to venture as far north as the Big Ice. So far.

Which is lucky for him, since the Syrena hide all things of importance under the frozen shield, down in the depths of the Cave of Memories—Grom's destination. Within the cave, he'll find the Ceremony Chamber, and possibly a way out of his own impending ceremony, the one that seals him to the house of Poseidon for the rest of his miserable life. The punishment for being a firstborn, third-generation Triton Royal.

Several times en route to the cave, Grom spots an occasional ice chunk bulging out more than the rest, so as to resemble a bulbous nose. If he lets his eyes relax enough, the crevices and icicles surrounding it could blur into the dour face of his father, the Triton king—or at least, the face his father made when Grom had told him he didn't particularly *want* to mate with the Poseidon princess.

But to complete the king's fury, Grom would need to somehow add ten shades of blotchy red to the ice, one shade for each time his father had said, "But you're firstborn, third-generation Triton. You *must* uphold the law of

Gifts." Or, on second thought, maybe one shade of red for each time Grom had said, "The law is outdated!"

Whether or not the law really *is* outdated, Grom couldn't say. The law of Gifts was brought into effect long ago by the great generals, Triton and Poseidon, to ensure the survival of the Syrena. At least that's what the Archives say. But so far, the Gift of Poseidon hasn't occurred in many generations. Not that the Syrena are starving, by any means. But as more and more humans invade the oceans, the more important the Gift of Poseidon will become, especially since they all share a common food source—fish. The humans have their nets. The Syrena have the Gift of Poseidon.

As for the Gift of Triton, not even the Archives can remember the last time anyone saw evidence of it. In fact, there is continual debate about what the Gift of Triton actually is. Even the Archives—the very ones entrusted to remember such things—continually debate about Triton's Gift. Some say speed. Some say strength. But if the *Archives* can't remember, who's to say it actually still exists?

But one thing Grom *is* sure of is that the survival of the Gifts couldn't possibly hinge on his mating with the ugly Poseidon princess. The Archives must surely be mistaken on that point.

Nalia, Nalia, Nalia. Just thinking her name makes him snarl.

He'd only ever met her once, years ago when her mother died. Etiquette had forced the Triton Royals to pay their respects to the mourning house of Poseidon. Well, etiquette, and the close friendship between Grom's father and the Poseidon king, Antonis. But for Grom, it was strictly etiquette. Especially considering how Nalia had treated him. *And I was just expressing my condolences!*

Thirteen mating seasons old at the time, he was already being groomed to rule the Triton territory, already given the respect of a future king. But Nalia was a haughty little mess, even at a mere nine seasons old. He remembers how careful he was in reciting each word of his mother's comforting speech, saying noble things about death and loss and love, even as Nalia sneered up at him in apparent disgust. Most of all, he remembers how those swollen red eyes made her look like the result of what would happen if a puffer fish mated with a rock. She'd said, "How could *you* understand my loss? You didn't even know my mother!"

Which wasn't true at all, of course. Grom's parents had been fast friends with the Poseidon Royals for many years. That is, before the precious princess came along. After giving birth to the spoiled bullshark, the Poseidon queen never fully recovered, and preferred to stay in the Royal caverns rather than venture out to any social functions.

To be fair—or at least, pretend to be fair—Nalia couldn't justly be blamed for the queen's death, no matter how closely her sudden decline coincided with the birth of Puffer Fish Face. *Or maybe she's more like a hammerhead, since her eyes are set so far apart.*

Grom smirks to himself as, at that moment, he passes a slab of ice with two deep-set holes spaced an arm's length apart. "Nalia," he says to the contorted, makeshift face, "still so icy after all these years?" He even allows himself a chuckle at her expense. *Why not? After we're mated, everything will be at my expense.*

After a long stretch of brooding, Grom senses the two Trackers guarding the entrance to the Cave of Memories. No doubt they sensed him before he sensed them, possibly as soon as he set off on his journey. Which has always amazed him. All Syrena can sense each other within close proximity, but Trackers have a special sensing capacity. The ones who impress him the most are the elite Trackers who can sense their kind even from opposite sides of the world. Only the elite can stand guard at the Cave of Memories. Only the elite can be trusted with such precious relics.

And to Grom, none of those relics are more valuable at this moment than the answers which lie in the Ceremony Chamber, the place where all of Syrena history is documented. Matings, births, annulments, deaths. With any shimmer of luck, Grom will find evidence that he's not third-generation. Or that he's not firstborn. Or, better yet, he's not even of Triton descent! He'd take any of those options over the last one: He is all of the above, and he will mate with Nalia and her hammerhead eyes.

When Grom senses the Trackers directly below, he swoops down and approaches them at the entrance. Both—one from each Royal house—move aside for him.

"Is there a Royal function here today, my prince?" the Triton Tracker says.

Grom pauses before he passes. "No. Why do you ask?" And then he senses her. Nalia. *Why is she here?*

The Tracker nods when he sees that Grom recognizes Nalia's pulse. "Her Highness arrived not long ago, my prince. We just thought . . . " The Tracker shrugs, unable or unwilling to theorize further.

Grom presses his lips together in a tight line. "Did she say why?"

This time, the Poseidon Tracker shakes his head. "She did not, my prince."

Grom nods. "As you were, then." Careful to hide his grimace until he passes, he makes his way into the enormous first chamber, a cavern filled with long rocks that look like icicles dangling from the top and protruding from the bottom. It reminds Grom of the mouth of a piranha.

You don't have to see her. Just find what you came for and leave. But the more he winds through the maze of caverns, the more his heart sinks. He passes the Scroll Chamber, full of human and Syrena relics, none of which are actual scrolls. All the true scrolls, the ones scrawled onto papyrus and birch centuries ago, have disintegrated into bits of nothing to be stolen by the current. Then there's the Tomb Chamber, the final resting place for all Syrena dead preserved by freezing water and, most importantly, kept from washing ashore on any human beaches. He eases past the Civic Chamber, full of monuments from many human civilizations. Each tunnel, each chamber, brings him closer and closer to the Ceremony Chamber—and closer to *her*.

Finally, he reaches the entrance, and the female Tracker on guard meets him with a surprised look. "Your Highness," she says, bowing her head in reverence.

Grom scowls. Nalia's pulse pounds against his chest, his head, his entire body. He doesn't remember her pulse being this strong, this intrusive. *She's in the Ceremony Chamber. Why, why, why?*

"As you were," Grom nearly growls, making his way through the elongated opening.

The Ceremony Chamber is nothing but century after century of Syrena records etched and carved into aged rock—a much more practical material than the humans' papyrus, Grom is sure—stacked atop one another, maintained for an eternity by the Archives, the Trackers, and the freezing water. Grom has always been in awe of this chamber, even before it meant something to him personally. Before it meant his possible escape from the law. He's always felt as if past lives, past experiences called out to him from the stone tablets, as if this place held answers to future questions he might have one day as a Triton king.

But now, it feels as if this place has closed off access to itself and been replaced by the suffocating pulse of *her*.

Deciding the meeting is inevitable—he knows she senses him just as clearly as he senses her—he chooses the diplomatic course and follows her pulse until he finds her draped over a stone tablet in a far corner of the cave.

Nalia is all grown up.

From head to fin-tip, she takes up the length of the tablet and then some. She's twisted her long black hair into a braid and tied a knot at the end to keep it in place. Though a strand of seaweed is wrapped tightly around her torso in the traditional female cover, it doesn't quite hide the swell of her breasts. Without looking up, she says, "What are *you* doing here?"

Though her voice is full of disdain, it's not unpleasant. In fact, it has a rich texture to it, velvety as a fin, and it fills up the cave with her presence. He doesn't like it. Not at all. Grom clears his throat. "I might ask the same of you, princess."

She huffs, but still won't look at him, which is sure to drive him mad. "Yes, you might."

It occurs to Grom that he really does want to know why she's here. *Is she here for the same reason I am? Does she seek a way out of this arrangement, too?* Hope licks at his insides, but then a sense of rejection instantly quells it. After all these years, she still dares to snub him.

I won't have it, not again. Not with all the females I have throwing themselves at me at every change in the current. What makes her *so special?*

Then Nalia, third-generation, firstborn Poseidon heir, looks up.

And Grom almost falters. "You've . . . you've changed, princess."

Yes, it's the same pulse he remembers from years earlier. But it's not the same face. Not the puffer fish face with hammerhead tendencies. No, this face, this new Nalia, this *grownup* Nalia, is breathtaking. Her eyes are still huge, yes, but in a way that makes his mouth go dry despite the ocean around him. And the color of them! Didn't he remember them being dull and plain? Could they always have been this vibrant, this crystalline violet? And her lips. So full. So alluring. So pouty.

So contrary.

"You haven't changed at all," she counters, crossing her arms. "Except, your mouth hangs open wider than I remember."

Grom clamps his mouth shut.

"And you still haven't answered my question. What are you doing here?" she says.

Grom offers his most charming grin, but by the look on her face, the effort is wasted. "Surely, you know. I'm here to make sure there is no mistake in the records. That I am the *only* Syrena *lucky* enough to be your mate."

Her eyes declare him full of whale dung. "Liar," is what she says out loud.

"I swear by Triton's trident." He places three fingers on his Royal birthmark, the small image of a trident embedded into his skin just before stomach turns into fin. "I had to make sure you were mine."

She uncrosses her arms. "You and I do not like each other."

"Is that so? I didn't realize."

If Nalia narrows her eyes anymore, they'll close. "You were mean to me when you came to my mother's entombing ceremony."

Beautiful, but dumb as a clam. Such a shame. Grom cocks his head at her. "Was that before or after you attacked me?" *Attacked me, then bit me when I tried to restrain her. How convenient that she doesn't remember.* Their parents had found them wrapped up in each other, her in his best headlock, him trying to pry her vicious little teeth from his stomach. That's when the ridiculous rumor had started that they had taken a liking to each other. Complete nonsense.

"You told me I killed my mother."

"I didn't say that. Not exactly." Pretty close, though, he recalls. "We could start over, you know. Forget about the past." *Over my lifeless fin.*

Nalia must notice that he's making his way closer, because she presses herself against the tablet. Grom swears she swallows with the familiar vulnerability of an awestruck female. "Why would we do that?" she says.

He stops within a fin's length of her.

"Why are you looking at me like that?" she says, her hand flitting to her throat. But he can tell by her face that it's the same kind of reflex of alarm he's feeling—and it has nothing to do with danger. Her eyes, too, are full of the same kind of whirlwind he feels tightening in his chest. And he doesn't like it. Not at all.

He floats closer, growing more delighted as she allows him to devour the distance between them. *Who's the awestruck one now, idiot?* "Like what?" he murmurs, his nose almost touching hers. Grom decides Nalia is the exact opposite of ugly. She has the same features as every other Syrena. Smooth olive skin, dark black hair, violet eyes. But hers are all arranged in just the right way to make her stunning.

Nalia gasps, licking her lips. She keeps her eyes locked on his. "Like . . . like . . ."

"Like I found what I was looking for?" he offers.

He's answered with a sharp jab to his throat. "Like you're looking to die," she whispers, pressing whatever weapon she has into the soft flesh under his jaw bone. "This is a lionfish spike. If you even flick your fin, I'll inject its venom."

His eyes lock on hers, a silent battle raging between them. "You won't do it."

"You don't know me."

"I want to. I do." *Right after I murder you.*

She scoffs. "I'm going to leave now. You're going to stay right here." She whirls them around in one fluid motion and backs away from him, toward the entrance. A tantalizing smirk curves her lips. "You must have bumped your head on the way in," she says, tucking the blade behind her, probably into her braid. "To think that would work on me."

Grom never takes his eyes off her. "And what do you think will work, pray tell?"

She shrugs. "I don't suppose it matters much." Nalia glances back at the stone tablet she'd been reading. "Since I don't have a choice one way or the other." Then she speeds away with such force that a swish of water slaps at his face in her wake.

When the length of her elegant fin disappears behind a bend in the cave, he glides over to the tablet. He could go after her. He could even call her bluff on the lionfish venom—she wouldn't keep such a deadly threat tucked against her bare flesh. Or, he could let her bask in this small victory. Let her think he's weak.

His eyes scan the tablet, but his attention is still overwhelmed by the memory of her. If she didn't find what she was looking for here, then it's not likely that he will either. Their future course is set. One day, they will be mated. It's a battle neither of them can win. He knows it. She knows it.

But today, Nalia started a new battle. One that he's intent on winning.

The one for her heart.

Grom finds his mother in her private chamber, right in the middle of her usual routine of caring for her human relics. She uses her finger to gently swipe off a layer of silt from a tall clear cylinder which she claims the humans use to contain fire for light. After it's spotless, she moves onto a small white box, her favorite of them all. "I can't touch this one anymore," she says without looking up. She puckers, then blows a gentle stream through the delicate flowers carved on the lid. A slight cloud of black wafts up, just before the surrounding water absorbs it. "Last time, I chipped one of the small green pieces. See?"

Grom swims forward and squints, more in a show of interest, rather than actual interest. "Are you sure it wasn't already like that? You did recover this from a wreck, after all."

She bites her lip. "I'm sure. I cried when I did it."

"You and your human treasures," he says, not unkindly.

"Oh, not you, too," she says, waving her hand. "Do I not get enough complaints from your father? Is it so wrong to want to preserve beauty, even if it's made from human hands?"

"Of course not." Grom smiles. "Otherwise, the Cave of Memories would be outlawed. Besides, I didn't come here to complain."

"Excellent! I do get weary of having to defend myself. What can I do for you, my son?"

"It's about Nalia."

The queen groans. "Oh, Grom. You know that's the one thing I can't—"

"I want her for my mate," he blurts.

"I . . . You do?" She clasps her hands together. "Because I was certain that you'd rather mate with a rock fish. In fact, I think you've said as much on several—"

"Things changed. *She* changed. But I want her to want me, too." Sort of. He wants her to want him, so he can reject her the way she rejects him. But that explanation won't convince the queen to help him.

"Truly? Do you . . . do you love her, then?"

"No," he says, even as he feels Nalia's pulse thrum through him. Ever since their meeting in the Ceremony Chamber, he can't shake it. Sometimes it's light, almost like a phantom tickle, easily brushed aside. Other times, it's maddening, strong and intrusive, so that he can't think of anything else but her. And apparently talking about her triggers the madness. He doesn't like that. Not at all.

"Then why?" His mother's lips press into a line.

Grom chuckles, hoping it doesn't sound as fake as it feels. "Have you *seen* Nalia lately, mother?"

The queen gasps. "Are you shallow as a clam pool, boy?"

"Triton's trident! Ever since she was born, you and Father have twisted my fin to accept her. Now, you're upset that I'm *willing* to mate with her. I do wish you'd make up your minds."

His mother grimaces in obvious shame.

"Truth be told," he says, almost choking on the words, "I think it's more than love. I think it's the pull."

"The pull!" she says, gliding over to him. "Grom, are you sure? What makes you think so?"

Grom shrugs. He should have looked into the whole ridiculous legend further before going around spewing "the pull" all over the place. He has no idea of the supposed symptoms. And symptoms they are, since Grom has always considered the pull a mental defect, at best. The idea that nature could force a couple together in order to produce stronger offspring has always been nonsensical to him.

"Do you think about her all the time?" The queen's eyes lit up. "Do you always sense her, no matter how far apart you are?"

There is nothing fake about his scowl as he realizes he does. *Not possible. It's not possible that I actually do feel the pull for Nalia.* He clears his throat. "Er . . . yes." The words taste like squid ink in his mouth.

"Oh, this is wonderful. I can't wait to tell your father."

"No! Do we have to tell anyone? I mean, it doesn't matter if it's the pull or not, right? We would still have to mate, even if it's not."

"But wait. If you feel the pull toward her, shouldn't Nalia feel the pull toward you? Isn't that how it works?"

Triton's trident, what a stupid legend. "I'm sure she reciprocates, mother. But given our history, she might be stubborn enough to fight it." Again, Nalia's pulse jolts through his veins. He grits his teeth. "And that's what I need your help with. I want to charm her. Win her over."

Grom swears he hears pity in the Triton queen's chuckle. "Oh, my dear boy. Who could resist your charms? I'm sure you'll have no trouble at all stealing her heart. You don't need my help. The little princess has no idea what's coming for her." With that, his mother flits out of the cave in a wave of feminine innocence. And Grom is sure he's just been had.

He follows Nalia's pulse to the shallow waters off the coast of the Old World, in Triton territory. *What is she doing in the Human Pass? Is she brainless?*

The Human Pass is just that—a stretch of barren waters where the humans pass through in their underwater death ships. As best as Grom can figure, these humans think this is their territory, and they do their best to patrol it regularly. It's a dangerous place for any Syrena, and a careless place for a Poseidon Royal.

Which is why he's not really surprised to have found her here. In the weeks since their confrontation in the Cave of Memories, he's found her in all sorts of unpredictable places. Unpredictable seems to be her specialty.

As he nears her pulse, he senses another one, the female Tracker he first met at the entrance of the Ceremony Chamber: Freya, Nalia's accomplice in all things bad. He finds them both in Blended form on the bottom of the passage, their bodies mimicking and reflecting the color and textured look of the rocky muck. Not bothering to Blend himself, he swims down to the barely discernible shapes. "Why are we hiding?" he says loudly.

Nalia materializes before him and rolls her eyes. "What are you doing here?" she hisses.

Grom crosses his arms. "I'm here to rescue you. I was very alarmed to find my future mate in dangerous waters. I've come to help."

She Blends again and huffs. "You can help by Blending, and shutting your mouth."

"What are you doing?" he asks, exasperated.

"I don't answer to you." Grom is left imagining just what kind of superior expression she has on that lovely face.

"No, but *she* does." He raises a brow at the transparent silhouette next to Nalia.

Freya materializes. "We're waiting for one of the long boats to pass so we can ride it."

"Freya!" Nalia hisses.

"What?" Freya says, her voice full of whine. "I have to answer him. He's a Triton Royal."

Nalia appears again, and scowls up at Grom. "Look, if you're not going away any time soon, then would you please just Blend so you don't blow our cover?"

"You're both out of your minds. Don't you know how dangerous—"

"Shhh! They can pick up sounds down here somehow. They'll come and investigate," Nalia whispers.

Grom doesn't even want to know how she knows this. He Blends and crouches down next to her, tucking his fin under him. "So, this is your plan? To get yourself killed so you don't have to mate with me?" He's glad she can't see the dejection he knows is all over his face.

She scoffs. "Not everything is about you. If you must know, we come here all the time. And since you're here, I was going to invite you to come with us, but if you're too scared—"

"I'm not," he says, though he's not sure he believes it. Hitching a ride on any human boat is dangerous, but hitching a ride on a human death ship is downright madness. Their sole purpose, as far as he can tell, is to pick fights with other human death ships, which makes them all moving targets. But begrudgingly, he admits he's a little thrilled that she thought to invite him this time. He'd love to reject the invitation, but if he does, it will look like as if he's afraid, instead of that he's just plain rejecting her.

Nalia seems pleased. "Good. One should be along soon. Here, take this. You'll need it to hold on." She hands him a chopped-off tentacle of what used to be a very large squid. The suckers are as big as his face. He wants to believe it was dead before she found it. But he doesn't.

He swallows, turning the tentacle over in his hands. "You're not serious?"

"Change your mind?" she coos. Freya giggles.

Grom swallows. "No."

"Shhh! Here it comes."

All three Syrena stiffen, almost invisible against the current. In the distance, a shadow emerges, slow and stealthy, like a wary shark. A giant wary shark. It glides through the water, looking every bit the predator it is. When it's just overhead, Nalia and Freya shoot up expertly, leaving Grom behind in the wake of their swirling muck. He watches as Nalia's clear form latches on to the metal hull with her squid tentacle. Dangling by one arm, she materializes just long enough to grin down at him.

Stupidly, he grins back. And he's thankful he's still in Blended form. Otherwise, she might think he's flirting with her. *Am I flirting with her?* In the next second, he springs up and attaches his own tentacle to the hull, his half grunt full of disbelief and thrill.

Up close, the ship doesn't look as smooth. Where the metal is chipped in places, rust rings have settled in, and even a few barnacles have taken up residence in sporadic clumps along the length of it. But Grom suspects the humans aren't so concerned about the beauty of it as they are about the deadliness of it. And deadly it is.

He keeps an eye on Nalia, who is now sneaking her way to the top of the vessel. He copies her movements as she sticks and unsticks her tentacle, careful not to make noise. Which is why his heart almost stops when Nalia starts pounding on the metal with a rock.

"What are you doing?" he says, feeling foolish for bothering to whisper.

She snickers, and knocks again in an unmistakable rhythm. She materializes briefly, and presses her ear against the hull, motioning for Grom to do the same. "She really is insane," he mutters as he does as he's told. Inside the vessel, he hears a squall of human commotion. Each time Nalia knocks, the humans chatter in an alarmed tone, in a language Grom doesn't understand. Then they knock back.

Nalia makes her way down to Grom at the middle of the death ship while Freya maneuvers to a long ladder on the side. He watches as the Tracker wraps her fin into rungs, to give her arms a rest.

"They always knock back," Nalia says, proud. "Not just this one, but all of them."

Grom smiles at the excitement in her voice. "What does it mean?"

"Not sure. My knocking doesn't mean a thing, but I think theirs means something to them."

Grom looks around. "We're heading into deeper water. How long do we plan on risking our lives? I'm getting hungry."

Nalia laughs, a genuine, tickled sound, and Grom realizes it could be his new favorite sound in all the ocean. *Get a hold of yourself, idiot. This is your game. Play it.*

"Sometimes we can drive them crazy enough to surface," she says. "Then Freya likes to make faces in their little hole at the top. That really drives them mad."

"Triton's trident! How have you not been caught?"

Nalia materializes. "Who says we haven't?"

"You've been caught by the humans? Does your father know?"

"Oh, yes. Of course he does. Because I tell him of all the illegal things I do." She rolls her eyes. "No, we've never really been caught. Freya came close though. Sometimes, she misplaces her intelligence."

Freya materializes long enough to stick her tongue out at them. Nalia laughs, removing all doubt that it's his new favorite sound.

Then a loud, foreign pitch startles him, one that seems to promise impending doom. He accidentally releases his tentacle and in a shaved second, he's falling behind the vessel. "What's that sound?" he shouts to Nalia, trying to keep up, not caring if the humans on board can hear him.

"It means there's another ship somewhere around here. An enemy one." Her face is full of dread.

Grom's gut wrenches. "Let go! Don't be stupid. Please!"

"I can't! Freya's stuck on the ladder."

Indeed, Freya wriggles within the confines of the ladder as if it's a living thing keeping her trapped. Nalia is right. Freya really does misplace her intelligence. It would be a simple thing to free herself, if she would just calm down long enough to think it through. But he can see the panic settle in, the calm leaving her eyes. She's working on survival instinct alone.

Then Grom sees it. In the distance, a huge shadow moves toward them.

No, toward the human death ship. With speed, with confidence, with purpose, as if the two vessels were connected by a rope and their coming together is as natural as high tide.

Only, the other ship is much, much bigger—and there is nothing natural about this gross imbalance.

Freya sees the shadow, too—and loses what little control she'd been harboring. She cries out, her wiggling becoming more frantic and only serving to make her more stuck. Finally, Nalia reaches her, just as the sound of the alarm from the other vessel reaches them through the current. With one sweeping motion, Nalia shoves Freya's fin through the last rung of the ladder, bending the tip at a painful angle. But even Freya recognizes the necessity of it, and nods her thanks to her friend as she swims from the metal monster.

Then another sound, metal against metal, resonates through the water. *Our death ship is firing.* Grom watches in horror as a cloud of fire lights up the front, then disappears, showing only a trail of a shadow leaving the ship. Unable to look away, he holds water in his lungs, unable to breathe it out until he sees that the missile missed the other ship.

Which is the worst-case scenario.

"They're going to fire back!" Grom shouts to Nalia and Freya, who are still too close to the ship. "We have to get out of here!"

"Yelling at me won't help anything!" Nalia points down. Freya's bent fin is making it impossible for her to keep a steady direction. Nalia bites her lip. "Leave us, Grom. There's no reason for us all to die."

He rolls his eyes and swims toward them. Grasping Freya's other arm, he jerks her forward and gives Nalia a hard look. "Let's. Go."

Nalia nods. Grom stamps down a feeling of admiration when her expression changes from hopelessness to determination. Together they drag Freya, one on each arm, but it feels like slow motion, as if the water has thickened, as if the ocean itself is working against their escape.

The dull thud in the distance lets them know that the other ship has fired. And they are still too close. Freya screams and writhes from his grasp to turn, to see something launching toward them at the speed of death. Grom considers knocking her unconscious. But there's no time.

Impact. Heat. Suddenly, the whole world seems pushed forward. Even Nalia screams. Grom decides he never wants to hear that sound again. Gritting his teeth, he pulls both of them toward the sea floor. "Get down!" he orders. "Lie flat."

They do as they're told. Debris, sharp and heavy, showers down on them like bits of fallen prey. A rush of hot swooshes over them, between them, finding even the smallest space to fill. A hand grasps his. He doesn't need to look down to know it's Nalia's.

When the loudness ends, and the silence chases behind it, Grom looks up. The ship is gone. Obliterated. As if it never existed. He squeezes Nalia's hand. "Are you alright?"

She eases up, shaking off the silt like an octopus coming out of hiding. Her lip quivers and she points to the back of her head. Grom tries to swallow his heart. "You're hurt."

She shakes herself and reaches around to pull a tangle of hair forward. "My hair," she says, her eyes bigger than he'd ever seen them. "It's singed."

Grom cocks his head, flirting with the idea of strangling her. "Seriously?"

She shrugs, dejected. "I know it sounds petty. It's just that . . . well, I really loved my hair." She dangles it in front of her as if it's a crispy, dead eel.

They both seem to remember Freya's existence when she groans. Apparently something else had done the job of knocking her out without Grom's assistance.

Nalia snaps out of it first and helps her friend, who gasps at the sight of her. "Oh, your hair! What will your father say?"

Grom pinches the bridge of his nose. *Has the entire world gone mad?* "It's just hair," he grits out. "It'll grow back."

Freya scolds him with a look. "It's never just hair, your Highness."

"No," Nalia says quietly. "He's right. It's time I let it go." Throwing Freya's arm over her shoulder and hoisting her up, she looks at Grom. "My father always said my hair was the exact same color as Mother's. It felt like keeping a part of her with me, I guess."

Grom stares at her, stunned. "I'm sorry. I didn't mean—"

"Freya, you simply have to cut it for me," Nalia says, setting her jaw.

Her friend pulls back, eyes wide. "Oh, no. Not me. I'm not doing it. Your father will have me arrested."

Nalia settles her gaze on Grom. "Will you do it?"

He tries to look away, but the pleading softens him. He nods.

She scans the floor, picking up pieces of debris and inspecting them, presumably looking for something with a sharp-enough edge. Grom and Freya can't bring themselves to help. At least Freya can claim an injury, he thinks to himself. *But how can I cut off her hair if it means that much to her?*

Finally, Nalia finds what she's looking for. She swims it over to Grom and hands him a thin piece of metal, disfigured and burnt, but sharp enough on one side to accomplish the task at hand.

He palms it, inspecting its capacity for cutting hair, and doubting his own. "You're sure?" he says, unable to look at her just yet. "You're sure this is what you want?"

"Someone's coming," Freya says, stiffening into the classic Tracker pose. "Better get on with this."

Nalia nods. "Do it," she tells him. "Before anyone sees me like this." She turns her back to him and offers up her burnt locks.

He turns the metal shard in his hand. "You're sure?"

"Poseidon's beard, just do it already!"

Before she's done yelling, he's holding her severed hair in his hands. She gasps and whirls around. He hands it to her. "I'm sorry."

She cradles it in her hands like one of his mother's human relics. Then, of all things, she laughs. "Can you *believe* that just happened? And we lived through it?"

When he doesn't immediately respond, she shakes the mangled locks in his face. "Admit it, Triton prince. That's the most exciting thing that's ever happened to you. And you're welcome."

Grom bites back a smile and swats her hand away, but she persists until he's forced to grab her wrist and restrain it behind her back. By now, he too senses Yudor, the Tracker trainer, approaching with others he doesn't recognize. "I saved your life, then cut your hair," he says, letting her go. "*You're* welcome."

The smile fades from her face. She looks back, obviously sensing the party coming to investigate the explosion. She turns back to Grom, hesitant. "About that," she says, inching closer. The water between them seems to heat up, but that can't be right, can it? When her nose almost touches his, she says, "Thank you for not leaving us." Then she presses her lips against his, soft and slow, and he feels an explosion, just like the one from the death ship, only this one is coming from inside, and it feels like a hundred electric eels slithering over him, every part of him, shocking him to life.

There's no reason to think about pulling her closer; his hands do that all on their own. There's no reason to worry about who sees. He couldn't care less. There's no reason to think about his plan to woo her, then reject her. He knows now that there will never be a time when he will reject these lips.

These lips, this kiss, they're everything he never knew he wanted.

Nalia pulls away suddenly, looking every bit as stunned as he feels. She clears her throat. "I'd better get going." But her expression tells him that maybe she'd rather stay, that maybe she'd rather keep kissing.

Grom nods in agreement with it all. She'd better get going. He wants her to stay. He wants to keep kissing.

She lets the carcass of her hair slink to the mud below them and, for the longest time, she'll stare only at it, not meeting his eyes. The Tracker party is close, within sight Grom knows, but still she stays, immobile and hesitant and stunning.

Then without another word, without meeting his eyes, she turns and swims away.

He finds her with Freya, sitting on the outer rocks of The Crag, the deep chasm etched into the sea floor where you could swim down for hours and never touch bottom. They're both peering over the edge of the cliff, as if they're actually contemplating going down there.

"Don't even think about it," Grom says. "Your lionfish spike won't work on a giant squid." He's amazed how natural it feels to settle down next to Nalia and hang his fin over the ledge.

She smirks up at him. "We waited for you. You're slow."

He laughs. Freya would have sensed him for a while before he arrived, but did Nalia? *Can she sense me as strongly as I sense her?* "Some things are worth the wait."

"You're slow *and* delusional," she says without bluster. She peeks back down into The Crag. "I want a tooth from a dangle fish."

Grom shakes his head. Dangle fish live in the deepest, darkest parts of the ocean, where they dangle a light in front of themselves as a lure to attract unsuspecting fish. Their teeth are as long as his hand. The Crag is a good place to hunt for dangle fish. "What could you possibly need that for?"

She scrunches up her face.

Grom raises a brow at Freya, who sighs in defeat. She has gotten used to this game. "She wants it to make a gift for you. For your mating— Ow! Poseidon's teeth, Nalia. He's a Royal!"

Nalia points her finger in Grom's face, almost up his left nostril. "You need to stop bullying her. Sometimes it's not your business."

Grom captures her hand and uses it to pull her closer. Her eyes go wide as she glances at his lips, but she doesn't squirm, doesn't try to move away. He feels himself melt a little at her touch. His bones feel like the water around him. "You were making me a gift?" He glances at Freya. "Freya, how rude would it be if I asked you to—"

Freya shrugs, then spirals up and over them. "Some Triton Trackers found a new human mine," she says, winking at Nalia, who flinches as she passes by. "Guess I could go help them set it off." Freya says that whenever the Trackers come across a mine, they set off the explosion from a distance, using rocks they hurl from the surface. She says when one of the floating metal balls burst, they all do.

"That sounds exceptionally fun," Grom calls after her. When she's gone, he grins at Nalia. "Don't tell me you're all of a sudden shy, Princess. We've seen each other every day for the past month."

Nalia lifts her chin. "I heard you feel the pull for me."

That is unexpected. From the sound of her voice, she doesn't like the idea. And he takes slight offense. Suddenly, the tiny pearl in his hand feels like a burning rock from the hot beds. "Is it so bad for me to *want* to be your mate?"

"That's just it. The pull is mindless. It tricks your feelings. It's not what *you* want, it's what *the pull* wants. To make stronger offspring. But I want something real."

A whirlpool of relief swirls through him. *She wants something real—from me.* "But you have to mate with me, pull or no pull. What does it matter if the feelings are real? There could be no feelings at all, and we'd still have to mate."

"I'd rather there were no feelings at all than be tricked by the pull." She crosses her arms. He's spent enough time with her to know this is her gesture when she's unsure.

"And if I don't feel the pull for you?" He caresses her lips with his eyes. She swallows. "Don't you?"

"Hmmm," he says. "I'm not sure. Wouldn't you feel the pull toward me if I felt it toward you?" He's hoping his mother knows what she's talking about, hoping that she didn't just make this ridiculousness up.

She considers. "I suppose so. That's how it's supposed to work, anyway."

"And?"

"And I suppose it would make sense for us to be pulled together." She tucks a short piece of hair behind her ear. "Firstborn, third-generation Royals, right? To pass on the Gifts of the Generals to our fingerlings. If anyone would be pulled, it would be us."

"And?"

"And *what?*"

"Do *you* feel the pull for *me?*"

She bristles like an anemone. "Oh, just forget it!" She turns away, but he catches her arm and whirls her around.

"I don't believe in the pull," he blurts. "I think it's a bunch of superstitious muck. Besides that, I think the pull would pale in comparison to the way I feel about you."

She lets out a tiny gasp, swirling the water in front of her and spooking some fish close by.

Grom pulls her closer, wanting this moment to be right, wanting the right words to appear in his mouth, wanting the contrary ones to disappear from hers. "If it was the pull, surely it would have brought us together before now. I've been old enough to sift for a mate for three seasons now. Don't you think that if the pull were at work, I would have sought you out already?"

"I hadn't thought about that."

"Well, I've been thinking about it a lot lately. About you and me. And . . . not long ago in the Cave of Memories," he says, "you told me that I was mean to you when we first met, at your mother's entombing ceremony all those years ago. Do you remember that?"

She bites her lip. "I was just a fingerling when she died. Nine mating seasons old. It wasn't what you'd said. It was how you said it. As if I was unimportant. As if it were a bother for you to be there."

Grom nods, cringing on the inside. That had been exactly how he felt when he'd had to make an appearance at the ceremony—imposed upon. "I'm so sorry." He brushes her cheek with his fingers, something he wishes he'd done all those seasons ago. Something, *anything* to comfort her instead of set her on edge like he did. If he wouldn't have been so self-occupied, maybe they wouldn't have avoided each other all this time, missed out on each other. Maybe they'd already be mated. The thought bears down on him with the weight of a great whale. "I have no excuse," he says softly. "But something you said back then stuck with me. Do you remember what you told me? When I offered you my condolences?"

Nalia shakes her head. Then she sends the thrill of a thousand electric rays running through him when she rests her hand on his. "No."

"You asked how I could understand your loss when I didn't even know your mother. But you were wrong. I did know her, before you were born. And I liked her." He offers his fist between them, then opens it. When he picks up the black pearl, her eyes go round and soft, luring him closer like the light of the dangle fish she'd wanted to hunt down. "I remember she had a pearl like this one," he tells her. "I remember how happy she was when my mother gave her a human string for it. She put it through the pearl and wore it around her neck, always."

Nalia accepts it into her palm, rolling it around with her finger. "She was entombed with it," she breathes. "I wanted to keep it, but I thought it would be selfish, so I didn't ask Father for it." She lifts her scrutiny from the pearl to his face. "This looks exactly like hers. It must have taken you forever to find one just like it." She bites her lip. "That's what you've been doing in the shallows every day before you come to meet me and Freya."

He nods. Every single day since he was forced to cut off her hair, he'd been harvesting in the oyster beds. Sure, Freya could have used her Tracker abilities to locate him. But by Nalia's expression, he knows that's not the case. "You can sense me, then. The way I sense you."

"Is that the pull?"

He grins, scratching the back of his neck. "I thought we just agreed that the pull doesn't exist?"

"Then why do we feel this way?"

"I was thinking of calling it 'love.' Of course, I can't speak for you—" He's cut off by her lips on his, her body against his, her arms wrapped around his neck. This kiss is even better than the first. This kiss wraps heat around them, between them, through them. It makes the ocean seem inconsequential, the moon unimportant, everything else nonexistent.

It fills all the empty spaces inside him, the ones he didn't know were there, and the ones he thought he'd already filled. And the future is laid plain before him. Their future.

"We're almost there," Nalia giggles, keeping her hands pressed tight over his eyes as he swims clumsily forward. He warbles a little, for effect. She giggles again.

Grom smiles. "Did you pick the furthest island from our parents, then?" Syrena custom normally calls for the males to pick the mating island, to find a private, uninhabited place for the newly mated couple to consummate their vows, which they can only do in human form. But Nalia had asked—no, *begged*—for him to let her pick the island and set it up for their stay there.

"Sort of. But the surprise part isn't who we're *furthest* from—it's who we're *closest* to."

Finally, after what seems like an entire season, his fin skims sand. "Are we there yet?"

She uncovers his eyes, and he's shown the underwater landscape of a slowly ascending ocean floor littered with coral reefs and rocks and colorful fish. They couldn't be more than thirty fins deep, which means the shoreline is close.

Nalia pops to the surface and motions for him to do the same. She points to their destination, and Grom drinks in the small island, the breeze dancing through the luxuriant green canopy, the lazy waves of ocean licking the shore. He holds up his hand to shield himself from the sunlight mirrored off of the bright sand, almost blinding him as his eyes adjust to dry air. Then he sees it. "Nalia," he says, his mouth gone suddenly dry. "You can see the big land from here."

She claps like a seal. "You noticed! Aren't you excited? But that's not the whole surprise. Let's go ashore." She pulls his hand, but he holds back.

"You'd better just tell me the rest of it. Because we're not going on shore so close to the human land."

Her face falls. "But that's the surprise."

Grom pinches the bridge of his nose. One thing he adores about Nalia is that she's adventurous, fearless. She could never be boring. But this is a bit much. This is not a small law to break. This is the biggest. Through gritted teeth he says, "Why would we want to go to the big land?"

She won't meet his gaze now, finding something terribly interesting to look at beneath them in the water. "Well, for one thing, it's fun."

"Please don't say that means you've done it."

She bites her lip.

"How?"

"I have what the humans call a rowboat. I do feel bad about stealing it, but I needed it to take me to shore after I change into dry human clothes on the island. I feel bad about stealing those, too—"

"How long have you been doing this?" His voice sounds gruffer than he intended.

She crosses her arms now, apparently in short supply of shame. "Why don't you ask your mother?"

"My *mother*?"

"Ask *her* where she gets her human treasures. You can't really believe that she scavenges for them herself."

Actually, he did. The idea that his mother has known about—no, *encouraged*—Nalia's escapades makes his insides catch fire. "This has got to stop!" he says before he can hold it back. Before he can twist the words into something more diplomatic.

The way her eyes pool into huge drops of water on her face. The way her mouth curves into a soft frown. The way her crossed arms seem to relax into a gentle self-hug, as if she's trying to hold something in and comfort herself all at the same time. She's disappointed in him.

Without another word, she slinks below the surface.

And he learns something new about Nalia. She is very fast. He cannot keep pace with her, but finds that the best he can do is not get left behind altogether. She moves further and further ahead, deflecting the attempts of others who try to greet her. They toss confused looks in his direction as they realize he's actually chasing her, calling out to her. And she's ignoring him.

He can't imagine the size of the spectacle they're making, but right now he doesn't care. He knew they would eventually have their first fight. Triton's trident, they started out fighting, didn't they? He knew they couldn't live in euphoria over their next two hundred years together. But he'd been expecting to argue about silly things first, like who is the better kisser, or what to name their first fingerling. Things that he'd be more than willing to surrender on.

But this fight is big. It's not just about her interest in humans, and he knows it. It's about her freedom. And about how much control he'll have over it once they're mated. This is not a fight he'd anticipated. He's always known she was fiercely independent, but he thought he could reason with her, coax her into seeing that there was always more than one point of view to any situation. And maybe he could have, if the first words out of his mouth hadn't sounded like some unbending command.

He curses under his breath. "Nalia, please stop," he calls out. "Please."

She doesn't. Already, they've passed the central hub of Syrena society, and they're well on their way past the Human Pass, where they were nearly killed. Just one more sandbar and they'll be close to another human shore altogether.

He reaches the hump of the last sandbar. And freezes.

She tries to stop, too, but her momentum catches up with her and she slides into the human mine. Hundreds of round metal balls floating above long chains, waiting to be touched, to be set off, to explode. It's a trap meant to kill humans, but now Nalia, *his* Nalia, is inside the mess of it, the slightest move of her fin setting the chains to swaying haphazardly. There's barely enough room for her to fit between them, let alone maneuver with any kind of speed. It's a miracle she's still alive, that the wake of her entrance didn't knock two of the balls together. It will be an even greater miracle to get her out.

"Don't move," he says, terror clutching at his throat like an actual hand. *This can't be happening.*

She nods, eyes wide. "I'm sorry," she whispers. "This is my fault."

"I'm going to get you out," he tells her, but he has no idea how.

"Grom. Don't come any closer. Get away."

He eases forward. "Be still."

"If you come any closer, I'll set them off on purpose."

"Nalia. Don't be stupid. I can help."

"This is how it's going to work. You're going to swim in that direction until I can't see you anymore. Then I'm going to get myself out of here."

He crosses his arms. "You've lost your mind if you think I'm leaving."

"There's no point in both of us . . . just go. I can get out. But I can't concentrate with you so close to—just go. *Please.*"

They both hear it at the same time. Two distinct *plunks* from the surface. Grom looks past Nalia. Two metal ovals, distinctly human-made, with a red angular symbol painted near the tail. Two miniature death ships falling sinking falling.

No no no no.

There is no time.

A flash of light. Once. Twice. Uncountable times.

Deafening thunder.

Devouring heat.

Blackness.

Quiet.

He senses Freya first, the closest to him. Then his mother, his father. Even Nalia's father, King Antonis. But the pulse so familiar to him, the one he cherishes most, the one he'd sense half the world away, is gone.

He knows. Before he opens his eyes. Before he looks up at what he knows will be Freya's stricken face. Before he feels the pain of his burns over the length of him. He knows.

"She's dead," he says. There is no question.

"I'm sorry," Freya chokes out. "I'm so sorry, Grom."

It takes a great effort for him to open his eyes, since he doesn't see the point in doing so ever again. He drinks in the somber faces surrounding him, keeping their distance from him and each other in different corners of his chamber. He tries to push himself up out of the pit where he sleeps, but groans when pain shoots through him.

Antonis swims over to him, but doesn't offer to help him up. Instead, the Poseidon king hovers over him. "What did you do to my daughter?"

Grom's mother gasps. "Antonis, please—"

But the Poseidon king holds up his hand, cutting her off. "I'm not talking to you. I'm talking to your son." He returns his glare to Grom. "Answer me."

Grom swallows, suddenly aware of how it all looks. People saw them in a disagreement, saw him chase after her, saw her angry with him. "We got into an argument. She got angry and left. I followed her. Into a mine. A new one. She was trying to get out, but the humans set off the explosion." It's as if he's recounting what he ate for his morning meal. The words feel hollow, meaningless, callous as he says them, and he wonders if they sound that way, too, or if it's just the numbness taking over, oozing out from the vicinity of his heart.

Nalia is dead.

Nalia is dead.

Nalia is dead.

"What were you arguing about?" Antonis says, his voice condescending.

Grom closes his eyes again. What is he to say? That Nalia admitted she made regular trips to the Big Land? That his own mother was part of it? That she wanted to continue to break the most serious of all Syrena laws?

No, he can't say that. He won't. He will not allow the memory of her to be tarnished in that way. Will not allow the guilt his mother will go through. No, he'll absorb the responsibility for it all. Keep it close to him. Antonis can think what he wants.

"I'd rather not say," Grom says, finally.

"Grom," his mother coaxes.

"No." He sets his jaw. Stares at the knobby rock ceiling of his chamber.

Antonis comes unhinged. "Of course you'd rather not, you slithering eel. Because you killed her! Because you've hated her since the moment you saw her, and you found a way out of your mating ceremony and took it."

"Antonis, old friend, don't be unreasonable," Grom's father interjects.

Antonis turns on the Triton king. "That's very easy for you to say, isn't it, *old friend*? Especially when you know I can't prove any of it. Don't worry. *Your* only heir is safe." He whirls back to Grom, nostrils flared. "But I swear by Triton's trident, *you'll* never mate. Not ever. Your seed will die with you."

Grom is about to tell him that he'd never want to mate with anyone other than Nalia anyway, but his mother interrupts. "What are you saying, Antonis? The law pledges your firstborn heir to him, to pass on the Gifts of the Generals. Your next heir must be mated to—"

He laughs then, a laugh full of bitterness and loss and poison. "There will be no heir. I will never take another mate. The Gifts of the Generals will die with his generation."

"Antonis, I know you're hurting," she says. "But this is not the proper way to mourn. If you do this, the Gifts—our future—will be lost. Both kingdoms will suffer."

"*Both* kingdoms?" he snarls. "There is only *one* kingdom. The Triton territory no longer exists." With this, he leaves. Freya presses her back into the wall and bows her head, giving him as wide a berth as possible.

Grom's mother grasps his hand. "Don't you worry about any of this, son. Antonis will come around."

Grom knows she's wrong. Antonis has lost too much. His mate. His daughter. His reasons to care. But all the things Antonis lost today, so did Grom. His mate. His prospect for offspring. His ability to care what happens next.

Even so, Grom can't help but think the Syrena lost more than both of them. A princess, a future queen, yes. But also a hope, one passed down from generation to generation. A hope for a prosperous future. A hope for protection from the humans once they inevitably invade every part of the ocean.

Not just a daughter, a mate, a princess, a queen. All of these things, yes. But so much more.

Today, they lost the Gifts of the Generals. Their legacy.

Shadow and Bone
978-1-250-02743-6

Of Poseidon
978-1-250-02736-8

Struck
978-1-250-02740-5

Monument 14
978-1-250-02738-2

Stay up to date on all the Fierce at:

facebook.com/fiercereads

macteenbooks.com